RUNNING OF THE BULLS

CHRISTOPHER SMITH

DEDICATION

For my great friend, Margaret Nagle.
Thank you for everything

ACKNOWLEDGMENTS

http://www.christophersmithbooks.com

10 9 8 7 6 5 4 3 2 1

For their help with this book, the author is particularly grateful to Erich Kaiser, Ross Smith, Ann Smith, Margaret Nagle, Matt Bialer, Ted Adams, Antonio Gragera, Constance Hunting, Deborah Rogers, Tim Moore, Caroline Moore, Suzie Irby, R.J. Keller, Laura Baumgardner, Martine Bound, Jamie Clark, David H. Burton, Misty Rayburn, Sandy Phippen, Keri "The Book Heroine" Rico and Matthy Matturro Terrill.

The author also would like to thank the amazing team at the Chief Medical Examiner's Office in New York City; the City of Pamplona, Spain (and the bulls the author ran with which were kind enough not to trample him); Ivan Boesky for his inspiration, however unintended it was on his part; for supportive readers everywhere who send along the best, most encouraging mail; to those men and women who introduced the author to the real Wall Street while he researched this book; and to friends, old and new, all of whom either helped to shape this book or who offered support as it was written.

Thank you.

BOOK ONE

PREFACE

NEW YORK CITY

Bebe Cole was an apparition that moved forward without sound, an enigma in the center of the dim foyer, where she turned on unsteady feet, unbuttoned her full-length cashmere coat, and let it fall to the gleaming marble floor.

She was naked, bloody, bruised.

"They've killed us," she said.

Still stunned from the beating, Edward Cole stared at his wife from the doorway of their Fifth Avenue apartment, unable to answer her, unable to speak.

The bandage they'd wrapped around his chest was too tight for him to breathe with any comfort; the drugs they'd pumped him full of were too much of a chemical blow for his body to handle. He brought a hand to his ruined face and felt its altered shapes and swollen cheeks. He smoothed his fingertips along the uneven curve of his broken nose and wondered how he'd ever explain this to a public who would want to know.

"You said they'd show restraint."

Her voice sounded as though it came from the far end of a winding tunnel, and Cole had to concentrate to hear it. He tried to focus on the petite figure that was his wife, but she was disappearing, vanishing, becoming one with the darkness rapidly unraveling along the edges of his vision.

"You promised we would be safe."

He shook his head at her in frustration, took a step toward her and was not aware that he'd fallen until he lifted his head from the cool marble floor and tasted the fresh surge of blood rushing into his mouth.

Again, he tried to speak, but words wouldn't come. And so he lay there, listening to the shallowness of his own breath, watching with fading eyesight as Bebe's shoes turned toward the dark library, stopped, and then backed up quickly as shoes that weren't hers raced forward. Too weak to comprehend or to even care, Cole slipped into unconsciousness.

When he woke, he saw his wife first.

Strapped to a Queen Anne chair in the center of the foyer, her carefully dyed blonde hair tousled and hanging in her face, Bebe was surrounded by four tripods, each holding a digital video camera trained on her. She was naked, shivering, gagged. There was a scrape on her forehead, cuts and bruises on her breasts. She locked eyes with him and moaned.

Cole forced himself to focus, pushed himself into a sitting position.

Bebe shook her head at him, tried to spit out the gag, but couldn't. She struggled to release herself from the rope that bound her hands and legs to the antique chair, but it was impossible. She turned her head to the left.

Cole followed her look.

There, sitting in the shadows beneath van Gogh's White Roses was a man Cole had never seen before. He was handsome, athletic, wore black pants and a fitted black turtleneck. In his hand was a gun.

The man rose from his seat, nodded at Edward and stepped beside Bebe, who followed his every move with her terror-filled eyes. "It's about time you woke up," he said to Cole in a relaxed voice. "We've been waiting hours for you." He kissed the top of Bebe's head. "Haven't we, dear?"

She jerked away from him and looked to Cole for help.

But Cole couldn't move--fear had rooted him to the floor. Powerless, he watched the man remove the gag from Bebe's lipstick-smeared mouth, press the gun against her temple and cock the trigger.

Bebe started. Her shoulders drew in and she looked imploringly at her husband, whose own lips had parted in shock. The gun,

Edward saw, had a silencer. The four video cameras surrounding Bebe hummed.

"Your wife needs you and yet you sit there," the man said with disappointment. "After everything she's done for you, after the way you've used and humiliated her in this marriage, couldn't you at the very least do something to help her?"

Edward rocked to his knees, pushed himself to his feet. He stumbled and leaned against a wall. His entire body ached. He was aware of his coat falling open, exposing his fat nakedness, the bandages at his chest, but he didn't care. The man was running the barrel of a gun along the bloated curves of his wife's bruised face.

"I want you to think of all your sins," the man said evenly, turning one of the cameras on Cole. "I want you to think about every one of them. Right now. Think."

"Who are you?" Cole asked.

"I want you to think about betraying your friends," the man said with anger. "I want you to think about selling out to the SEC, taking that witness stand and sending one of your best friends to prison when you yourself should have been rotting there in his place." The man cocked an eyebrow at him. "Mr. Cole, I want you to think about all of it."

Bebe moved her head slowly, carefully away from the gun. In a quiet, barely restrained voice, she said to her husband: "It's Wolfhagen."

The man kissed her on the cheek. "The canary sings."

"He's hired this man to kill us."

"So he has," the man said, and fired a bullet into her brain.

Edward's whole body went tense with disbelief. Bebe's unseeing left eye was blinking, her upper lip quivering, mouth working, foot twitching, yet she was dead, had to be dead. Part of her head was on the floor.

A hand gripped his arm.

Cole turned and saw the woman just as she jammed the gun into the small of his back and urged him forward, toward his bleeding wife, the man in black, the humming cameras. "Fight me," she said, "and I swear to God you won't die as quickly as your wife."

She came around and pulled him across the foyer with a hand far steadier than his own. The man had dragged Bebe off to one side and now was placing a matching chair where she had sat. Cole was led to the middle of Bebe's spilled blood. Now, the cameras surrounded him.

"Are you thinking about those sins, Mr. Cole?"

They'd murdered his wife. They'd do the same to him. If he broke now, it would be over for him. He forced himself to think, to somehow remain calm.

"Are you thinking about taking that witness stand? Do you remember the look on Wolfhagen's face when you burned him?"

He ignored the man, looked at the woman. Tall and attractive, thick brown hair framing an oval face of cool intelligence, her eyes the color of chestnuts and just as hard. She wore black leggings and a black shirt, no jewelry.

The man moved behind her, his face partly concealed behind the video camera now poised in front of him. "Get rid of his coat," he said to the woman.

She got rid of it.

"Now the bandages."

She ripped them from Cole, who stared into the camera's opaque lens and saw his own ruined face floating up at him from the dark, rounded glass. And he knew--Wolfhagen would be viewing these tapes.

The woman took a step back, looked with revulsion at Cole's bloody chest, then turned that look on him. "So, it's starting again?" she said. "You were there last night? You let them do this to you?" She shook her head at him in disgust. "How could you let them do this to you?"

"Because he asked for it to get off on it," the man said. "Isn't that how it works, Mr. Cole? You and your wife asked for it, but this time, it got a little out of hand."

Cole held their gaze and said nothing. He willed himself to believe that he could get through this. It wasn't too late for him. Everyone had a price, everyone could be bought. Hadn't Wolfhagen taught him that much?

"I have money," he said to them. "Millions. I'll triple whatever Wolfhagen's paying you. Both of you can walk out of here right now and never have to do this again. You'll be set for life. Just let me live."

The woman's lips, rouged red, broke into a half-smile. "Did you really think he'd let you get away with it forever?"

Cole shook his head as if he didn't understand, but he understood. He knew this day would come. Still, his belief in the power and the influence of money galvanized him. They would not kill him if he offered enough. "Millions," he said.

She lifted the gun.

* * *

Pamplona, Spain

Six Months Later

Ever since he was a child, Mark Andrews had longed to run with the bulls.

As a boy in Boston, he would sit on his grandfather's lap and listen to the old man's stories of his days in Spain, when he was still young and single, and traveling the world on the trust fund his father gave him upon graduating from Yale.

Mark would marvel at the man's retelling of La Fiesta de San Fermin, the week-long orgy of bull worship that honored Pamplona's patron saint San Fermin, who was martyred when bulls dragged his body through the city's narrow, dusty streets.

Mark's grandfather had run with the bulls. He had stood among the thousands of men in white shirts and red sashes impatiently waiting for the first rocket to signal their release.

Even then, some thirty years ago in his parents' home, Mark could hear the thunderous clacking of hooves as the twelve beasts came crashing down Calle Santo Domingo, through Plaza Consistorial and Calle Mercaderes, their horns sharp and deadly, their murderous rage focused on those foolish young men running blindly before them.

Now, at thirty-nine, Mark Andrews himself stood among fools in white shirts and red sashes, the early morning sun beating down on his face, the delicious anticipation of the impending event flooding his senses.

Pamplona was a city gone mad.

All week long, fifty thousand people from around the world had participated in La Fiesta de San Fermin, known to the locals as Los Sanfermines. They paraded drunkenly through the streets with towering, colorful *gigantes*, went to the afternoon bullfights, drank gallons of wine, made love in alleyways, and rose each morning from brief catnaps to watch the spectacular running of the bulls.

Earlier in the week, the mayor had kicked off the festivities at noon by lighting one of many rockets from the Ayuntamiento's balcony. And now, as Mark waited along with nearly a thousand other men for the rocket that would signal the beginning of *el encierro*, he watched and listened to the cheering crowd that looked down at him from open windows, wrought-iron balconies, the Santo Domingo stairs, as well as the Plaza de Toros itself.

Never had he felt more alive. He would run as his grandfather had.

He felt a hand on his arm. Mark turned and faced a stranger.

"Do you have the time?" the man asked. "I left my watch at the hotel. They should be firing the first rocket any minute now."

Mark smiled at the man, delighted to be in the company of a fellow American. He checked his watch and said: "In a few minutes, we'll be running like hell from twelve very pissed off bulls." He extended a hand, which the man shook. "I'm Mark Andrews," he said. "Manhattan."

The man's grip was firm, his teeth bright white when he smiled back. "Vincent Spocatti," he said. "L.A. What brings you here?"

"My grandfather," Mark said. "You?"

The man looked surprised. "Hemingway," he said, in a tone that implied there could be no other reason why he had traveled thousands of miles to be at this event. "I even brought Lady Brett with me." He pointed down the barricaded street, toward a building where a young woman stood at a second-story balcony, her dark hair and white dress stirring in the breeze. "That's my wife, there," he said. "The one with the video camera."

Mark looked up and caught a glimpse of the woman just as the first rocket tore into the sky to signal that the gates of the corral had been opened.

He felt a rush. The sea of young Spaniards and tourists lurched forward. A cheer went through the crowd and rippled down the narrow streets, reverberating off the stone walls, finally blooming in the Plaza de Toros itself. Moments later, a second rocket sounded, warning the crowd that the chase--which usually lasted only two minutes--had begun.

Mark ran. He heard the bulls galloping behind him, felt the earth trembling beneath his feet and he ran, knowing that if he stumbled, if he fell in the street, he would be trampled by the men running behind him and then by the 1,800-pound beasts themselves.

He moved quickly and easily, suddenly euphoric as he shot past the Calle La Estafeta and the Calle de Javier. He thought fleetingly of his grandfather and wished he could have been here to see this.

The crowd of spectators was screaming. Shouting. The terrific pounding of hooves filled the morning air with the intensity of a million small explosions. Mark shot a glance over his shoulder, saw the American, the crush of young men behind him and the first of the twelve bulls that were rapidly closing the distance between them all.

He was delirious. He was beyond happy. He knew that not even the day he testified against Wolfhagen could compare to the rush he experienced now.

He was nearing the Plaza de Toros when Spocatti, fan of Hemingway's lost generation, reached out and gripped his arm.

Startled, his pace slowed for an instant and he looked at the man. Now, he was running alongside him, his face flushed and shiny, his eyes a shade darker than he remembered. Mark was about to speak when Spocatti shouted: "Got a message for you, Andrews. Wolfhagen sends his best. Said he wants to thank you for ruining his life."

And before Mark could speak, before he could even react, the man plunged a knife into his left side. And then he did it again. And again, sinking the knife close to his heart.

Mark stopped running. The pain was excruciating. He looked down at his bloody side and chest, and fell to his knees, watching in dazed silence as the man named Spocatti leaped over one of the barricades and disappeared into the jumping, thrashing crowd.

He had fallen in the middle of the street. Hundreds of men were darting past him, jumping over him, screaming as the bulls drew near. Knowing this was it, knowing this is how he would die, Mark turned and faced the first bull as it loomed into sight and sank its lowered horns into his right thigh.

He was thrown effortlessly into the air, a rag doll tossed into the halo of his own blood, his right leg shattered, the bone jutting from the torn flesh.

He landed heavily on his side, so stunned that he was only dimly aware that more bulls were trampling him, their hooves digging into his face, arms and stomach.

The men rushing past him tried to move him out of the way, tried to grasp his shirt and pull him to safety, but it was impossible. The beasts were upon them. There was nothing anyone could do but watch in horror as twelve running bulls ripped apart a former prince of Wall Street.

When it was over and the bulls had passed, the thing that was Mark Andrews lay in the street--its body bruised and broken beyond recognition, its breathing a slow, clotted gasp. It looked up at the narrow slit of blue sky that shined between the buildings on either side of it.

In the instant before its mind winked out, its failing eyesight focused on Lady Brett Ashley herself. She was standing just above on one of the building's wrought-iron balconies, smiling as she filmed its death with the video camera held in her outstretched hand.

CHAPTER ONE

DAY ONE

NEW YORK CITY

ONE MONTH LATER

At the Click Click Camera Shop on West 8th Street, Jo Jo Wilson cranked up the dial on the dented green oxygen tank between his legs and eyed the camera in Marty Spellman's hands. "Beauty, ain't it?" he said through the mask covering his mouth. "Just hit the market. Knew you'd want it. Called you first. The strings I pulled."

Marty looked over the camera. It was the latest digital Nikon-- the best and latest in their series--and it was impressive. God only knew how Wilson got hold of it. It had the sort of lens that was so powerful, it could capture a cheating husband's contented look four football fields away. Holding it made his heart melt.

The problem was that it had been used before. There were hairline scratches on the black casing. Oily smudges on the lens. Marty gave it another once-over and shook his head. There was no way he was paying twenty grand for this camera.

"Too bad it's hot," he said.

Wilson looked surprised, genuinely offended. He sat back on the stool and blinked, his great round belly expanding before him like a comic strip balloon. Seventy years old and he'd eaten himself into a three-hundred-fifty-pound birthday suit. It was a medical wonder his heart continued to pump. "What the fuck you talkin' about?" he said. "That camera ain't hot."

"Don't lie to me," Marty said.

"I'm not lyin' to you."

"Then show me the invoice."

That silenced him.

"And where's the box?"

Jo Jo looked away.

"You can't keep lying to me, Jo Jo. You're no good at it. I've been onto you from the first day we met, when you were stupid enough to try and sell me a directional microphone that had no direction. Why haven't you smartened up by now?"

Wilson snapped his fingers on either side of his head. "Can't hear you, Spellman. Emphysema's eatin' away my ears, too."

Marty removed fifty $100 bills from his pants pocket and fanned them out on the dirty glass counter that separated them. "Five thousand and you pay to have it delivered to my apartment tomorrow. That's a fair price, Jo Jo. We both know it."

Wilson had no trouble hearing that and he looked at the cash as though it were a great pile of stinking shit. He gulped air and shook his pale moon of a head. "You got more money than God, and this is what you offer me? Five fucking grand?" He pushed the mask aside and spat imaginary spit. "Ten grand or nothing."

Marty put a finger on one of the $100 bills and dragged it to the left. "And my offer dwindles. Your call."

"That camera's worth twenty grand and you know it!"

"And you probably got it for two grand." He dragged another bill aside. "Look at that. It's magic. The money just disappears."

"Look," Wilson said. "Give me a break. Doris went to the doctor last week. She's gotta have an operation. I need the cash."

Even if this were true, Marty knew for a fact that Jo Jo Wilson was far too clever a man to have reached seventy without having secured health insurance. This was just another ploy.

"Times are tough for all of us, Jo Jo. Have you seen the economy? It's in the shitter. Just yesterday, I saw an elderly woman roasting a pigeon over a metal trash can in the South Bronx." He pulled another bill away, crumpled it in his fist. "Imagine what she'd do with this money."

"I can't even imagine you in the South Bronx."

Marty put a finger on another bill.

And Wilson caved. He took the money and counted it twice before stuffing it in his shirt pocket. "Generosity ain't your middle name, Spellman, I'll tell ya that. What do you need a camera like that for, anyway? You workin' another case?"

"I'm always working another case, Jo Jo."

"What's this one about? Another murder?" He sucked air. "Or are you hangin' some society slick for cheatin' on his wife?"

Marty didn't know. The call came yesterday morning from Maggie Cain, a best-selling novelist whose books were currently enjoying critical acclaim. She was his ex-wife's favorite writer. In their brief conversation, Cain asked if they could meet today at six but offered nothing more. "I'd rather speak to you in person," she said. "I have lots of reasons for not trusting telephones or cell phones."

That interested Marty. You got jaded at this job. He got her address, said he'd be there and hung up the phone.

Six o'clock was forty minutes away.

He looked at Wilson, who was turning off the oxygen. "Well, at least leave yourself a trickle," Marty said. "I want you alive so that camera is delivered tomorrow."

"Yeah, yeah."

"Love ya, buddy."

"Bullshit."

"It's true."

"Then recommend a movie for me. The wife wants a heartwarmer."

"In your condition? It better be 'Cocoon'."

"Fuck you, Spellman."

With a grin, Marty left his camera sitting on the countertop, stepped out of the store and took a right on Fifth.

* * *

Maggie Cain lived on West 19th Street.

When Marty arrived at the narrow brownstone, he noted at a glance the boxed summer flowers at each window, the bronze knocker on the carved mahogany door and what must have been a freshly swept walk.

He knocked.

When she met him at the door, he was faced with a mere slip of a woman in her early thirties with shoulder-length brown hair. She wore clothes that suggested someone too busy to care about frills-- faded jeans and a white T-shirt. She wore no make-up, which Marty thought was unusual because if she had, it would have helped to conceal the faint scar that stretched from the corner of her left eye to the side of her mouth.

She extended her hand, which Marty shook. "It's nice of you to come," she said.

Her grip was strong and firm, as self-assured as her voice. "It's a pleasure," Marty said. "I've been looking forward to this."

"So have I." She stepped aside and revealed an entryway that stretched before them in varying degrees of light and darkness. "I know you're busy," she said. "Come in and let's talk."

He followed her down a hallway lined with bookcases, paintings, drawings that caught his eye, and into the living room, which smelled of roses in their prime. He noted a grand piano in the corner of the room, photographs framed in silver on its lowered lid. On the windowsill behind it, a black cat sat poised and alert, gazing out at the city.

"That's Baby Jane," Maggie said, indicating the cat with a nod. "Rescued her from the street years ago. She's the real woman of the house."

"So, I should be talking to her?"

Maggie laughed. "Actually, she'd probably answer back, but I'm afraid you'll have to settle for me. Would you like something to drink? I have just about everything, but if you'd prefer something cool, I just made a pitcher of iced tea."

"That would be perfect."

In her absence, he took the opportunity to look around. While he knew she was a successful writer, he also knew enough about the publishing business that few writers, regardless of their success, could afford the drawing by Matisse he glimpsed in the entryway.

He crossed to the piano and looked at the photographs. A little girl with blonde hair; an older couple posing in front of a tropical sunset; a handsome man stacking wood beside a snow-covered cottage. The rest were of Maggie Cain.

In each photo, she was younger, perhaps in her late twenties at best, and as Marty studied them, he saw that in none of these photographs was her left cheek scarred.

He wondered again why she made this appointment.

Her voice came from behind him: "How much do you know about Maximilian Wolfhagen?"

She was walking toward him, the light from the surrounding windows catching the red highlights in her hair. He took the glass of iced tea she held out to him. "The arbitrageur?"

"You know another Maximilian Wolfhagen?"

Marty smiled. Wolfhagen wasn't exactly an unknown, and his name certainly wasn't common. "As a matter of fact, I don't."

Maggie leaned against the piano, her narrow frame fitting neatly in its gleaming curve. "I remember a time when everyone wanted to be him," she said. "People dressed like him, wore their hair like him, went to the same restaurants as him. You couldn't turn on a TV or open a newspaper without seeing those crowded teeth of his. You know what happened to him?"

"He was indicted by the SEC for insider trading."

"That's right," Maggie said. "And five years ago, he spent three years in Lompoc because of it." She nodded across the room. "Would you like to sit down?"

"I'd rather stand." He watched her step to the gold brocade sofa in the center of the room, where she put her glass down on the table beside her. "When we spoke on the phone, I think I told you I'm a writer."

Marty nodded. He'd stayed up late the night before skimming through two of her four novels, remembering those characters Gloria had loved and hated, cheered for and despised, recalling those times he'd fallen asleep with his head on her stomach while she turned the pages. It wasn't something he wanted to think about now. "My ex-wife's a big fan."

"Just your ex-wife?"

She was teasing him. Most of his clientele had airs about them. She didn't seem to have any. "I've read some of your books. In each one, you seem preoccupied by humiliating men of power.

Exposing men like Wolfhagen. There was a time when Gloria and I wondered if there was a reason for that."

"Gloria's your ex-wife?"

"She is."

She shrugged. "I guess a writer always has a reason for writing. That reason could be as simple as making money or as complicated as finding out some truth about themselves or the world in which they live."

"What's writing for you?"

"A little of both. Five years ago, when I wrote my first novel, I learned more about myself, my strengths and my weaknesses, than any counselor could have unearthed."

Marty looked at her scar and wondered how much of that was true.

"The reason I asked you here is that I'm writing a book about Wolfhagen. A biography, which is new for me. Too new for me. The problem is that my publisher is expecting the first draft by November, which is nuts but I agreed to it, so the blame is on me. Still, there's no way I'll be able to finish it in time without someone to help me do the research."

"And you need my help?"

"That's an understatement."

"What do you need?"

"While I'm interviewing people here in New York, I'd like you to fly to California and watch Wolfhagen. He's been out of prison for two years, and he's done a fine job keeping a low profile. I want to know everything about his life after prison. I want to know how he spends his time, who his friends are now--the lot of it. If you give me basic information--and by basic information, I mean dull, everyday stuff--I'll pay you your standard fee. But if you give me something the world can sink its teeth into, something that'll push this book onto bestseller lists, I'll double your fee--and throw in a bonus. Does that sound fair?"

He liked that she was direct. What he wasn't sure of is whether she'd like his rates. "I get $250 an hour," he said. "Plus expenses. If you double my fee, that'll come to $500 an hour. I should probably be asking you how fair that is."

Maggie came over to where he was standing. Watching her, he wondered if she knew of how attractive she was and decided that once--before the scar that drew a line down her face--she must have known.

"If there's any book I can't screw up, it's this one. My publisher paid a lot for it and I need to deliver. I asked you here only after I learned from friends that you're the best. I know you're worth those rates and I'm happy to pay them if you'll take the job."

"Do you mind if I think about it?" he asked. "I have two daughters. Usually, I work here in New York so I can be close to them. They mean everything to me."

"Of course," she said.

"Is tonight too late to call with a decision?"

"Not at all," Maggie said. "It's just me and the cat. We'll be home all evening."

They moved into the foyer and Marty stepped outside. When he turned to say goodbye, he saw just behind Maggie that the cat, Baby Jane, was sitting on the very edge of a hand-carved table, her tail flicking as she looked at herself in the dim glass of an enormous beveled mirror.

There was a moment when Marty thought the cat was studying him, appraising him. And then it leaped onto the floor and Marty suddenly was looking at himself--a tall man with sandy brown hair and shoulders so wide, they suggested a swimmer's build.

"I do have one question," he said. "Wolfhagen--have you two ever met?"

Maggie tilted her head and started to close the door, her hair spilling over the scar on her left cheek. "No," she said. "Never."

CHAPTER TWO

Half an hour later, Marty stood in the hallway outside his ex-wife's apartment.

He removed a set of keys from his pants pocket, knowing--but not really caring--that Gloria would be angry that he hadn't called before coming by.

He'd already taken care of the doorman. In the lobby, he asked Toby not to call Gloria and tell her he was here. Better to just walk in, make the call to Roz and visit with his girls. Gloria might even be out.

He stuck the key in the lock and opened the door. Soft music, soft lights and Gloria met him in the entryway. She was standing at a curving chrome side table, a glass of bubbling champagne in one hand, a spray of tulips in the other.

Without so much as a glance at Marty, she put the glass of champagne down beside a framed photograph of her dead mother and started placing the tulips one by one into the vase filled with water. Her voice was cool when she spoke. "What are you doing here?"

It wasn't the response he was hoping for, but he'd certainly heard worse.

Nudging the door shut with his elbow, he stood looking at the woman he had married twice, divorced twice and unfortunately still loved. Tall and slender, her skin as pale as the cream silk suit she wore, Gloria Spellman had the contented look of a woman enjoying life. "Sorry, I didn't call," he said, looking past her into the living room. "Are you with someone?"

She didn't answer.

"Mind if I come in?"

"You are in."

"Why are you dressed like that?"

"What business is it of yours?"

"It's just a question, Gloria. You look nice."

She turned to him. "That's sweet. Jack Edwards is coming by to look at my paintings. He feels I'm ready for another showing. He should be here soon. Why are you here?"

It was interesting, Marty thought, to note how much she had changed in the six months that had passed since her first showing. This wasn't the shy, introspective woman he'd fallen in love with fourteen years ago. Success had freed her. Rarely one to voice her opinions, Gloria now looked people in the eye and shared those opinions with confidence. Her hair, once light brown and shoulder length, was now black, angular and severe. She wore makeup and narrow glasses, smoked clove cigarettes and spoke of reincarnation. She was an evolving woman in a constantly changing shell.

"I'd like to see the girls," he said. "They around?"

"Of course, they're around. But now isn't a good time to see them."

Nevertheless, she glanced at her watch and stepped aside so he could move past her. At least she understood how much they meant to him. "Fifteen minutes," she said. "And not a second more. They're in their bedroom."

"Can I use your phone first?"

"It's your fifteen minutes," Gloria said. "I could give a rat's ass how you use it."

She certainly was a bitch tonight.

But as Marty walked down the hallway and picked up the telephone, he understood. His choice to focus more on his job than on their relationship had twice cost them their marriage. Psychiatrists and psychologists all gave him the same textbook reasons about why he was so screwed up now--his parents were murdered when he was a boy. They'd lived in a rough section of Brooklyn. His father was a cop who paid too much attention to the local gangs. When he was on the verge of bringing down a gang leader, three gang members shot him and his wife dead in their apartment while Marty, seven at the time, hid under a bed.

A cascade of sketchy foster parents ensued. At eighteen, he was able to go to university on scholarship, where he received a film degree because, as a boy, movies were the one thing that offered escape.

And better yet, they didn't require the sort of commitment a relationship required.

The phone was answered by a friend of his at the FBI. "Roz, it's Marty. Got a minute? Great. I was wondering if you'd run a check on someone for me. Name is Maggie Cain, otherwise known as Margaret Cain, the writer."

Gloria turned to him with interest.

"If she's in your files, do you think I could have a background by this evening? Find out where she got her money. The woman has a goddamn Matisse in her entryway. I know, right? Next time the pasta's on me."

When he hung up the phone, Gloria was standing behind him. "You're investigating Maggie Cain?"

"I don't know what you're talking about."

He stepped past her and moved down the hallway to the girls' bedroom. His professional life was the one thing he shared with no one--and Gloria knew why. Too many times in the past he had been threatened by someone who learned of his surveillance. Marty didn't take the repercussions lightly, especially after what happened to his parents.

"I can't believe it," Gloria said. "Maggie Cain! She's one of my favorite writers. You know I love her books. What's she done?"

"Nothing."

"Oh, please."

"Leave it alone, Gloria."

"Just give me something."

Behind them, the service telephone rang.

Gloria stopped mid-stride and went to answer it. When she returned, she was all business. "That's Jack and he's early. I need you to leave. This is a night for art, not ex-husbands."

"Define art."

"You wouldn't understand it."

"See how little you know about me? Consider what you've done with your makeup. Now, that's art." He glanced at his watch. "I've still got ten minutes to see my daughters."

RUNNING OF THE BULLS

"Mom's got a new boyfriend. Met him yet?"

Marty closed the door behind him and entered the one room Gloria had been banned from redecorating when she overhauled the rest of the house. Large and dim, the purple- and green-striped walls peppered with posters of that month's hottest teen idol, his daughters' bedroom had become in the year since his second divorce from Gloria a sort of battleground for Katie and Beth.

Clothes were missiles that had exploded on the floor, desks and bureaus. The beds were fortresses piled high with tapes and magazines, books and stuffed animals. In a large glass container, three hamsters raced frantically through an alarming network of scratched yellow tubes--perhaps seeking exercise, but maybe, Marty thought, trying to escape. Guilt had prevented Gloria and him from demanding the girls keep their bedroom clean.

Beth's question lingered in the air.

"Have you two become hoarders?" he asked.

"You're dodging the question."

Seated in the middle of her bed, her tanned legs crossed at the ankles, she looked at her father with the same level gaze she had inherited from him but had perfected by imitating her mother.

In an effort to buy time, Marty kissed her on the forehead, turned to where Katie was sitting on her bed and kissed her on the cheek, then looked around the room for a place to sit. Since divorcing Gloria, he had never been comfortable discussing her private life. While he knew she dated, it was somehow easier living under the illusion that Gloria's life revolved solely around her painting, this apartment, the two girls. But he sensed Beth needed to talk and so he sucked it up, despite the sinking sensation he felt in his gut.

"No," he said, sitting on the edge of her bed. "I haven't met him. I wasn't aware your mother was seeing someone."

"She's more than just seeing him," Beth said. "He practically lives here. Last night, they woke Katie and me up. It was fucking embarrassing." She caught the look on his face. "Sorry, but it was. Mom kept saying his name over and over. Jack this and Jack that. Please, Jack, please. Oh, Jack, oh. I just wanted to die."

What, Marty thought, was he supposed to say to that?

"Like, I don't mind if Mom sees someone," she said. "But if she can't keep it down, Katie and I are thinking of moving in with you. Is that all right?"

He'd take them in a minute, but each time he tried to get custody, he failed. "You know what the judge said."

"Weekends and holidays, I know. But what about what we think?"

"The judge thinks you're better off with your mother."

"Why? That's sexist. We'd rather be with you."

"And I'd rather have you with me."

"Can I talk to the judge?"

"You can certainly write him a letter. Both of you can."

"Great. We'll get on that."

In the growing silence, Katie glanced at him out of the corner of her eye. She had stopped flipping through a magazine and now was nibbling the inside of her cheek. Nine years old and almost as tall as Beth. Blonde hair to her shoulders and lips as full as his. She looked at him now with an impatience he had never seen in her before.

He cleared his throat. "In the meantime, I'll speak to your mother about her... behavior."

Beth rolled her eyes. "What good'll that do? She doesn't listen to you anymore. If anything, she'll put on more of a show just to spite you."

At what point, Marty wondered, had Beth become so comfortable talking about sex? She was thirteen years old, for God's sake. What had happened to the child?

"You leave your mother to me," he said. "I pay the rent on this place, not her."

Beth looked amused. "Oh, Dad, please," she said. "Don't you see what's happening? Mom's going to be famous. She's going to make a lot of money and won't need you anymore. She told us so this morning."

* * *

There had been a time when the sound of Gloria's laughter had left him feeling whole and well, fit and strong. Her smile, broad as the map of America, could get him through the worst of days. But now, as he left his daughters' room and moved toward the living room, the sound of her laughter unleashed feelings in him he wasn't sure he was ready to face.

Gloria was moving on. He was losing her to another man. And what that touched in Marty was an emotion he hadn't felt in years-- a sudden, deep jealousy.

He entered the living room.

Gloria and Jack were standing across the room, in front of the painting of a red wheelbarrow she'd hung on the north wall. Their backs were to him and they were discussing the painting. While Marty stood there, watching, Edwards reached out a hand and lightly brushed the nape of Gloria's neck.

Marty cleared his throat.

Edwards dropped his hand casually to his side and turned with Gloria, whose pale skin now had a rosy glow. From laughing?

"You must be Marty," Edwards said.

Marty came across the room, his mind like a camera, photographing this moment. Immaculately dressed in tan silk trousers and a white button-down shirt, Edwards was taller than he expected, in decent physical shape, his balding head tanned, his smiling mouth bright as the moon. Forty years old, Marty thought. Maybe forty-two.

He shook Edwards' smooth, manicured hand and noticed the carat diamond glimmering on the man's little finger. With raised eyebrows, Marty looked at the ring. Then, with disappointment, he looked at Gloria, who was standing behind Jack, looking brave but uncomfortable. "Yes," he said with a smile. "I'm Marty."

"It's a pleasure," Edwards said. "Gloria's told me a lot about you."

"I haven't heard anything about you."

"She says you're a private investigator," Edwards said. "And a movie critic. How does that happen?"

"Magic." He turned to Gloria, whose decorated lips had drawn into a thin line of discomfort. "Can I talk to you?"

They walked toward the twin glass doors that opened onto the terrace and stepped outside. Marty closed the doors behind them. His voice was low when he spoke. "I'll keep this brief."

"You've got no choice."

"Are you aware that Beth can't sleep at night? All she can hear is you and Edwards having sex. Same goes for Katie. Now, look. You know I won't tell you how to live your life, but when you sleep with this guy, at least show some respect for the girls and keep it down."

Gloria lifted her eyes to his, Manhattan's Upper West Side sparkling behind her in the late-afternoon sun. "I knew you wouldn't be able to handle this," she said.

The coolness in her voice took him off guard. "Handle what?"

She paused to tap out a clove cigarette from the rumpled pack she'd brought with her. "My seeing Jack." She lit the cigarette with a match. "You can't handle it. He's intimidated you and you feel threatened. Admit it."

"The man wears a goddamn diamond on his pinky, Gloria. He doesn't threaten me."

"That's a lie. You can't stand seeing me with another man."

"You're probably right," Marty said. "But what I hate even more is what you've become. Look at yourself. You're not even the same person anymore. You've redefined yourself. You've sold out and become the very kind of person you and I used to mock when we were young. Who are you, Gloria? Do you even know?"

She shook her head sadly, the gesture somehow condescending. "You're asking me if I know who I am, Marty? Let me ask you this. Since your parents were murdered, how many times have you asked yourself that very question?"

He turned to leave and when he did, she laid a hand on his arm. "I'm sorry," she said. "That was below the belt. But I'm happy. I've met a man who's got his act together. I've found a man who's willing to put me first. Don't blame me for wanting this. Don't blame me for being angry because you couldn't give it to me."

"Just keep it down in the bedroom," he said.

And he was gone.

* * *

Later, in his own apartment, Marty poured himself a glass of Scotch before calling Roz. "Tell me you hit the jackpot."

"Still working on it. Give me thirty and I'll call you back."

He clicked off the phone and went to his study, which offered one of the better views of Central Park. On his desk was his computer. On the screen was his blog. In his spare time, he reviewed movies. It was just a sideline meant to clear his head and retain his connection to his first love--film--but it had become an unexpectedly popular sideline, with tens of thousands of people visiting the site daily.

Right now, he was working on the review of the Blu-ray release of Billy Wilder's "Double Indemnity." Just a few additional paragraphs and it would be finished.

While he waited for Roz to call back, he sat down to have a look at the review. Last night, he pulled his favorite scene from the movie so he could discuss it. He read it again.

NEFF

Look, baby, you can't get away with it.

PHYLLIS

Get away with what?

NEFF

You want to knock him off, don't you, baby?

PHYLLIS

That's a horrible thing to say!

NEFF

Who'd you think I was, anyway? A guy that walks into a good-looking dame's front parlor and says, "Good afternoon, I sell accident insurance on husbands. You got one that's been around too long? Somebody you'd like to turn into a little hard cash? Just give me a smile and I'll help you collect." Boy, what a dope I must look to you.

PHYLLIS

I think you're rotten.

NEFF

I think you're swell. So long as I'm not your husband.

PHYLLIS

Get out of here.

NEFF

You bet I will. You bet I'll get out of here, baby. But quick.

Marty smiled at the passage, admired the dialogue and was about to reflect on its importance in the movie when the telephone rang. He reached for it. Roz.

"Learn anything?" he asked.

"Oh, I've learned something," she said. "But it's not going to be enough for your tired white ass. If I'd had clearance to her file, I would have learned more."

Marty stood and went to the windows overlooking the Park. Two helicopters were sailing toward one another, their blades glinting in the fiery light of the setting sun. For a moment, it looked as if they were going to collide. "Clearance to her file," he said. "She has one?"

"She has two files, sugar, and one of them's top secret. Can't lay my pretty black hands on it. But I do know this much--since 2006, Maggie Cain has been under surveillance by the FBI."

CHAPTER THREE

Marty hung up the phone and sat at his desk. He went to his computer, began a file on Cain and entered everything Roz had told him.

Years ago, Maggie Cain had been in a relationship with Mark Andrews. Mark Andrews had been one of Wolfhagen's bond traders. His testimony helped to send Wolfhagen and two others to prison.

He died last month. Trampled by bulls in Pamplona.

Maggie Cain's relationship with Andrews explained the Matisse Marty glimpsed in her entryway. With the money Andrews had at his disposal during the height of the stock market, he easily could have bought her that drawing--and maybe even her home in Chelsea. And if they were involved during the time the FBI was watching Wolfhagen and those closest to him, wouldn't she have been under surveillance as well?

Marty would have.

But none of this explained why she was under surveillance now. Why did the FBI still have an interest in Maggie Cain? It had been five years since the trial. Her connection to Mark Andrews was severed with his death. What could they possibly suspect her of doing that was considered top secret? And since Cain had been in a relationship with Andrews, obviously she knew Wolfhagen.

So, why had she lied to him?

He got up from his desk and went to the window. There was so much smog and haze, he barely could see the sun set beyond the trees of Central Park. He wondered what a sensible man would do with this information.

The answer came at once.

A sensible man would confront the source.

* * *

In thirty minutes, he was at Maggie's townhouse and Manhattan was lost to the night.

Marty looked across the deserted street to the building's façade, where inside it seemed as though she had left on every light. The windows, shielded by lace curtains, punched bright bands of gold into the darkness.

He paid the driver and stepped out of the cab, noticing as he crossed the street that the living room window was open. The curtains moved in the air, parting slightly, giving brief, frequent glimpses into the room beyond.

Maggie was sitting at the piano. Her back to him, she appeared to be studying the many photographs framed in silver on the piano's lowered lid. In her hand was a glass of wine. Curled beside her on the bench was Baby Jane. If it weren't for the movement of the cat's tail, Marty also might have been looking at a photograph.

He went to the lighted door and rang the glowing buzzer.

It was a moment before Maggie answered. "Yes?"

Marty watched the peephole darken, felt himself being watched. "It's Marty."

He heard her say his name before unlocking the door and opening it wide. There was a mixture of surprise and curiosity on her face. "I thought you were going to call."

"I decided to stop by instead. Is it all right if I come in? There are a few things I'd like to ask you."

She gave him a puzzled look, but stepped aside so he could move into the living room.

"I hope I'm not interrupting something," he said.

"Not at all. Would you like something to drink?"

"I'm good, thanks."

She motioned for him to sit down on the gold brocade sofa and took her own seat in the chair opposite him. She crossed her legs and for a moment simply studied him, her index finger tracing the rim of the wine glass she held in her hand. "Have you made a decision?" she asked.

"I haven't," Marty said. "First I need to ask you a few questions. Do you mind?"

Maggie hesitated, and Marty sensed she wasn't at all comfortable with the prospect of being questioned. But then, perhaps seeing no way out of the situation, she finished her wine and placed the empty glass down on the table between them. "You can ask me anything."

"That Matisse in your entryway. Did you buy it?"

Her eyes widened slightly. "As a matter of fact, I didn't."

He turned in his seat and looked at the sculpture of a ballerina that stood on the mantle above the fireplace. Her feet in fifth position, the original pink ribbon in her hair, the sculpture was one of Gloria's favorites and had been sold at auction a year ago, after the suicide of its previous owner. Marty noticed it when he walked in. "And the sculpture by Degas? Did you buy that?"

Maggie smiled.

"I know about your relationship with Mark Andrews," he said.

"It's no secret. I loved Mark. He was everything to me."

"Did he buy you the Matisse and the Degas?"

"I do well, but not that well. He also bought me the piano."

"How about this house?"

Maggie shook her head. "I bought the house--Mark just helped me furnish it."

"I want you to tell me about your relationship."

"I want you to tell me why it's important."

"It's important because I've just learned from a friend that for years, you've been under surveillance by the FBI. I have a feeling you do know Wolfhagen. I have a feeling you're writing this book for reasons other than insight or commercial success. I don't like being lied to, and if I'm going to work for you, I expect you to tell me the truth."

Maggie looked at him for a moment, the expression on her face wavering between anger and resentment. She stood and went to the piano, where there was a pack of cigarettes on the padded bench. She shook one out, lit it with a gold lighter. "You've run a check on me?"

"I run a routine check on everyone who wants to hire me. It's standard procedure. You weren't singled out." He let a beat of silence pass. "Are you aware of the FBI's surveillance?"

"Of course, I'm aware of it. They aren't exactly subtle."

"How long has this been going on?"

"Too long--I don't know. Years."

"Do you know why they're watching you?"

Maggie laughed. "Do I know why they're watching me? Jesus, Marty, I was involved with a man who helped to steal hundreds of millions of dollars from people around the world. I lived with a man who passed briefcases filled with cash to people in Central Park and who was partly responsible for the stock market collapse. Mark did all these things without my knowing it--until the day the FBI knocked on our door and read him his rights.

"Now, look," she said. "I've asked you to watch someone for me. If you take the job, I'll pay your fee. While I'm flattered by your interest in my personal life, I'm sure as hell not going to share it with you. It's none of your business. You can take this job or not. As for the FBI, they've been watching me for years--they're probably listening to us right now--but I don't care because I've never done anything wrong. I don't have any of Mark's stolen money stashed away in some Cayman account. I was a victim. By writing about Wolfhagen, by exposing the truth about him, I'll finally be able to close that part of my life and move on. That's why I'm writing the book. That's why I want to hire you."

It wasn't enough. "How well do you know Wolfhagen?"

Maggie closed her eyes. "Well enough to know that he deserved far more than the three meager years he spent at Lompoc." She looked at him. "I hate the man, Marty. He's a cruel son of a bitch and I'm going to burn him with this book."

In her anger, he saw something else. Vulnerability? Fear? There was something more here and it went beyond mere anger.

He was about to speak when she raised a hand. "That's it," she said. "That's all I'm offering. Yes, I know Wolfhagen. Yes, I lied to you and I'm sorry. But to be honest, I'm not going to tell you my entire life history when we've only known each other for a few hours. I don't even know if I can trust you."

Marty decided that was fair. He certainly wouldn't tell her how his commitment issues had twice cost him his marriage to Gloria. But still he was uneasy. He could see she was shaken. There was something she wasn't telling him, but if he could earn her trust, he felt she would eventually reveal it.

They fell into a silence. Maggie stood looking at him, drawing on her cigarette. Marty searched for something to say, but everything that came to mind seemed inadequate. It was Maggie who spoke first. "So, will you help me and take the job? Or have I spoiled everything?"

He needed something to take his mind off Gloria.

"I know you're good. I think we could work well together."

Her toughness was a facade.

"You haven't spoiled anything," he said.

"Then you'll take the job?"

Here was the perfect opportunity to do what came naturally-- lose himself in his own movie, one in which even he didn't know the ending.

"I'll start tomorrow."

CHAPTER FOUR

Carmen Gragera paused outside the building on Wall Street and looked through the tinted wall of glass. The uniformed security guard was there, seated at the circular front desk, his face glowing blue in the flickering light of a television she couldn't see.

Watching him, she lifted the lapel of her black business suit and spoke into the tiny wireless microphone Spocatti hid there earlier. "He's alone," she said. "Start filming. I'm going in."

She pushed through the revolving doors and moved across the lobby, her attaché case swinging, her heels clicking like drum taps on the shiny marble floor. The man looked up from the television as she approached. "I have an appointment to see Gerald Hayes," she said. "He's expecting me."

"Your name?"

"Maria Leonard. From the Times."

The man swung around to his computer, typed her name into the machine and smiled at her while waiting for confirmation. Carmen smiled back. She lowered her gaze in a way an American woman might and glimpsed the gun holstered at his waist. Had he ever used it before? Carmen doubted it.

And he certainly wouldn't use it on her.

The computer screen flashed and the man nodded at the illumined wall of elevators behind him. "Mr. Hayes is on the 20th floor, third office on the right. I'll call and let him know you're coming."

Carmen crossed to one of the elevators and stepped inside. She punched the button marked 20 and leaned back against a mirrored wall as the elevator began its rapid ascent.

Late last evening, she arrived from Salamanca and hadn't slept. Instead, she and Spocatti spent the entire night talking, planning, exchanging ideas and stories, speaking on the phone with Wolfhagen and deciding how this would play out and who would be next. In spite of getting no sleep, she felt absolutely alive.

The elevator slowed. Carmen glanced up at the lighted dial and saw the number 20 highlighted in blue. She felt a prickle of anticipation.

The doors slid open, revealing a tastefully decorated corridor accented with 19th-century furniture, paintings on the hunter-green walls, alabaster lamps casting umbrellas of soft light on the otherwise bare tables. Carmen stepped out. She could feel the gun concealed behind her buttoned, loose-fitting jacket. Hayes' office would be at the end of the hall, third on the left.

She started toward it, recalling her conversation with Wolfhagen, a man she and Spocatti hadn't met in person, but only spoken with on the phone.

Gerald Hayes had been one of Wolfhagen's most trusted friends, and still he became an undercover agent for the Department of Justice, going so far as to tape a recorder to his chest and trick Wolfhagen into admitting that he had traded, time and again, on inside information. Hayes had done all this for personal immunity. He'd sat on the witness stand, pointed a finger at the man who had made him millions, and sent him to prison with his testimony.

Now, at fifty, Hayes was reestablishing himself in a world that had shunned him only a few short years before.

While the SEC had banned him from trading domestically, they couldn't prevent him from trading abroad and it was this foreign business that Hayes now capitalized on. But that was no surprise to anyone who knew him. Before destroying Wolfhagen in court five years ago, Hayes had been revered as one of the men who had turned Wolfhagen's millions into billions, and his mind was sharper now than ever.

Earlier that morning, Carmen phoned Hayes for an interview. "It's time you set the record straight," she said to him. "People are tired of Wolfhagen and his lies. Now they want your side of the story and I want to help you tell it. Can we meet? The Times is promising prime space."

Hayes agreed, but only after quizzing her about her career as a journalist. If he was going to tell his story, it wouldn't be to an amateur. Carmen told him that she had been nominated for a Pulitzer for her reporting on international terrorism. For Hayes, it had been enough. For Spocatti, it had been a grave mistake on Carmen's part. If Hayes decided to Google the names of the nominees for that award or her position at the Times, he'd know she was a fraud.

His office door was closed. Carmen knocked twice and waited. It was a moment before the door swung open, revealing Hayes, his richly appointed office and the long array of windows behind him.

Carmen sized him up in a flash. Gerald Hayes was taller, more athletic than she expected, but there was something else, something in the stubborn set of his jaw, that caused her to pause. "Mr. Hayes," she said, extending a hand. "I'm Maria Leonard from the Times."

Hayes looked at her hand but ignored it. His cheeks were flushed and his tie was loose. Carmen sensed he had been drinking. "You're late," he said. "You said you'd be here an hour ago." But Carmen had specifically asked to meet him at 10 p.m. She was about to disagree when Hayes raised a hand, silencing her. "Forget it," he said. "I had a report to finish, anyway." He stepped aside so she could walk through. "I was about to fix myself a drink," he said. "Care to join me?"

The door clicked shut. Carmen said she was fine. She followed him out of the main office and into one that was much larger but with none of the former's warmth. Furnished with spare iron sculptures and abstract prints, the ivory-colored walls a shade darker than the bleached hardwood floor, Gerald Hayes' office was virtually without color, suggesting the man had bled all emotion from his life.

He motioned to the chair opposite his desk. "Have a seat," he said, stepping to the bar. "I'll be a minute."

But Carmen went to the windows beside the pale leather chair and faced the building across the way. Though it was late, she could see, in one of the building's few illumined windows, a cleaning woman pushing a vacuum over a beige rug. In another window, a man was talking into a cell phone while rifling through a file cabinet. Several floors above, two women were locked in a passionate kiss.

She didn't look for Spocatti or for the office he'd rented two weeks ago. She knew he was there, poised behind a rifle, filming this for Wolfhagen through one of the darkened windows, listening to and recording everything she and Hayes said.

"So tell me," Hayes said from the bar. "Why is everyone suddenly interested in Wolfhagen? First you call for an interview, then Maggie Cain calls for one. The man was a goddamn crook, for Christ's sake. What do you people see in him?"

Carmen turned from the window. "Someone else is doing a story on Wolfhagen?"

Hayes came over with his drink. "More than just a story. Maggie Cain is writing a book. She told me this afternoon that she'll interview everyone who's ever been linked to Wolfhagen, starting with those of us who testified against him in court." He took a hit of Scotch. "Or what's left of us. With the Coles and Mark Andrews dead, she may have a slim book on her hands. And I haven't even agreed to the interview."

He sat down at his desk and indicated for Carmen to do the same. "But if I know Maggie, she'll pull it off. She's good at what she does. She's smart and disarming. She'll probably even get me to talk."

Instinctively, Carmen knew that Wolfhagen would want to know about this book. She sat opposite Hayes. "Who is Maggie Cain?"

Hayes lowered his eyebrows. "She's a writer," he said slowly. "She was once involved with Mark Andrews." Something in his face darkened and Carmen realized her mistake--a reporter from the Times would at least have recognized Cain's name. "Do I have to tell you who Mark Andrews is, Ms. Leonard?"

Carmen said that he didn't.

"How about Edward and Bebe Cole?"

"I knew the Coles," she said, and half-smiled at how she knew them.

Hayes finished the last of his Scotch and leaned back in his chair. "All of them are dead," he said grandly. "The Coles murdered in their apartment over Bebe's van Gogh, Andrews trampled by bulls in Pamplona. Maybe all of us will pay after all," he said. "Maybe the immunity our government promised us has finally run out."

He shot Carmen a look. "The press would love that," he said. "They've been bitching for years about how easily we twelve got off, and maybe they're right. Maybe we did get off easy." He shrugged. "Doesn't matter. In the end, all of us will pay for our hubris. Even you, Ms. Leonard."

Something in the tone of his voice set her on edge. Carmen looked at him.

"Who are you?" he asked. "You're not from the Times and you were never nominated for a Pulitzer. I checked." He folded his arms. "Suppose you tell me what you want from me. Suppose you tell me why you deliberately lied to me this morning and asked for this interview."

It was exactly what Spocatti feared.

Carmen was searching for an answer when she noticed, on the sleeve of Hayes' maroon and white striped shirt, a tiny pinpoint of red light. As she watched, the light moved up Hayes' arm to his shoulder, hesitating at the base of his neck before curling around his chin and stopping to dance on his right temple. *Spocatti*, she thought.

"Answer me," Hayes said. "Tell me what you're doing here."

The laser beam flashed across Hayes' face in a brilliant streak of scarlet. Thrilled, Carmen watched it disappear into the man's hairline before darting out and appearing in the center of his forehead. There, it wavered like a flame.

"Do you always betray your best friends, Mr. Hayes?"

Hayes, who had been expecting an answer to his own question, looked at her as if he didn't understand.

Carmen opened her jacket, reached inside for her gun and stood. She pointed it at him. "Wolfhagen was one of your closest friends and you betrayed him," she said. "You told all his secrets in court, you sent him to prison for three years and you've never regretted it. Did you really think he'd let you get away with it forever?"

Hayes straightened in his chair and stared at the gun. He seemed neither frightened nor surprised. "What do you think you're doing?"

Carmen came around his desk and motioned for him to stand.

But Hayes made no effort to rise. He was twice her size and he knew it.

"On your feet," she said firmly.

But Hayes didn't move. He continued looking at the gun, his eyes narrowing, doubting she would shoot. Carmen cocked the trigger and pressed the cool metal barrel hard against his temple. "Move," she said. "Or I'll blow your fucking head off."

Hayes pushed back his chair and stood, rising to his full height of six feet four inches. He was just drunk enough to believe he was invincible. He looked down at her and said, "You think you can come in here and threaten me? You think you can intimidate me with a gun?" His voice rose in anger. "Your face is on every video camera in this building. Touch me and your ass will be in jail for the rest of your life."

Carmen leaned back against the edge of his desk. Beside her was a heavy marble paperweight the size of a baseball. She put her hand over it and said, "Mr. Hayes, I've killed drug lords, politicians and religious leaders. I helped murder the Coles and Mark Andrews. I've been doing this for seven years without fear or interruption. Surely, I can do the same to an old man like you and get away with it."

She swung her arm around and threw the paperweight against the side of his head. The blow took Hayes by surprise and he collapsed to the floor, his left temple crushed, his body jerking as though he had been electrocuted. Blood vomited from his mouth in a brilliant fan of crimson. His eyelids fluttered. A sound came from his mouth that wasn't human.

Carmen holstered the gun, stepped over his body and was happy to note that the building was so old, the windows opened. And so she opened one. The air was warm and humid and smelled faintly of salt. She looked out but saw no traffic on Wall Street. At night, lower Manhattan became a ghost town.

She glanced over at the building facing her and saw only the cleaning woman pushing her vacuum, oblivious to the murder next door.

But Carmen knew Spocatti was watching.

She turned to Hayes and was startled to find him on his knees. His mouth was open and working, dripping blood and saliva on the gleaming hardwood floor. His eyes were bulging and he was breathing heavily. The gurgling in his chest was growing deeper. His lungs were filling with blood and he was trying to stand while he literally drowned. He was dying, but he was too dazed to know it.

Carmen was seized by a sudden urge to do something different from what she and Spocatti had planned.

At the bar, there were cloth napkins. She rushed to it, grabbed a few and wiped her prints from the window. Then, she went over and helped Hayes to his feet. He was confused and disoriented and looked at her as though they'd never met. He leaned on her shoulder as she led him to the window. She could smell alcohol on his breath and expensive cologne on his skin. He murmured something in her ear though she wasn't sure what. Blood spooled from the corner of his mouth. Her own heart hammered.

They reached the window and she pressed his finger tips against the glass. She took his hands and pressed them down on the window sill and then on the lip that lifted the window. Carmen looked again for the cleaning lady, didn't see her, and lowered Hayes' bleeding head to the warm night air. With a supreme effort, she shoved him through.

He made no sound as he tumbled through the air. His arms flailing at his sides, his feet wavering as though detached from his body, he simply fell, head first, into the darkness.

There was no time to hear him hit the concrete.

Carmen rushed across the room and into Hayes' private bath. She retrieved a pale blue towel from a wide bar, wiped her prints from the marble paperweight, replaced it on the desk, then cleaned the blood from the floor with a special fluid she had in her briefcase case. The blood vanished. It couldn't be traced.

She looked around the office and knew she had touched nothing else. She hurried around the desk and retrieved her briefcase from beside the leather chair. She opened it, tossed the bloody towel onto several large stacks of cash and removed a pair of white gloves, which she put on.

She crossed to the bar. Hayes had been drinking Scotch. She grabbed the half-empty bottle and brought it back to the desk. From her inside jacket pocket, she removed the suicide note Spocatti wrote that morning and drenched it with the alcohol, blurring the handwriting that had been a perfect match to Hayes' own slanting scrawl.

With a last look around, she dropped the note and the bottle of Scotch onto the desk, reached for her briefcase, left the room.

Time was running out.

With the $100,000 in her briefcase, Carmen had a security guard to bribe.

CHAPTER FIVE

From the opposite building, Spocatti watched in disbelief as Gerald Hayes fell to the concrete pavement. None of this was part of the plan. Carmen intentionally deviated from it and he was furious with her given the potential situation she'd just put them in.

He filmed the man dropping to his death, filmed his cartwheeling hands and wide-open eyes, filmed his last few moments of life before his head exploded on the sidewalk and his body collapsed on top of it in a broken heap.

For Wolfhagen's sake, he held the shot for a lingering moment before he jerked the camera back to the open window, where Carmen was hurrying about the room, covering her ass.

Why did she go against the plan? She was supposed to have knocked Hayes unconscious, wipe her prints from the gun and then place it in his hand while firing a bullet into his brain. It was simple. It had been her idea. So, why did she change her mind? Why did she deliberately take this chance?

The fool was going to get caught.

He watched her move quickly and efficiently, her eyes missing nothing. When she was finished, she grabbed her briefcase and left the room. Thirty-five seconds, maybe forty. Though he hated to admit it, Spocatti doubted whether he could do better.

Still, she had to get out of the building.

He adjusted his earphone and listened to her run down the hallway to the bank of elevators. His mind like a camera, he imagined her stepping into the car, punching the button marked "L" and composing herself in the reflection of the mirrored doors as the elevator plummeted twenty floors.

"That one was for you, Vincent," she said into the microphone. "I would have given him a kiss on the lips before showing him to the window, but I didn't want to make you blush."

Spocatti was having none of it.   She'd taken a stupid, unnecessary risk. If she didn't get out of the building safely, if she somehow got caught, the police would know that the deaths of the Coles and Mark Andrews were related, leaving Spocatti with a far more difficult task when it came time to kill the other men and women on Wolfhagen's list.

He glanced at his watch, then lifted the binoculars from his neck and looked down at the sidewalk. Hayes had been on the ground for several minutes and still no one had found his body. Spocatti looked up and down Wall Street, saw no one on its deserted sidewalks, no cars on the barren street. He listened to the elevator doors whisk open and heard Carmen's shoes click across the marble-tiled floor.

Her breathing was controlled. There was a firmness in her step that suggested confidence. "The lobby's empty," she said in a low voice. "Just me and the security guard. Shouldn't take more than five minutes to get the tapes and I'm out of here."

But Spocatti was no longer listening to her, couldn't listen to her, because down below on the street, a woman was moving hesitantly toward Hayes' body.

He lifted the binoculars to his eyes and leaned toward the window, bringing her face into focus. She was Hispanic, had long, wiry black hair and was wearing a faded blue work uniform. Her hands were buried in the fold of her bosom. Her face was pale with horror. She looked up at the open window from which Hayes was pushed and put her hand over her mouth. Though Spocatti couldn't hear her, he knew the woman was screaming.

And then he heard, in the distance, the faint wail of police sirens.

He pressed a finger over his earphone and listened for Carmen, but her voice had been severed, cut short by static. He tapped the device, heard nothing and checked the radio that was their only link. The dial was at zero. Somehow, her microphone was disengaged.

Incredulous, he turned back to the window. Sirens blaring, blue lights flashing, two police cars shot around William Street and pulled alongside Hayes and the woman standing over him.   The officers stepped out of their cars, looked at what had been one of Wall Street's most powerful financiers and immediately radioed ahead for help.

Spocatti moved to the semi-automatic rifle that was anchored to the window beside him.

He looked down through the powerful telescope and brought one of the officers into view. He gently squeezed the trigger and watched the laser's tiny pinpoint of red light appear on the back of the man's head. If the situation got out of hand and Carmen needed help, Spocatti would kill these officers and that woman. He would fire five neat holes into the backs of five shaken people.

He didn't know how long he stood at that window.

As word spread of Hayes' death, the area outside the building gradually filled with the media and the curious.

Photographs were being taken of the body. The woman who found Hayes had been taken away by the police. Inside Hayes' office, detectives were picking through the remains of a life. There was no sign of Carmen.

He was fearing the worst when he heard the jangling of a key and the door behind him swing open.

And there she was, her white silk blouse and black, loose-fitting jacket stained with the blood of a dead man. She moved to the center of the room and stood there, her eyes like a light turned to his face. She tossed the attaché case onto the floor and it popped open, exposing the bloodied, pale blue towel, the white gloves and the surveillance tapes.

Spocatti was about to speak when something in her expression caused him to pause. For a moment, he forgot his anger and listened.

"The book," she said. "Maggie Cain," she said. "Everyone on our list is being interviewed by her. We need to call Wolfhagen now and let him know."

But when they called his La Jolla estate, there was no answer.

CHAPTER SIX

Wolfhagen danced.

He arrived in New York just as the lights of Manhattan were beginning to shine, took a cab from LaGuardia, rented a room at The Plaza, snorted four lines of meth and had wine sent to his room.

He twirled.

No one knew he was here and that's how he wanted it. He came to play and to cause a little trouble, and he wanted to do so as quietly as he could for as long as he could.

This was an important trip.

He poured himself another glass of wine--his third--sipped it and tripped into the bathroom. He was high, blissfully high, the drug threading like needles through his system. Earlier, he lit candles, several scented candles, and the bathroom now glowed with the rich smells of vanilla and jasmine.

He put the glass down on the marble vanity and began to undress. He reached for the phone next to the toilet, tapped out Carra's personal number and slammed down the receiver when she answered. He looked at his reflection in the wide spotless mirror and marveled at the shadows stealing like thieves across his arms and chest.

He opened his leather shaving kit and exposed the glimmering gold blade. He wiggled out of his pants and swung his veiny rope of a penis from side to side--smack, smack, smack. He flexed his muscles and knew at this moment that his body was indeed beautiful.

He wouldn't look at his face.

He drank more wine and did a jig in front of the mirror. He closed his eyes and breathed in deeply, his mind spinning out and grasping the memory of the little nothing shit who came to his home in La Jolla that morning to tell him in her stupid lilting star-struck voice: "Your wife has decided to sell, Mr. Wolfhagen. We'd like to show the estate at noon."

He'd shut the door in her face and called Carra, who told him in that fucking controlled voice of hers that if he dropped this ridiculous alimony suit of his, he could have the damned house and everything in it. "But you'll never get a cent of my father's money, Max. Not a penny. I won't let it happen. He made his fortune without your help, he willed it to me and it's staying with me."

And so Wolfhagen danced.

He picked up the phone and dialed again. This time the line rang longer, but it was Carra who answered, her voice quick, all business. "What is it, Max?"

"I'll tell them everything," he said. "I'll go to all the papers and tell everyone. I don't care. I'm in New York now. I have nothing to lose. Don't you fucking dare sell my home. Don't you fucking dare try it. I'll ruin--"

"You're in New York?"

"That's right."

"Why?"

"I'm going to smash that fucking face of yours."

The line went dead. Wolfhagen hit the redial button but this time Carra didn't answer. The line rang and rang and rang--and his rage grew.

He dropped the phone to the marble tile and tripped back into the bedroom. He grabbed the can of shaving cream from his open suitcase, tossed it high in the air, reached out blind hands to grasp it, and laughed, laughed, laughed when it struck his bare shoulder, hit the carpet and rolled toward the television, where CNN played without sound.

Wolfhagen turned up the sound.

He picked up the can of cream and tip-toed back into the bathroom. The high was evening out, but he was determined to maintain it, determined to make it last. He danced and he danced, moving his arms and swinging his head, rolling his eyes and baring his crowded teeth. The shadows on the walls moved with him in wild, jumbled rhythms.

But it was fruitless. He was losing it. He swung his hips harder and turned in complete circles, glimpsing his face once, twice, three times in the mirror. And that killed it. The illusion snapped. He stopped to stare at his face. That face. God, how he hated it. The hooked nose, the crooked teeth, the slanting eyes. This wasn't him! It was wrong! He was better than that face!

Before he showered, he would shave.

The shaving cream went on easily. He smoothed it on his arms, chest and stomach, rubbed it over his buttocks, through the stubble at his groin and down the length of his legs. He was fastidious in his application. His hands moved slowly and carefully, covering the two-day's growth with broad, foamy sweeps. Five days ago, he had his back waxed. It would be another week before he needed to go there again.

He rinsed his hands in the sink and left the water running. He took the gold straight razor and went to work, scraping away the hair he hated.

How could he have been born this way? Why had God done this to him? When he was thirteen, he had been taunted in the school showers by the other boys. He was made fun of because of the dense black hair that crawled up his back, covered his forearms and stomach, flourished with the stubborn determination of weeds in the peaks and valleys of his chest. His legs were sheathed with it.

At the time, Wolfhagen's parents were poor and couldn't afford a doctor to tell them that their son suffered from an acute imbalance of testosterone. They were uneducated and couldn't know the psychological scars already carved into their child's mind. But they were not insensitive. They weren't blind to the faults of nature. And so in the summer of his fourteenth year, only days before he started a new school year, Wolfhagen's mother began a ritual that lasted a lifetime--with soap and water, she shaved him.

"It hurts, Mama. Stop!"

"Stand still."

"But I'm bleeding!"

"It's either this, or you'll catch it from those little bastards at school."

As he matured, his skin toughened along with his soul. While the hair may have vanished, the jeers from his classmates didn't. They knew he shaved. They could see the stubble on his arms and legs in gym class, could smell it on him as though it were an odor, reeking and awful. They called him a freak to his face. Some spit on him in the halls.

At lunchtime, anonymous arms swung out to strike, while anonymous hands reached out to slap. Through it all, Max learned more than any of them. He learned the darkness of the human heart and just how deeply a person could hate.

His escape became books and literature. He found sanity in the lives of fiction's characters. He graduated second in his class, earning a four-year scholarship to Yale School of Management, where he redefined himself and became so much more.

He needed to call Carra again. He knew she was having a party tonight and he was going. All it would take was one threat. One potent little threat. Then he could revel in all the shocked faces that greeted him while he humiliated her.

He was slicing away the hair on his chest, maneuvering carefully around the peak of his left nipple, when he heard on the television the news of Gerald Hayes' death.

Wolfhagen stepped out of the bathroom, his body dripping a mixture of hair and shaving cream onto the Oriental rug. He moved to the center of the bedroom and stared at the television.

Hayes was dead, a possible suicide. There was an eye-witness, Maria Martinez, who was in the opposite building when Hayes fell past her window. The police were questioning Martinez and would make a statement by morning. They were not ruling out murder.

Neither was Wolfhagen.

He reached behind him for a chair and instead caught a glimpse of himself in the full-length mirror on the wall to his right. A thin river of blood was running from his chest down the length of his muscled stomach, stopping to pool in the foam at his groin before dripping from the head of his penis to the carpet.

He looked down at his bare feet and saw that they were speckled with blood and shaving cream. The sight startled him. He usually was so careful. He couldn't remember a time when he had last cut himself. As he stood there, watching, he felt a sudden, deep rush of shame and embarrassment.

He put his free hand over his slippery, bloody penis and the shame turned to rage.

CHAPTER SEVEN

Spocatti paced.

He walked past the window, walked past Carmen, walked back to the window, paused and looked across at Hayes' office. In silence, he watched the police rifle through the man's desk, bag folders, make notes, say little. He saw one of the detectives pick up the marble paperweight on the edge of the desk and wondered again just how carefully Carmen had cleaned it.

He stepped away from the window and looked at her. She was seated cross-legged in the center of the room, his MacBook humming in her lap, her face glowing in the bluish black. She wouldn't look at him. She knew better. Her fingers raced over keys he couldn't see.

"What's the number, Carmen?"

"Almost there."

"You said that a minute ago."

"The wireless in this place is shit."

She typed faster, stopped, leaned toward the screen and read off the number.

Spocatti removed his cell and dialed his contact at the First Precinct. It was late. Chances were she wouldn't be in.

But the woman answered. "This is Rice," the detective said.

Spocatti smiled. "Brenda," he said. "And I thought you'd be home in bed, fast asleep in the arms of your lover."

Silence.

"You know who this is?"

"Of course."

"Can you talk?"

"Hold on."

The sound of a chair sliding back, a door clicking shut. Then her voice, lower than before. "Okay," she said. "What is it?"

"I need a name."

"A name."

"And an address."

"An address."

"And whatever else you can find out about the woman who saw Gerald Hayes fall from his office window."

"Right," she said. "When?"

"Put it this way," Spocatti said. "You get back to me in twenty minutes with the information I need, and I'll personally see to it that money won't be a problem for you or your family ever again."

* * *

It took her fifteen minutes to secure her future.

Spocatti picked up the phone and listened. "Her name is Maria Martinez," Rice said. "Lives on 145th Street. Has a daughter, five years old. Three priors for drug trafficking, two for prostitution. Had an addiction to heroin and crack. This was six years ago. Now's she's off welfare, off drugs and has three jobs, one of them cleaning offices in lower Manhattan for Queen Bee Cleaning. Looks as if she's turned herself into an upstanding member of the slums."

Rice paused. "And you're going to kill her."

"I don't know what you're talking about," Spocatti said. "I've never killed anyone. Tell me what she knows."

"She didn't see anything," Rice said. "Said she was cleaning a window when she looked out and saw Hayes hitting the concrete."

"She didn't see anyone in Hayes' office?"

"No."

"What does our beloved Chief Grindle think?"

"He thinks she's lying."

"So do I. Give me her exact address."

She gave it to him.

He thanked her, hung up the phone and looked at Carmen, who had moved across the room and now was stuffing her blood-stained clothes into a gray duffel bag. Spocatti watched her change into black pants and a black top. She pulled her hair away from her face, secured it with an elastic and lifted her pant leg. She holstered her gun in the calf strap. "Are you expecting an apology from me?" she asked.

He didn't answer.

"Because I won't apologize," she said. "You would have done the same thing had you been there."

"No, I wouldn't have."

"I've seen you do worse."

"I won't deny that," he said. "But I wouldn't have pushed Hayes out that window. It wasn't necessary. It was juvenile. You're too proud to admit it and that's what disappoints me." He started to walk past her. "But that's your age and probably your gender, so I can look past it--this time."

He shot her a sidelong glance, his eyes bright despite the dark room. "It'll be interesting to see how you handle Maria Martinez."

CHAPTER EIGHT

The van, a slate-blue Ford Spocatti picked up in Queens, farted little clouds of exhaust as it ribboned through the city.

It was rust-spotted and fender-dented, but its engine was strong and it drew no attention on these streets, which, Carmen knew, was the reason he bought it in the first place. He hit a string of green lights and sailed to 145th Street, just off the Harlem River, where he parked across from Maria Martinez's tenement and sat waiting with the engine off for the police to bring her home.

Carmen rolled down the passenger window and watched the activity on the street. It was almost midnight and the sidewalks were alive with the homeless, whores and pimps, pushers and addicts, their sunken faces occasionally caught in the trembling headlights of passing cars. Here, the streetlamps were dark. The city refused to pay for bulbs that were constantly being smashed by gunfire. Instead, the major source of light came from a storefront, where a couple was freebasing coke.

"Stay here," Spocatti said.

He opened the door and stepped out. Carmen looked in the side mirror and watched him move down the sidewalk until the shadows and the night slid over his back and engulfed him. She didn't know where he was going or what he had in mind, but his trust in her had weakened and she was surprised by how much that bothered her. She'd been in this business seven years and she'd never been caught. Her hits were as daring as his, her reputation just as solid. She had nothing to prove and yet she obviously tried to impress him when she pushed Hayes out the window. Why? What was it about him that made her want to be viewed as an equal in his eyes?

What was it about herself?

She leaned against the seat.   What had Martinez seen? Anything? It all happened so quickly, Carmen couldn't be sure. She played the movie of her memory through her mind and saw only a badly edited, disappointing blur--Hayes kneeling, mouth bleeding, head lowered, falling through.   Everything else was lost in the dizzying rush of adrenaline that had overwhelmed her at that moment and she realized now just how wrong she'd been to go against the plan.

She looked for him in the side mirror, but all she could see was a dim stretch of empty sidewalk fading into darkness. It occurred to her that being here was not about killing Maria Martinez or learning what she might have seen. Rather, this was about saving face, fixing the past, re-instilling faith in Spocatti, and moving on with what they'd been hired to do. If she failed? Spocatti might shut her out completely.

The door swung open and he stepped inside. Carmen cupped a hand over the interior light and waited for it to dim. She glanced down at his hand and saw in it a tiny plastic bag, a spoon, a syringe. He tossed it all onto the dash and looked across the street. "Anything?" he asked.

She looked at the gleam of that syringe and shook her head.

Spocatti reached for the bag and the warped metal spoon with its blackened tip. The bag was filled with white powder. Cocaine or heroin, she couldn't be sure. He emptied it into the spoon and told her to hold it.

She held it.

He heated the spoon with a lighter. The powder liquefied and boiled. A curl of smoke swirled. He dropped the lighter in his lap, reached for the syringe, filled it.

He gave it to Carmen. "Martinez was once addicted to heroin," he said. "Tonight, she saw a man commit suicide. She saw his head explode and she saw what was left of him while she was questioned by the police. She's lost her faith in God and mankind. She's tired. She lives in this wasteland.   She works three jobs and still she struggles. No one's going to be surprised if they find her pumped full of this shit."

Carmen nodded.   It would work.   And then something--a glimmer, a flash of light--caught her eye and she looked across the street, where a patrol car was slowing to a stop alongside Martinez's apartment building.

Carmen watched a woman open the passenger door and step out. She was a cop and she was immediately followed by the driver, a tall man in uniform. The people on the street parted and walked their separate ways. Maria Martinez, seated in the back of the cruiser, made her appearance last. She was still in her pale blue work uniform. She was saying something Carmen couldn't hear.

And then Spocatti's voice, low, closer to her ear than she would have liked: "This is a simple hit," he said. "Nothing but an accidental overdose. Don't disappoint me again."

* * *

They waited for the police to leave before alighting from the van and moving across the street. Martinez lived on the second floor. Carmen followed Spocatti up two flights of stairs and down a dim hallway. The building seemed exhausted in the August heat, as though its slanting walls and sinking ceilings, desperate for relief, were trying to lean against one another for support. Here, the temperature was well past eighty and the air, heavy with humidity, stank of something sour.

Martinez's apartment was at the end of the hall, last door on the right. Spocatti moved past it and stepped into deep shadow. He drew his gun, cocked the trigger and tapped his foot.

Carmen knocked twice on the door and waited. There was a silence followed by a woman's voice, so high and thin that Carmen questioned whether it belonged to the heavyset woman who just emerged from the cruiser.

"What?" the woman called. "What is it?"

Carmen checked the hallway, saw in a thin tunnel of light a cat strolling in her direction--golden eyes flashing, white paws padding, tail held high against the stained wall. Dangling from the cat's jaws was a mouse, its wiry gray tail flicking at the very tip.

"Mrs. Martinez?"

Silence.

"It's the police, Mrs. Martinez. Could you please open the door? We need to ask you a few more questions."

"Come back tomorrow."

"It'll only take a minute."

"Me and my kid are tired."

Kid...? "Please."

Martinez started unbolting the locks.

Carmen glanced over her shoulder at Spocatti, but couldn't see him in the shadow. She turned back as the door parted on its slender metal chain. Maria Martinez peered out, her mocha pudding face and bloodshot eyes stamped with fatigue.

In the room behind her, Carmen saw a pretty young girl sitting at the brightly lit kitchen table. The sight caused her to pause. She didn't know Martinez had a daughter. The child had dark hair and dark skin, a narrow nose and a delicate build. She was sitting in a straight-backed chair, her eyes closed, face on the table, dead asleep. If Carmen had a daughter, it might resemble this child....

"Who are you?" Martinez asked. "You wasn't just here."

Carmen showed Martinez the badge Spocatti gave her upon leaving the van. "I'm Detective Martoli," she said. "Chief Grindle sent me to speak with you." She looked the woman full in the face and waited for some sign of recognition. There was none and Carmen questioned whether this woman had ever seen her. "May I come in?" she asked. "It'll take just a minute."

"Your minutes take hours. I wanna get some sleep."

"It's only a few questions."

"I already told you people what I know."

"The chief has a new lead. He wants me to discuss it with you. I promise this won't take long. Three questions and I'm gone."

Martinez glanced past Carmen to the very place Spocatti stood in shadow. She hesitated, moved to speak, but then shook her head and removed the metal chain. She opened the door. Carmen watched her face, tried to read her expression. Had she seen Spocatti? Wouldn't she have slammed the door shut if she had? "All right," Martinez said. "But only a second. I've got jobs tomorrow."

Carmen stepped inside and glanced fleetingly at the child, who now was sitting up, her head bobbing, then lifting to dip again. She seemed oblivious to Carmen's presence, as though she already was lost to the vague world of sleep.

* * *

Martinez closed the door and went to her daughter, moving easily, fluidly, not self-conscious at all. "Before we talk, my kid's going to bed." She scooped the girl into her arms. "She's had it worse than I have tonight."

Carmen nodded, pleased. She didn't want the child here. Things would go smoother without her. "That's fine," she said. "Take your time."

Martinez murmured something and left the room.

Carmen was about to follow but decided against it--Martinez only could go so far. She reached into her shirt pocket and removed the heroin-filled syringe. There was enough here to kill Martinez. But her child? No way.

And Carmen was happy for that. She'd never admit it to Spocatti, but she liked children. One day, she wanted to have a child of her own. There was no reason for this girl to die. Carmen was certain she hadn't seen her. Unless she missed something, the girl appeared to be asleep the entire time.

She wondered if Spocatti would take that risk? If he were here, would he be willing to take the chance that Martinez's daughter had seen him in the few moments they had shared the same space? Probably not. He'd kill her, too.

But how would the police view this? If Martinez's death was to look like an overdose, she wouldn't have given her daughter the drug. So, the girl could live.

She held the syringe at her side and moved to the center of the small kitchen, looked around and appraised the details that made up Maria Martinez's life. Photos of herself and her daughter decorated the refrigerator door; a rainbow of dirty dishes rested against one another in the stained sink; a large plastic crucifix was nailed slightly askew to the wall above the kitchen table; and on the sweeping orange countertop, paperback books were stacked three deep, some so frequently read, their covers were torn or missing.

Carmen chose one of the books and turned it over in her hands. Her brother had been a voracious reader, sometimes finishing several novels in a week. But years ago, when AIDS stole his eyesight, it was Carmen who read to him, Carmen who sat at his bedside, Carmen's voice that rose and fell along with the respirator that had become his lungs. Though twelve summers had passed since she buried him, she missed him fiercely.

She put the book down and stepped to the refrigerator. In one of the photos, Martinez was laughing, her smiling face wide as the sky. Did she know things that could ruin Wolfhagen? Was there something she wasn't telling the police? Only a moment ago she had been reluctant to let Carmen inside.

Had she seen Spocatti waiting in the hall?

Carmen glanced at her watch, then turned to the doorway through which Martinez had carried her daughter. Ten minutes to put a child to bed?

She slipped the syringe back into her shirt pocket and left the kitchen. The living room was tiny, so dim it seemed almost gaslit. The brown, threadbare carpet was unyielding beneath her feet. There was a door in front of her, another off to her right. Both were closed. The air was slightly cooler here, as though somewhere there was a breeze. She listened but heard nothing in the adjoining rooms, no sounds of a mother comforting her child, no soft, murmuring voices. Just the breeze.

And Carmen knew.

Martinez had known who she was all along.

She lifted her pant leg and removed the gun strapped to her calf, opened the door to her right and glimpsed the empty bathroom before charging forward to the next door, which was locked. Locked!

She slammed her fist against it in frustration. She stepped back and kicked the door once, twice, but it wouldn't give, it wouldn't open, she wasn't strong enough and it infuriated her.

Behind her, the front door crashed open and Spocatti rushed in. He called out her name, ran into the living room with his gun drawn, listened to her, glared at her and drew back a foot, slamming it hard against the metal knob.

The door gave easily--splinters flew like confetti.

Carmen groped for a light switch and turned it on. The bedroom was empty, sucked free of life. Beside the unmade bed was an open window, its pale yellow curtains lifting to expose a rusty black fire escape shining blue in the light of a waxing moon.

Martinez had taken her daughter and run.

CHAPTER NINE

DAY TWO

The telephone was ringing, endlessly ringing, pealing throughout the apartment with the stubborn determination of an alarm that wouldn't stop. Marty turned his head and looked at the clock on the bedside table. It was 6:32 on a Saturday morning in New York City. Who the hell was calling him at this hour?

Finally the machine picked up and his disembodied voice instructed the caller to leave a message after the tone. Then a woman's voice, high and clear despite the machine's walnut-sized speaker:

"Marty, it's Maggie. Are you there? It's important."

He grabbed the phone from his bedside table. "What's important?"

"Have you seen the Times?"

"Generally, I don't see anything this early."

"Gerald Hayes is dead."

Marty sat up in bed. "Who is Gerald Hayes?"

"Wolfhagen's former business associate and friend. He helped Wolfhagen make his fortune, then turned against him on the witness stand."

"How did he die?"

"He fell from his office window. The police are thinking suicide."

"Did he leave a note?"

"Apparently. But it doesn't end with Hayes. Last night, Judge Kendra Wood was found dead in her townhouse on 75th and Fifth."

Marty closed his eyes. He knew Wood, had met her over the years at private parties and political functions. She sentenced Wolfhagen and two others to prison for securities fraud. "What happened?" he asked.

"She was decapitated. Someone broke into her home and took an ax to her throat."

Now, he was up and pacing on the cool floor. "What time was she found?"

"Just after one in the morning."

"And Hayes?"

"Just after 10 p.m."

For a moment, they were quiet.

"So, what do you think?" Marty asked.

"Anyone could have killed Wood. The woman had a reputation for being tough, especially on minorities. Whoever broke into her home could have been sitting in prison for years, just waiting to be released. But Hayes' death is off. Yesterday afternoon, I called to ask him for an interview for the book. He was in good spirits. Now this. Why would he kill himself? He was making a fresh start. People were calling him again. It doesn't make sense."

"What does?"

"Seven months ago, Edward and Bebe Cole were shot dead in their apartment. Last month, Mark was trampled by bulls in Pamplona. And now, on the same night, Gerald Hayes and Judge Kendra Wood are found dead. All of those who've died--with the exception of Wood--were once close to Wolfhagen. And yet they betrayed him. Wolfhagen must have been furious."

"You're thinking he's behind this."

"I don't know," Maggie said. "He's such a smart son of a bitch, I can't see it because it's too obvious. He'd be more subtle. He'd know that sooner or later, people would start suspecting him."

"Maybe that's what he wants people to think."

"Why?"

"Sometimes, if something appears too obvious, it can work in your favor. Wolfhagen has been out of prison for only two years. Common sense says he wouldn't want any attention like this, and yet he's getting it. It's something he could make an argument for if anyone questioned him."

"I'd buy that."

"What are our other options?"

"My mind keeps coming back to Ira Lasker and Peter Schwartz. They were partners with Wolfhagen about a year before everything fell apart."

Marty knew the names, had read about them. Ira Lasker was the young investment banker Wolfhagen hired to be a mole at Linder, Gleacher and Loeb. Book smart but greedy, Lasker was so taken by Wolfhagen, he agreed to sift through the partners' files and look for hints of possible mergers.

Peter Schwartz, a veteran investment banker in his forties, had done the same for Wolfhagen at Stein, Goldsmith. In hopes of a lighter sentence, Wolfhagen quickly turned each into the SEC before either could strike immunity deals. Each did his time, just as Wolfhagen had.

"Where is Lasker living now?" Marty asked.

"In a penthouse on Fifth."

Oh, to be an ex-felon, Marty thought. "What do you know about him?"

"Not much," Maggie said. "I've never met the man. Last I heard he's working out of his home as a financial consultant."

"And Schwartz?"

"He lives on 77th and Fifth. Mark and I had dinner there once. Unbelievable home. You'd think the Met had opened a new wing there. Word's out he's writing his autobiography."

"Were they called to testify against Wolfhagen?"

"They were and they did."

"And I suppose since he turned them in, Wolfhagen also testified against them?"

"That's right. And Wood worked each case. She sentenced them all to prison. Do you have the paper in front of you?"

"I can get it."

"Don't bother. You can read the story when we hang up. Some cleaning woman from Harlem saw Hayes fall from his office window and smash onto the sidewalk. She may know something the police haven't told the press. Is there any way you can find out?"

It was his Saturday to be with the kids. He intentionally chose an evening flight to California to watch Wolfhagen so he could have lunch with them. "I'm not sure," he said. "Are you going to be at home?"

"I'll be here until noon. The rest of the day, I'll be tied up in interviews. Any way you can get back to me before then?"

He was supposed to meet Katie and Beth at noon. Gloria would have a field day with this if he canceled. "I can try."

"I'd appreciate it."

"I'll do my best." He hung up the phone, went to the front door and got the paper. Gerald Hayes and Judge Kendra Wood were on the front page of the Times, not for the first time--and certainly not the last.

He focused on the Hayes article. Though suicide was probable, murder wasn't being ruled out. Marty finished the story and sat in thought, his mind picking over the facts. Gerald Hayes had been trading successfully in the foreign markets. Investors were coming to him again for advice. He must have been fueled by the renewed sense of power.

So why jump out a twenty-story window and end it all?

He read the Wood article. As he suspected, the story offered few details that could help him. By the time they went to press, her story was still unfolding.

No problem.

Marty reached for the phone and dialed the one person in Manhattan who would know as much about this case as the cops-- Jennifer Barnes at Channel One.

She answered on the third ring, her sleepy voice a reminder of things better left forgotten. "Jennifer, it's Marty. I think it's time we have that breakfast."

There was a silence. He heard her turning over, the bed creaking as she shifted position. "Who is this?"

"It's Marty."

"Marty?"

"That's right."

"And you want breakfast?"

"That's what I said."

"You've got to be kidding...."

"I'm not kidding."

"All right," she said sleepily. "I've got food here. You know where to get the coffee."

"Perfect."

"What's this about, anyway? I thought you needed more time?"

"This isn't about us, Jennifer."

"Sure it isn't."

"I'll see you in an hour.

CHAPTER TEN

Jennifer Barnes lived four blocks south on 67th Street.

Marty crossed over to Sal's on 66th, bought two large coffees and left thinking of all the mornings he came here after spending a night with her. It was a brief, six-month affair and it didn't end well. But in many ways, the time they spent together was a necessary distraction from a marriage that had fallen into disrepair.

The doorman recognized him on sight.

Marty nodded and strolled past him into the building. He stepped into the dark warmth of a mahogany-paneled elevator and pushed a button until it glowed. Channel One paid its star reporter a salary so handsome, it allowed her to live on the eighteenth floor, just high enough to offer a glimpse of Central Park.

Jennifer met him at the door with a gun.

She pointed it straight at his heart, took a step forward and pulled him inside by the arm. "I ought to put a hole straight through you," she said.

Marty moved past her and put the coffee down on a side table. He took the gun from her hands, checked the barrel, saw that it was loaded, snapped it shut. "Cute," he said. "What if it had gone off?"

"You probably would have died."

"And if I had?"

"One less bastard walking the streets of New York."

"Just the one?"

"I'll find the others. They always seem to come to me."

She took one of the coffees and started into the living room, her curtain of blonde hair swinging. "I don't know why you're here," she said. "But it had better be good. I still can't believe I've agreed to see you, especially after I read your blog and Netflixed that movie you raved about.   Second biggest waste of time in my life."

"You read my blog?"

"Apparently, everyone does.   People talk about it at work.   It's their go-to source for finding a good movie.   I'm not nearly as enthusiastic."

"Which movie did you watch?"

"'The White Ribbon.'   And can you just tell me what you were smoking when you wrote that review?   That was the bleakest, darkest movie I've seen in years.   And it had subtitles.   I hate subtitles."

It was a fantastic movie, but he wasn't going to argue with her. With raised eyebrows, Marty took his coffee and followed her into the living room, where she stood at the great window, her back to him, coffee on a side table, hands on her hips.

He loved this apartment.   Much like his own home, books, magazines and newspapers were piled everywhere--on the floor, leaning against tables, towering alongside each end of the sofa. There was nothing pretentious about it, nothing that suggested a designer's stamp.   Marty always felt that he could breathe here, high as he was above the congested streets of Manhattan.

"Why are you here?"

They had met nine weeks after his separation from Gloria.   He was just shaking off the cobwebs of a deep depression when the call came from Paul, his good friend from college, asking him to dinner.   "There's someone Laurie and I want you to meet."   The dinner was small and informal--an eclectic group of eight people eager to have fun and to be themselves.   Jennifer Barnes was seated at his right.   Her quick wit and easy laugh was like a tonic.   Soon they were falling into conversation.   For the first time in years, Marty found himself flirting.

"Don't just stand there, Marty.   Tell me why you're here."

For a while things were good.   They dated steadily for three weeks before Jennifer asked him to spend the night.   "Look," she said.   "I'm thirty-five years old, do what I want, choose whom I like. Can't we get this out of the way?"

Sleeping with her was like throwing away the ghosts of his past. Unlike Gloria, who rarely enjoyed sex, Jennifer was sexy and fun, uninhibited and wild, her aggression a welcome reprieve from

Gloria's disinterest.   Marty had never met anyone like her--professional, healthy, happy, remarkably settled considering her position at Channel One--and to this day, he regretted hurting her the way he had. She wanted a relationship and, naturally, he didn't. End of their story.

Or was it?

"I need your help," he said after a moment. "A favor."

She turned away from the window, her eyebrows arching.

"Gerald Hayes and Kendra Wood.   Are you covering their story?"

She reached for her coffee and peeled off the plastic lid. She sipped and gazed across the room at him.   "This really is about business, then?"

He nodded.

"You didn't come here for another reason?"

"No."

The disappointment on her face was unmistakable. "Then you should already know the answer to your question. Of course, I'm covering what happened to them. Didn't you see my piece last night?"

"I didn't."

"Naturally, you didn't.   Probably withdrawing into another movie."

She left the window and sat down in the middle of the overstuffed sofa. "You need a favor from me?" she said. "Well, I don't give favors.   In my business, favors are a commodity, exchangeable on the open market. But I'd be willing to trade."

Always the shrewd one. But then he knew this wouldn't be easy. "What do you want?"

She stretched out her legs and eased back against the sofa. "You're obviously investigating their deaths for someone," she said. "And while I don't necessarily care who that person is, I'd hope you'd be willing to share any insights you might come across during your travels. You're good at your job, Marty. We both know that. But we also know that Hayes didn't kill himself. At least I know that. Especially after what happened last night. As for Wood, don't you find it interesting that whoever chopped off her head also left with it? Why would someone do that? What are they planning to do with Kendra Wood's severed head?"

She paused, the Styrofoam cup pressed against her bottom lip as she watched Marty's brows draw together. "But I see you know nothing about that. Maybe, we can help each other."

He'd be a fool to turn her down. In many ways, they were equally well connected, only in different circles. "All right," he said. "Fair enough."

She smiled, her blue eyes shining. "So sensible," she said. "And so unusual. I'm impressed. Are you a new Marty, or are you still the Marty who can't make a commitment and who leaves when things are just starting to make sense?"

"Jennifer...."

She held up a hand. "What's the favor?"

"Wood and Hayes," he said. "What wasn't written about them in the Times?"

"Plenty."

"Such as?"

"Such as what was smeared in blood above Wood's bed. But Hines asked me not to include that in my report. You know our deal--he gives me exclusive information that won't compromise the investigation, I put him in front of the camera and make him a star. Blah, blah, blah. Last night, all I was allowed to mention about Wood is that her head was missing at the scene and that the job was done professionally, whatever the hell that means. Are their professional rules for cutting off someone's head?" She shrugged. "Despite a sophisticated security system that included a video camera hooked to a DVR, someone got inside."

Marty sat down beside her. Detective Mike Hines was obviously working Wood's case. Good, Marty thought. They were friends. "Has anyone checked the DVR?"

"That's all I know."

"Who has access to the apartment other than Wood?"

"Far as I know, no one."

"No husband? Ex-husband? Lover? Children? Relatives? Friends?"

"Kendra Wood wasn't close to anyone, Marty. She was a loner, protective of her privacy, consumed with her work. You two would have loved each other. And you should have seen her home. Shit piled everywhere, books stacked to the ceiling. She never married, never had children, doubtful if she ever took a lover. I think she was a hoarder."

"Apparently, being a hoarder is in vogue."

"What does that mean?"

"Nothing."

"Are you saying I'm a hoarder?"

"Don't be ridiculous."

"I may not be the neatest person in the world, but I'm no hoarder."

"I was referencing my girls' bedroom, which is a wreck."

"Whatever. As for Wood's friends, where are they now? By the looks of that townhouse, something tells me that Wood never got close to anyone. But here's the most interesting part, perhaps even the most telling--her family hates her. They live in northern Maine, have nothing, literally nothing, and they don't want a thing to do with Wood or with her funeral arrangements. Seems that Kendra wrote them off years ago. They haven't seen her since 1982 and they certainly don't mind that they won't be seeing her again."

Marty thought about that for a moment, thought about the dynamics of hatred within a family, and sipped his coffee. "What was written above the bed?"

"I can't tell anyone that."

"But you'll tell me."

"And lose a contact because of it? Forget it."

Later, he'd call Hines and ask him. "Anything else on Wood?"

"That covers it."

"Then what about Hayes? Why are you convinced he was murdered? The Times hinted at suicide."

"The Times also went to press about an hour before Maria Martinez and her daughter were found dead in a Dumpster on 141st Street." She lifted her head. "You do know who Maria Martinez is, don't you?"

Marty could guess. "She the woman who saw Hayes hit the sidewalk?"

"She's the one."

"Christ."

"Gerald Hayes wasn't suicidal, Marty. His business was doing well. The man was on his way back, even if it was through international markets. The only way he would have jumped is if it was onto a bed of blue-chip bonds. Somebody murdered him."

Earlier, Marty came to the same conclusion. He sat down on the couch.

"Martinez's death is obvious," Jennifer said. "Whoever shoved Hayes through the window must have known that Martinez was a possible witness. Somehow, they found out where she lived and murdered her and her daughter. Why the bodies were dropped in a Dumpster four blocks away is beyond me. But I do know this-- whoever killed Maria Martinez has one less witness to worry about in the death of Gerald Hayes."

They fell silent.

Jennifer finished her coffee, crumpled the paper cup into a tight ball and hurled it across the room to the overflowing wastebasket beside her writing table. She hit the top of the towering paper heap and smiled despite the avalanche of old notes and passé story ideas that tumbled to the floor. She rose from the couch.

But Marty remained seated. "Just a minute," he said. "I've got another question. Edward and Bebe Cole. Did you cover their deaths?"

"Of course, I did. But that was months ago."

"They were murdered over a painting, weren't they? Something by van Gogh?"

"Among other things, but, yes, the van Gogh was the item hyped by the press. Cole paid $40 million for that painting. He and his wife were celebrated for it. God knows where Boob Manly was going to sell it."

And then Marty remembered.

Robert "Boob" Manly was the small-time crook who had been tried and convicted of second degree murder in the Coles' deaths. After initially pleading not guilty, he was advised by his lawyer to plead guilty to the reduced sentence when the van Gogh and the murder weapon were discovered in a storage area rented under his name.

Manly maintained his innocence, said he'd been framed. But when he learned that his prints were on the gun and on the painting--and that there was a witness who could place him at the crime scene--he followed his lawyer's advice and reluctantly changed his plea to guilty, thus avoiding an expensive trial and a jury that could have sent him to prison forever. Instead, Manly was now serving twenty-five years to life at Riker's. Parole in eight to twelve years.

Marty was intrigued. Maggie Cain must have known that Manly admitted to killing the Coles, so why hadn't she mentioned him this morning? Why did she deliberately overlook him to suggest that Wolfhagen, Ira Lasker or Peter Schwartz were the murderers? Did she believe in Manly's pleas of innocence? Did she have reason to?

Jennifer shot him a quick, knowing look. "I get it," she said. "You're thinking the deaths are related. And actually that would be a neat fit. But I covered Manly's hearing, Marty. I saw the creep. Manly had a penchant for stealing art. He had a rap sheet that would have impressed even you. He confessed. He did it." She paused to study his face. "You might as well forget Mark Andrews," she said. "He was trampled by bulls. Thousands of people saw it happen. Murder's unlikely."

"Unless he was pushed."

Jennifer held his gaze. "He died last month, didn't he?"

"That's right," Marty said. "And now Wood and Hayes are dead. See the pattern? There was a time when all of their lives collided in Wood's courtroom. Now they're dying. Coincidence?"

"But those people have been out of the public eye for years," Jennifer said. "If someone wanted to bump them off, they would have done so years ago. Why wait all this time?"

"Sometimes, it's best to wait."

She shook her head at him. "I don't know. It doesn't feel right. In any given week--never mind over a period of seven months--I could find something that would link five of the city's unexplained homicides, but that doesn't mean that one person did the killings. And what about Manly? If you were innocent of murder, would you ever have pled guilty? I wouldn't have. I'd fight to the death, regardless of what my lawyer said."

She held out her hands. "But what do I know? If I've learned anything it's that in this city, anything is possible. Even a hunch. Look into it. Maybe something else connects their deaths. Something that can't be explained away."

She walked him to the door.

"If I were to tell you that I've missed you, what would you say?" she asked.

At first Marty wasn't sure if he heard her right. She was standing in front of him, her back to the closed door, her face partly concealed by shadow. Marty could see the faintest hint of a smile on her lips. He told her the truth. "I'd say that I've missed you, too."

"Would you mean it?"

"I'd mean it."

"Then you're smarter than I thought."

She opened the door and was about to let him pass when she said: "I'm going to give you another chance."

A part of him froze.

"Oh, for God's sake, relax. It has nothing to do with us, and everything to do with a good movie. It's Saturday night and I'm staying in. I know, I lead a thrilling life. I want to Netflix something, but obviously it needs to be something I can stream. What do you recommend?"

"What are you in the mood for?"

"Right now? Something about a doomed couple."

"I've got something, but it has subtitles."

"I told you earlier that I hate subtitles."

"That's because you're broadcast, not print. Of course, you hate subtitles. It involves reading."

"I'm going to pretend you didn't say that."

"Great. And besides, the movie will make up for it. 'Let the Right One In.'"

She screwed up her face. "I hear that's bloody."

"Bloody brilliant."

"Isn't there an English version out?"

"There is, and it's good, but watch this one first."

"Alright," she said. "'Let the Right One In' it is." She stepped aside so he could move past her. "You'll call me when you have something?"

"I will."

She started to close the door. "And maybe even if you don't?"

Once again, she caught him of guard. Marty was about to speak, but was saved when the door clicked shut.

CHAPTER ELEVEN

Carmen heard the rat before she saw it.

She was in the safe house on Avenue A, curled up with her cheek to the hardwood floor, and she could hear it. Rummaging, chittering, pushing its luck.

She opened her eyes and saw it sideways.

Ten feet away, larger than she had anticipated, eating the remains of the pastrami sandwich she bought last night at an all-night deli in the Village. Slate gray whiskers twitching, jaw chewing, eating her breakfast. Without a sound, Carmen lifted the gun nestled beneath her ribcage, checked the silencer and took aim.

"Hey," she said. "Rat."

Their eyes met--and suddenly the rat was a dripping gray-red smear on the crumbling brick wall.

She sat up and looked around the spare room, the floor of which had an angle steep enough to cause concern even among the most jaded of New Yorkers. Her skin was damp, sticky. Her dark hair clung to her neck in crisscrossing webs. She'd stripped down to her underwear sometime in the night, but it hadn't helped. Despite her efforts to shut it off, the ancient iron radiator tucked beneath the open window had continued to tick off the seconds with quick bursts of steam.

She wondered if Spocatti had returned.

She got up, slipped into shorts and a T-shirt, and went into the flat's only other room, which was small and dim in the shade-drawn light. There was a gas stove and a refrigerator here, a dirty metal sink with exposed pipes and a square metal table, on which sat Spocatti's computer, printer, modem and a spray of red tulips arranged in a pale blue plastic water jug that hadn't been there when she went to sleep.

She looked up and saw Spocatti hanging from the ceiling.

He'd screwed two U-shaped metal bars into one of the three exposed rotting beams and he was doing pull-ups. Save for the pair of black nylon shorts that hugged his ass, he was naked. His back was to her. Splinters of wood fell down on top of him, collecting in his hair and on the rounded curve of his shoulders. His muscles rippled with each pull and he did the exercise quickly, with absolute ease.

Carmen didn't know what to say to him or where she stood with him. Last night, he'd been so furious with her, he'd sent her back here and left to take care of Martinez himself. In the time that had passed, she didn't know what had happened or if he'd even found her. She'd waited until dawn for him to return before giving up and going to sleep.

She went to the refrigerator, pushed aside his clouded bag of vitamins and removed the carton of orange juice. She unscrewed the cap and drank, watched him go up, down, up. She wouldn't be surprised if he asked her to leave.

He dropped from the ceiling, stretched, shook the splinters from his hair, twisted his back, cracked the spine. He turned, acknowledged her with a nod, came over to where she stood and took the carton of juice from her hands. As he drank, he looked at her over the dew-drop gleam of sweating cardboard. She was almost convinced she could feel the heat of his body pulsing straight through her own.

"What time did you get back?" she asked.

He emptied the carton and crushed it, raised his dark eyebrows and said nothing.

"Did you find Martinez?"

"I did more than just find her, Carmen. I killed her and her daughter." He tossed the carton into the trash and nodded at the newspaper lying on top of the computer. "Take a look at the front page of the Times," he said. "There's a story that might interest you."

She went over to the table, looked at the newspaper, saw Wood's photograph in the lower left corner and skimmed the story that ran alongside it. Wood was dead. The details were sketchy. Carmen felt a sinking in her gut. Spocatti went ahead without her. "You killed Wood yourself? You did this without me?"

"I had nothing to do with her death. I assumed you did it."

Wood was on their list. "I didn't."

"Then who?"

"I have no idea."

"Well, that's intriguing, isn't it?" He dropped to the floor and started doing push-ups.

"Does Wolfhagen know she's dead? Have you talked with him?"

"Oh, I've talked with him," he said. "This morning and last night. We couldn't reach him because he wasn't in California. He's here, in New York. Staying at The Plaza." He put one arm behind his back and continued. "Wasn't too happy with you, Carmen."

"I'm sure he wasn't."

He switched arms. "You had an off night. You made a few bad decisions. We've all been there. I sympathize."

He jumped to his feet and ran his hand down the length of his muscled torso, wiping away the sweat. "Anyway, things have changed. Wolfhagen wants to move on this. He wants us to get through the list by the end of the day. The police are already onto it. They're making connections. They suspect Martinez saw something and they're probably right."

He paused, plucked a tulip from the arrangement, turned it over in his hands and lifted the delicate red cup to his nose. "But now, she's dead and that's going to be enough for the police. They'll know Hayes was murdered and they'll connect him to the rest. Before the others make that connection, Wolfhagen wants them dead. It'll make for one hell of a day, but I've agreed."

"But we've already discussed this," Carmen said. "If we move too quickly, the police will suspect him. Wolfhagen's got motive. They'll know it's him. They'll burn his ass."

Spocatti tossed her the tulip. Carmen snagged it with one hand and stared at him.

"Wolfhagen knows the risks, but he's no fool. He's willing to take them because he's going to be everywhere when each murder happens. When they die, he'll have alibis. He plans to be with this person, that person, at this public event, that restaurant. It's not a bad plan. As long as he remains in public when we take out the others, he should be fine. And besides, after my last job here, I'm tired of New York. I've been here too long. I want this over with.

It's time for something new. He wants those people dead by the end of tonight? Fine. I'm all for it. You should be, too."

"Tell me how we're going to do this when we have to let everyone know why they're being murdered and catch everything on film?"

"I mentioned that to him and he's willing to be more lenient. If the situation allows for it, great. But if we need to take a rifle and shoot someone in the back of the head in an effort to be more efficient, that's what we do."

He stepped beneath the U-shaped bars, jumped and gripped them tightly. Up, down, up. "One other thing," he said to her. "Maggie Cain? Wolfhagen wants us to kill her first, but not before we've found every trace of what she's written about him and burned the manuscript." Up, down, up. Eyes hard and narrowed and suddenly fixed on hers. "I'll take care of Cain. In the meantime, I'll need you to search her apartment for that manuscript." Up, down, up. "Oh, and there's one other thing. Just a small thing. I also need you to figure out how we finish off the rest by midnight tonight."

CHAPTER TWELVE

Even before Marty reached the cutting room, he could smell the stench of formaldehyde and human decay. When he entered the building, he swiped Vicks beneath his nose, which helped to a point, but as he approached the room, there was nothing he could do about the eerie scream of a Stryker saw as it bit down into bone just beyond the closed doors.

He was at the Chief Medical Examiner's office on First Avenue. It was hot outside, but here the circulation of refrigerated air wasn't as welcome as one might expect. It cooled the area, sure, but it also got the stink of death so far up into your nose, it was enough to make your stomach clench.

He pushed through the doors and looked across the room at Carlo Skeen, the chief medical examiner whose gloved hands were buried deep in the chest of an elderly man. He was pulling on something that wouldn't come loose.

This was a breeding ground for bacteria and as they feasted on the dead flesh of the several other bodies in the room, the gasses they emitted were as cutting as anything Marty had experienced. It was a smell he'd never get used to. Just being here made him want to vomit.

And it got worse.

In the far corner of the room, a male intern started humming as he hunched over the head of a middle-aged woman. He started the Stryker saw again and appeared oblivious as the saw's note deepened and sometimes caught as it glided across her milky white skull.

On the four other necropsy tables, those who were next in line were being drained of what had once kept them alive.

Marty focused on Skeen and moved toward him. He tapped him on the shoulder just as the man wrenched free one of the elderly man's lungs. Typical of Skeen, he never flinched. He'd been aware of Marty's presence the entire time.

"Are you never late?" Skeen asked.

Marty glanced down at the lung clutched in Skeen's hands-- black, pockmarked, cobwebbed with tar, it literally smelled of nicotine. His stomach tightened. "Nope."

"Gloria ever slow you down?"

Marty watched him turn the lung over in his hands. Each time he did so, it stirred the air. "Yup."

"Then you must have been late at some point in your life."

"I drive fast, walk fast. Look," he said above the whining saw. "Thanks for seeing me. Can we talk?"

"Sure." Carlo placed the lung onto a scale spattered with blood and peeled off the heavy latex gloves. Marty decided he couldn't look at the lung any longer. He glanced down and, with a jolt, found himself looking into the body's cavity, which was peeled open and exposing the man's organs. He turned away and focused on Skeen's hands. Large, pink and smooth, the nails clipped close.

"So, what's up?" Carlo asked.

"I need a favor."

"Name it."

"Maria Martinez and her daughter? They here yet?"

"Came in this morning."

"I don't suppose you've done them yet?"

Skeen laughed. "You're funny, Marty. Really. You're a scream."

"It was worth a try."

"Not really," he said. "But I can give you a preliminary. The mother was shot twice in the back of the head at close range. The child's neck was broken. That's all I've got."

"What about Judge Wood and Gerald Hayes?"

"They're different," Skeen said. "They came in last night and they've got priority. Ain't power and position grand? We're working on them now."

"What've you found?"

"Nothing on Hayes," Carlo said. "He's still being drained. But Wood's almost finished, except for some lab work. Want to take a look?"

They moved across the room to the table where Judge Kendra Wood lay beneath a shimmering white sheet, her legs lifted and parted in stirrups. With a flick of Skeen's wrist, the sheet was gone, exposing what was left of Wood's headless body. Marty looked at the "Y" sliced into her chest and asked himself that very question.

"It'll take some time to know for sure, but it appears that she died from an overdose of methamphetamines and alcohol. Time of death occurred between three and four yesterday afternoon. Decapitation approximately nine hours later."

Surprised, Marty looked at his friend. "Someone cut her head off after she was dead?"

"Hours after she was dead."

"Why?"

Skeen shrugged. "That's for you and the police to figure out. I can only tell you how she died and what happened to her after death."

Though the story in the Times didn't say so, Marty assumed from his conversations with Maggie and Jennifer that Wood had been murdered. "Did she kill herself?"

"Maybe. But if she did, she probably didn't do so intentionally. See these marks on her arm? And these here on her left ankle? She's been shooting up something for the past year and a half. Had quite a little habit too. It's a wonder she didn't die sooner."

"What was she was using?"

"Not sure yet, but probably heroin."

Heroin--the ultimate cure for someone with low self-esteem. Just one shot could make you feel invulnerable, beautiful, godlike. But why would someone in Wood's position need it? She had looks, power, celebrity. She was respected, even feared. Marty thought of the few times they had met and remembered a confident woman, comfortable and serious. Had she been high then? Worse, had she been high while handing out sentences on the bench?

"There's more," Skeen said, reaching for the box of latex gloves on the table beside him. He removed a pair, slipped them on and said while glancing at Marty: "I'll apologize for this now."

His hands went between Wood's legs to the freshly shaved area of unyielding flesh above her vagina. His fingers fanned out and parted her labia, exposing the gray, sunken clitoris between the drained web of waxy flesh.

"Come closer," he said to Marty.

Marty hesitated, then took a step forward and leaned into the light shining above them. The smell of death and rot and formaldehyde were stronger here, only slightly masked by the citrus scent of Skeen's cologne, which made it somehow worse. Marty held his breath and watched Skeen press the clitoris down and to the left, exposing a deep green tattoo half the size of a dime.

"It's an animal of some sort," Skeen said. "Here. Take a look."

He lowered the lighted magnifying glass above them and positioned it so Marty could view the tattoo, which looked like a blob with two points on top of it. He was about to step back when he noticed the tiny puncture wound in the tattoo's center. "What's that?"

Skeen moved the magnifying glass aside. "Her clitoris was pierced," he said. "Earlier, I removed a tiny gold hoop from it. That's when I noticed the tattoo." He looked at Marty. "The hole and the tattoo are at least ten years old. She had her nipples pierced around the same time, but she let them heal." He paused. "And it gets worse. Her rectum was torn. Ripped. Last night, after Judge Kendra Wood had been lying dead in bed for nine hours, somebody had anal intercourse with her."

It was too much. Marty had to leave. Skeen saw it and followed him to the door. "Why don't we have coffee," he said. "My office."

"I have a better idea," Marty said, stepping into the hallway. "Why don't we get out of here? I need some air."

* * *

When they left the building, a band of clouds--thick, dark and as high as the buildings in Midtown--had stretched across Manhattan, swallowing the sun and giving needed relief from the heat. Carlo looked at Marty, moved to speak, but hesitated. "There's more on Wood," he said. "Want to hear it?"

Marty nodded.

"Her PERK was a disappointment," Carlo said, referring to her Physical Evidence Recovery Kit. "I swabbed, but found nothing, no residue of semen. Whoever had intercourse with her used a lubricated condom."

"Wouldn't you on a corpse?"

"Bad joke."

"What about hair?"

Carlo shook his head. "We found only a few that were consistent with hers. My guess is that we're dealing with someone who's familiar with the system, somebody who shaved himself beforehand, knowing that any stray hairs could lead to a positive DNA match."

"What about the tattoo and the piercing? Have you done a search?"

"NCIC's computers are down," Carlo said. "They'll be up soon. But Jimmy contacted VICAP this morning. We should be hearing from them by tomorrow afternoon at the latest."

He looked at Marty. "I wouldn't get my hopes up, though. Body piercing is bigger than ever. I can't tell you how many young men and women I've come across in the past few months with rings through their nipples and gold rods through their genitalia."

"I get the twentysomethings," Marty said. "But on an adult judge? And the tattoo on her clitoris? It sets her apart from the rest."

"Not really. You don't see what I see on a daily basis. The poorest person can be wheeled in and they have none of that shit. The wealthiest person can be wheeled in and they have all of that shit. Kink doesn't differentiate between social boundaries, Marty. People lead secret lives, which you likely see in each case you take. Until we know what that tattoo is supposed to be, you're out of luck. We've sent photos to VICAP hoping they can match it to something in their files. But if they can't, I don't know what to tell you."

"You were there last night, weren't you?"

"I was."

"What did you see?"

It began to sprinkle, the light breeze driving the rain against their backs, the cars parked at the curbside, the trees dotting the sidewalk. "I could tell you, but I won't because it wouldn't do you any good. I was there for three hours last night. If you can swing it, this one you need to see for yourself."

CHAPTER THIRTEEN

At first glance, the townhouse on East 75th Street was as elegant as its counterparts--narrow casement windows shielded by heavy lace curtains, leaded glass windows in the carved mahogany door, a gleaming brass knocker above the brass nameplate, which read, rather simply, K. Wood.

But upon closer examination, cracks could be seen in the bricks and the foundation, the black iron bars that protected the windows from possible intruders were beginning to rust, and high above on the roof, birds were nesting in the white eaves.

Marty stood in front of the house and wondered about the secret lives of Judge Kendra Wood. She'd been a respected judge, she'd amassed enough power and wealth to live just off Central Park, and she had risked it all for a world darker than most could comprehend.

He looked up at the birds circling above him, watched them hover and peck insects from the side of Wood's house, and wondered when it was that she let them roost on the roof. When had she ceased to care?

A door clicked shut behind him.

Marty turned and saw a woman leaving the house opposite Wood's. She looked at him, then at Wood's house, then slowly back at him, her eyes narrowing.

Marty nodded at her. The woman's lips formed a tight line that dropped the temperature in Midtown fifty degrees as she walked away. Tall and diet-slim, her silver hair framing an oval face that would defy age as long as medically possible, she moved with all the grace and cool aloofness of a woman who only had known privilege.

She was everything his ex-wife wanted to become.

A car horn sounded beside him. Marty turned just as a black Dodge Charger pulled to the curb, music pumping, bass thumping, low fans of water rising at the wheels as the driver parked in a Tow Away Zone. Earlier, it had stopped raining. Detective Mike Hines, his angular face chiseled and tanned, looked through the open passenger window.

"Jesus, Spellman. Don't you eat?"

He shut off the engine, threw open the door and stepped out of the car. Mike Hines clearly ate enough for two. At six feet eight and pushing three hundred pounds, he was one of the tallest, most physically fit men Marty knew.

"Thanks for coming," he said.

Hines shrugged. "Provided the deal's the same, it's my pleasure."

It hadn't always been so easy. Eight years ago, when Marty first approached Hines for help, the man insisted on knowing who hired Marty and why, sensing that the person might somehow be connected to the victim's death. But Marty refused to tell, claiming client confidentiality. Hines only acquiesced after Marty agreed to divulge everything he learned in a report, given exclusively to Hines, and from which Hines ultimately solved the case. It was the beginning of their friendship.

Hines reached into his pants pocket, produced a key attached to a yellow evidence tag and unlocked the front door. He pushed it open. Marty followed him inside.

The entryway was small, dim and opened to a larger room with cathedral ceilings. Hines went into the gloom, but Marty remained at the door, looking around, the damp, heavy air enclosing him like a fist.

"There was no forcible entry," Hines said in the foyer. He turned on a desk lamp and the room took shape, exposing mahogany-paneled walls and a sweeping staircase that curved to the second floor. A layer of dust coated everything. The air smelled of old books and leather. "The alarm didn't malfunction, either."

Marty looked at the keypad on the wall beside him, saw the flashing red button that indicated the alarm wasn't in use, and then glanced up at the high gray ceiling, where a video camera was trained down on him. The system was one of the best on the market. "You've viewed the contents of the DVR?"

Hines nodded.

"What was on it?"

"Just Wood coming home and deactivating the alarm, which cuts off the camera."

"She didn't reset it?"

He shook his head. "Let's just say she wasn't thinking clearly."

"What time was this?"

"Oh five hundred hours," Hines said. "The time and date's imprinted on the footage."

Marty nudged the front door shut with his elbow and stepped into the foyer. "She was just getting in at five in the morning?"

"That's right."

"From where?"

"No idea. But wherever she went, I'd say she had one hell of a time. You should see her on the DVR. She could barely work the alarm. By the looks of her, I'd say she was crashing hard from whatever drug she was on."

"Can I see the footage?"

"Absolutely. I'll get a copy to you later."

"What about her neighbors?" Marty asked. "Anyone see anything?"

"The people in this neighborhood would rather eat off Chinet than talk to the police, Marty. They shut us down with the standard B.S. about seeing and knowing nothing."

Unfortunately, Marty knew that was true. This area of Manhattan was a haven for old money and older secrets. If they could avoid it, few people here would get involved in a any kind of police investigation. Still, he would try on his own. People tended to open up to him.

"What about work?" Marty asked. "Wood ever go in?"

"Are you listening to me?" Hines asked. "She was in no condition to work. And besides, she had the day off. I've seen her calendar. Wood took every third Friday off."

Hines took a step back toward the winding staircase, anxious for Marty's reaction to the bedroom. But Marty didn't move. He looked through the shadows at Hines. "Who found her? If the alarm wasn't set when she returned home, then someone must have called it in."

Hines started climbing the stairs, his back to Marty as he spoke. "You and I both know who it was. The same person who severed Wood's head dialed 911 with the news. We got here in five but Wood's head was already missing. You want to see the rest, then I suggest you follow me."

Marty followed. "The person who dialed 911--man or a woman?"

"Whoever called used a device that altered their voice. We're looking into it."

Wood's bedroom was at the top of the stairs, to the right of the balustrade, through a door that had been left open. Hines stepped inside. Marty remained in the doorway.

The human body contains six liters of blood, enough to paint a small apartment. Over the years and through countless investigations, Marty had come into the homes of strangers and seen just that--blood covering the walls, blood slicking the floors, blood staining the furniture, blood everywhere.

But Wood's bedroom was different in that she had died hours before decapitation. Her blood, thick and cool and pooled in the well of her buttocks, had remained mostly in her body. Only a small amount leaked from the wound at her neck, staining in an almost perfect black oval the bare, pale yellow mattress.

But it was not this that rooted Marty to the doorway. It was what was smeared in blood above Wood's bed that caused him to pause and wonder about the human soul and all the darkness that could lurk within it.

November 5, 2007

NEVER
FORGET!

Marty looked at the date and those words and wondered how they fit into the puzzle of Wood's death. He looked over at Hines and saw on his face a range of emotions that mirrored his own-- empathy for Wood, disgust for the person who had desecrated her body, irritation for his own limitations as a detective.

"Collins dusted this place twice," Hines said, referring to Sharon Collins, the chief fingerprints examiner. "She found nada, nothing, zip. Wood must have been a fucking recluse by the looks of things. Except for a few partials, her prints were the only ones lifted."

Marty stepped inside and shook his head. "Wood was no recluse," he said. "She may have lived here alone, she may have refused company, but people don't party alone, especially if they're shooting heroin. On that crap, you want to be seen."

He looked around the bedroom. It was here that Wood must have spent most of her time while at home. Her computer was here, as were her law books, a photocopier, a printer and a flat-screen television. There were two telephones, an exercise bike and even a small refrigerator, which sighed at him from the far corner of the room.

"All right," Hines said. "Give it your best shot."

"Wood was into kink," Marty said. "We know that from the tattoo and the piercings. But where did she go at night? Why did she take every third Friday off from work? To recoup from every third Thursday night? That's a no brainer."

"So, she belonged to a club."

"Absolutely," Marty said. "But which one? This city is filled with underground clubs that feature an a la carte menu of anything you want. Some are public, others are private. Some even take food stamps, but you probably don't want to go to those. Or maybe you do. The problem is that most are mobile--they rarely meet at the same place twice. They rent a space, have their fun, shut it down when they're finished. Have you talked to Vice?"

"Not yet."

"When you do, mention the tattoo. See if they can match it to anything in their files. If they can, you might get your club." He nodded at the message scrawled in blood above Wood's bed. "Maybe even the person who can't forget November 5, 2007."

Hines' cell went off. He slipped his hand into his pocket and answered.

While he spoke, Marty looked at the bloody mattress that had become Wood's final imprint on the world, thought of the tattoo and the piercing, and wondered how a federal court judge, that bastion of morality and justice, could have become engaged in something so far on the fringe. When had the balance of her personal judgment tipped?

He looked around the large room with its heavy velvet curtains and sturdy iron bed, its bookcases brimming with law books Wood either had memorized or written, the pale yellow wall smeared with its mysterious message, and wondered what secrets it held. What did this room know about Judge Kendra Wood that the world was only just now finding out?

Hines clicked the phone shut, turned to look at Marty. "Now this is getting interesting," he said. "That was the chief. Remember Maximilian Wolfhagen? The guy who was busted a few years back for insider trading? The guy Wood sent to prison? Guess whose head just showed up at his room at The Plaza Hotel?"

CHAPTER FOURTEEN

Hines's Charger was as neat as Marty had come to expect from a man who demanded order in everything. Together, they got inside, shut the doors and drove across town.

"All right," Hines said. "Who'd send Wood's head to Wolfhagen? Who'd know he was at the Plaza? Grindle said he just got in last night."

"What time last night?"

"A little past seven."

"Why's he in New York?"

"Chief didn't say."

Marty nodded and looked out the passenger window. He wasn't comfortable with any of this. Already, the investigation was turning into more than Maggie Cain had promised, more than he had planned. But was it more than Maggie planned? Had she sensed from the beginning that Boob Manly had nothing to do with the Coles' deaths? And if that was the case, why was she keeping quiet about it now?

Look at the facts, he told himself.

This morning, she had sounded upset--not surprised--when she phoned to tell him about Wood and Hayes. It was as though she had been anticipating their deaths, or, at the very least, expecting someone else to wind up dead who was connected to the others. He wondered again why she lied about her relationship with Wolfhagen. What happened between them that she was covering up?

"What do you know about Wolfhagen?" Hines asked. "You two ever meet?"

"No."

"But I thought you and Gloria knew everyone."

"Gloria knows everyone. She just took me along for the ride."

Hines lit a cigarette. "Wolfhagen comes to town and two people from his past wind up dead--the first a man whose testimony sent him to prison, the second the judge who put him there. You heard about Gerald Hayes?"

"I was going to ask you about that later."

"Why's that?"

"Because I have an interest in his death, too."

"Think there's a connection?"

Maggie Cain certainly did. "I don't know. Why would Wolfhagen cut off Wood's head, send it to himself and directly associate himself with the case? Either he's next or somebody is setting him up."

Hines shot across the Park. "If I had plans to kill Hayes and Wood, sending myself Wood's head might be exactly something I'd do."

"Why?"

"Because, if I did do it, I'd need an alibi. Sending myself the very head the cops are accusing me of chopping off is the perfect one. Actually, if it turns out to be true, it's brilliant. Wolfhagen wasn't caught with her head. Instead, it was *sent* to him. Big difference. It makes it look as if he's being targeted."

Marty chewed on that for a minute and decided it made sense.

They turned onto Fifth and pulled behind one of several television remote-broadcast vans parked in front of the Plaza. The entrance was peppered with reporters, among them Jennifer Barnes, who joined the rest of the crowd by surrounding the car and shouting questions Hines wasn't prepared to answer.

He stepped out of the car.

"Can you give us a statement?"

Towering over the crowd, he pushed forward. "On what? I haven't even gone inside yet."

"Word's out she died of an overdose."

"Can't confirm that."

"What can you confirm?"

"Nothing. Now, please let me through. I'll brief you when I know something."

But these people weren't budging. Like a smashed nest of hornets, they rose up and enveloped him.

* * *

While Hines fielded the press, Jennifer emerged from the crowd and put her hand on Marty's elbow. "So, maybe your hunch was right. Wolfhagen clinches it. These deaths are connected."

"Seems that way."

She moved closer to him, her voice a whisper he had to strain to hear. "Have you discussed this with anyone else besides me?"

He could smell her perfume. "Just Hines."

"What's he thinking?"

Marty told her about Hines' alibi theory.

"That's a twist," Jennifer said. "But I don't buy it. Wolfhagen would have to be nuts to send himself Wood's head. He's not stupid."

"That's what I said."

"Of course, we're probably wrong, Hines will bust this case wide open, he'll get a promotion and we'll look like fools."

"It'll be good for his esteem," Marty said dryly. "I'm happy for him already."

"You've been to Wood's?"

Marty nodded.

"Anything I might have missed?"

Despite the agreement they'd made earlier, Marty was keeping quiet until he knew more about Wood's case. He wasn't saying a word about the tattoo or the piercing until he knew more. "I doubt it," he said. "You don't miss a thing." He paused. "What do you make of the date smeared above her bed?"

"Two of my assistants are looking into that now. One's Goggling, the other is going through old newspapers and court records. Before this happened, I was thinking Wood may have sentenced somebody on November 5th. Maybe they just got their walking papers and decided to pay her a visit." She shrugged. "Or not. I don't know what to think."

"Good," Marty said. "Because it didn't happen that way."

She folded her arms. "Then how did it happen?"

He decided he could tell her a little. "Wood wasn't murdered," he said. "She died of an overdose. Her head was severed approximately nine hours after death. Whoever wrote that date and severed her head knew her. That much we know."

Jennifer scribbled in her notebook.

Marty lowered his voice. "Our agreement is the same," he said. "You don't use any of this until I give you the word. If the wrong information gets out, it could ruin this investigation and after what I saw today, I'm not letting that happen. Agreed?"

"Agreed. But I can't keep quiet forever. Every reporter in town is on this case. If I feel somebody is ready to scoop me, I'm going live with it."

"That's fair."

"What else do you know?"

He looked up at Hines, who was pressing closer to the Plaza's entrance. If Marty was going to get inside, he needed to join him fast. "I'm about to find out. I'll call you tonight if I have anything." With Wolfhagen in New York, he wouldn't have to go to California. He could watch him here.

"I've got a better idea. Why don't we meet at my place tonight?"

He was surprised by the invitation. "Sorry," he said. "I'm busy." If Wolfhagen went out, Marty planned on tailing him, just as Maggie Cain would expect him to do. "It'll have to be by phone."

"Then call me at eight. You know the number. And try not to be late. With Wolfhagen here in New York, I might be going out myself."

CHAPTER FIFTEEN

On the Plaza's fourth floor, a young officer nodded at Hines and Marty as they approached room 406. Sunburned and thin with an easy smile and an easier laugh, he was leaning against the door with an attitude that suggested none of this touched him, the fact that he was guarding a federal court justice's head in one of the world's most exclusive hotels. He didn't know Marty and stared openly at him.

"Who's this?" he asked Hines.

Hines looked down at him, his patience still short from his run-in with the press. "What the hell do you care?"

"I'm supposed to ask."

"Is that so?" Hines said. "Well, how about that. You asked."

He opened the door and they looked inside. Carlo Skeen, the M.E., was standing at the far end of the room, changing the lens on his camera with gloved hands. His eyes flicked up and met Marty's. They nodded at each other.

"You might want to plug your noses," the kid said with a grimace. "It's pretty bad in there. Smells like she's been dead for weeks."

Hines leveled him with a look. "Remember that smell," he said as they stepped past him. "One of these days, it'll be you."

Despite the warning, nothing could have prepared them for the smell. The air reeked of death. Hines expelled a rush of air through his nose; Marty caught his breath and held it. He was about to move farther into the room when a sergeant he'd known for years came forward to enter their names, time of arrival and Hines' shield number into the crime scene log.

He nodded at Marty. "How's it goin', Spellman? Long time no see."

"No offense, O'Hara, but I could have waited longer." He looked across the room to Skeen, who now was taking photos of the large blue Tiffany box placed in the center of a shiny round table. In it, Marty could just make out the top of Judge Wood's head.

"What time did it arrive?" Hines asked.

"Ten thirty," O'Hara said. "By messenger."

"I don't suppose anyone got an ID on the messenger?"

The man looked at him with raised eyebrows. "You're kidding, right? The stuck-up pricks at the front desk say they know nothing. Couldn't even give us the color of the perp's hair. May have been brown, may have been black. Some chick with a stick up her ass thought it was a woman, her hair pulled up in a cap. Who knows? Just dropped it off for Wolfhagen and took off out the door. It's not like they're trained to notice these things, Mike. They check people in, they check people out. That's their job. That's their miserable fucking lives."

"They have surveillance cameras here," Hines said. "Did you get the footage?"

The surprise in the man's eyes gave him away. "Working on it."

"Right. Where's Wolfhagen?"

"Downtown with the chief."

"Have you seen him?"

"I was first on scene."

"So, talk."

"He's scared. Freaked out. When I got here, he was standing in the middle of the room, starin' at that box like it held the truth to every one of his nightmares." He pointed beside the unmade bed, where there was a dark stain on the carpet. "He lost it after opening the package. Tried to make it to the bathroom but couldn't. After washing out his mouth, he called the front desk, who called us. We got here in ten."

"Along with the press," Hines grumbled. He started toward the box. Marty and O'Hara followed. "Wolfhagen happen to mention what he did last night? Where he went? We know he checked in around seven. I assume he didn't stay in."

"He didn't," O'Hara said. "He ate dinner in his room, then left to visit his wife. Or is it his ex-wife? They divorced yet?"

"On the verge," Marty said. He looked at Hines, then at O'Hara as Skeen's camera flashed. They stopped just short of Wood's head. "What time did he get back in?"

"This morning," O'Hara said.   "About an hour before he received the package."

"He spent the night with her?"

"That's what he said."

"Has she confirmed that?"

"We haven't contacted her yet."

"Don't," Hines said. "I'll talk to her myself." He looked at Skeen, who was standing behind the table, writing something down on a note pad. "Mind if we take a look, Carlo?"

Skeen shrugged. "Why not? Green's your color."

"Shit like this don't bother me."

"We'll see."

Hines peered inside the box.   Marty hesitated, then did the same.

Wood's neck had been severed at such a steep angle that her head leaned back against the stained cardboard, her ruined face lifted to his. In a flash, Marty saw the sagging curve of her grayish right cheek, the fleshy hook of her twisted nose, the torn lips drawn back in horror over teeth that had been smashed to dust.

Wood's skull no longer had the gentle curve of the living--it had been crushed by something blunt.   Blood and bits of bone peppered her face in a swirl of scarlet. Her light blonde hair was now a deep reddish brown and matted in thick, coagulated clumps. Her eyes were missing. Someone had gouged them out.

Marty looked away. Wood had been dead nine hours and still someone had done this to her. She cheated them of murdering her, so they smashed her face, ripped off her head and sodomized her to satisfy their rage.

This was personal.

But would Wolfhagen have done this? The man had motive, but would he have gone this far after so much time?

Hines turned to O'Hara. "Why's Wolfhagen in New York?"

"Never said."

"Didn't you ask?"

"No," O'Hara said. "I didn't. The guy wasn't exactly in one piece when I got here."

"Neither was Wood," Skeen said, and the young officer at the front of the room barked out a laugh.

Hines wanted to smack the kid. "He thought the box was a gift?"

"It had pretty ribbons on it. Wouldn't you?"

"He must have smelled it."

"Her head was sealed in plastic," Skeen said. "Likely to prevent leakage, but also to conceal odor."

"Who'd he think it was from?"

"He didn't know," O'Hara said. "People like him are used to getting gifts."

"What was his reaction when he opened the box?"

"I told you," O'Hara said. "The man freaked. Seeing Wood's head scared the shit out of him."

"And it's your opinion that his reaction was genuine? Not rehearsed?"

"Why? You think he's behind this?"

"I'm not thinking anything yet. It's just a question."

"It really don't matter what you think," O'Hara said. "I know people. I know what I saw. Wolfhagen didn't get anything past me. He was telling the truth. There's no way in hell he knew what was inside that box."

CHAPTER SIXTEEN

Once out of the Plaza and away from the press, Hines offered Marty a lift to Gloria's. "I can get you there quicker than any cab."

They climbed into the Charger. Marty checked his watch. He'd promised his daughters he'd be there at noon to take them to lunch. Now, it was 12:30. "I owe you one."

Hines pushed a button and the windows receded, sucking warm air and exhaust fumes into the car as they sped away. "You owe me more than that," he said, "but we'll discuss that later."

For awhile, they were quiet. Marty closed his eyes and leaned back against the hot seat. He tried to clear his mind, but it was impossible. All he could see was Wood's smashed head staring up at him from the tight confines of the Tiffany-blue box.

"Far as I see it, we got three ways we can look at this," Hines said. "One--Wolfhagen's guilty as hell. He killed Hayes, chopped off Wood's head and sent it to himself for the alibi. Two--he's being framed. Somebody thinks he didn't spend enough time in the hole and wants him to spend the rest of his life rotting there. Three--Wolfhagen's next. Whoever killed Hayes and Wood wants Wolfhagen dead, too. But they're going to play with him first, send him squashed heads to scare the shit out of him, break him down before his own head winds up in a cardboard box."

"It's all possible," Marty said.

"I'll know more when I've checked Wolfhagen's alibi and talked to him and Carra myself. I can't get you into see him, but I can get you a copy of everything he says to Grindle, along with a copy of Wood's surveillance tape and the call to 911. Tomorrow morning all right?"

"Tomorrow morning's fine. I'd appreciate it."

"No problem," Hines said, cruising across Ninth. "It's part of the deal. Remember?"

Marty remembered. Soon, Hines would be expecting Marty to deliver something relevant to Wood's case, or Marty would be on his own.

"If you want to know about Hayes, you'd do better to talk to the First P yourself," Hines said. "It's their case."

"Who's assigned to it?"

"Linda Patterson," Hines said, smiling. "Know her?"

Hines knew damn well that he knew her. Marty tried working with her in the past on the high-profile murder of Emma Wilcox, the mayor's sister, but Patterson's cocaine addiction was so out of control at the time, her work so sloppy, he found the help he needed elsewhere and cracked the case himself. Patterson never forgave him for it. That case was her ticket to detective first grade.

"If you ask nice, she might be willing to help you," Hines said. "Maybe even tell you what happened last night to Maria Martinez and her daughter."

Not before helping herself to my wallet, Marty thought. Unlike Hines, Patterson helped no one without first being handed a check. "I'd rather you tell me about Martinez."

They were on West End Avenue now, moving Uptown at a speed that was twice the legal limit. "What little I've heard ain't gonna help you, my friend. Right now, my life is Wood and will be until I find the pervert that took her head. Just talk to Patterson. She'll know what's up with Martinez and Hayes. Patterson might be dirty, but she's sharp. If you play her right, she might help."

Hines cut right, narrowly missed the side of a delivery van, and cruised to a stop in front of Gloria's building.

"Thanks, Mike."

"No problem, man."

Marty left the car and pushed through the building's revolving doors. The doorman rose as Marty stepped past his desk. "You just missed them, Mr. Spellman. They left ten minutes ago."

Marty felt a sinking in his gut. He promised the girls that he'd be here. He knew what his absence would mean to them. "Did they say where they were going?"

The man shook his head. "Just that they were going out."

"Were they alone?"

"They were with Ms. Spellman's new friend. They left in his car."

Marty felt a rush of anger. He had never been late picking up the girls. Gloria knew that. She could have waited for him. "Would you leave her a message for me, Toby?"

"Of course, sir."

"Tell her I'll be here next weekend at noon to take my daughters to lunch."

The man wrote the message down on a yellow slip of paper. "Anything else?"

There was plenty Marty wanted to say to Gloria, but it would be to her face, not through this man. He turned to leave. "Just tell her I won't be late," he said. "And thanks, Toby. I appreciate it."

* * *

At home, there were two messages left on his machine--the first from a Sister Mary Margaret asking for a handout, the second from his ex-wife informing him that he was late, but not to worry, Jack was taking them all to lunch. Marty went into the kitchen, grabbed a can of Diet Coke from the fridge, cracked it open, knocked it back.

Unbelievable.

He'd call Mary Margaret back with a contribution, but as far as Gloria was concerned, she could go to the very place the good Sister feared most.

He was hungry. He went to the refrigerator, took out the fixings for a turkey sandwich, carried it all to the counter. He sliced and he spread and he stacked. He was cutting the sandwich in half when the service telephone rang. He licked mayonnaise from his fingertips and reached for the phone. "Carlos," he said. "Talk to me."

"Jennifer Barnes to see you, sir."

Marty laid the knife on top of the sandwich. He and Jennifer had agreed to talk at eight. What was she doing here now? "All right," he said. "Send her up." He hung up the phone and waited for the doorbell to ring.

It didn't.

The front door clicked shut and Marty heard the familiar sound of her heels clicking down the hallway. Jennifer stopped in the kitchen's arched doorway and simply stared at him, her face flushed, as if she'd taken the stairs.

"How?" he asked.

She reached into her purse and removed the key he once gave her in a rush of affection. She held it up, a winking curve of metal. "I never gave it back," she said. "I just held on to it. Don't ask me why, I'd only lie. Do you want it back now?"

"I don't know," he said tentatively. "Why are you here?" He knew why she was here. He could see it on her face.

"Oh, Marty," she said. "Why do you have to ask so many damn questions?"

She came over to where he was standing and kissed him hard on the mouth. Still kissing him, she tugged at his shirt and started unbuttoning it, her fingers brushing his nipples, skimming his chest, smoothing the thin trail of light brown hair that snaked down his stomach to his groin.

Marty moved to speak, but Jennifer put a finger to the lips. "Don't," she said. "Why ruin it? Just let it happen. We both want this."

* * *

Later, in bed, exhausted and sucking air, Marty looked up at Jennifer as she slowly slid off him. "My God," she said. "The neighbors must be looking for wolves right now. You didn't hold back at all. You actually let yourself go."

"I was horny."

"That wasn't it," she said. "You're different. I saw it this morning. You've changed. You've never come like that."

Marty smiled at her. "I am different," he said, patting his flat stomach. "About ten pounds different, right around my middle."

"That's not it," she said. "You're more relaxed. Your guard is down. You seem more settled. It's as if you've let something go."

She lifted the damp hair off his forehead and combed it back with her fingertips. "Can I ask you something?"

"Shoot."

"Why did you leave?"

At some point, he knew she'd ask that question, but he was surprised by the suddenness of it here. "I don't know if I can answer that," he said tentatively.

"Can you try?"

He owed it to her, but how to get it out properly? "I needed to get my act together," he said. "When I met you, I was still in love with Gloria. We had two kids together. I love my kids. I miss them every day. I thought maybe there was another chance for us-- even a third chance. Until I straightened my head out, I decided it was cruel to be in a relationship with you if all of me wasn't here for you."

"Where do you stand with Gloria now?"

"We're finished," he said. "We have been for a while."

"Are you in love with her?"

Marty thought about that, thought of all the years and all the guilt and all the love won and all the love lost, and wondered what it all had meant. Was he a better man now for having loved Gloria? Besides his daughters, had anything good come out of those thirteen years together?

"I'll always love her," he said. "She gave me Katie and Beth. We have a history that I can't just swipe away. But she's changed into somebody I don't recognize. She wants to be something else. She wants to be a celebrity, which I don't understand. It's a different kind of love I feel for her. It's not sexual, but based on our past. We made two fantastic girls together, and that's about all we got right. Does that make sense?"

Jennifer bent to kiss him on the lips. "I always knew you were a good man. I waited for you, you know?"

"You waited for me?"

She shrugged. "I love you," she said. "I've always been in love with you. Of course, I waited for you. I knew at some point you'd come around and we'd give it another try." She paused. "If that's what you want."

Marty was still for a moment. He felt overcome and grateful, but not confined. He realized he also loved her. And for the first time since he'd known her, he told her so.

CHAPTER SEVENTEEN

Spocatti threaded through the crowds on lower Fifth, Maggie Cain so close he could reach out and slice her throat.

He'd been tailing her since early afternoon and he was enjoying it. She was attractive. Dark brown hair falling to her shoulders and swinging like scarves. Olive green shorts, white shirt, matching green shoes, legs tanned and shining in the sun. The scar on her cheek made him go weak with the mystery of it. He wondered how she smelled and how she tasted. She reminded him of the only woman he had ever loved, dead now ten years by his own hands.

He cut left and hung back to give her some room. On the street, a city bus rumbled past, its joints squealing like stuck pigs, a flood of yellow cabs pooling around it like an impatient school of fish.

Maggie Cain paused to look behind it. The sun hit her square in the face and lit up her eyes. Spocatti thought she was striking. In the past hour, he'd followed her to two bookstores, her agent's office on 13th Street, and the post office.

At the first bookstore, a trio of young women recognized her, pulled her books down from the dusty brown shelves and tentatively surrounded her, their mouths split wide and smiling. Spocatti watched her sign her name. She listened and nodded and laughed with them, but none of it was real--her thoughts were elsewhere. And that intrigued him.

But not as much as her scar.

She stopped on the corner of Fifth and 8th, and waited. The light turned, traffic stopped, the WALK sign flashed, but she didn't move. She didn't cross and Spocatti had no choice but to stroll past her. It would be too obvious if he didn't. He walked by and caught her looking at him out of the corner of her eye, saw what might have been a smile on her lips. For him?

He moved to the other side of the street, lost himself in the crowds, shielded himself on the other side of a hot dog kiosk and turned back to look at her. Now she was facing uptown. He followed her look and saw only the crush of a thousand cars bearing down on Washington Square.

Carmen.

He removed his cell and hit her number. Two quick rings. Her voice: "What?"

"Are you inside?"

"Of course, I'm inside."

"How long?"

"Thirty minutes."

"Any problems?"

"Her security system's good, but not that good."

"What have you found?"

"Nothing. Not even a hint of something on Wolfhagen."

"Not even a hint," Spocatti said. "That certainly seems strange for someone writing a book about the man, wouldn't you say?"

Carmen didn't say.

"Maybe she isn't writing a book," Spocatti said. "Maybe you got that wrong, too."

"You heard what Hayes said, Vincent. I wasn't imagining it."

"So you weren't," he said, and paused. Cain was checking her watch. "You've checked her phones?"

"I've hit the redial button on every one I've come across."

"And?"

"A call to her agent, one to her dry cleaner, another to someone in L.A."

"Who's the someone in L.A.?"

"I have no idea. No one picked up. No answering machine."

"You've scanned the numbers?"

"No, Vincent, I've ignored them. Jesus, give me some credit. Where is Cain now?"

"Corner of Fifth and 8th."

"What's she doing?"

"I have no idea. She's just standing there."

"You have no idea," Carmen repeated. "Has she spotted you?"

He smiled. "She might have."

"Think you can handle this, Vincent?"

"Touché, Carmen."

He lowered the phone from his ear as Maggie Cain stepped to the street. He watched her lift the strap of her handbag higher onto her shoulder and finger her hair away from her face. She waited and Spocatti saw what she was waiting for.

A black limousine pulled sharply to the curb and the rear passenger door shot open. Looking tense, Cain leaned down, said something, shook her head, glanced at him and then stepped inside.

Spocatti pushed forward to the street.

The limousine pulled away from the curb, took a left on 8th, drove straight past him. Vincent leaned down, but the tinted windows were so dark, he couldn't see inside. He searched the street for a cab, glimpsed one halfway down 8th, and swore to himself.

So far away and yet he needed that cab. He couldn't lose her now. He cut through the flock of pigeons dawdling on the sidewalk and ran in the wake of their beating wings.

* * *

Carmen stood just outside Maggie Cain's living room, looking across to the black cat poised on the edge of the grand piano. It was staring at her, its golden eyes gleaming. She stomped her foot at it, hissed at it, but it made no effort to move. She switched the phone to her other ear and said impatiently: "Are you there, Vincent?"

But he wasn't. He'd hung up.

She snapped the phone shut and glared at the cat. It would have to be black. In this business, luck was as important as skill and Carmen, raised by parents who instilled in her a fear of broken mirrors and the otherworldly, was superstitious enough to know with certainty that her luck was being challenged.

Time.

She had to move. She wanted to be out of here in twenty. She did another surveillance of the living room, but there was nothing for her here. She went back into the hallway, grabbed the knapsack she left at the front door, tossed the phone inside, and took the staircase to the second floor.

To the right of the bedroom was Cain's office, a large space that overlooked 19th Street--tall shelves lined with books, heavy damask curtains that pressed out the sun, an acrylic cylinder filled with tropical fish that stretched from floor to ceiling and cast blue flares of light along the pale hardwood floor.

At the far end of the room was a desk.

Carmen went to it and sat down on the brown leather wingback. At last, a writer's world--stacks of papers and thick green folders; a computer, printer, a telephone sitting atop a modem; books leaning against books; an ashtray overflowing with crushed cigarette butts; a dented can of Diet Coke, half-full.

With gloved hands, Carmen started opening the folders, flipping through the papers, skimming the pages for anything on Wolfhagen. But all she found here were letters from fans, bills Cain had yet to pay, several letters to her editor, three notes from Cain's mother, an old shopping list slashed with red marks, coupons that had expired.

She put the folders back, turned on the computer and while waiting for it to start up, she swept the room again. There had to be something here.

She leaned back and opened the desk drawers, found Cain's address book tucked beneath a sheath of plain white papers, tossed it onto the desk, and then swung around to look through the file cabinets behind her. Nothing. Not even a file on the man.

She stood and rummaged through the rolltop desk next to the bubbling aquarium. She checked the trash can beside the bookcase. There was a closet at the far end of the room, but nothing helpful within it. As much as Carmen looked, she came away with not so much as a scrap of information on Wolfhagen. She went into the bedroom, searched everywhere, but it fruitless.

Was Cain even writing a book?

Carmen returned to the office, knowing she couldn't leave here without something.

She crossed to the desk and removed a flash drive from her knapsack. She connected it to Cain's computer, downloaded the contents of her hard drive, and reached for Cain's address book, soaking the pages into memory. She put it down and, as she did, her hand brushed against the telephone.

And Carmen felt a rush. She hadn't checked this phone.

She hit the redial button and listened through the loud speaker as the machine on the opposite end picked up. A man's voice, brisk, all business: "This is 555-2641. Leave a message at the tone and I'll get back to you."

Carmen severed the connection and searched for the man's number in the address book. She found it toward the back of the book: Marty Spellman, Private Investigator. The ink was dark red and appeared fresh. There was an address beneath it and the number to his cell, which she called on her own cell.

"Hello?"

She hung up.

A private investigator--and Maggie Cain was in contact with him.

Carmen smiled.

Bingo.

CHAPTER EIGHTEEN

Stretched out naked in the center of the bed, Jennifer lifted her head from Marty's chest and looked up at the telephone. "All right," she said. "First your telephone, now your cell phone. Who's calling and hanging up on you? What's her name? You break her heart, too?"

He looked at the number on his cell, but didn't recognize it. "Very funny."

"You must be seeing someone."

"What makes you think that?"

"Because you're so good looking," she said. "So charming. So intelligent. So much money."

"So full of shit," he said. "And besides, I don't know anyone with enough courage to date me."

Jennifer laughed. "Sweetheart, are you kidding? This is New York. Here, the women have bigger balls than yours."

"In the right parts of town, they do."

She put a finger to his lips. "I really don't want to know how you knew that," she said, wiggling down the bed. She tiptoed her fingers down the length of his penis, cupped her hand around its base and smiled as it swelled. "Amazing," she said. "I mean, look at it grow. I bet Brian Williams' cock doesn't do this." She winked at him. "Or Katie Couric's. If I had one of these, I'd never leave it alone."

Marty watched as she slowly masturbated him. "There was a time when I didn't leave it alone."

"Let's not talk about those months you were without me."

"I was talking about when I was a kid."

"Of course, you were."

"I'm serious."

She squeezed harder. "I'm sure you are. And let me tell you, Marty, the idea of you locked away in a bathroom with some skin magazine propped on your lap is certainly going to get my coals burning this afternoon." She tugged and pulled and thumped the head of his penis against her chin. "How big is this thing, anyway?"

"How big is a mile?"

"A hell of a lot longer than this." She flicked her tongue along the very tip. "I'd say it's a good three inches. Maybe four."

He patted her ass. "Aren't you sweet. Care for me to guess your weight?"

"I've got your balls in my hands. You sure you want to go there?"

"Probably not."

She continued to play with it. "It is big," she said.

"Your weight or my cock?"

"So clever."

She put her mouth over the head and reached up to pinch his nipple. Her tongue extended and curled, fluttered and did things to him that made him moan. He put his cell down and got on top of her. It occurred to him that this would be the third time in less than ninety minutes that they'd made love.

It occurred to him again just how much he had missed her.

* * *

"I'm supposed to be in editing," Jennifer called from the bathroom. "My producer is going to kill me."

She came out of the bathroom and crossed to the bed, where she'd laid out her clothes and started to dress. She leaned down to kiss Marty on the forehead, then on the lips, then on the nose and on each cheek. Her skin was free of makeup and it glowed from the heat of the shower. Her hair, loose around her shoulders, was damp and smelled of shampoo.

"Voice-overs?" he asked.

"Ad nauseam."

She started down the hall. Marty dressed and followed her into the entryway.

"We'll talk tonight at eight," she said, opening the door and stepping into the hallway. "You can tell me everything then."

Almost everything, Marty thought. He wasn't telling her about the tattoo and the piercing until he knew more.

* * *

When she left, he showered, brushed his teeth and dressed in a fresh change of clothes. He didn't know where his relationship with Jennifer was going or what the past few hours had meant, but he knew better than to second-guess anything. Right now, he was simply happy to have her back in his life. Whatever came of it.

He went to his office.

Maggie Cain asked him to call at noon, but now it was 3:30. *Time to get focused.* He tried her number, got her machine and left a message, saying he'd call her back as soon as he got the chance.

He sat at his desk, opened his address book and looked up Linda Patterson's extension at the First P. He didn't want to call her, didn't want to deal with her crap, but he had no choice. He picked up the phone and tapped out her number. She answered on the third ring. "Patterson."

"Linda," he said. "It's Marty Spellman. How are you?"

"Busy."

"Too busy to meet somewhere for a drink? I'm buying."

"You'd have to get me to sit down with you."

Coming from anyone else, Marty would have been insulted. But Patterson was such a wreck, so infinitely troubled, he couldn't help being amused by her little dig. And so he dug back, reaching back to her past when she'd been busted for drug abuse. "The reason I'm calling is that I just learned from a friend that IA is about to bust your ass for trafficking. All I wanted to do is buy you a drink before they finally kick your ass off the force. A parting gift of sorts to make up for the pension you'll be losing."

"Fuck you, Spellman."

"Charming as ever, Linda."

"Kiss my ass."

"I'd never be able to afford to."

She slammed down the receiver.

Marty called her back. "Do you think we can behave like adults now? Or is that out of the question?"

She didn't answer.

"All I want is to do is ask you a few questions."

"Why the hell should I bother talking to you?"

"I think we both know the answer to that question, Linda."

He heard what sounded like her pushing back her chair and closing her office door. "What questions?" she asked.

"Not over the phone," Marty said. "In person. How's 4:00 sound?"

"Forget it," she said. "I'm working a big case. Gotta be here. Gotta be now."

He had no time for this. He'd have to be blunt. "I can't exactly hand you a check over the phone or in your office, now can I, Linda?"

She went silent for a moment, then cleared her throat. "I don't know what you're talking about," she said. "My birthday isn't until next month. But what the hell? I haven't eaten lunch, so let's make it the earliest dinner New York has ever seen. Where do you want to meet?"

* * *

The Tarot Café was in the partitioned basement of an old warehouse on Prince Street. Owned by three psychic sisters from Flatbush, the café served imported coffees and herbal teas, ginseng extracts and mushroom shoots, exotic-looking desserts and homemade breads, soups, sandwiches, as well as glimpses into their clients' futures.

It was through Gloria that Marty came to this narrow, dim place that often smelled of patchouli oil, and it was through Gloria that he had met the three sisters Buzzinni--Roberta, Carlotta and Gigi.

Not a superstitious man, Marty had come to view the Buzzinnis' psychic powers as little more than a gimmick that had turned into a comfortable career of tea leaves and tarot cards, face readings and character analyses. Gloria, however, swore by them. "They're good," she said, after her first visit. "One of them held my hand and told me I have two daughters. Another read my cards and learned that I paint. They said I'm going to be famous."

Now it was Gloria who was saying that.

Roberta Buzzinni, his favorite of the three sisters, had taken the cafe's reins while Carlotta and Gigi worked to open their new satellite café on Christopher Street.

She was seated at the rear of the empty café shuffling a deck of cards when he stepped into the quiet gloom. She looked up at him with raised eyebrows and immediately cut the deck, drew the top card and held it as high as the hair on her head. "This," she said, smiling, "is your future." She looked at the card and her smile faltered. She drew the next card and her frown deepened.

Amused, Marty threaded his way through the many tapestry-covered tables and wispy, gray-blue slips of incense smoke. Today, the café smelled of tomato soup and myrrh. "That bad?" he asked.

Roberta buried the cards at the bottom of the pile and put the deck away. "What the hell do I know?" she said. "I'm just a psychic." She stood up and enfolded him in heavy arms. "Where have you been?" she asked. "We've missed you."

"I've been working," he said. "What else?"

"I can feel your bones," she said, squeezing him. "You're not eating. You're too thin."

"It's all muscle, baby."

"Yeah," she said, stepping back. "Kinda like me."

He gave her a kiss on the forehead and inhaled the sweet scent of plums in her thick, curly black hair. "Sorry it's been so long," he said. "But I did stop by three Sundays ago. The place was closed."

"We had a little fire in the kitchen," Roberta said as they sat down. "Carlotta saw it coming two weeks before it happened, but couldn't zone in on the exact date. Gigi and I tried like hell to tap into it, but our own Information Superhighway was on the fritz. Too much static in the summertime--too many souls buzzing in and out of our lives. But the fire turned out to be great. No one got hurt and we got a new kitchen out of the blaze, courtesy of Fabrizzi's Insurance. Gigi's in heaven. No more rats!"

Marty laughed. "How's the new place?"

"Opening next month. And wait until you see it. Spirits speak to you in there. The place is brimming with energy."

"Just be careful who you tell that to."

"What are you talking about? I'm telling everyone."

"How are you?"

"Fatter than ever, but happy as hell. It's you I'm worried about. Where have you been? Two months I haven't seen you. Gigi was asking for you the other day. I told her I didn't know anything, which surprised all of us because, you know, I tend to know things without knowing how I know them. Gloria disappeared years ago, but you, you hung in there. You came to see us. You cared. Then, poof! You're also gone." She shrugged. "Doesn't matter. You're here now, so you might as well eat. I'm feeding you. Lotta made a tomato soup this morning that'll make you cry. It's on me."

"Bring tissues."

"You'll need them."

She got up from the table with a bit of a struggle. She was a large woman with hips like barrels and breasts so heavy they rounded her back. She pushed sideways through the swinging set of kitchen doors and returned a moment later with soup, bread and chilled herbal tea on a wooden tray. "Enjoy," she said, placing the food in front of him. "There's more where that came from."

He knew better than to argue. He started to eat and became aware that she was studying him.

"You're giving off a helluva lot of energy, sweetie, and that either means you've met someone, or you're working a new case. I think it's both, but let's start with the new case."

Marty spooned soup and evaded the subject. "I meant to tell you that I'm meeting someone here."

"I knew that," Roberta said, sitting in the chair opposite him. "Now, give me your hand."

"Let's not start that crap, Roberta."

"Just give me your hand," she said. "I had a bad feeling when you came in. I need to make sure of a few things."

"I'm not superstitious."

"Neither am I," she said. "Just gifted. So, humor me. Something's off."

Reluctantly, Marty gave her his hand. Roberta held it for a moment, then turned it so the palm faced the tapestry-covered ceiling. She closed her eyes and massaged the soft center with her thumb and index finger. She was silent for a moment before she spoke. "This new case of yours," she said. "It's not what you think."

Marty sipped his tea.

Roberta's forehead creased with thought. Her dark eyebrows stitched together and became one. "You're in over your head. You're being lied to. You're in danger and you don't even know it. Someone's not what they seem."

"Few people are," Marty mused. "Take Gloria, for instance."

"No," Roberta said, looking at him. Her eyes were serious. "Don't be flip. I drew the Death card when you came in. You're at risk. I'm sure of that. For once in your life, listen to me. It's possible you might not come out of this alive."

Marty tried to pull his hand back, but Roberta hung on.

"Three women," she said. "One of them loves you, one of them resents you, the third is keeping secrets from you. They're in danger, too, but only one knows it and she doesn't care. She's got murder in her heart. She wants someone dead. I don't know if it's you, but you're involved. She might kill you."

She released his hand.

"You've got to listen to me," Roberta said. "This is real."

At that moment, the front door swung open and Linda Patterson stepped inside.

CHAPTER NINETEEN

Linda Patterson was not the woman Marty remembered from two years ago.

Dressed casually in beige linen pants and a white top, her light blonde hair just reaching her shoulders, she moved toward Roberta and Marty with the air of a professional, which was a radical difference from the last time he'd seen her.

Where was the hardened, strung-out cop he once caught freebasing coke in the back of a tenement on Avenue C? Where were the deeply rouged cheeks, brittle red hair and dumpy looking clothes that once aged her? Today's Linda Patterson looked nothing like her past and instead gave the clever illusion of city chic--until she opened her mouth.

"Oh, this is perfect, Spellman," she said, looking around. "A Tibetan massage parlor. Last time I caught a whiff of incense was 1969 and Mama Cass had yet to choke on her chicken bone."

"You and your urban legends. It was a ham sandwich."

"Whatever. You and your freaky joints. I suppose you're into holistic home medicine, too. Acupuncture. Aroma therapy."

"Good manners."

"Bullshit responses."

Roberta shot him a glance. Marty returned the look and stood. "Linda," he said, "I'd like you to meet Roberta Buzzinni. She's one of the owners of the café."

Unfazed, Patterson turned to Roberta and blinked. "You a psychic or something?"

Roberta nodded.

"And you admit it," Linda said. "Now, that's interesting." She said 'interesting' as though it were the least interesting thing in the world. She lowered her shiny leather handbag onto the table and put her hands on her hips. "Okay," she said, "I'm game. Tell me my future."

Roberta lifted an eyebrow at Marty, then pushed back her chair and stood. "Ms. Patterson," she said, "something tells me you wouldn't be able to handle it."

"I've been a detective with the NYPD for eight years," Linda said. "Before that, I was an assistant at the M.E.'s office. You have no idea what I can handle. Try me."

Roberta's face became set, expressionless. It was the face of a woman addressing a problematic child. Marty saw tolerance in her eyes, but also a hint of something else. Mischief? "All right," she said. "Give me your hand."

Linda held out her hand, which Roberta took and just as quickly dropped. "You won't live to see your fiftieth birthday. You'll be shot dead in the street--a hole right through that Botoxed forehead of yours. The number of people who show up at your funeral will reveal just how cruelly you've lived your life." In the silence that fell, Roberta excused herself and swung sideways into the kitchen. Marty heard her bark out a laugh as he sat back down.

Patterson took the chair opposite him. "What the hell kind of a woman is that?" she said angrily. "Won't live past my fiftieth birthday. What kind of a thing is that to say to someone? I'm forty-nine now, for Christ's sake. My birthday's in a few months. She saying I'll be dead by then?" She shook her head. "No wonder this dump is empty."

"Can't handle it, Linda?"

"I wanted to know something nice," Linda said. "I wanted to hear something good, just like we all do. I didn't need to hear that crap. That woman's got nerve."

"I believe she could say the same about you. You insulted her and her business."

Patterson ignored the comment and rummaged inside her handbag--blunt red fingernails clicking, hands grasping and pulling out a rumpled pack of cigarettes. She shook one out, lit it with the strike of a match and inhaled, holding the smoke before blowing it above their heads. "Look," she said. "I meant it when I said I was busy. I'm giving you fifteen minutes. What do you want from me?"

He looked at her cigarette. "Smoking isn't allowed in here."

"I'm a cop."

"Doesn't matter."

"We'll see. I'm seeking information."

"Surprise, surprise. What about?"

"A couple of things. But let's start with Maria Martinez and her daughter."

Patterson drew on the cigarette and sat looking at him, her eyes and face betraying nothing. "Maria Martinez?" she said. "Since when are you interested in the welfare mothers of the world, Marty? Martinez didn't live in a penthouse on Fifth. She was no murdered socialite. Why would you of all people be interested in her and her daughter?"

"I'll ask the questions, Linda."

"That may be," Linda said. "But it's up to me whether I answer them, isn't it?" She took another pull off her cigarette and paused, her face hardening, jaw tightening, wheels turning. "Look," she said. "I'm not giving you shit until you've handed over that check you promised me."

Marty removed the check from his shirt pocket and pushed it face-down across the table.

Patterson picked it up, glanced fleetingly at the amount and tucked it in her handbag. "That's less than before," she said. "You're getting cheap. But seeing as though I've only got a couple months to live, I'll take it. What do you want to know?"

"For starters," Marty said, "I'd like to know about the people who saw them being dumped in that Dumpster on 141st Street."

Patterson started nibbling her lower lip, a nervous habit she'd picked up in rehab. "Aren't you the clever one, Marty. How'd you find out about that?"

"I get around."

"Yeah," Linda said. "Like the clap."

The kitchen door swung open and Roberta appeared with a steaming cup of tea on a metal tray. She put the cup and the saucer down in front of Linda, plucked the cigarette from her hand and said with her eyes lifted to the ceiling, "This will help even you out. It's my own special blend. It's my suggestion that you drink it while thinking positive thoughts, if that's possible. There's no charge. Don't smoke in here again." Without another word, she went back to the kitchen. Linda looked at the cup of tea--which had a faint ammonia scent to it--moved to pick it up, but instead pushed it away. "She took my fucking cigarette."

"That's because it's against the law to smoke here."

"Whatever. About Martinez. Only one person came forward. The other disappeared."

"I assume we're dealing with a prostitute here?"

"You assume correctly."

"And her john took off."

"Wouldn't you?"

"Who's the hooker?"

"LaWanda Jackson," Patterson said. "Twenty-seven. Been on the streets since she was fifteen and is angry as hell because of it. Until last night, she lived behind that Dumpster. Had a mattress stained with blood and crawling with God-knows-what. Now I don't know what'll happen to her."

"What did she see?"

"Plenty."

"Care to elaborate?"

Linda shrugged. "I'll give you your money's worth. Jackson said she was giving some sleazoid suit the blowjob of a lifetime when Martinez and her daughter ran into the alley, followed by some man with a gun. Before Jackson could react, the man had Martinez against a wall and was pumping two bullets into her brain. He pushed her to the ground and snapped the little girl's neck. Jackson said she'd never seen anything like it, which I doubt. In sixty seconds, the man murdered two people and tossed their bodies in a Dumpster. He never broke stride. The friggin' end."

"What did he look like?"

"Jackson didn't get an ID," Linda said. "Too dark."

"She saw nothing?" Marty said. "Oh, come on, Linda. She must have seen something. Even the color of the man's hair."

"She didn't see anything, Marty. Zero. I believe her."

And you're a goddamn liar. "How can I get in touch with her?"

Patterson laughed. "Are you serious, Spellman? Did you hear anything I just said? Jackson lives on the street, not in the sort of glitzy Park Avenue high-rise you're used to. Do you get the distinction? She's a homeless whore. I'd be lucky to find her again."

Suddenly impatient, she glanced at her watch. "Look," she said. "I've given you your fifteen minutes. I've told you what I know about the Martinezes. You got something else you want to ask me? Because if you don't, I'm out of here."

"Then let's talk about Gerald Hayes."

Patterson leaned back in her chair as Roberta came through the door with a clutch of sage. She lit it on fire and walked past the table in great swirls of smoke. "Gets rid of the negative energy," Roberta said. "I should be more thorough, but I don't want to interrupt, so I'll make this quick."

She said something beneath her breath and waved the sage near Linda. Then, with a final shake that released a plume of smoke, she left.

"What the fuck is this place?" Linda said. "Now I smell like Thanksgiving dinner."

"Can we talk about Hayes, please?"

Linda shook her head. "No, Marty, that's something I'll never give you. Did you really think I didn't know where this was going? Did you really think I'd give you anything on Hayes after the way you screwed me over on Wilcox?"

She smiled at him. "I had you pegged for an idiot, but this is ridiculous. You burned me once. I gave you everything I had on Wilcox and you went public with her murderer. You broke your promise. You said you'd give me the son of a bitch and you didn't. I'm going all the way with this case. Hayes' death was a high-profile blessing from God. I'm getting Detective First Grade out of it."

"I doubt that," Marty said. "But I am curious. If you knew I was fishing all along for Hayes, why'd you give me anything on Martinez? Their deaths are obviously related. You've helped more than you know. So why talk?"

Patterson patted her handbag. "Because I wanted the money," she said lightly. "Pure and simple. And, besides, what I gave you wasn't worth shit compared to what I know about Hayes. Certainly nothing you couldn't have found out without me. So, it was an easy two grand. Lucky me."

She rose from her seat, all cool lines and silky curves. She reached for her handbag and looked down at him. "Here's something else, Spellman, a little advice. If you interfere in any way with this case, if you cross me, I'll bust your ass for obstruction.

This case is NYPD property. Do you understand me?" Her voice was absolutely calm. "You're not a cop. You have no authority. Screw with my case, and I'll get a court order that'll nail you to the wall."

Marty smiled up at her. "Sweet, Linda. Really, I'll keep it in mind. But I'm a registered private investigator, and that also gives me rights. Before you leave, there's something you should know. That check I gave you? It isn't signed. I gave you an unsigned check. You did just what I knew you'd do. You only looked at the amount. You never even thought to look for a signature. Too greedy. Too predictable. Too much like the old Linda. So, unless you forge my name, which I wouldn't suggest since it's a crime, it looks like it's you who's just been nailed to the wall."

* * *

"I don't like that woman, Marty. She's evil. She's no good. And it's not because she insulted my place. She's got a darkness in her that even I won't go near. Why do you hang around people like that? They sour your soul."

Marty reached in his pocket for his cell and tapped out Hines' number at the 19th. Roberta, busy making tea for the party of five that had just stepped in, shot him a sideways glance. "And I'll tell you something else," she said. "My prediction is right. That woman will be dead by fifty. Just you wait and see."

"I wish you wouldn't talk that way, Roberta. You've got me on the list, too."

"But you can do something about it," Roberta said. "You can drop the case now, before it goes any further. You could listen to me."

"Roberta, if I listened to you, I'd be penniless. Do you realize that every time I take a new case you're telling me I'll be dead."

"This time you might be."

"Whatever happened to optimism?"

"Oh, please," she laughed. "Are you serious? When they legalize pot, I'll be optimistic."

Hines answered. "Can't talk," he said. "Just busted the perp on another case. Son of a bitch drove stakes through his wife and kids. Thought they were vampires. Admitted to all of it. Said Stephanie Myers told him to do it. In there smiling at me, like he'd do it again if he had the chance. Call me back later."

"Two questions," Marty said. "That's it."

"Make 'em fast."

"Where's Wolfhagen?"

"Not at The Plaza," Hines said. "Checked out this afternoon. Said the place gives him the creeps."

"Where's he staying?"

"With his wife."

"With his wife?" Marty said. "Then his alibi checked? He was with her last night?"

"He was at a party of hers last night," Hines said. "A big deal that lasted until two in the morning. Thirty people can and will vouch for his presence. I talked to Carra Wolfhagen myself and she confirmed everything. She says he spent the night with her and there's nothing I can do about that. Now, I gotta go. Call me later. You know, when you've got something."

The line went dead.

Marty hung up the phone and caught Roberta's concerned glance. She was standing beside him, slicing a lemon, adding the curving yellow wedges to the steaming pot of tea.

Slice, slice, slice.

"Everything's going to be fine," he said.

But Roberta, whose face now reflected a sadness he had never seen in it before, shook her head. "No, Marty, this time it isn't."

CHAPTER TWENTY

Spocatti stood between the heat of two double-parked vans, looking across to the grimy brick building Maggie Cain had just entered. He was in the roughest part of the South Bronx--Hunts Point--where the haze of poverty and decay was so strong here, it clung to his clothes and cut off his breath.

He knew this neighborhood.

When he was a boy, several family members lived here. At that time, his father owned a successful restaurant in Little Italy, and so, because they had money, it was Spocatti's family who drove here on Sundays to visit the relatives. Then, Spocatti would sit next to his father and listen to his two uncles discuss their hopes and dreams to find better jobs and move their families out of this place.

It didn't happen. Though they wished for a better future, his uncles' alcoholism and drug abuse prevented them from having it.

That was thirty years ago. And while this place had seen a push in the '80s in an effort to revitalize it, the attempt failed. Looking around, Spocatti thought it looked worse than ever, particularly after the recession.

Even now, on the cusp of sunset, transvestites and prostitutes were working the streets and street corners, drug deals were being made in backrooms, private clubs were thriving in shadowy basements--and disease was running rampant.

With the Meatpacking District now bright with boutiques and trendy restaurants, the South Bronx, in a sense, had taken its place among those areas in the city where the fringe could thrive. Were you a trucker in need of a blowjob? Come to Hunts Point. Married businessman into a bit of kink? Come to Hunts Point. The area was morphing even deeper into the corrupt underworld some craved.

Spocatti was amused to find how comfortable he was here.

He looked at his watch. Cain had been inside three minutes. Whoever had dropped her here was gone. He looked across to the two scantily clad transvestites clicking toward the building and watched them walk down the narrow cement steps. They rapped on a door he couldn't see, screamed something above the sudden roar of music, and were let inside.

Private party.

Password protected.

He'd seen it before. The people who threw these parties gave every queen and whore working these streets a password that allowed them entrance. If business was slow, they could come to a party, perform for the guests, earn that night's dinner. Maybe even a taste of whatever drug was circulating that day.

So, why had Maggie Cain come here?

He left his shiny metal enclave and stepped into the street. Trucks rumbled past. At the street corner, four transvestites were leaning against a black Mercedes. They tapped on its hood, shook their asses in front of the darkened windows, bent down to blow kisses, circled and posed. One of them looked up at him and smiled.

Spocatti smiled back.

The easiest way inside that building was on her arm.

* * *

She said her name was Diva Divine.

She was taller than him and black, her platinum blonde hair worn in a teased flip. The long white gloves that stretched up her emaciated arms hid the veins she'd ruined with needles, but her makeup--heavy and smeared in the moist August heat--couldn't conceal the day's growth of beard that shadowed her face in a dusting of black. Spocatti thought she had the exhausted, sunken look of someone who had seen every rotten thing twice--and remembered it.

He led her behind a large truck and listened as she spoke.

"You got the fiercest queen in the city, baby. Fiercest. Diva's gonna rock your world."

Her drag was a tight white tube dress that was fraying at the hem, stained with food, blotched with sweat. Her four-inch heels--red as her lipstick but more even in color--were badly in need of repair. She snapped her fingers above her head and swayed slightly, as if she were drunk. But she wasn't drunk. She was coming off a high. Her eyes were the same as his brother's had been just before the high left him--bright brown panes of glass.

He pointed to the building Maggie Cain had entered. "I need to get inside that building," he said. "As in now. Can you do it?"

Divine fluffed her wig with long, chipped-black nails. "You got enough cash, Diva D. can take your beautiful ass anywhere you want to go."

"How much?" he said.

"Lots."

"Be specific."

She sank against the truck and reached up inside her tube dress, eyelids fluttering as she scratched something he couldn't see.

A limousine swung in front of the building. Spocatti turned and watched a well-dressed couple leave the car and hurry down the cement steps. A rap on the door, a firestorm of music, silence.

Ten minutes had passed. Maggie Cain could be anywhere.

He gripped Divine's arm. "How much?"

Startled, she reared back.

"How much?"

Real fear in her eyes. She shrank away from him. "I don't know. Let go of me. You're hurting me!"

He gave her a hundred.

* * *

The door was large and solid, painted black, windowless. Spocatti could see strobes of red light pressing through the cracks around the edges. In the space beyond, he could hear the driving, crashing beat of industrial music. Here, the air smelled of something spoiled, as if the building itself, along with its inhabitants, were failing in the searing summer heat.

Divine knocked twice, waited, knocked again, and the door parted on its heavy metal chain.   Music and light blasted the stairwell.   Divine stuck her face into the two-inch crack and shouted: "It's me, Frankie! I gotta guest!"

"Private party, Divine. No guests."

"Don't play that shit with me, Frankie. Let me in!"

"No guests."

"Oh, for Christ's sake, he ain't a cop!"

"You know the rules."

"You want the damned password?"

"It ain't gonna help."

"Then what I really know is you." She turned to Spocatti, eyes suddenly focused, alert.   "The greedy mothafucka wants some money. Gimme another hundred."

Spocatti moved right, looked at Frankie's profile through the four-inch crack. He was tall and muscular; bulging, black leather pants; black leather vest; black leather head mask with an open zippered mouth.   His nipples were pierced with shiny silver lightning rods. His torso and arms were a colorful palette of bold tattoos. He leaned down to pull on his boots.

He was alone.

Spocatti dipped his hand into the pouch at his waist and gripped the gun. "I don't have another hundred," he said.

"Then gimme what you got."

He checked the silencer, flicked off the guard, looked around him. Nobody. But Divine, who missed nothing on these streets, saw the gun and put her hand over his. She shook her head at him, reached inside her bra, removed the hundred he'd given to her, stuck it through the crack. Frankie snagged it.

"You satisfied now, Frankie?" she called. Her eyes never left Spocatti's. "You happy now, darlin'? That'll buy you a week's worth of meds and God knows your infected ass probably needs it. Bigger tramp than me."

She forced the gun back into its pouch. "No," she said to Spocatti. "No."

Spocatti lifted an eyebrow at her. "You're telling me what to do?"

"This is how I eat, baby. This is what I do. I don't need no trouble here. Just be cool. I'll get you inside."

And she did.

The door closed, swung open again and Frankie stood there, folding the bill into a neat square. He smiled at Spocatti, reached out to slap Divine's ass. "Welcome to Heaven," he said.

*   *   *

Heaven was straight down a staircase that leaned left.

Lights flashed and skidded up the black walls, giving the illusion of movement within shadows too dark to judge depth. The floor thudded with the driving beat of industrial music. The air was cooler here, and it smelled of sweat and rotting wood. At the top of the staircase, Divine turned to him. "I got friends here," she shouted above the music, backing down the stairs, white gloved fingers tiptoeing along the rail. Itching to get away from him. "I gotta see them. You'll be okay alone? Just a few minutes?"

Spocatti moved down the staircase after her. "Is this the only way out of here?"

She nodded.

"You're sure?"

"Yes, baby. Why?"

He looked over her shoulder and saw in the sudden ricochet of light the moons and planets of six faces peering up at him from the darkness of the stairwell, only to disappear and reappear again in different order. It was as if this universe was realigning itself, unraveling. He took Divine's arm and led her down the stairs. "Tall woman," he said in her ear. "Early thirties. Shoulder-length dark hair. Scar on her left cheek. Striking. Name's Maggie Cain. Find her and you'll get your money back, plus another grand."

"Plus another grand?"

They paused at the bottom of the stairs and looked left. The basement was as cavernous as it was captivating. Low ceilings were strung with spinning lights, thick rotting beams jutted at odd angles from the dirt floor, crowds of naked people were twirling to the music.

In one of the twelve metal cages lining the walls, someone in a Bush mask was sucking face with Obama's twin. In front of them, a train of men trotted past, their identities smeared and distorted by the plastic wrap wound around their grinning faces. In the moment before he left her, Spocatti looked at Divine and saw on her face the wall she'd been building since childhood. Anger. Despair. Resentment. A surprising vulnerability. Never had she suspected that this would become her life, yet here it was.

Her tough luck.

He moved through the shifting wall of bodies and saw Maggie Cain almost immediately. She was across the room, her face pressed between the bars of a metal cage. Inside the cage, a heavy-set woman with nothing but a ball gag in her mouth and a pink ribbon in her hair was circling an elderly man lying naked on his back, his Tinker Toy legs lifted and parted in stirrups. Cain was talking to the man, who seemed disinterested in what she was saying.

Spocatti was interested.

He pushed forward and stepped within earshot, but he was too late--Maggie Cain was already pulling away. "You're a fool, Alan, just like the rest of them."

As she turned, Spocatti turned with her, showing her his back as she slipped into the crowd. He waited to make sure she wasn't moving toward the exit before turning to glance at the man in the cage. He pressed a coke inhaler against his nostril and made kissing noises to the woman while he snorted the drug. He giggled and he laughed, and Spocatti, who never forgot a face, recognized him from the photographs Wolfhagen sent months ago, when the job was initially proposed and accepted.

He was Alan Ross, another of Wolfhagen's former moles, who had testified against Wolfhagen for his own personal immunity. He'd stolen confidential information for Wolfhagen but he'd done no time in prison for the millions he'd ripped out of the world's hands. He was on Wolfhagen's list and he was to be murdered along with the rest of them.

Had Maggie Cain come here to warn him?

He looked around for her, saw her talking to a man at the makeshift bar, and knew that if she had warned Ross, he couldn't let the man leave here alive.

He also knew that if he didn't do this quickly, he'd lose her.

He moved to the rear of Ross' cage and swung open the door. The woman looked around and growled a low warning at Spocatti as the club's lights fanned out and dimmed to blackness. Ross' head jerked up. "Who's there?" he whispered.

Spocatti stepped right, eyes on the woman.

"Mama?"

The lights again, all of them, lifting from floor to ceiling.

"Tell me it's you."

Spocatti bent down and gripped the woman by the throat. "Get out of here. Now. I'm fucking him, not you."

The woman started to laugh, but Spocatti stopped her with a slap across the face, which startled and thrilled her. He could see that she was high, so he slapped her again, this time so hard that the ball gag sprang free from her mouth and for an instant, her eyes became clear. "Get out."

The woman left on all fours.

Spocatti leaned down and cupped Ross' face in his hands. He brushed away the sweaty white hair cobwebbing the man's forehead and traced a finger around the man's mouth. He kissed him, felt Ross's tongue slide across his lower lip, tasted the man's self-hatred on his breath, sensed him relaxing beneath his touch, and became aware of shapes and shadows moving closer to get a better look at the man in street clothes kissing the freak. One by one, they left, disinterested.

Spocatti waited for the lights to dim and finally they did. He pulled out his iPhone, set it to record and discretely put it next to Ross. He shielded it with his lowered body so nobody could see it. Now, the camera faced Alan Ross' head.

He curled his lips away and said just loud enough for Ross and the camera to hear, "You sent Wolfhagen to prison and now he's having you murdered. Tell me how it feels, Alan."

The man blinked in recognition at the sound of Wolfhagen's name. His eyes flicked up to Spocatti, then across to the iPhone, where the room's lights were causing an electrified firestorm to gather and crash in the center of the device's glass panel.

"Who are--?"

Spocatti gripped the man's head and, in an instant, twisted it. The sound of neck bones breaking was dulled only by the sharp

blast of music. But Spocatti heard it and, as he gently rested Ross'
head back onto the table, he slipped the iPhone into his pocket and
stepped away just as the man lost control of his bladder and colon.

Lights still low, Spocatti moved away from the cage and into the
crowd. He glanced back and saw pooling on the floor all of the
rotten life that was leaving Ross.

He stared at it for a moment and knew that in this crowd, it
wouldn't go to waste. It would attract an animal of a different sort.

CHAPTER TWENTY-ONE

In Heaven, Maggie Cain's scarred profile, caught in the ceiling's spinning lights, flashed across the blackened walls in a million jigsaw shadows that would never fit if pieced together.

She was sick from being here. Revolted.

She looked up at the woman hanging above her from the black trapeze and wanted to snap the damn cords. But why bother? This woman would feel nothing if she fell. Her eyes were wide open yet unseeing, windows that looked into empty rooms. The things she'd seen, the secrets she knew, were stamped within the lines of her face.

Fool.

Maggie looked at her watch and again around the club. He wasn't coming, even though he'd sent his driver to pick her up and bring her here. She was disappointed but not surprised. When they spoke, she'd warned him what was going on, but didn't answer his questions. She wanted to see him in person to tell him the rest of it, if only so she could try to reach him with the gravity of the situation before it was too late. Although he told her he came here every Saturday at this time, he'd obviously backed out.

Something soft and fleshy brushed against her leg.

Startled, she looked down and saw an enormously fat woman walk past her on all fours. She stopped to rest beside a man with a glass slipper perched atop his head. Maggie watched him reach down to pat the woman's head, then she turned and looked in the direction from which the woman came.

She saw him almost immediately--the man from the street. He was leaving Ross' cage, closing the door behind him, now sliding along the walls as he moved in her direction. He passed through ribbons of red light and Maggie saw with a start that he was looking at her. His mouth tightened, their glances crashed, hers fell away.

He was following her.

She'd seen him at the bookstore, the post office, her agent's office on 13th Street. She'd dismissed him as a curious fan.

She stepped back into shadow. He wasn't FBI, didn't have the look. Who, then? And why had he been in Alan Ross' cage?

Two hundred feet and a wall of bodies separated them. She moved away from the bar and in the direction of the exit, where a tall black transvestite with a teased platinum wig turned to look at her with interest.

The queen's lips parted in what could only be a look of recognition and now real fear burned in Maggie's throat. He'd blocked the only exit with a sidewalk whore, who straightened and looked briefly behind Maggie before coming down the last step and staring her hard in the face.

Heaven's lights dimmed to blackness.

The crowd surged to the right in a tidal wave of flesh and Maggie felt hands on her body, hips and shoulders slamming into hers. She started to rush back when one of the hands reached out and snagged her arm, hooked it in a death grip, pulled her forward and held her firm. Maggie twisted back, struggled against the man, and was about to scream when his deep voice hissed in her ear: "Shut up, fool." It was the transvestite. "You wanna live, then you better move your ass outta here now. Right now. Hear me? There's a crazy fuck in here that wants to kill you."

* * *

Spocatti knew the moment Divine leaned toward Maggie Cain's ear that she was telling her to run. And so he ran through the crowd, leaping over the fat woman pretending to be a dog and a dozen other people behaving like dogs as he sprinted toward the exit.

But in the wild maze of flashing lights and twirling bodies, he couldn't see clearly, couldn't seem to move forward without someone getting in his way and slowing him down. With mounting frustration, he saw Cain look over her shoulder, spot him and then, with fear on her face, she rushed up the stairs, which led to open air and freedom.

Spocatti ran toward the white light wavering at the exit, saw the cool glare that was Divine's face as it slid into shadow and disappeared, but he had no time to seek out that face and bash it in. He hit the stairs as Maggie Cain shot past Frankie the doorman and burst through the door. He caught a glimpse of her dark hair in the sudden blast of sunlight and knew that she was his.

But Frankie, foolish in the bravado of his high, stood in front of the door, pulled off his leather mask and folded his arms around his muscular chest in an effort to create some kind of intimidation.

Spocatti raced toward him, the gun in his hand exploding along with the back of Frankie's head. Frankie collapsed in front of him but Spocatti didn't lose momentum. He was through the door, up the stairs and on the street. Heart hammering, eyes blinded by the white-hot sunlight, he saw only shiny trucks rumbling by and the three whistling whores walking alongside them.

He whirled in a complete circle.

Maggie Cain was gone.

* * *

Wolfhagen stood at the top of the staircase, listening.

Down below, in the library, Carra was straightening chairs, moving about, wanting to be heard. The only rugs in this house were threadbare antiques worth a fortune and her shoes clicked across them without apology.

He imagined her stopping in front of mirrors and glimpsing the rage on her face. He imagined her damning him and his presence in her home.

He imagined her dead.

Now she was in the hallway, now the living room. Click, click, click. Wolfhagen leaned over the railing and looked down at the bright entryway, remodeled with his money while he was in prison. The central air conditioning hummed but it couldn't deaden the sounds of those heels. Would she never leave?

Finally, her heels in the hallway, her shadow stretching, Wolfhagen stepping back, floorboards creaking, door swinging open, banging shut.

He hurried into her bedroom and crossed to the window overlooking 68th Street. He parted the heavy damask curtain and peered out. On the sidewalk, Carra was approaching the black limousine waiting for her curbside. She wore a wide-brimmed hat that concealed her face and a tailored red suit that showed off her legs. The driver opened her door and she stepped inside. Wolfhagen had no idea where she was going or how long she would be, but he had threatened her and so she'd left. If he was going to look at this DVD, he'd have to do so now, before she returned.

His suitcase was across the room on the wide iron chair.

Wolfhagen unzipped the bag and removed the disc from beneath the stack of neatly folded clothes. He turned to the cabinet behind him, opened the pale wooden doors, and switched on the television and the DVD player. He inserted the DVD, grabbed the remote, walked backward to the bed, sat down and pushed PLAY. As the screen faded to black, he stared at it.

Time passed. The disc spun. He sat completely still and watched Gerald Hayes tumble through the air and strike the sidewalk. He was shocked by the violence of the act, but not repelled by it. He viewed the scene again and again, marveling at the woman's cool as she smashed in one side of Hayes' head and then led him to the open window and shoved him through.

And of course the woman's words, over and over the woman's words: "Wolfhagen was your closest friend and you betrayed him. You told all his secrets in court, you sent him to prison for three years, and you've never regretted it. Did you really think he'd let you get away with it forever?"

Wolfhagen rewound the DVD, watched it a fifth time. Hayes had just been shoved through his office window when the bedroom door snapped shut.

Startled, Wolfhagen turned.

Carra was at the rear of the room, looking at the television screen, her decorated lips twisted back, her body rigid. He'd been so intent on Hayes' murder, he didn't hear her come in.

Immediately, he stood and shut off the television. How much had she seen? Why had she come back? His mind raced. "It was sent to me," he blurted. "It came in the box with Wood's head. There was a note--it told me to take it. Someone's trying to frame me."

But Carra, whose hat was now in her hand, took a step back.

"It's the truth," he said.

Carra's eyes said it wasn't and she shook her head firmly. She was a woman known for her composure and she didn't lose it now.

She reached out a hand and gripped the doorknob. "I was standing right here," she said. "I heard what that woman said. You killed Gerald. You killed Wood. You've killed every one of them."

* * *

Carmen's face glowed in the light of the computer.

She was in the safe house on Avenue A, reading the information she'd downloaded from Maggie Cain's computer. Her eyes skimmed the information Cain had been compiling since the death of her lover, Mark Andrews.

When she was finished, she sat back in her chair. In all her years in this business, she'd seen some sick shit, usually created by her own hands, but this was a new low. This would be enough for Wolfhagen. Cain and her private investigator were as good as dead.

Carmen picked up her cell and hit Spocatti's number. The line rang, but he didn't answer. She hung up the phone and opened another file, this one marked "Marty Spellman." She read quickly and then stopped at one paragraph. She read it again--and again.

Could this be true?

Again, she tried Spocatti and this time he answered. She told him what she knew and Spocatti told her where to meet him. "His name is Marty Spellman?"

"That's right."

"And he's working with Cain?"

"They're investigating Wolfhagen. They've already involved the police."

"Run a check on him. Find out where he lives."

"I already know."

"That's resourceful, Carmen, good for you. What do you recommend?"

"It's no longer just Cain. We take both out. Now."

"Agreed. Let me call Wolfhagen and tell him our priorities have shifted."

CHAPTER TWENTY-TWO

The light in Manhattan had changed to the deeper glow of late afternoon when Marty left Roberta's. The sun had dipped below the jagged skyline and now deep shadows were stretching across the city, thick fingers reaching out, perhaps in search of a breeze.

Or a neck.

He walked on auto pilot to Washington Square Park, his own shadow dancing before him on the pavement. He watched people he didn't know step all over him, cars race over his head, a city bus cut him in half, a kid on a skateboard sever his legs. His invincible shadow collided with all of New York and it didn't hesitate or flinch. It simply charged forward without feeling, rippling over curbs, growing slowly by inches.

Wolfhagen.

Now this was an interesting turn of events. Marty had to smile. So the man might not be out, after all. He put his hands in his pockets and strolled across the park's wide expanse of cracked cement. Had Wolfhagen really flown 3,000 miles to attend a party given by the woman he was suing for thousands a week in alimony?

Marty read the Post. Like the rest of New York, he knew the Wolfhagens were in the middle of a bitter divorce battle. Carra was fighting him with a team of lawyers hell-bent on giving him nothing of her personal, inherited fortune. She had publicly spoken out against him. Editors continued to showcase the unfolding story with headlines that demanded attention. Had they come to some sort of reconciliation in the few days that had passed since he read the last story? Unlikely. But even if they had, would Carra really have invited him to come cross country to one of her parties? To spend the night at her home? That he couldn't believe.

He left the park and started up Fifth, allowing his thoughts to wander around the possibilities. If Carra hadn't invited Wolfhagen to her party, then why had he flown to New York? To confront her face to face about their divorce? That was a possibility. But if it was the case, then why had Carra allowed him to stay with her now?

Did she have a choice?

He turned onto West 8th Street. Ahead of him and to the right, the Click Click Camera Shop reared its ugly face to the world. Marty stepped inside.

A shirtless Jo Jo Wilson looked up as Marty strolled toward him. He dropped the tattered issue of Big Jugs he was holding and scowled, his pitted lips parting in protest. "This better not be about your camera," he said. "I sent it to you, just like you asked."

"The camera's fine," Marty said. "I need to use your phone."

"You need to use my what?"

He continued across the narrow, dingy little store and put his hands down on the dusty glass countertop. Jo Jo leaned back on his rusty metal stool. "Your phone," Marty said. "I need to use it. My cell is almost dead."

Wilson's hand skidded left, behind a stack of boxes that had the words "POISON" and "!DANGER--LIVE ANIMALS!" stamped in red all over them, and came back with a dirty gray cordless phone that once had been beige. He handed it to Marty, who dialed Maggie Cain. Again, he got her machine. Still, she wasn't home. He left another message, this time asking her to call his cell immediately. He hung up the phone and stood there, wondering where she could be. He needed to speak to her. She knew the Wolfhagens.

"Trying to reach somebody?" Jo Jo asked.

"Oh, that's brilliant, Jo Jo. That's smart."

"Tense as usual?"

"I'm not tense."

"Right. And I'm not sittin' here dyin' right in front of you." He paused to take a breath. Even the shortest conversation could leave him winded. He glanced down at the oxygen tank beside him and put a hand on the cloudy mask. "So, what's the problem? Ex-wife givin' you shit again?"

"You could say that."

"Sorry you divorced her?"

"She divorced me, Jo Jo. Twice. Remember? And no, I'm not sorry. In fact, today I'm particularly happy that she did."

"Miss your girls, don't you?"

Marty looked at him.

"That's it, isn't it? You're missing your girls."

How could this unfeeling, sloppy grotesque be so intuitive? It made no sense, but it was one of the reasons Marty had come around for the better part of fifteen years. Every once in a while, Jo Jo Wilson tapped into whatever worldly experience he had and was able to see straight through him, cutting right to the core of whatever was bothering him. But Marty wasn't willing to go there now. "I think you need a hit of oxygen, Jo Jo."

Jo Jo took a hit. "I'll show you what else I need." He reached down and retrieved the half-empty bottle of Scotch from the open drawer at his feet, put it between them on the cluttered counter. "Want a drink?" He unscrewed the bottle cap and clicked it down on the glass counter. "I guarantee you this little honey will take care of all your problems."

For a moment, Marty believed it would. But right now, he needed to keep his head clear and so he declined. "No, thanks," he said.

"Shit's good."

"I'm fine."

"You sure?"

"Trust me."

"Trust you? Spellman, if anyone needs a drink right now, it's you. You look like shit. And I know that look because I see it on my wife's face every time she turns to look at me. It's like she just saw a horror movie. But whatever. Your call."

And so Jo Jo, seldom a generous man, wasn't about to ask again. Instead, he reached for a dirty glass hidden within arm's reach behind the towering stack of boxes. He picked up the bottle of Scotch and began to pour, his gnarled, unsteady hand causing the amber liquid to slosh. When he drank, he did so in little gasps that fogged the glass.

"I'll see you later, Jo Jo."

"Right on, brother."

* * *

He left the store, caught the E-train at West 4th, and shot uptown to 53rd and Third. As the train rocked, he thought of Judge Wood and her high-brow neighbors on 75th and Fifth.

Even if someone hadn't seen Wood being dropped off yesterday morning, wasn't it likely that over the years someone had seen something unusual in her behavior? Wood leaving late every third Thursday night? Wood coming home drugged out of her mind the next morning?

Marty knew. This was New York. Here, prying eyes missed nothing, knew everything, collected information like a computer. If only the mouths would speak. But how to get them to talk?

Think.

Who did he know on 75th who lived near Wood? There must be someone--Gloria would have made sure of it. She cultivated friendships on Sutton and Beekman, Fifth and Park. She was the ultimate address snob, the quintessential climber. Live in a penthouse on Fifth? Come on over for a cocktail. Have an apartment overlooking the Park? Let's do dinner. Marty never understood it.

Gloria.

Right now, she was the last person he wanted to speak to. But there was no question she would know a neighbor or two of Wood's. No question she was still friends with those people and could get him inside.

Her influence could make all the difference.

He needed to call her. He reached into his pants pocket and pulled out his cell. He was down to one bar, but if he was quick, it might be enough.

Gloria picked up on the fourth ring, her cool voice an absolute change from the woman he once loved.

Gloria, his latest contact.

Gloria, helping him out on a case.

Sweet Jesus.

* * *

"You want me to do what?" Gloria asked.

"A favor," Marty said. "I want you to do me a favor."

"Let me get this straight," Gloria said. "You miss lunch with your daughters and you want me to do you a favor? Oh, that's rich, Marty. That's perfect."

"I didn't miss lunch," Marty said. "I was a few minutes late."

"You were thirty minutes late."

"It was unavoidable."

"It was inexcusable. Obviously, the excuses won't end with you."

She paused and Marty could feel her mind working.

"Why were you late? Does it have to do with Maggie Cain?"

He could hardly lie to her--Gloria would know. "Yes," he said. "She's also the reason I need your help now."

"Is she in some sort of trouble?"

"She might be."

"You know she's my favorite writer. You know I love what she does with words. She paints with them. She creates landscapes, murals, art. She has an ability to generate entire fields of engrossing characters. Her plots are something to be studied and admired."

Marty said nothing.

"You've never asked me for help before," she said suspiciously. "Why now?"

"Because you're the only one who can help me." That wasn't exactly true, but it wasn't exactly a lie either. At home, Marty had a list of names and addresses of all their friends and acquaintances. He could have gone there, skimmed the list himself for someone they knew on 75th, called them up, and hoped they'd agree to see him.

But it was too much of a risk. These people adored Gloria and her rising star. They're the ones who put her on a pedestal and applauded first before the rest of the art world followed suit. He had been her absentee husband, writing his little movie reviews and bringing down wealthy people not unlike themselves. That's what he was known for--being hired by the rich to take down the rich. If he was going to break into this crowd, he'd need her influence.

"What do you want from me?" she asked.

He told her.

"No way."

"Come on, Gloria."

"They don't like you, Marty. None of my friends like you. I'm not risking my reputation because of you."

"What about for Maggie Cain?"

"This will help her?"

"This could change everything for her. It could save her."

"The situation is that dangerous, then?"

He laid it on thick. "It's worse."

A silence passed. Marty could feel her weighing her options.

"Alright," she said. "But there's a condition."

Of course, there was. "What is it?"

"I want the girls for Christmas."

He almost hung up the phone.

CHAPTER TWENTY-THREE

Carra Wolfhagen stood to the right of her third-story bedroom window, a sleeve of red curtain pressed against her cheek as she looked down at the street, where the media and the curious had come to catch a glimpse of her and her murdering thief of a husband.

What were they thinking, knowing he was here with her now? That she'd had a change of heart, supported him, welcomed him into her home and taken him back?

If only she had the courage to tell them what she'd kept secret for years.

She moved away from the window and glanced across to the locked bedroom door. Fear of him rooted her here. She thought of the gun sitting ten feet away in the top drawer of her nightstand and knew if she could kill Max--right now--and get away with it, she'd do it. She'd find him in this house and take his life for the one he continued to steal from her.

Where was he now? In his guest suite? On the phone with his lawyers? Or maybe he was watching that disc.

That disc. If she phoned the police now and they came, she knew Max would somehow find a way to destroy the DVD before they made it to him. He'd burn it or smash it or crush it and flush it. He'd find some way to get rid of it. Still, at some point, she'd have her opportunity. When the time was right and she felt safe, she'd grab that disc, contact the police and be rid of him forever.

But now? Now she wanted out of this room.

She went to the door and pressed her ear against it, heard nothing, unfastened the lock and opened the door. She looked into the hallway and saw only her cat, Sasha, strolling by.

Carra went after it, scooped the animal into her arms, listened. The house was quiet. The cat purred against her breast.

Behind her, a door opened and clicked shut.

Though the hallway was generous in width, Carra pressed her back to the wall as her husband, naked save for the shaving cream dripping from his body, stepped out of the bathroom with the gold straight razor clutched high in his hand.

He was bleeding from the peak of each nipple, but he didn't seem to notice. Too angry and too high to notice. He did a little jig in the middle of the hallway and twirled around twice, glaring at her each time, fanning out his sopping arms, nearly knocking off a side table the expensive vase she'd bought at auction with his stolen money. With his arms pinwheeling, he came over to where she was standing, stopped and then scraped the razor down the length of his stomach. With his head cocked, he flicked the blade hard and sprayed her face with a mixture of stubble, shaving cream and blood.

Carra turned her head and gasped.

She dropped the cat, ran the back of her hand across her face and smeared her lipstick with the cool pink foam. She tasted his blood on her lips and thought of HIV as she frantically wiped her sleeve across the tight line that was her mouth.

Furious, repelled, she reached out to slap him but he snagged her wrist first. She raised her other hand to strike, but he dropped the blade and grabbed it before she could. He stuck his face in hers. His pupils were tiny islands of black sand drowning in rough blue waters. His eyelids trembled from the nerves he'd fried with meth. There was nothing she could do when he was like this, only pray to God he wouldn't beat her as he had in the past.

His lips curled back to expose the uneven, crowded yellow teeth he'd never had fixed because he knew how they could intimidate. "Remember," he said. "I've got a video of you, too, Carra. Burn me, and everyone in this town will know the real Carra Wolfhagen."

"Get your hands--"

"What was that?"

"You're hurting--"

"What was that?"

She struggled against him, but he only tightened his grip on her wrists, cutting off the circulation to her hands, hurting her more.

"I didn't do it!" he shouted.

"You killed the Coles! You killed Gerald!"

"I'm being set up!"

"You had them murdered!" she screamed. "It's on that disc! You've murdered before! You know I know that. How could you ever think I'd forget that night? How could you expect anyone to forget what you did? You   killed--"

The first blow sent her to the floor. The kick to her stomach sent her to the gray edges of unconsciousness. Her head fell to the side and she saw through the whirlwind of black flies now clouding her vision that the middle toe on each of his feet was missing. He'd had them removed.

Now, his feet resembled hooves.

"If I am responsible," he said angrily, leaning close to her ear, shaving cream and blood dripping onto her nose and cheek and lips, "you can be damned sure you're next."

And with that, she violently swung her body around, swept her legs under his feet and sent him toppling to the floor, where he fell face-first on the marble floor.

Her only chance was flight.

He was stronger than she was, but right now, he wasn't moving. She pushed herself up just as he rolled onto his side. He was bleeding from the mouth. He'd split his lower lip. He blinked at her in confusion and put a hand over his mouth in an effort to stop the blood, which was pooling on the floor.

Behind him, in the bedroom he was using, would be the disc and a telephone. He'd been shaving. He would have kept them close. They'd be in the attached bath.

Youth had left her years ago, but she'd kept in shape, and so she leaped over his body, though not high enough. He lifted a hand as she jumped, tripping her. She went down hard, sliding across the floor.

For a moment, she was dazed, but adrenaline was as powerful as the sound of him making an effort to stand. She looked over her shoulder and watched him push himself to his feet and lean against a wall. He was naked, he was bleeding and he was vulnerable, but rage was at the forefront and that's what propelled him toward her now.

As quickly as she could, she was on her feet.

Wolfhagen reached out a hand and swung toward her head. She could feel his fingers brush through her hair as she lurched toward the table beside her.

On it was one of her prize possessions--an original crystal Lalique Bacchantes vase that could send fifty New Yorkers into early retirement. It was thick and it was heavy, but Carra was able to grab it and smash it in tiny piece at his bare feet. She did so as he was still coming toward her, but the moment the broken glass lodged into the bottom of his feet, he stopped in pain and looked incredulously at her. All around him was a circle of sharp glass. He was trapped and he knew it.

"You're going down," she said, backing away from him and toward his bedroom. "You're out of my life now."

She darted into the room, slipped into the bath, saw the disc on the vanity and grabbed it along with the cordless phone on the wall beside the sink. She took each back into the hallway, the phone poised above her head and ready to strike in case he was waiting for her.

But he wasn't. He hadn't moved. He was still standing in the growing round of his own blood.

With the blood dripping from his mouth, the remnants of shaving cream still clinging to his body and the patches of thick hair he'd yet to shave off, he looked like a monster to her--which, of course, he was. His voice was muddled when he spoke, but he was so oddly calm, she could understand him in spite of his smashed lip.

"You won't win," he said. "I video taped everything we did back then. There's a safe deposit box with each tape. If anything happens to me, my lawyers have access to all of it and they have orders to release the tapes to the press. It's then that the world will know the truth about you."

"I'm not worried about the tapes, Max."

"You should be."

"Why? I'm not on them."

"I've seen you on them."

"No, you haven't. I thought about it this morning, after you threatened me with them last night so you could come to the party and stay here. You've got nothing on me. I knew where you hid the cameras back then. I knew where not to stand. But if you think I'm wrong and that you've got something on me, I'll take my chances."

"Like you're doing with the police? They're going to question me again, Carra. They're going to wonder what happened to my face and my feet."

She looked down at his feet. "You're going to show them your hooves, Max? Is that it? Please. Here's what I know about you. When I leave here, you'll pull the glass from your feet and you'll fix your lip. Your too vain not to do otherwise. And if you do tell the police what happened here today, I've got my own story. We had an argument and you attacked me. Guess who lost?" She kept her eyes on him, turned on the phone and tapped numbers.

"I wouldn't call the police, Carra."

"Who said I am? Tonight, it's all about business and you're going nowhere." She cocked her head at the bedroom as the phone started to ring. "That's where you're staying from this point forward. You'll have no access to a phone, to this disc, and no way to ask for help. What you will have is four men standing guard outside your door. Make one move when they get here, and it'll be your last."

"People can be bought, Carra."

"Not these men, Max."

"You don't know a thing about money or people."

"Then prove me wrong. We'll see who's right." She held up a finger. "But if you try it, know that they'll have orders to kill you."

"Death doesn't frighten me."

And there it was--his greatest lie yet. For the first time since he came back into her life, she felt as though it was she who had the upper hand. And, so, she pounced. "That's a lie," she said. "I think you really believe you have a chance to be on top again and because of that, I think you fear death more than you hate your body, more than you hate your childhood and more than you hate your miserable fucking existence."

BOOK TWO

CHAPTER TWENTY-FOUR

5:52 p.m.

When Marty arrived on East 75th Street, he wasn't surprised to find the media parked outside Wood's home. It was nearly six o'clock and time for the evening news. If all of New York wasn't already talking about this case, soon they would be. The fame that had found Kendra Wood in life was about to catapult her to new heights in death.

He left the cab and scanned the confusion of cameras and cables and vans and people for Jennifer, found her reading her notes in front of the police barricade, and smiled to himself. Around her neck was the necklace he gave her when they first dated.

The cab sped away and Jennifer looked up, but not at him. She said something to her cameraman, laughed with him and lifted her face to the dozens of birds darting above them in the umbrella of trees. He heard her say, "If one of them shits on me, I swear to God I'm smearing it on that bitch from Fox 5."

Marty called out her name.

Jennifer spotted him in the crowd and waved him over. "What are you doing here?" she said, smiling. "I thought we were going to talk at eight."

"We were," Marty said. "But I need to talk to you now. Got a minute?"

"I don't know." She looked at her cameraman, a short man with a cap of white hair who was nearly twice her age. "How much time?"

"Seven minutes and your pretty face will be smiling at half of New York."

She touched the man's forearm. "That's sweet," she said. "My pretty face. If I had a fan club, Bob, I'd make you president."

"If you had a fan club, I'd be working elsewhere."

"Oh, come on. You'd Tweet me if you had the chance."

"Not unless you took your ass to the city clinic first." He raised a finger before she could speak. "Careful. You don't want me to fuck with your lighting, girl."

Jennifer kissed him on the cheek and followed Marty across the street. "Isn't he great? You don't find cynicism like that just anywhere. I love him." She squeezed Marty's hand. "What are you doing here? Something tells me it isn't just to see me."

"You're right," Marty said. "It isn't. Though this is a nice surprise." He cocked a thumb at the row of houses behind them. "Emilio DeSoto and Helena Adams. I'm interviewing them."

Jennifer's eyes widened. "How'd you swing that?"

"You don't want to know."

"Sure, I do."

"It was Gloria," he said.

"Gloria?"

"Just got off the phone with her."

"But I thought you were pissed at her."

"I am," Marty said. "But I knew she could get me inside so I said to hell with it and called her."

"She really does know everyone, then."

"She makes it her business to," Marty said. "It's what she does."

"Think they saw something?"

"It's what I'm hoping."

"Anything I can do to help?"

"Actually, there is," Marty said. "What are you doing after this?"

"Bob was going to buy me a drink but I can get out of that," she said. "Bob's a pushover. He loves me, too."

"Enough to Tweet you?"

"Oh, please. He'd Tweet the hell out of me if he was straight."

Marty smiled. "Too much information. If he's willing to take a rain check, I was wondering if you'd drive over to Carra Wolfhagen's and keep tabs on her husband. He's staying with her."

That was enough for Jennifer. She took him by the arm and led him farther down the street, away from the other reporters. "Wolfhagen's there?" she said in a low voice. "But they can't stand each other."

"You think?"

"Why would she let him stay with her? She's divorcing him. Everyone knows how they feel about each other. You'd think he'd find some other place to stay."

"It is interesting, isn't it?"

"What else do you know? You're holding back--I can tell."

"I'll tell you everything later," he said. "But only if you'll watch him."

"Of course, I'll watch him."

They walked back toward the crowd of reporters.

"Bring your cell," Marty said. "Call me on mine and follow him if he leaves. I don't know when I'll be able to join you, but I'll get there eventually." He looked at her. "You're okay with this?"

She frowned at him. "Oh, please. It's not like I haven't pulled surveillance before. Remember Gotti?"

How could he forget? At that early point in her career, she may have been a young reporter, but she'd tailed the mob boss for three weeks without getting caught. She'd gone undercover and dated the man's son to extract information about the family. She won a Peabody for her report, which exposed sides to Gotti he never wanted made public. And it made her a star.

She squeezed his hand. "I'll see you after you interview DeSoto and Adams. It'll be fun, like old times." She winked at him. "And do me a favor--wear those tight jeans I like so well, the ones that show off your ass. You never know. You might just get lucky again."

With that, she crossed the street, stood in front of the camera, skimmed her notes and took a breath as the camera's floodlights flashed on. Bob pointed a finger at her and Jennifer began speaking to half of New York, as did the other reporters around her.

* * *

Marty turned to the building behind him.

Emilio DeSoto's home was tall and narrow and painted bright white--bright white door, bright white bricks, bright white awnings over the wide white windows. The steps were painted white, the trim was painted white, the wrought iron railing that ran alongside the house was painted white. The only hint of color here was on the door--the number "21" in pearl gray. Marty knocked twice and waited. Experience told him that gaining entrance to this home might take awhile.

E, as he was known in the New York art circle, was one of Manhattan's premiere minimalist artists. A close friend of Gloria's, his mere presence at her first showing had given her career the kind of boost every debut artist desires. He had purchased the smallest of her paintings--a tiny stamp in a collection of sprawling canvases--and whispered in her ear all evening. When asked by the media what he thought of this new artist's work, E surprised them all by answering in a complete sentence: "Her work is arresting."

Her work is arresting. Those four words helped Gloria and the gallery net seven figures in sales by evening's end.

The door opened slowly, carefully, finally exposing a sliver of E in white silk pajamas, white satin slippers, his head and eyebrows shaved clean. He was a thin slip of a man with skin so pale, it was almost translucent. They'd met only once--here, for tea with Gloria--but E hadn't spoke to him, only stared when Marty commented on the man's paintings.

Now, Marty wondered how in hell he was going to get this odd man to talk to him about Judge Wood and what he may have seen over the years as her neighbor. But Gloria promised he would talk. "Death fascinates him," she said. "It's a major force in his work, especially during his black period, which coincidentally coincided with mine. And he's different when he's alone. He's different when he doesn't have an audience. You'll see. You won't be able to shut him up."

But looking at E squinting at him, frowning at all of the colors that made up Marty's clothes, he couldn't be sure. "Thanks for seeing me, E," he said. "I know you're busy and I appreciate it."

E said nothing. He looked past Marty to Wood's home, moved to speak, but then pursed his lips into a tight pale line and said nothing. He lowered his gaze and with an almost imperceptible inclination of his head, invited Marty inside.

A long white corridor stretched before them like a tunnel of snow. Strategically placed lights were hidden in the ceiling, concealing shadows, casting others. There was no furniture, no paintings on the walls, no signs of life present or past. E locked the door behind them and wordlessly turned to walk down the blinding hallway.

Intrigued, Marty followed.

How did this little, peculiar man survive in New York? Was it all an act, as Gloria suggested, or was it something deeper, some unexplained disturbance he had never resolved?

As they moved forward, Marty watched the man list left, then right. They reached the end of the hallway and E's shoulder struck the edge of the doorway. The blow took him by surprise and he lurched sideways, almost falling into the room but righting himself at the last moment.

He tripped across the living area, bumped into one of the few white chairs arranged in the center of the room, sent it toppling and pushed forward, toward the table along the far white wall.

Marty couldn't tell if the man were sick, drunk or simply unable to make out the subtle shading that defined where this chair was, that couch, that table. He stood in the doorway and watched E grasp the small white urn at the end of a table. He unscrewed the lid, reached inside and removed a short white stick.

The stick was a joint. Marty stepped inside and watched E fire it up with the white lighter beside the urn. He closed his eyes and inhaled deeply, the blue smoke rising before him in thick little clouds. It wasn't until after he had exhaled that he finally looked at Marty and said to him in a thin, exasperated voice: "Glaucoma." He sighed and for a moment, Marty thought he understood him.

"I need to ask you a few questions," he said. "But if now isn't a good time, I can come back when you're feeling better."

E screwed up his face and sucked harder. He coughed and brought a hand to his chest, which he gently patted once.

Marty looked at the fingernails on that hand. With the exception of the thumbnail, which was clipped close, the nails on the remaining four fingers were long and slender, curving and yellow. Marty glanced at the nails on the other hand and saw that they had been chewed to the skin.

And E sucked.

"Did you know Kendra Wood?" Marty asked.

E finished the joint, snuffed the roach in a clean glass ashtray and put a finger to the very tip of his narrow nose. His eyes were clouded and unfocused. His body occupied space, but his mind was far away. He coughed again and gazed across the room toward Marty. His upper lip twitched.

Marty wasn't sure if the man had heard him. "You've been her neighbor for six years. It would be helpful if you could tell me anything you might know about her."

E turned his head and traced a finger along the urn's curving white lid. He gave no indication of pending response.

"Perhaps I should be more blunt," Marty said, keeping the frustration from his voice. "Last night, Judge Wood was found dead in her bedroom. Her head was severed and, until this morning, was missing. The evidence suggests she lived two separate lives. I'd like to know if you've seen anything unusual in her behavior over the years."

"Yes," said E.

Finally, thought Marty. "Could you tell me about that?" he said. "What have you seen?"

"Things," said E.

"Such as?" asked Marty.

"People," said E.

"Who?" asked Marty.

"Rodents," said E.

And that stopped Marty.

He watched a wave of disturbance flash across E's face, which was somehow paler than before. The air in the room seemed to shift and turn in on itself. Marty could sense it tightening. "I need you to be more specific," he said. "Can you do that for me?"

"No."

"She was decapitated, E."

"Life lops heads."

"Please, tell me what you know."

"I know they'll be looking for a new judge."

"And I know your routine is an act."

E recoiled.

"Gloria told me that you were a good man. She told me that you would help me. She said that death fascinates you."

"Life is the new death."

"What did you mean by 'rodents'?"

E's eyes flicked up to meet his. "Rodents eat their young."

"What does that mean?"

"Rodents eat their own."

"You're saying Judge Wood was a rodent?"

"Yes."

"Who ate her, E?"

But E had spent his words. Like a child, he turned his back on Marty, folded his arms around himself and behaved as if he'd offer nothing more.

But Marty was having none of it. He'd be damned if minimal Emilio was going to dangle a carrot in front of his face and snatch it away.

"The police will be here, E. Kendra Wood was a federal court justice and they're going to question everyone on this block. They'll question you and they won't be as understanding as I am. They'll harass you. They'll make you talk. They'll know you're hiding something and they'll force you to tell them what you know. They'll humiliate you. They'll get subpoenas. They'll bring in the FBI. They'll call you a freak. Everything will be leaked to the media. It will be a circus. You'll have to talk to everyone."

E lifted his head toward the ceiling.

Marty lowered his voice. "But if you tell me what you know and I solve the case, you'll never even have to deal with the police." Which was a lie, but time was short and Marty needed answers.

"You don't know me," said E.

"I don't need to," said Marty.

"You're not an artist."

"What does that have to do with a dead woman?"

"Artists see things differently."

"You're probably right."

"You and I can't communicate."

"I believe we are now."

"Communication isn't harassment."

"No one is harassing you."

"Life harasses me."

"I'm trying to solve a crime."

E turned to him. "It wasn't a crime."

"What does that mean?"

"Rodents eat rodents."

"Cut the bullshit, E."

"It's the truth."

"Tell me what you know."

"I know you were a bad husband."

"You're hiding something."

"I hide everything."

Marty pulled out his cell. "One call and your life changes."

"One call to Gloria and so does yours."

He dialed Hines' number.

"This is what I know."

He listened to the phone ring.

"I know you hurt your family."

He refused to let this man in.

"I know your daughters will never have a normal life."

Hines' answering service picked up.

"I know you're a shitty critic."

Marty focused on Hines' voice.

"And I know you need to get out of my house."

Marty snapped the phone shut. "You'll regret this, E."

"I never regret truth."

"Have a look at yourself and tell me that."

"I'll tell you this. I'm incubating. Tonight, I change."

And without another word, E went to one of the plain white chairs in the center of the room and sat down. He put his face in his hands and positioned his body in such a way that his limbs drew close to his body and appeared to make him even smaller. The lines of his body shortened. His will to vanish quickly became the strongest statement he'd made thus far.

There would be nothing more forthcoming.

Marty turned to leave. But when he reached the door, E's voice lifted and carried down the hall. "Those rodents are going to eat you, too, Spellman."

CHAPTER TWENTY-FIVE

6:26 p.m.

Helena Adams' home was four houses to the left of DeSoto's and almost directly across from Wood's. It was three stories of bricks and shiny casement windows, black shutters pressed with winding ivy, a carved mahogany door with stained glass and reinforced, Marty suspected, with at least two inches of steel.

He looked down the street, toward the Park that was so close at the end of it, and watched the dozens of people rushing by on the sidewalk. They were either hurrying up Fifth or hustling to move down it. He pressed the glowing buzzer and waited while trying to clear his mind of the scene he'd just had with DeSoto.

"Those rodents are going to eat you, too, Spellman."

As he played their conversation over in his head, there was a part of Marty that now thought DeSoto told him more about Wood than he'd originally thought. The man spoke in code. Who were the rodents?

A young Asian woman answered the door.

"Mr. Spellman?" she asked. By her expensive, fitted pale blue suit, Marty guessed she was Adams' secretary.

"Yes," Marty said.

"I'm Theresa Wu, Mrs. Adams' personal assistant. We're having tea in the library. Mrs. Adams would like you to join us there."

She stepped aside so he could move past her, then closed the door and motioned for him to follow her down a cool hallway lined with delicate antique tables and paintings on the walls. Marty looked at the tables and saw without surprise the silver-framed, black and white photographs of film stars from another era. Most were signed with love or affection, and none were studio shots.

These were from Adams' personal collection. Somewhere, a central air conditioner whirled cool air into the room.

They turned right at the end of the hall and entered a library whose walls were filled from floor to ceiling with books.

At the far end of the room, where the light was flattering, sat Helena Adams. She rose from her seat to greet him. "Marty," she said. "God, it's good to see you. Please, come in."

Except for her hair, which was now a shorter, elegant silver bob that hugged her famous face, she looked no different from the woman he'd spent an evening with two years ago, at a fundraiser for AIDS research. Tall and slender, still striking in her eighth decade, she had the kind of grace and elegance that could only be natural, not learned or practiced. He took her hands in his own and squeezed them gently. "Thanks for seeing me."

"I had little choice," Helena said. "Gloria told me this was important. Have you ever turned that woman down? Awful. All that tense silence. I don't have that kind of courage anymore."

But of course she did, and they both knew it. Throughout the 1940s, Helena Adams starred in nearly three dozen films, two of which earned her Academy Awards for Best Actress and turned her into a legend. Hollywood occasionally courted her, but Helena turned her back on them forty years ago to marry Cecil Chadbourne, the billionaire investor. In the few interviews she'd given since, she never explained why she gave up a career as promising and as powerful as hers was then.

"Theresa," Helena said, turning to her assistant. "Would you please get this kind man some tea?"

"Of course."

Helena smiled at Theresa and they watched her leave the room. "She's a super girl," Helena said. "I'd be lost without her." She turned to Marty and asked him to sit in the embroidered chintz chair opposite her. "I'm dictating my autobiography to her," she said casually, sipping from her own cup of tea. "Now that Cecil's gone, I can finally tell everything. We're nearly finished and I can say this, Marty--I've had one hell of a life."

"I don't think anyone would question that, Helena."

But Helena shook her head. "You don't understand," she said gravely. "I've done things no one knows about. I know things about Hollywood and New York society that everyone is going to question--especially the FBI." She raised her hands. "Oh, I can't wait till they get their greedy paws on this book. That'll be an especially trying day. But I'm old and I don't care. Keeping secrets can be a terrible burden, don't you think?"

He nodded.

"Yes, in your business, I thought you might. It can ruin you, make you give up your dreams, throw away your life for one that doesn't matter. It can even make you marry someone you hate. I'm ending that cycle now. I'm telling the truth about both towns. I'm burning my bridges and I love it. It's something I should have done years ago. This is my '60s liberation five decades later. I'll never eat lunch in either town again."

She smiled at him, mysterious as ever. "You'll have to read my book to know what I'm talking about, dear. I'm being vague on purpose. Part of my charm, I'm told, this vagueness of mine. Cecil told me that just before his accident."

She stared openly at him and Marty had to wonder. Cecil Chadbourne died in a freak fall late last winter. Broke his neck after slipping on a patch of New York ice. Helena the widow had been too upset to attend her husband's funeral. After all, right in front of her, she watched Cecil bleed out through his smashed head, take his last few breaths and die. Friends understood her absence, particularly when the business and entertainment media started camping outside her door. In an effort to get away from them, she flew to Paris to comfort herself in the lush confines of their apartment overlooking the Seine.

Theresa returned with a silver tea service. She put the tray down on the table between Marty and Helena, poured Marty a cup of the steaming tea, offered him milk, sugar, NutraSweet, the works, and then asked Helena if she would like another cup.

But Helena shook her head and waved her hand expansively. "I'm fine, dear, fine. Really, you're like a well-paid, attentive nurse, rather than an assistant. Why don't you sit down and join us? Mr. Spellman here is about to ask me to help him with something important--I can see it on his face--and I'm curious to know what on Earth that could be."

Theresa sat in the chair beside Marty and crossed her legs. She was a fit, beautiful distraction with hair that dipped past her shoulders and a face that reflected intelligence and something else.

A mild flirtation? She tilted her head and smiled at him, her eyes lowering a bit.

Helena straightened. "Well?" she said. "Come on, Marty, you know I hate suspense. What's this all about? Somehow, you managed to get Gloria involved, so it has to be good if you were willing to go there. Are you reviewing one of my movies? Did you want an exclusive interview? Is that what you're seeking?"

Marty looked away from the smiling Theresa Wu and said: "Actually, it's about Judge Wood. Did you know her?"

Helena touched the diamond brooch fastened to the pocket of her white silk blouse and looked disappointed. "This is about that Wood woman?"

Marty nodded.

"Nothing else?"

"I'm afraid not."

"Not even one of my movies?"

"You know I love your movies."

"Obviously, not enough to review them. I read your blog, you know. The young people who leave all those enthusiastic comments should know about my work, don't you agree?"

"I do," he said. "'Private Affair' is coming out on Blu-ray next month. I plan to cover it."

"That would be nice. And, you know what? It's held up well. I was nominated for it, of course, but lost to that Crawford bitch when she started her smear campaign against me. Meanest person I ever met and there she was winning for being slapped across the face by that brat in 'Mildred Pierce.' Davis and I used to talk about her for hours. We'd rage against her. Bette would say that she wanted to snatch her bald, whatever that meant, though I expect it had to do with the fact that Crawford had trailers filled with wigs." She waved her hand again. "But that's all in the book and obviously my career isn't why you're here. Why are you interested in Wood?"

"I can't say, Helena."

"Not even to me?"

"Not even to you."

She shrugged. "Well," she said. "It was worth a try. Don't you think, Theresa, dear? Always try. But I suppose it doesn't really matter, anyway, because I know nothing about the woman. I told the police that this morning. A very tall detective with the bluest eyes I've ever seen came here to question me. Beautiful. What was his name, Theresa?"

"Hines."

"That's right. Hines. Those shoulders of his were *incroyable*. I wanted to make up things just so he'd stay, but that would have been illegal and I've broken enough laws in my life, as you'll soon find out. So, I played it smart and told him the truth. I didn't know her."

And you also didn't want to get involved in an investigation, Marty thought. *Especially one of this magnitude.* He sipped his tea, wondering how best to play this. Meanwhile, Theresa tilted her head to the other side and recrossed her legs.

"Whatever you say to me will be kept private," he promised. "It'll never come back to you. You will only ever be known as a source. I give you my word on that, Helena."

"I'm sure you do," Helena said. "But it changes nothing. I still didn't know that woman. Like everyone else in New York, she kept to herself. Oh, there was a time when I tried to get to know her, but that was years ago, after she became famous for sentencing those men to prison for securities fraud. But it came to nothing."

"Would you tell me about that?"

Helena shrugged. "It was Cecil," she said dismissively. "He spoke about that woman every day for three weeks. When Wood became popular, he asked me to invite her to dinner. The stupid man was fascinated by her, had a little crush on her, wanted to know everything about her. But she never returned my calls or answered my invitations. The woman would have nothing to do with us. Nothing. It was as if we weren't--us. You couldn't imagine how that upset Cecil. He wasn't used to being refused anything and went on about it for days."

"Did you ever notice anything unusual in Wood's behavior?"

"Like what?"

"You two were neighbors," Marty said. "You must have seen her coming and going at some point."

"Well, of course, I did," Helena said. "But that was hardly an everyday event."

"Doesn't matter," Marty said. "You saw her. You were able to draw conclusions, even if you were unaware of it at the time."

Helena looked away and finished her tea. She fingered her brooch and said nothing. Theresa Wu shot him a concerned glance, which Marty ignored. Like Emilio DeSoto, Helena knew something. He saw it the moment she turned away from him.

"Come on, Helena," he said. "This is important. Did you ever see anything unusual? Wood leaving late? Or maybe coming home drunk the next morning?"

"Now you're describing half of New York," Helena said, but it wasn't with any real conviction. She turned to the window beside her and looked across the way. The reporters were packing up and leaving Wood's home. Helena watched them go and her thin, narrow shoulders drooped a little. She sighed. "Oh, all right, Marty," she said. "I'm too old for this and you're too good. Yes, I know something. I was even considering putting it in the book, but I give up. I'll tell it to you."

She looked at him, her eyes suddenly and surprisingly hard. "But this goes nowhere. If it comes back to me, I'll deny it all and make you look a fool. People believe old women like me. It's one of the few treasures of being my age, this universal belief that the elderly are too sweet to lie. And even though I haven't made a movie in decades, I haven't lost my bag of tricks. I'm still one hell of an actress. Understood?"

Marty understood.

"When Cecil died, I had trouble sleeping. He was a big man in every way--this home became a vacuum without him in it and I wasn't used to the silence. So I would wander around the house at all hours. I'd read or I'd phone friends in Europe or I'd watch television. Sometimes, I'd even turn on the radio and listen to music while thinking about the past and all I gave up for one man.

"One night, about a month after Cecil's death, I was standing at my bedroom window thinking about that piece of ice that killed him when I saw a car pull up in front of Wood's house. It was big and black and expensive, the kind of car you'd expect in this neighborhood, the kind of car Cecil would have bought for himself."

"What time was this?" Marty asked.

"Late," Helena said. "Past three."

"In the morning?"

"Yes. It was winter and it was cold."

"Could you see who was inside the car?"

"Just let me talk, Marty."

He listened.

"No," she said. "I never saw who was inside that car. But when Wood came rushing out of her house and swung open the passenger door, I saw from the interior light that the car was filled with people." She lowered her voice a notch. "And all of them were naked, just as Wood was."

Theresa excused herself and left the room.

Marty watched her go and felt the moment stretch. At first he wasn't sure he had heard Helena right, but of course he knew he had. He thought of Wood's tattoo, of the date smeared in blood above her bed, of her missing head, and wondered again where all this was leading. "She came out of her house naked?" he asked.

Helena nodded.

"You're certain of this?"

"I think I know a naked woman when I see one, Marty. Kendra Wood wasn't wearing a stitch of clothing. And neither was anyone in that car."

* * *

Later, as Marty was leaving, it was Theresa Wu who stopped him in the entryway.

She pressed a manila envelope into his hand and said in a quick, nervous whisper, "Early yesterday morning, while Mrs. Adams was still asleep, I saw this woman leaving Judge Wood's home. I'm positive it was her. I'd know her anywhere."

"Who is it?"

"You'll see. And you mustn't tell anyone I told you this. I'll deny it all, just like Mrs. Adams. Neither of us wants a scandal right now. Neither of us can afford being connected in any way to this. But you'll look into it, won't you? I think she might be involved in what happened to Judge Wood. She was carrying a large box when she left that house. She looked frightened. Terrified. But there was something else on her face--rage, I think."

Wu opened the door and asked Marty to leave. "Mrs. Adams mustn't know," she began in earnest, but Marty never heard the rest. By then, he had already opened the envelope and shaken out the paperback book Wu had placed inside it.

He turned it over and looked at the photo on the back cover. And when he did, his skin shrank away in chill.

The familiar, scarred face of Maggie Cain was smiling back at him.

CHAPTER TWENTY-SIX

6:49 p.m.

Maggie Cain.

She had lied about her relationship with Wolfhagen. She was under investigation by the FBI. She must have known that Boob Manly had pleaded guilty to the Coles' deaths, and yet she had overlooked him for Wolfhagen, Lasker, Schwartz. And now this. Now Marty had an eyewitness who could place her at Wood's home on the day of her death. An eyewitness who had seen her leaving with a box big enough to house a head. An eye witness who had seen fear on her face. Rage.

Maggie Cain was the biggest mystery in this investigation.

As many questions as he had about Wood and Gerald Hayes, the Martinezes, the Coles and Mark Andrews, his thoughts always returned to Maggie and to everything she wasn't telling him. Had she hired him to research a book on Wolfhagen? Or did she have other motives?

He thought of Roberta and her warning about the three women. Was Maggie Cain the woman with murder in her heart? Or was that Linda Patterson?

He looked across the street to Wood's home.

The crush of reporters was gone and now only the birds remained, dozens of them, roosting in the pale white eaves, swooping down in twos and threes to pluck insects from the umbrella of trees that canopied the shady street.

Despite all the streetlamps and all her neighbors--and knowing she might be seen--Kendra Wood had left her house naked, joined her naked friends in their dark car and was driven off into the night. But where did they go? To which club?

Did they all have the same tattoo?

Marty pulled out his cell and called Skeen's private number at the M.E.'s office. It was late. Chances are he wouldn't be in.

But Carlo answered. "Skeen."

"It's Marty. Got a minute?"

"For you, I've got three. What do you need?"

"Gerald Hayes. Have you done him yet?"

"Finished him two hours ago."

"Tell me he had a tattoo. Tell me it was like Wood's."

"He had a tattoo. It was like Wood's."

Marty closed his eyes. "Where was it located?"

"On the head of his penis."

The deaths were connected. Things were moving. Patterson and Hines would be comparing notes, consulting Vice for a list of possible clubs. "What was the tattoo a picture of, Carlo?"

"My best guess?"

"Your best guess."

"I think it was a bull. There was a tiny gold hoop going right through the center of it, just like Wood's."

Marty lowered the phone from his ear. Cars shot by on the street. He looked behind him and saw, at the street corner, a man in a wheelchair blowing kisses at the sky. "I need you to do me another favor."

"Shoot."

"Edward and Bebe Cole. Did you do their posts?"

Skeen was silent for a moment. "That was what? Eight, nine months ago?"

"Seven."

"I don't think so," Carlo said. And then, remembering: "No, I know I didn't. I was at a conference when they were murdered. Hatlen did them."

"All right," Marty said. "Would you mind pulling their files? See if they had the same tattoo?"

"Will do."

"And thanks, Carlo."

"Don't mention it."

He clicked the phone shut, stepped to the curb and flagged a cab. The driver was straight out of the Third World, with a bright red turban wrapped around his head and a grisly black beard that hugged his pock-marked face in thick dark coils. Marty gave the man his address, repeated it, and hoped he'd get there before nightfall.

He looked out the side window and watched the city skate by. Skeen was right. Though crudely rendered, Wood's tattoo had been a picture of a bull. What looked like a smudge with points on the top, actually was a bull with horns. The tiny hole had gone clean through its snout.

A Wall Street bull.

Marty leaned back against the seat and thought of Gerald Hayes. There was a time when he had been one of the most prominent men on Wall Street. A time when hedonism and greed had marked an era. Then, the bulls on Wall Street had known no limits. They had stolen and cheated and deceived a nation. So why not push things beyond the boardroom and the DOW and prove themselves elsewhere? Screw hedge funds. Why not hedge your life, take things farther and create the ultimate club, where the price of initiation was a tattoo, a tiny gold hoop and God knows what else?

But the membership wasn't exclusive to only those who controlled the money on Wall Street--Wood's involvement proved that--which led Marty to believe that this club was more about power than anything else. And what better symbol of power than a bull?

So, who else was involved? Wolfhagen, Lasker and Schwartz? How many people in how many different positions of power?

The cab stopped for a red light and Marty looked out the front window. The crowds at the street corners were beginning to cross. His gaze lingered on the profiles of people he didn't know while his stomach tightened.

This case was bigger than him. The people involved in this club obviously were aware of the murders and the police involvement. They knew their cover was threatened and Marty knew they'd go to any length to protect that cover. This was the kind of case that destroyed careers.

This was the kind of case where people murdered to keep others quiet.

* * *

At home, he dropped the mail and Maggie's novel onto the kitchen table, checked his answering machine and found no messages. He went to the refrigerator, grabbed an apple from the top shelf and wondered about Maggie. With Wood's security system disabled, she'd been able to walk straight into the woman's house.

He went to his office, sat at his desk, reached for a pen and a pad of paper, and started to outline the facts as he knew them.

Wood came home yesterday at 5:00 a.m. Hines said she'd been a mess and forgot to reset the alarm. Then, at some point, she went upstairs to her bedroom, overdosed on meth and died in bed between three and four o'clock that afternoon. Theresa Wu had seen Maggie leaving Wood's home that morning, though she hadn't given Marty a specific time.

Marty took a bite of the apple and chewed. He opened his address book, looked up Helena Adams' telephone number and called her. It was Theresa Wu who answered. "Theresa, it's Marty Spellman. Can I ask you a question?"

"If you're quick."

"What time did you see Maggie Cain leaving Wood's home?"

"6:30."

"You sound pretty sure about that."

"That's because, I am. I take my run at that time each morning. If I miss it, like I did today, I run at night. I was leaving when I saw her."

"Did she have a car?"

"She did. She put the box in the trunk and took off." Wu paused and dropped her voice to a whisper. "What do you suppose was inside that box?"

"I'm trying to figure that out," Marty said. He thanked her and hung up the phone.

All right. Wood was alive when Maggie made her visit. But why the visit? Was it an interview for the book? Marty dismissed the idea. Wood never would have scheduled one that early. She'd know she'd be coming home high. So Maggie must have come unannounced. But why so early? What was she seeking? Wood with her guard down?

Marty finished the apple, went back to the kitchen, tossed the core into the trash, grabbed a can of Diet Coke from the fridge.

Maggie knew about that club. He could feel it. She knew about Wood's involvement and had gone to her home on that specific day and at that specific time so she could catch her at her worst. She wanted the upper hand. She needed something from Wood and she left with it in that box.

Marty was wondering what it could be when the telephone rang.

He picked it up, expecting Jennifer, but it was Maggie Cain. "I'm being followed," were her first words to him.

There was fear in her voice, an edge of panic.

"Where are you?" he asked.

She didn't answer. "This was all a mistake," she said. "I never should have involved you. I had no idea so many people would be involved." Her voice was unsteady. Marty could sense that she was shaking. "Kendra Wood committed suicide because of me, Marty. She did it because of me."

Marty felt a river of questions rise up within him but he stamped them down. Now wasn't the time to ask questions. First, he had to get her to a safe place and then talk.

He listened to the silence for clues. She wasn't outside--no sounds of traffic. Wherever she was, it was quiet. *Good*, he thought. *She isn't on the street.* "I can help you," he said calmly. "But you'll have to trust me. Can you do that?"

Silence.

"Maggie?"

"I don't know."

"Will you try?"

"You don't know what you're asking."

"It won't work any other way. You're going to have to trust someone. I'm a third party. I'm impartial to all of this. I think you hired me for that reason."

It was a moment before she spoke. "All right," she said. "I'll trust you."

"Who is following you?"

"A man."

"Have you lost him?"

"I don't know," she said. "I think so. I'm not sure."

"Tell me where you are. I'll come for you."

Silence.

"Tell me where you are, Maggie."

"They've murdered someone else," she said.

Marty felt a needle of ice dart up his back.

"I'm standing over his body."

CHAPTER TWENTY-SEVEN

7:52 p.m.

Marty went to his office, removed his gun, a stainless steel Walther PPK, from the top drawer of his desk, loaded it and slipped it into his shoulder rig, which he put on along with a lightweight blazer.

He pocketed his cell, left his apartment, hailed a cab at curbside and gave the driver the address Maggie Cain gave him. He did all this with automatic efficiency. The cab swung through the city, lurched through traffic, but he paid no attention. He was not aware of anything but Maggie's words, still sounding like an alarm in his head: "His blood is everywhere."

The building was on 77th Street, not far from Fifth. Large and gray with wide stone steps that led to the heavy black door, the building reflected wealth, security, establishment.

In spite of the fact that the sun had slipped below the Manhattan horizon, there was not one light on in the building, not one sign that a frightened woman was waiting inside for him. The cab made three passes and Marty saw no one on the sidewalks, no one in the cars parked at the curbsides, nothing that suggested Maggie Cain was being watched or followed. He asked the driver to drop him at the end of the block, handed her a ten and stepped out.

The sidewalk that stretched before him was lined with great black sacks of trash piled high between the slender trees. The air here was heavy and sour, shot through with rot, laced with the exhaust of the city, so rancid it was almost nauseating. Despite being one of Manhattan's more elegant neighborhoods, when it was trash day, there was no escaping how fair the city could be to everyone, regardless of class.

Save for the sound of the air conditioners cooling the town houses he passed, the street was quiet. Marty kept left, moved down the sidewalk and looked into every shadow, every stairwell, anywhere a person could dip out of sight. Twilight was pressing down on New York and casting everything into its faintly surreal glow.

He moved at a brisk clip, his head slightly lowered.

When he reached the building, he discretely checked the sidewalks, saw nobody peering at him through the windows of the surrounding houses and climbed the steps. He tapped once on the door, but it didn't open. Maggie wasn't waiting for him. He felt a spark of anger, tried the handle, found it unlocked, pushed and stepped into an arctic blast that revealed a dark entryway. No sign of Maggie, only shapes that loomed left and right, objects he couldn't make out clearly.

He closed the door behind him and listened. He could hear nothing but the insistent whirring of air conditioners he couldn't see. The house was an icebox. The unmistakable, coppery scent of blood was everywhere.

He drew his gun and called out Maggie's name, got no response, said it louder, heard nothing and wondered if he was too late. Was the smell of blood also hers?

He reached into his pants pocket and removed the small penlight attached to his keychain--a gift from Katie. He turned it on, shined the weak amber light down the narrow hallway and saw a table lying on its side--late eighteenth century, intricately carved sides, clawed tiger paws at the end of the gently curving legs. A spray of roses past their prime fanned out around the table in a half-moon, their dark red petals resting not in spilled water, but in broken glass.

Marty's heart beat a little faster. He knew he should call Hines, knew by being here he was destroying a crime scene, but he was in too deep. If he called the police now, he'd have to go to Hines again for information. And that was something Marty wasn't willing to do. Still, he knew protocol and so he reached into his pocket and pulled out paper shoe coverings. He slipped them on and then put on rubber gloves.

He looked around, spotted the alarm console on the wall to his right and saw by the flashing red light that it was disengaged. Again he called out Maggie's name but there was no answer, nothing that suggested she was in this house.

He moved down the hallway, keeping the penlight on the upended table, listening for clues in the dark. To his left was an arched doorway that opened to a room facing 77th Street. Marty stepped over the table, the roses and the broken vase, shined the light once more down the hall, saw the staircase that lifted to the second floor, the coiled end of the brown banister, and quietly entered the room.

An air conditioner blew cold air and the smell of something rotten from the window opposite him. Outside, on the sidewalk, streetlamps flickered to life and started to burn, casting crisp slants of gold into the otherwise dark room.

Marty stood just inside the doorway and listened. His gun was held at arm's length. He wasn't sure what to expect but he was ready just the same. The scent of blood and decay was stronger here. He panned the room with the tiny flashlight but it was useless. The beam wasn't strong enough. All he could make out were glimpses of cloth, splashes of color, the sharp edge of something solid, shadows in the light. A van was approaching on the street. Marty waited for it to pass.

He'd have to turn on a light.

The Tiffany lamp on the table beside him punched rainbows of blue, purple and green onto his face and the paneled walls. He turned to look across the room and saw the body of Peter Schwartz sitting upright on the blood-soaked sofa, his legs crossed at the knees, his hands clasped in his lap as if in prayer, his head tilted back to expose the gaping wound at his throat.

Save for the pair of black rubber underpants and knee-high black leather boots he wore, he was naked. His skin was greenish-red and streaked with blood. As Marty walked over to him, he noticed with revulsion the maggots crawling into and out of the man's nose and open mouth.

The smell was cutting, like boiled pork gone sour and bad. He forced a sharp rush of air through his nose but it was useless. The smell had settled in for the long haul. He closed his eyes and willed his stomach to settle. A fly buzzed past him, heading straight for

Schwartz, where it dived into the man's open mouth and disappeared down his throat, where it would plant a new clutch of eggs.

Schwartz didn't seem to mind.

Looking at the man and the maggots consuming him, Marty was repelled but not surprised. This was the middle of summer in New York. Outside, on the sidewalk, the piles of trash were roasting in the August heat. Flies had wended their way into this house and laid thousands of eggs in Peter Schwartz's eyes, nose and mouth. The eggs had hatched and now maggots were feasting on the rotting tissue of a dead man. When a forensic entomologist was let loose on this scene, they'd be dizzy with elation.

If he was going to do this, he'd have to pull a Skeen and follow his advice--look at Schwartz as though he were nothing more than an object. Resolved, Marty took his gun and pushed the barrel underneath the man's right hand. It lifted easily--no rigor, which was expected since Schwartz obviously had been dead for awhile.

He holstered his gun and pressed the inside of his wrist against the man's forearm. The flesh was cold and clammy, as if Schwartz had broken into a sweat. With the air conditioners running on high, it was difficult to say just how long he had been dead, but Marty had learned enough from Skeen to take an educated guess. The color of Schwartz's skin, the presence of insects feeding on his body, the smell of decay and the lack of rigor all suggested at least 48 hours, likely more.

He looked down at the dead man and saw beneath the layer of blood what his family and friends eventually would be seeing--Schwartz as beautiful corpse.

He was a small, powerfully built man who had never married--his handsome good looks were apparent even in death. The face that had photographed so well in the press after his indictment by the SEC would now be forever young--firm jaw, narrow nose, high cheekbones, curly dark hair matted only slightly at his forehead with blood. Marty looked at the man's careful pose of folded hands and legs, the rubber underpants and high black boots, and knew without question that Schwartz would have that tattoo, that picture of a bull imprinted on his penis, that same shiny gold hoop going clean through its snout.

He looked closer at the body and at all the inconsistencies it offered. Schwartz hadn't been wearing these clothes when he was murdered. His carotid artery had been severed. Fountains of blood had sprayed onto the floor and sofa, covering the man's arms, torso and legs. But his underpants and boots were untouched, suggesting they had been put on after death.

After death.

Schwartz hadn't died in this position. He wouldn't have gone down without a struggle. Someone murdered him on this sofa, dressed him up and posed him pretty. Someone wanted him to be found in these clothes.

His cell sounded, cracking the silence in three piercing bleats. The sudden intrusion sent a jolt through Marty and he took a step back, away from Schwartz. He removed the device from his side, glanced down at the number flashing in the illumined window and knew who it was before Maggie Cain answered.

"Where are you?"

"Three blocks away."

"Why aren't you here?"

She was out of breath, her words clipped and shortened from lack of air. "Why do you think? I was scared. I didn't know how long you'd be. I got the hell out of there." She paused and Marty could hear the traffic rushing past her. Car horns sounded in the distance. "Have you found the body?"

"Yes."

"How long has he been dead?"

"I don't know," he said. "Maybe two days. Maybe longer."

"That's three people today, Marty."

He walked over to the Tiffany lamp and clicked it off. In the darkness, the buzzing of the flies and the humming of the air conditioner seemed to grow louder. He looked once more at Schwartz and saw the moon of his face glowing in the dark. It seemed oddly separated from his body, frozen yellow in the city light.

His body--bloody save for his clothes.

And Marty wondered.

"It was you, wasn't it, Maggie?"

"What are you talking about?"

"Schwartz. He wasn't murdered wearing those clothes. There's no blood on them and God knows there should be. Someone dressed him after he was dead. I want to know if it was you."

"Are you saying I murdered him?"

"Did you?"

She barked out a laugh. "Are you serious?" She didn't wait for an answer. "No, Marty, I didn't murder him. I found him. What the hell is wrong with you?"

"Not a thing. I'm just tired of being lied to. Why were you here?"

"I had an interview with him," she said tightly. "And what do you mean you're tired of being lied to?"

Marty ignored the question. "Schwartz was dead when you got here. I want to know how you got inside."

"The door was unlocked. I rang the buzzer twice and then tried the handle. I called out his name and got no response. The air stank. I saw the table lying on its side and knew that something was wrong. I found him in the living room. I called you and then his telephone started to ring. It scared me. I got out."

"You did more than that," Marty said. "There's no way you were here and didn't look around. You're smarter than that. You're after something. Tell me what you found."

"I didn't find anything. I got out of there."

"You said Wood killed herself because of you. I know you were there the day she died. I have an eyewitness who saw you leaving her house with a box. Obviously, you threatened her. I want to know with what."

"We'll talk about that later."

"What's your relationship with Wolfhagen?"

"We'll talk about that, too."

"What's the importance of November 5, 2007?"

Silence.

"Talk to me, or I swear to God I'm out."

A van passed on the street, taillights burning red. Marty left the living area and stepped back into the cold hallway, his shoes crunching on the broken glass. He removed his paper slippers, shook them and put them in his pocket. It was a moment before Maggie spoke.

"All right," she said. "I'll talk to you. But not over the phone. I'll come there."

"When?"

"Now. And while you're waiting, look in Schwartz's bedroom. Push past the clothes in his closet and see for yourself what we're up against. You have no idea, Marty. None. You're close to the truth, but you don't know all of it. Look in that closet and see what I've suspected for years."

CHAPTER TWENTY-EIGHT

8:19 p.m.

Marty pocketed the phone, turned on the hall light and took the stairs to the second floor. He looked right and saw the door to Peter Schwartz's bedroom hanging off its hinges like a broken jaw. Splinters of wood led into and out of the room in concentric half-circles, as though scattered there not by force, but by a careful hand.

Unmoving, he stood just outside the room looking in.

Shafts of yellow light touched down from the opposite window, the bright shards of a wall mirror glinted like a splintered, frozen pond in the center of the embroidered rug, the smell of death, even here. He reached inside for the light switch and turned it on.

Tried to turn it on.

He flipped the switch up and down but nothing happened. No light would shine.

He listened, heard only the air conditioner, the gentle rippling of a curtain he couldn't see, and removed the penlight from his pocket. He swept the room with the waning amber light and spotted a lamp on the side table next to the window. He went to it and turned it on.

Two bureaus, both with their drawers stuck out like dry wide tongues, were along the wall in front of him. Each had been emptied for inspection, their contents stuffed back haphazardly. The large, unmade bed was beside him, its high pale posts stretching to the ceiling, cream-colored sheets crumpled, pillow cases missing. The door leading to the adjoining bathroom was open. The closet was beside it, its double set of doors shut tight.

Marty went to it, swung open the doors.

Two rows of suits and shirts and folded pants on wooden hangers lined the top and bottom bars. Marty pushed the upper rack of clothes aside. In the sudden rush of air, he smelled the faint, unmistakable scent of leather and rubber--and knew. He parted the lower set of suits and glimpsed a waist-high door painted red against the dark wall. He cleared an area large enough to walk through and turned the black handle. He pushed.

On the street, a car alarm began to scream.

Startled, he glanced over his shoulder, toward the window and listened to the bleating. It was coming from one of the cars parked curbside and he cursed it. Schwartz's neighbors would be looking out, noting the lighted window, filing it away unknowingly.

He needed to leave, but not before learning what Maggie Cain already knew. He ducked his head and slipped under the lower bar. The door gave easily. A light flashed on automatically, surprising him to the point that he drew his gun. The room was narrow and deep, floor painted black, air heavy and still.

Marty holstered his gun and stood.

Along the pegboard to his left were leather head masks with zippered mouths, full rubber body suits, heavy metal chains and gleaming handcuffs, a coiled noose, a birch switch, nipple clamps, feathers, dildos, knives. In another investigation, he'd seen something like this before. But then, Marty had never seen knives displayed for sexual pleasure, and now he could only guess what Peter Schwartz had done with them. Or what they had done to him.

He stepped deeper into the room, which opened to become surprisingly large and well appointed.

On the wall to his right were file cabinets, a desk with a computer, a telephone and an answering machine. Toward the back was an entertainment center, complete with a massive, flat-screen television, a DVD player, camcorder and stacks of DVDs, each listed in descending order by month and year. Marty scanned the dates, which began in the fall of 2001, and noted with interest that there was no DVD for November 2007. The final DVD was for July, just a month ago.

Marty grabbed it, went to the television, turned it on, popped the DVD into the player, found the remote and hit PLAY.

The screen brightened to a lighter shade of gray and suddenly he was looking at a row of well-fed white men with soft arms and softer stomachs sitting naked on a long wooden bench, their faces concealed with leather hoods.

Above them, a single bare light bulb swung from a black cord, casting shadows, throwing light. The camera panned left and Marty saw the object of their desire--in a large metal cage, a woman was lying naked on a gleaming metal necropsy table. She was young, fit, attractive. Cocooning her in duct tape was an older, powerfully built man, his dark hairy arms rolling her over and over, hoisting up her ass, shooting the tape through and around, pulling it tight. The woman's lips moved and her head lolled sluggishly. She raised her head and seemed to scream, but there was no sound on this disc, only silence.

Marty clenched his jaw as the camera swung left.

The space was huge, open, industrial. Black walls, floor, ceiling. No windows. Smoke in the air. Strobe lights strummed at the rear of the room, briefly catching the jerky movement of other bodies, all wearing the same leather hoods, all naked and dancing. He thought of Judge Wood, of her naked friends and their dark car, and wondered where they were in this crowd.

The camera panned, stopped and zoomed in on the several people sitting across the room at the makeshift bar. And finally Marty saw faces. He leaned forward and saw *faces*. The leather hoods had come off and people were sitting on wide wooden stools. The bartender wore a black rubber apron and nothing else. He swung his hips and cracked open beers. He laughed while he served them.

Marty was startled to find that he knew the man, had seen his face time and again on television and in the press. He was Jackie Diamond, the well-known, right-wing, bible-waving, oil-rich, big-nosed senator from Arkansas. He was worth millions, hundreds of millions, and here he was wearing black rubber and serving canned beer to a group of naked men and women probably just as wealthy and as powerful.

The camera panned up and Marty glimpsed the image of a bull painted money-green on the wall above the bar. He pushed pause and the image froze. The bull was enormous and towering. It leaned over Diamond's shoulder with bulging eyes and flaring nostrils, as though it would tear him apart if given the chance. A gold hoop shot clean through its snout. The rack of spotlights nailed to the ceiling illuminated it in a half-moon. The head was an exact replica of the tattoo he'd seen on Wood.

Marty turned off the television, ejected the disc and put it back in the stack. His hands were trembling. He was beginning to see all of it now. This club wasn't just New York, it was nationwide and he was right in the middle of it.

He and Maggie Cain.

The car alarm stopped. Marty checked his watch, went to the file cabinets and pulled open the drawers. Empty. He turned on the computer and looked for files. None. They had been purged, the hard disk cleared and reformatted, which wasn't a problem because the information was still ghosted there, assuming the person didn't fully wipe it.

He opened the desk drawer and found empty folders, pens, pencils, a stack of printing paper, the usual. But what, if anything, had been in those folders? And why leave behind the DVDs? He checked himself. Why leave behind every DVD save for the one marked November 2007? It was no coincidence the disc was missing--November 5, 2007 had been scrawled in blood above Wood's bed. He knew what was on it--more of what he'd just seen on the July DVD. Whoever took it obviously was on it. They didn't want to be seen.

Was it Maggie Cain? She'd just been here. But not long ago, so had the person who killed Schwartz. So who took it?

He checked his watch. Forty minutes had passed and still she wasn't here, and yet she said she was only three blocks away. He couldn't wait for her. He'd already been here too long. He turned off the lights, slipped through the small door that was in Schwartz's closet and stood in his bedroom.

And when he did, he was forced to rear back.

Facing him were two people--a man and a woman.

Marty went for his gun but the woman moved forward with such speed, he couldn't get to it in time. She wrenched his arm behind his back and the man came forward. He removed the gun from Marty's holster, patted him down and nodded once at the woman, who released Marty and said, "We will kill you if you move."

She had an accent. Spanish? He looked at the man. Italian? "Who are you?"

The man cocked his head. "Mr. Spellman, we're the end of your life."

CHAPTER TWENTY-NINE

8:37 p.m.

For Spocatti, Spellman was just the beginning of a long night.

He appraised the man standing in front of him and could sense him trying to calculate a way out of the situation. Spellman was solid and well-built, and Spocatti sensed he probably was quick on his feet. But right now, without his gun, he was powerless. "Sit over there."

"Which chair?"

"The chintz," Spocatti said. "You couldn't pull off the Stickley."

He watched Spellman cross to the chair and sit down.

"Before I kill you, you're going to answer some questions."

"Before you kill me, I'm answering nothing."

"Not quite." He looked at Carmen, who was standing beside him, her hands on her hips. "Make the call."

She withdrew her cell and Spocatti watched Spellman lean forward as she dialed. She put the phone on speaker and they listened to the ring. And then Spellman's daughter, Katie, answered the phone.

"Hello?"

Spocatti drew his gun, pointed it at Spellman's head and put a finger to his lips. "Is this Katie?"

"Who's this?"

"A friend of your father's."

"Which friend?"

"It's Mark," he said. "We met a year or so ago at your sister's birthday party. I was wondering if I could speak to your mother?"

"She's out."

"Oh," he said. "Do you know how long she'll be?"

"She's with the creep," Katie said. "We were told ten. I'm betting midnight."

"That's several hours away," he said, disappointed. "And my wife and I are about to leave the city. Here's what's up. Your father is on a case and he wanted me to get you something quickly. He said it was important. If we stop by on our way to the airport, would you mind ringing my wife up so she can give it to you?"

She hesitated. "I'm not allowed to do that."

"Can you call your mother and ask?"

"My mother only wants to be reached if it's an emergency."

Spocatti was unfazed. "I see," he said. "Well, this isn't one."

"Then I can't help you."

He locked eyes with Spellman. "Look," he said. "I'm supposed to keep quiet about this, but time is running out and we need to catch our flight. Can you keep a secret?"

"I guess."

"Our dog had puppies a few weeks ago and your dad bought one for you and your sister. He wanted to bring it by tonight, but he got hung up and so he asked us to do it instead. He knows we're leaving town for a few weeks and he didn't want you to wait."

"Dad bought us a puppy?" The thrill in her voice was unmistakable.

"He did."

"What kind?"

"I can't give away everything," he said with a laugh. "Do you mind if we drop by? You can see what it is then. I'll be in the car, but Michelle, my wife, will run the dog up to you."

The moment Katie agreed, Carmen snapped the cell phone shut. Spocatti ignored the tension on Spellman's face and looked at Carmen. "You know the address. Go there and wait. I'll call you if he doesn't cooperate."

"I'll cooperate."

They turned to Spellman.

"What do you want from me?"

"It's simple," Spocatti said. "We need Maggie Cain. We know she hired you. We know there's an investigation. Tell us where she is."

"I wish I knew."

"Bad answer."

"It's the only answer I've got. I don't know where she is."

"Then call her and tell her to meet you here. Tell her what happened to Peter and that you need her here immediately. Tell her it's critical."

"Do you want to reach for my cell or do you want me to do it?"

Carmen walked over to him as he stood. She dipped her hand into his pants pocket and pulled out the phone, but not before copping a feel. She looked at Spocatti. "I know where to shoot him first. You can't miss it."

"Just hand him the phone, Carmen."

She did.

"Is she at home or is she out?"

"I don't know."

"Call her at home first," Spocatti said. "Put the phone on speaker. If she answers, do what I told you to do."

They watched him dial. Outside, on the street, there was the faint sound of an ambulance.

The phone rang. Standing there, in the darkness, they listened to it while the ambulance's lights started to illuminate the street. It was a ways off, but its siren was growing louder. Spocatti nodded at Carmen, who went to the windows across the room and looked out. She craned her head into an awkward position and said, "I can't see it."

Maggie's phone picked up. It was the answering machine. Her voice was barely audible above the ambulance's alarm. "This is Maggie. Please leave a message."

Spocatti reached over and snapped the phone shut. "Dial her cell."

He looked over at Carmen and saw the ambulance's sweeping red lights start to whip across her face. "What's going on, Carmen?"

"I can see the lights, but I can't see the ambulance."

"Tell me when you can."

"It's the city, Vincent. Relax. People die."

"You don't say?"

The ambulance's wail grew to a roar.

"I can see it now," she said.

Spellman held out the phone as it started to ring.

"It's not stopping here. It's going too fast. It's going to turn onto Fifth."

And in that moment, just as the ambulance raced past the windows with its sirens screaming, Carmen Gragera crumbled in front of them and dropped to the ground.

* * *

For Marty, the next few moments came in waves.

From the doorway next to the windows, Maggie Cain rolled into the room, kicked the woman's gun across the floor, lifted her own gun and started firing at the man named Vincent, but not before he dropkicked Marty and sent him flying over a chair. Marty went down with it, his cell slipped beneath him and he landed on top of it.

He was on his back.

He looked up to the sounds of muted gunfire and watched strobes of light reverberate off the walls. Maggie Cain was coming across the room, her gun poised in front of her, the determination on her face captured each time she fired.

With surprise on her side, she was shooting repeatedly at the man, but missing. He was taking his own shots at her, but missing. The room was too large and too dark to allow for accuracy, but with the chance for death so ripe, the space nevertheless was bright with fight.

Marty reached beneath him for the phone, tried to dial 911, couldn't. He broke it when he fell.

There was another shot and this time the man reared back, the gun in his right hand now covering a wound on his left arm.

Maggie closed in. She fired again and this time a portion of the wall behind him exploded into bits of plaster. As a wavering white veil drifted up to consume him, the man stood at the center of it, his head turning to the door to his right.

Behind them came a groan.

The woman named Carmen was attempting to stand in front of the windows, but her balance was off. In the city light, Marty could see blood on her head, confusion in her eyes. She was clutching her side. Instinct lifted her up.

As she struggled to her feet, the man rushed out of the room, his hand over his arm, Maggie Cain racing after him, still shooting even as he ran down the hallway, took to the stairs and fled from the building.

Marty was about to run over to Carmen and tackle her for questioning when Maggie Cain rushed back into the room.

"Leave her," she said. "This place is about to be filled with cops and I can't be associated with any of it. I need you to move, Marty--now!"

* * *

Deep in shadow and halfway down the street, where he was concealed behind the back of a Mercedes SUV, Spocatti watched the front door of Peter Schwartz's building open slowly before Spellman rushed out the building with Maggie Cain close behind him. He could see their guns in their hands. He knew they would shoot if provoked.

They came down the steps crouched low. When they hit the street, they intentionally slammed their backs against one of the cars parked curbside. The alarm went off, Spocatti looked up to see people coming to their windows or closing their curtains, and when he looked back, Spellman and Cain already were in flight and near the end of the block.

He watched them flag a cab, saw them snag one on their second try and then they were gone, fast into the night.

Spocatti wasted no time.

He ran across the street, entered Schwartz's building, took the staircase to the second floor. He called out Carmen's name and came face-to-face with her when he entered the room he'd left her in. When he saw her, she was standing with her back to the window, her gun raised and pointed at his face.

"Why did you leave me?"

He came toward her, knowing that time was running out and that they needed to leave. "I had no choice. She shot me. She ran after me shooting. I had to run or I would have been killed. You would have done the same thing."

She looked at his arm, saw what must have been a flesh wound given the absence of significant blood, but nevertheless kept her gun as steady as she could on him.

"What did she do to you?" he asked.

"She threw a bronze bookend at me. It hit me in the kidney and I went down."

He kept moving in her direction. "Why is there blood on your forehead?"

"I fell, Vincent. Guess what hit the floor first?"

"Put down the gun," he said.

"I'd rather blow your fucking head off."

"Just put down the gun."

"I should take you out now for leaving me here."

"I didn't leave you. I came back for you. I can't do this alone."

"Bullshit."

Maybe, he thought. But what he heard in her voice now wasn't so much anger as it was ego, and that was enough for him. He kept moving toward her just as, in the distance, the faint wail of police sirens started to sound.

"We need to get out of here," he said. "Those sirens are for us." He reached out a hand and lowered the gun. "We have to trust each other. If we don't have that, both of us will be dead." He cupped the side of her face with his hand. "I didn't have to come back. You saw what happened. I don't know where she learned to shoot like that, but she's no amateur. We can't forget that."

And with that, Carmen holstered her gun. "There are others on our list tonight," she said. "We'll chalk this up as a botched job and move forward." She moved quickly past him. "Unless you want to get caught, I suggest we get out of here. I need to clean your arm and bandage it before we start again."

They hurried out of the room, down the staircase and left the building. Outside, well down the street, a police car was speeding forward, its sirens mixing with the sound of the car alarm. Together, they moved to the end of the block, turned it and kept going at a steady pace.

"Who's next?" she asked.

He told her.

"Good," she said. "I need a little theater."

CHAPTER THIRTY

9:14 p.m.

In the cab, Marty told the driver to take them to the Tarot Cafe on Prince. Then, he leaned back against the seat and was quiet while the driver shot down Fifth.

He needed to call four people, beginning with either Katie or Beth, but his phone was busted. He asked Maggie if he could use her cell, she gave it to him, he dialed and listened to the phone ring. Maggie looked out at the city, her gun in her lap, the side of her head against the window. He put his hand over hers and motioned for her to conceal the gun, which she did.

Beth answered on the third ring, music blasting in the background.

"Hello?"

"It's Dad. Turn down the radio."

"Radio? God, you're old. It's my iPod."

"Whatever. Just turn it down. I need to talk to you."

She turned off the music.

"Is your mother home yet?"

"She won't be home until midnight. She said ten, but she always says ten. It'll be midnight. And then they'll be moaning and groaning all night long, as usual, which already wants to make me barf. Katie said something about a dog. Are we getting one?"

"Not tonight," he said. "There was a mix-up, but that will be cleared up soon. I need you to listen to me."

"You need me to listen to you after you deliver that shitty news?"

"Beth," he said. "This is important. It's as important as anything I've ever said to you and I need you to do as I say and do it quickly."

Maybe she sensed the urgency in his voice or maybe she was just playing nice so they'd get a dog, but there was a pause before she spoke again, and when she did, her tone was serious. "I'm listening."

"Are the Moores home?"

"Of course, they're home. They never go anywhere. I finished watching a movie with Andrea about an hour ago. Why?"

"I need you to take Katie and go down and stay with them. I need you to call your mother and say one word to her--blue. You don't need to know what it means, but she will and that's what matters. Call her now, get Katie, lock the apartment and go down to the Moores immediately. Say the same word to them. They'll also know what it means and then I need you to listen to them and do as they say."

"Are we in some sort of trouble?"

"Not if you do as I say."

"Then, we are in trouble. Why are you scaring me? Why are you acting weird?"

"I'm not trying to scare you."

"Then what's wrong?"

He couldn't answer that without alarming her more than he had. And if he lied to her now, what good was he to her? "It's complicated," he said.

"It has to do with us," Beth said. "That's obvious. I think we have a right to know."

She resembled her mother and also had inherited her mother's tenacity. He closed his eyes and tried to keep his voice calm. "I really need you to cooperate with me right now, okay? Can you just do that for me? I need you out of the apartment in five minutes."

There was a long hesitation before she agreed.

"I love you," he said.

"I love you, too, Dad."

"And I'm sorry if I've scared you."

"That dog better be cute."

She severed the connection and Marty stared at the phone. There was fear in his gut, but long ago, he and Gloria had devised a plan to keep the family safe in situations such as this. Gloria and the girls lived in a large building. If Beth did as she was told, they'd be safe.

This time it was Maggie who reached over. She clicked the phone shut and put her hand on his. "Are you all right?"

He moved his hand away. "You and I will talk when we get to the cafe." He opened the cell and dialed Jennifer Barnes.

"Hello?"

"It's me."

"It says it's Maggie Cain."

"I'm borrowing her phone. Are you at Carra Wolfhagen's?"

"I've been here since eight, when we agreed to meet. Why aren't you here?"

"I'll tell you everything later, but I can give you an exclusive now. Peter Schwartz is dead. His throat was sliced and now his body is home to a whole host of things you don't want to see. If you want the scoop, I'd run with it now for the 11 o'clock newscast before someone else does. You'll find him at his house. He's been dead for awhile, so be prepared. Wait for the police to arrive before you go anywhere near his house."

"I'm on it."

"Did you hear me?"

"I won't go near the house. I'll wait for the police."

"Promise me."

"I promise."

"One last thing. Are the Wolfhagens home?"

"Carra left about an hour ago. A limousine arrived and she left the building with a young, really built guy. A few minutes ago, I saw Wolfhagen pacing in front of one of the upstairs windows."

"I need you to get out of there now," Marty said.

"You don't need to tell me twice."

"What was Carra wearing?"

"That's a bizarre question."

"Things are getting bizarre. Wait until you have a look at Schwartz."

"She was wearing a black cocktail dress."

"Nothing else?"

"It's still in the 80s and humid as hell, Marty."

"What about her escort?"

"A black suit."

"Grab a cab," he said. "Watch your back. We'll talk later."

"Be careful," she said.

"I'll try."

"I love you."

"I love you, too."

He hung up the phone, thought for a moment and decided to call Linda Patterson first, Hines second.

This time, he dialed *67 to conceal his identity so neither knew whom he was working for. He told them about Schwartz, he came clean that he owed each a tip but that he was telling nobody else other than themselves. Now, it was up to them who got on-scene first and decided who was taking Schwartz's case.

Though Marty would be happy for Hines, he was pulling for Patterson. Hines was a friend Marty had helped countless times over the years, usually in ways that lifted his stature and his title within the department.

But in this case, which might prove the largest of Marty's career, he knew he needed to be smart. Winning over Patterson after he screwed her out of two grand was critical. With her contacts and ability to tap into information, having her on his side could be the game-changer he needed as this case progressed.

* * *

When they arrived at the Tarot Cafe, Marty was relieved to find it open. It was nearly 9:30 and the café's neon sign--a tarot card tipped into a coffee cup--punched a red halo of light into the night and across the faces of those on the street.

"We'll be safe here," Marty said.

Since she'd been secretive from the start, he was expecting her to put up a fight. But she didn't. Instead, she nodded and they stepped out of the cab. Marty went to the driver, handed him some cash and they went inside the cafe, where Roberta was across a room filled with hanging tapestries positioned in such a way that they diffused the light and created a mood.

Just inside the door was a rush of incense that smelled of something toasted and earthy. Candles burned low on the gnarled wooden tables. Marty swept the space and saw that only a few of those tables were occupied. Moroccan music played in the background. He caught Roberta's eye and immediately saw the concern on her face.

"Twice in two days?" she said. "Let me get tea. Sit in the rear booth, not the front. The energy is better back here."

They went to the back of the café and slid into the booth. Marty chose the seat facing the door. Maggie sat opposite him and looked around the room. "I've never been here before," she said.

He had zero patience for small talk. He removed his cell and looked it over. Physically, it seemed fine. He smacked it hard against the palm of his hand and tried it. Nothing. He smacked it harder, this time against the side of the table, and it worked like a charm. He gave her back her phone. "Let's get to it," he said. "If my kids weren't involved in this now, I'd be out."

"I'm sorry," she said.

"For which thing?"

"For everything. For the first day we met. For tonight. For lying to you. For all of it. I've been watching my back for years. I don't know who I can trust. I saw them enter the building tonight. I called the ambulance for a distraction so I could go inside without being heard. Did they hurt you?"

"I'm fine. But we're finishing this together and you're going to tell me what you know. Who were those two people tonight?"

"I don't know. Assassins?"

"Wolfhagen hire them?"

"I'm not sure."

"Why aren't you sure?"

"Because one thing still doesn't make sense to me. Wolfhagen wouldn't have sent himself Wood's head. I know him. He wouldn't have pointed the finger at himself."

"Not even for an alibi?"

She paused. It was obvious by her expression that she hadn't considered that angle. As her expression changed, he saw now how much sense it made to her.

"Would he do it for the alibi?"

"He might. Forcing the attention on himself would actually work in his favor if he did hire this out. That's how he thinks."

"What about Lasker?"

"He's a possibility."

"Where does he live?"

"On Fifth."

"You're not writing a book, are you?"

"I'm not."

"Then, what are you doing?"

"Trying to expose Wolfhagen. Trying to make him pay for what he did."

"He's already been to prison, Maggie."

She leveled him with a look. "That's right. For securities fraud."

"What else did he do?"

At that moment, Roberta arrived with two cups of tea, each smelling of cinnamon. When she handed Maggie hers, Marty noted that she intentionally brushed the side of her thumb along the curve of Maggie's left hand. Her eyes darted to his, but she kept her voice light. "So, who's this?"

"Roberta, meet Maggie."

Roberta held out a hand, which Maggie shook. "You seem familiar to me," Roberta said, still holding Maggie's hand. "Have we met before?"

Maggie looked down at her hand. "I don't believe so."

Roberta gave it a slight squeeze before releasing it. "I've seen you somewhere," she said. "It'll come to me."

Maggie smiled, which emphasized the scar on her face.

Roberta's eyes lingered on that scar before she turned to Marty and leaned down to kiss him on the forehead. "I'm glad you're here, because this has been killing me. Do you remember that joke I told you the other day about the three women?"

He looked at her for a moment and then remembered. It wasn't a joke--it was a warning. This was her way of reaching him covertly. Her words came back to him. *Three women,*" Roberta said. *"One of them loves you, one of them resents you, the other is keeping secrets from you. They're in danger, too, but only one of them knows it and she doesn't care. She's got murder in her heart. She wants someone dead. I don't know if it's you, but you're involved. She might kill you.*"

"I remember," Marty said, and in his mind's eye, he saw Maggie rolling into Schwartz's room, her gun held out in front of her and firing. No amateur moved like that, so where had Maggie Cain learned to? It took everything he had not to look at her. "But as usual, you forgot the punch line."

"That's because I'm old. And the worst part is that it's not even as funny as I remembered. Still, I remembered it. Want to hear it?"

"Why not? I could use a joke right now."

She kept her gaze squarely on Marty and though she tried to mask her emotions, she couldn't. In her eyes, he saw fear and sorrow. "The third woman killed him."

CHAPTER THIRTY-ONE

9:27 p.m.

With his children involved, the only way out of this was to see it through. To do that, he needed Maggie. There was no other option. She'd lied to him before, but Marty now sensed it wasn't with malice, but because she felt threatened by what was happening now.

She was scared and trying to protect herself. He felt she was finally being honest with him. Still, if she thought for one second that her fear would ever get in the way of him protecting his daughters, she was a fool. His family was in danger. To end this, he would do whatever it took.

He watched Roberta go back into the kitchen. "Alright," he said. "Go on."

"I need you to understand one thing," she said. "If my name is connected to any of this, I'll be dead in a week."

"You don't know that."

"I do know that."

"Then we'll keep your name out of it. Why were you at Wood's?"

"How did you know I was at Wood's?"

"It's what I do."

"She had a videotape I wanted. She had files on Mark. With him dead, there was no one else who could protect his memory from that tape and those files if someone didn't intervene and destroy them. So, I called and threatened her. I got from her what she never should have had."

"What was her condition when you got there?"

"She was high, but at least she had the box ready. I was there for about ten minutes. I left with what I came for."

"Why does the FBI have a file on you?"

"We've already discussed that. They think I have Mark's stolen money, but I don't. That's their only interest in me."

Marty knew the answer--he just wanted to see if she delivered the same response. She did. "Who would want to kill you?"

"Who do you think? You've seen the DVDs."

"I've seen one DVD."

"Fine, you've seen one. That's enough." She cocked an eyebrow at him. "Did you recognize anyone on that tape, Marty?"

"Senator Diamond from Arkansas."

"No one else?"

"Everyone else was wearing a leather mask."

"Then you chose the wrong DVD."

"Who else should I have seen?"

"Diamond was enough," Maggie said. "Take off those leather masks and you would have seen more senators. More players with power. People who could buy and sell your ass a hundred times over."

"Wolfhagen started this club?"

"He started it."

"Was it a sex club?"

"It was whatever they wanted it to be. A sex club. A place to relax. A kink palace. A place to drink and have your drugs served a la carte. You could participate or just watch. It was whatever you wanted it to be because that's what that crowd demanded. Anything they wanted. Admission wasn't free. Each paid millions to join."

"Who belonged?"

"Every bull who mattered on Wall Street, and then it grew to include others."

"Give me names."

"Lasker," she said. "Schwartz. Wood. The Coles. Gerald Hayes. Everyone who testified against him in court, and many others."

"What about Boesky? Milken? Levine?"

She raised an eyebrow at him. "What do you think?"

"Tell me about Mark's involvement. Did he belong?"

There was a sudden air of protectiveness about her. "He did," she said. "But not by choice. He was trying to please Wolfhagen even though he was nothing to Wolfhagen. Zero. Wolfhagen wanted to surround himself with money and power. Real money and power. Mark had neither. He was a pawn there to do what Wolfhagen wanted."

"I've been to the M.E.'s office. I've seen the tattoo. Did Mark have one?"

"I have no idea."

"But you were lovers."

"That's right."

"So, how couldn't you know? A ring went through its snout. At the very least, you would have felt that."

"Sure, if we'd been making love. Mark left me about a week after he joined the club, which is where they initiated people with the tattoo and the piercing. He moved into his own place. Said he couldn't be with me anymore. Wolfhagen was behind it. He wanted Mark for himself and he got him. He took away the one person in my life who mattered and I want him dead for it. Mark called me a week before he was murdered in Pamplona. He said he wanted to talk. He apologized for the mistakes he'd made." She leaned back against the booth. "And then he was dead."

"Why do you think he was murdered when he was trampled by bulls? There were witnesses who saw how he died. He could have just fallen. It happens every year there. Why murder?"

"Why not? Why would his death be any different from what happened to the Coles, Wood, Hayes and Schwartz? Someone could have pushed him and he fell. Someone could have tripped him while he was running. I'm convinced he was murdered."

"Did you belong to that club?"

"Not on your life."

"Mark didn't take you?"

"Mark loved me. He got sucked in, but he made certain I was never a member."

"You didn't answer my question. Did he take you to the club?"

It was a moment before she spoke, and when she did, the fear she was trying to hold back came right to the forefront. It was obvious she'd never spoken to anyone about this. "Yes," she said. "He took me. Once."

"When was this?"

"Years ago."

"Let me guess. Three?"

"How do you know that?"

"There was a date painted above Wood's bed. Did you do it?"

"What date? What are you talking about?"

It was the correct answer. They'd never talked about it and it still hadn't reached the press. If she'd said yes or no, she would have revealed that she knew about it. She was telling the truth.

"Somebody wrote a date above Wood's bed in her blood. Somebody also had sex with her after they decapitated her. Any idea who?"

"What was the date?"

"November 5, 2007."

She closed her eyes. "It could be any number of people. There were dozens who witnessed what Wolfhagen did that night. Even the sick ones--the real pervs--thought he went too far. They also want him back in prison."

"What happened that night?"

She looked over at Roberta as she swung through the kitchen door.

"I need to know."

She waited for Roberta to move to a table of customers before she spoke.

"Murder," she said.

* * *

"Start from the beginning."

She pulled her hair away from her face and looked up at the ceiling. It was almost imperceptible, but in this light, he could see that her eyes were welling with tears. The more he learned from her, the more he felt connected to her. When they first met, he thought she was rigid. Now, all he saw was a woman being stripped of her secrets because she had no choice but to share them with him. That took a level of trust he felt she'd likely only shared once in her life, likely with Mark Andrews.

"I wish I could have a cigarette."

"Do you want a drink?"

She shook her head. "I think we're in for it tonight. My head needs to be clear." She quickly wiped a finger under one of her eyes. "Do you want a drink?"

"Actually, I'd kill for one, but I'm with you. Tell me about the murder."

She took a breath. "Mark and I had been apart two months and I knew Wolfhagen was behind it. When I called to ask if he'd see me, he agreed, but only at his convenience, which was at midnight that evening."

"Midnight was his earliest convenience?"

"It had nothing to do with convenience. It had to do with power. I wanted to see him, he wasn't going to make it easy. It was midnight in his office or he wouldn't meet with me. Period. But when I arrived, Wolfhagen was putting on his jacket. He said a friend needed to see him. I could either talk to him in the limousine or I could forget about ever talking to him about Mark again. I knew he wouldn't give me another chance. I was desperate and so I went." She looked at him directly. "Have you ever loved somebody so much you'd do anything to get them back? Absolutely anything?"

Six months after his first divorce from Gloria, he'd started seeing shrinks, psychologists, counselors. He'd told them every rotten thing that had happened in his life in an effort to find out how he could handle the past so he could maintain a healthy relationship in the present. It didn't work, but he tried.

He lifted his eyebrows at Maggie and smiled.

"Then you know," Maggie said. "I loved Mark so much, I was willing to do anything to get him back. Even risk talking to Wolfhagen alone. And it was a risk," she said. "I knew whatever I said to him might get back to Mark, probably twisted around. But I didn't care. I had something on that son of a bitch. I planned on bribing him into letting Mark go."

"How?"

"Before I set up the meeting, I hired a private investigator who tailed Wolfhagen for two weeks. I had photographs of him cruising the meat packing district back when it was much more than just the meat packing district. I had photos of him at three in the morning screwing young girls in the back of his Mercedes, photos of him leaving The Eagle with men old enough to be his father. I had it all and I planned on going public with it if he didn't let Mark go."

But when she showed Wolfhagen the photographs, his reaction wasn't the rage or the fear she'd been anticipating, but delight as he casually flipped through them.

"He asked me which one I liked best," she said. "He actually looked me in the eye and asked which one would work best for the front page of the Post--the photo of him going down on the old man in leather, or the one with him pushing the naked prostitute out of his car."

She sipped her tea. "I thought I could intimidate him. I thought the photographs would be enough, but I was wrong. He set me up. He wanted me in that limousine for a reason, said if I was going to judge him, I'd better be prepared to judge Mark as well, because they were one in the same."

"What did he do to you, Maggie?"

"Oh, not to me, Marty--at least not yet."

That got his attention. "Then to Mark."

"The limousine had a television and a DVD player. Wolfhagen hit the remote, told me to watch the screen." She looked at him with a sadness and a rage that was so deeply entrenched, it hardened her face. "And there was Mark," she said. "Naked. In the middle of all these people. Wolfhagen turned up the volume, tried to make me listen to what they were doing to him, but all I could do was sit there wondering how in hell he'd superimposed Mark's face on another man's body."

The vulnerability he sensed she rarely showed anyone was back and alive. "How did you get that scar?"

"Wolfhagen."

"Did he cut you?"

"Actually, he shoved my head through the limousine's side window."

Though he was startled by the violence of it, he pushed forward without pausing, not wanting to lose momentum. "Why?"

"That video was playing. Everything I'd hoped for was gone. I'd brought a gun with me for protection, but when I went for it, Wolfhagen was quicker and he shoved my head through the window." She stopped at the memory of it. "I must have blacked out, because when I woke, I wasn't in the car. I was in his club and Wolfhagen had just murdered a man."

"Who?"

"I don't know."

"Did you see his face?"

She shook her head. "He was tied down. His forehead was strapped to the table. I could barely see his profile. There was too much confusion."

"What did Wolfhagen do to him?"

"He slit this throat."

"Why would he do that?"

"Because he was Wolfhagen. Because at that point, he was so high, he was delusional. He literally thought he was a god."

"What else do you remember?"

"Shouting. Things getting out of hand. People screaming. But I'd lost a lot of blood at that point and my memory isn't as clear as it should be. I think I was coming in an out of consciousness."

"Who was there?"

"A lot of people. When I got home, I wrote down the names of those I could remember. I think there are some who think I saw the murder, and those who don't. But I did. Wolfhagen would have killed me too if Peter Schwartz hadn't gotten him out of there. He would have killed me. And do you know what I keep thinking after all these years? You know what I go to bed with every night? A part of me wishes he had."

"Why didn't you go to the police?"

"Because I was scared. I thought they'd come after me. I've always thought that. It's why I took a self-defense course. It's why I took classes on how to shoot a gun. There are too many people who know I know what happened. I thought I'd be dead years ago. It's why I told you I can't be connected in any way to this because they'll come for me. I'm surprised I'm sitting here now."

"Wolfhagen filmed everything that happened at that club, didn't he?"

"He did, but only a few people knew about it. That whole club was designed for blackmail. That's the reason it was created. It's one of the ways Wolfhagen got his inside information. When he wanted a favor from a senator or from the president of a corporation, a bit of information that could make him a fortune on the street, all he had to do was invite them to the club. He'd slip something into their drink, they'd do something stupid, it was all caught on tape. Then, when it was time to collect, he'd pick up a phone, invite that person to lunch at his office, and if they refused his favor, he'd show them how well they performed at their audition. Maybe they'd be fucking a prostitute. Maybe it was a hell of a lot worse."

"How did you find out about the tapes?"

"Mark. When I was on that table, he threw a towel over my face. When I took it off, he put it back on and leaned down to my ear. He told me there were cameras. He told me not to remove the towel."

"But it was too late at that point. You already were on camera."

"That's right," she said. "And that's why I took the disc marked November 2007 from Schwartz's hidden room tonight."

"Where is it?"

"I destroyed it. There are more out there--there have to be--but at least I got one of them. At least I got that."

His cell phone rang, which startled each of them. Maggie ran a hand through her hair while Marty answered. There was static on the line. Movement on the other end. "Hello?" he said.

A man's voice: "Put Maggie Cain on the phone."

Marty's heart skipped a beat. Did somebody know they were here? Nobody had entered the cafe since they'd sat down, but that didn't mean that someone couldn't be waiting for them outside.

He looked at Maggie, who was now watching him intently, her slender body so taut, he could almost feel the tension as if it was a wire stretching between them. "There's no one here by that name," he said irritably. "Who is this?"

"Put her on the phone, Spellman."

"Who are you?"

"Put her on the phone."

"Not until you tell me who you are."

"It's Mark Andrews," the man said. "And I know she's with you. If either of you wants any chance of ending this, you'll do as I say and hand her the phone now."

CHAPTER THIRTY-TWO

9:38 p.m.

In the safe house on Avenue A, Carmen grabbed a satchel of supplies, followed Spocatti into their shithole of a bathroom and ripped open his shirt. She paid no attention to the buttons that popped off and ricocheted off the peeling walls. She was in a hurry. They needed to move.

She could sense Spocatti looking down at her.

"Horny?" he asked.

"Shut up, Vincent."

"Because I'd be happy to fuck you," he said. "Release some of this unnecessary tension between us. Consider it my way of apologizing for leaving you behind." He grabbed a handful of her ass, but she was fast. Just as quickly, she grabbed his crotch and squeezed it hard, so much so that he released his hand and, through the pain, put it on top of hers. He squeezed his crotch with her. "How does that feel?" he asked. "Big enough to make you forget you had a bad day?"

She knocked his hand away. "I don't need your mercy fuck, Vincent."

"It wouldn't be one."

"Let me fix your arm."

He put her hand back on his crotch and she was surprised by how much it had grown. "What do you say?" he said. "I fuck you, you do your nurse duties and then we get back to work?"

She'd be a liar if she said she wasn't attracted to him, but this isn't how she played it, and she knew it was the same for him. He was testing her, just as always.

She put a hand on his shoulder. "You're sweet, Vincent. And that's quite a package you've got. Your old man would be proud. But I'm going to clean your arm now, you're going to let me do it and then we're going back out. You know why?"

He had an amused look on his face. "Tell me," he said.

"Because if we don't finish this job soon, we'll have blown it. The police are onto us. So are Maggie Cain and her P.I., who now knows for certain that we're working for Wolfhagen. If this isn't front-page news by tomorrow, then it will be the next day. And all those people who once testified against Wolfhagen who aren't already dead will know that soon they will be. And then they'll flee."

"Schwartz won't flee."

Spocatti took him out days before Carmen arrived from Spain. There were two others in the city sitting in their own chilled living rooms, poised exactly like Schwartz. Only, those people had been dead longer. "No," she said. "Not unless those maggots sprout wings."

She removed the last of his shirt. He hadn't lost much blood. Cain's bullet only grazed him. Still, if she didn't clean and stitch it properly, it would become infected and then they'd really be in for it. Given their records, there were no hospitals available to them.

She removed a bottle of rubbing alcohol from the satchel and soaked a clean cloth with it. She pressed it against his arm and wasn't surprised that he didn't wince. "I'm not losing out on a $10 million bonus for you, Vincent."

"I don't expect you to. I was just offering you my cock, Carmen. Frankly, I'm offended you don't want it."

She looked up at him and was about to speak when the look on his face stopped her. Gone was any trace of humor. Back was the cold man with the hard eyes and the set mouth that reminded her again why she never could trust him.

He took the bottle of rubbing alcohol from her hand, poured it over the wound and allowed it to splash into the sink. He saved half for the clean-up and handed the bottle back to her.

"Get a needle," he said. "Stitch me up. It's past nine-thirty. I want to be out of here in fifteen. We have four people on our list and we're getting through them tonight."

She looked surprised. "I thought there were five."

"There were," he said. "But I had an opportunity to take out Alan Ross earlier today and so I did." She was about to speak when he held up a hand. "I'm not explaining it to you. Later, you can watch the footage yourself to see how it went down. Just stitch me up so you can take care of that scrape on your forehead and make yourself look pretty. We know Yates' routine. He'll be sitting at that bar in twenty minutes."

* * *

When they left the building, Carmen was a new woman.

Her face was clean, she'd applied fresh makeup, brushed her hair, concealed the scrape and changed into a short black dress that revealed long, slender legs and a robust bust. Her dark hair tumbled down her back and swung when she moved. In her ears were faux black diamonds that concealed tiny microphones. The brooch she wore was a camouflaged miniature camera. She was beautiful, she knew it, and just how deeply she knew it was reflected in the confident way she held herself.

She was wearing heels for the first time in what seemed like months and even though she hated them, she knew how important they were. This next job was all about illusion. As pretty as she looked right now--and as sexy as she was without going over the top--it was just a tool to generate the interest of one man.

Spocatti was ahead of her, climbing into the van parked curbside. Carmen went to the passenger-side door and slid in. She opened the small, jeweled black purse she'd brought with her, checked her gun to make certain it was loaded, looked for the syringe Spocatti had filled with a lethal dose of potassium chloride and, satisfied, snapped it shut.

The drove uptown in silence.

When they arrived at a private club called The Townhouse, which was just off Park on 67th Street and which Wolfhagen had made arrangements for Carmen to enter, Spocatti stopped at the street corner to drop her off.

"Stick to the plan," he said. "Don't pull another Hayes."

She lowered the illumined visor for a final check of her appearance. "I learned my lesson, Vincent. Don't worry about it."

"Yates is fat and lonely and old. This should be easy for you. I'm expecting you to be out of there in twenty."

"He's also worth billions, which erases age and weight. I have no idea what I'm walking into or which starlet will be trying to charm him when I find him. But I'll be quick. And I'm better looking than most. Expect to hear from me in fifteen."

"Don't use the gun."

She was growing tired of him. She was every bit as good as he was and he knew it. She applied a last swipe of lipstick, smacked her lips together, shut the visor and opened the door. She pulled her hair away from her face and turned to look at him. Her voice was steady when she spoke. "Cut the condescending bullshit attitude toward me or you're finishing this alone."

On the street, it was quiet. This was mostly a residential neighborhood, but there were a handful of restaurants and, of course, The Townhouse, which was two-thirds of the way down the street on the right.

Carmen moved down the sidewalk as if on air.

She was still in pain from the bookend Cain smashed against her side, but unlike most people, Carmen didn't mind the pain. Her awareness of it only made her focus more intently on the task at hand and so she moved through it, holding herself with the confidence of the rich, her black dress swinging along with her hair as she approached the building's red-carpeted entrance.

At the top step stood a middle-aged man in an expensive business suit. His hands were behind his back and he smiled at her as she approached. "Welcome," he said when she took the steps. "Beautiful evening, isn't it?"

She smiled at him.

"Are you here to meet someone?"

"No," she said. "I'm in town for the week and a guest of one of your members."

"May I ask who?"

"George Redman."

"Your name?"

"Sophia Bianchi."

From behind his back, he pulled out an iPad. Carmen watched him turn it on and, in the glow reflected upon his face, move his finger down the screen until he arrived at her name, which he clicked. "Perfect," he said. He stepped aside and opened the glass and bronze door. "Have you been to The Townhouse before?"

"First time."

"You'll find a lively crowd on the first level, a terrific new talent performing wartime standards on the second, and the lounge on the third. Waiters are throughout, so you won't want for a drink. But if you are looking to relax with a cocktail before potentially coming upon someone you know, I recommend the lounge first."

She moved past him and then, turning on her heel, stopped on the cusp of entering the crowded room. "Actually, I am hoping to find an old friend here tonight. Do you happen to know if Ted Yates has arrived?"

"You'll find him in the lounge."

* * *

When it came to taking a life in public, Carmen was no stranger.

She'd slit throats in Sicily during open-air operas, she'd broken necks in Paris while shopping for shoes in the Marais, she'd swept down the Alps and caused one especially difficult man to go flying into a tree, and on one job in Vienna, she'd taken down a pedophile priest (and a few unfortunate others who were there to absolve their sins) when she poisoned the wine being offered at Communion.

Now, as she walked into a room that harkened back to another time--dark mahogany woodwork reaching to the tall ceilings, Tiffany windows and fixtures splashing color along the golden walls, lights dimmed just low enough to flatter the well-appointed crowd--she felt suddenly recharged with the life she was about to take.

Ted Yates had earned his billions thanks to Wolfhagen and, in turn, Wolfhagen had earned at least part of his fortune thanks to Ted Yates. With their contacts, their knowledge and insights into national and international markets--not to mention Wolfhagen's ability to garner inside information--they once were an unassailable team, until Wolfhagen was charged, put on trial and had to face Yates when he took the stand to testify against him.

For his trouble, Yates was offered immunity, as was everyone. As a slap on the wrist, everything was taken from him save for his apartment on Fifth and all the money he'd managed to tuck away in Swiss accounts. In all, he'd lost close to a billion in cash, securities and property, but it was just a dent in what he really had at his disposal. Though people assumed but could never be sure, Ted Yates was among the wealthiest men in the world.

And today he would die.

"Can you hear me?" she asked Vincent while turning her head to toy with one of her earrings.

"I can hear you."

"And the brooch? You can see everything?"

"You're fine, Carmen. Move."

At the end of the room was the staircase that led to the two additional levels. There also was an elevator to the left of the staircase. In a glance, she could see it was the building's original elevator--this crowd would have it no other way--and that it likely was too slow for her needs.

And so Carmen moved through the smiling crowd, took to the stairs and passed the level on which a young woman was singing "The Memory of Your Face," which was just ironic enough to make Carmen smile. The woman was so good, Carmen longed to listen, but there was no time. She went quickly up the last flight of stairs and into the lounge, which was dominated by an enormous mahogany bar and just as crowded as each of the rooms below.

A man stopped beside her with a silver tray. "Champagne?"

She looked at the shallow bowls with their bubbling stems and couldn't deny that she wanted one. She looked at him and also couldn't deny that with his dark wavy hair, broad shoulders and classic Greek looks, that she wouldn't mind having him either. "I'm more of a martini girl."

"I'd be happy to get one for you."

"You're kind," she said, sweeping the bar and finding no trace of Yates. "But I think I'll just sit at the bar, if I can find a seat."

"You won't find one here," he said. "But there is room on the other side."

Other side?

Carmen followed him through the crowd and to the rear of the bar, where there was a wide arched doorway that led to another room. Here, it was somewhat quieter. The decor was the same and there was an identical bar, at which sat Yates, alone--just as they were told he would be.

The seats to his right were occupied, but to his left there were two open chairs. Carmen went to the one farthest away from him. The young man pulled out the chair, she smiled over her shoulder at him as she sat down, and then she heard him say to the bartender. "Martini here." He looked at her as Yates turned to do the same. "Straight up?"

"And with three olives."

"Belvedere?"

"I prefer the Goose."

Yates lifted his own martini in an amused toast to her comment and Carmen knew why. This was his drink, and Grey Goose was his choice of vodka.

She looked at him. "I suppose that is an odd way to put it."

"The French would love you for it."

"The French would be happy I was buying their vodka."

"The French know how it's done."

"The French almost made me an ex-pat."

She crossed her legs and put her purse on the bar. Yates, who was indeed fat and hovering somewhere near 80, glanced down at her tanned legs before taking another sip of his drink. "I haven't seen you here before," he said. "I'm Ted Yates."

"Sophia Bianchi."

"An Italian drinking French vodka?"

"Consider me a non-conformist."

"Non-conformist. Ex-pat. What do you believe in?"

"Freedom."

He laughed at that. "I would have thought Uvix for you."

Carmen waved her hand. "Vodka never should be made from grapes."

"It's actually rather good."

"As good as the Goose?"

"Probably not that good."

She smiled. "I didn't think so."

The bartender came with her drink and she watched Yates look around the room. It was starting to fill up, the din was rising and soon the chair between them would be occupied. "Are you meeting someone tonight?" he asked.

She shook her head and ate an olive. "It's just me. I'm in town for the week and a good friend who's a member thought I might enjoy stopping by for a cocktail."

"What do you think so far?"

"It's lovely," she said. "And obviously popular."

"How's the olive?"

She chose another and held it to her mouth. "Perfectly soaked in French vodka."

At that moment, a middle-aged gentleman pulled out the seat between them and started to sit down. Carmen saw the disappointment that crossed Yates' face and shrugged her shoulders at him, as if she wasn't sure what to do. The man caught the shrug and asked if anyone was sitting here. And Carmen took the opportunity.

"Actually," she said. "We were just starting to talk. Would you mind if I slid over and you took my chair?"

"Not at all."

She sat in the chair next to Yates and lowered her purse so it rested in her lap. She released the latch. The bartender, missing nothing, moved her martini in front of her. She touched glasses with Yates, who once again dropped his gaze to her legs. "This is a nice surprise," he said. "Nobody ever talks to me here."

"That's a curious thing to say. Did you throw a drink in someone's face?"

"No," he said, smiling. "But sometimes I'd like to. I'm just old and worn out and not very popular anymore."

"Sometimes, being unpopular with the wrong crowd isn't such a bad thing. But if it bothers you, why come?"

"Lot's of reasons," he said. "I live nearby. I once had terrific times here, especially when my wife was alive. And I still enjoy myself even if the mood has changed against me."

"Now you're creating a mystery."

He motioned for the bartender to bring two new drinks. "Allow me to deepen it. What I am is a man at the end of his life who's made his share of mistakes."

"Who hasn't?"

"They were public mistakes."

"I think you're probably more than that," she said. "Look at this place." Her words gave her an excuse to look around the room. People were talking closely and loudly in an effort to be heard. The room was near capacity, which was to her benefit. At the far right of the bar, vodka and vermouth were shaking with ice. Carmen noted that on this side of the bar, he was the only bartender on duty.

With distraction on her side, she reached her hand into her purse and grabbed the syringe. And then, as always when she was about perform a kill, she felt the rush of anticipation shoot through her body. "They don't just let anyone in."

He held out his hands as if in defeat.

She stuck out her bottom lip and took one of his hands in her own. She came up behind him, the syringe at her side. She looked down at his face and into his liquid blue eyes, and felt nothing when she saw hope, lust and embarrassment reflected back at her.

"And besides," she said, leaning in close so only she, he and the microphones could hear. "You're Teddy Yates. You could buy and sell all of these people. We both know that just as we both know that Maximilian Wolfhagen would one day make you pay for sending him to prison. Now, it's time to collect."

Yates' brow furrowed and then, just as quickly, his eyes widened with recognition as he saw what was about to happen.

But Carmen was quick. She leaned forward as if to kiss him on the neck, but instead, with her hair tumbling over and concealing her hand, she slipped the syringe into his carotid artery and pressed down hard so the contents mainlined into his heart.

It was over in seconds. His eyes growing wider, Yates placed his hand over his neck and tried to speak. But he couldn't. His heart was seizing up.

Carmen backed away from him and positioned her body so his last few breaths were caught on camera. She dropped the syringe into her purse, blew him a kiss and lowered her head slightly as she left him behind and moved through the enthusiastic crowd.

It didn't take long.

Behind her, she heard the crash of a chair hitting the ground, women screaming, men shouting for someone to call 911, and then she was on the stairs, hurrying past the singer who now was belting out something jazzy on the second level, and then she entered the first floor, where the crowd was tighter than before.

She slipped through it. As she neared the door and the doorman she'd encountered earlier, she was completely composed.

"Leaving so soon?" he asked.

"Afraid so," she said. "One drink limit. My flight leaves first thing. But it was nice to see Teddy even if he wasn't feeling well." She moved past him and took the stairs. "Good night."

He nodded at her and with that, she walked down the street toward Vincent, who was waiting for her in the van she could see at the end of the street. She stepped into it and he pressed the gas. "How long was I?" she asked.

"Just over twenty."

She couldn't still the disappointment that washed over her. She had promised him fifteen and she'd blown it.

Spocatti turned the wheel and they started moving toward their next target. Carmen stepped to the back of the van, where she changed into comfortable clothes and then checked the contents of a large satchel that was at the center of the van. It was all there. With an uneasiness that was alien to her, she moved back to the front passenger seat and sat down.

Everything was in place.

Spocatti broke the silence. "Killing Yates wasn't easy," he said. "But you pulled it off. You did well."

She pulled her hair away from her face and knotted it into a ponytail. "I'm worried about this next one," she said.

"I agree, but we need the distraction."

"There are other ways to cause a distraction."

"You're just a woman going for a walk. You're too sharp for anyone to know what else you're up to. I know you'll be discrete."

She pulled hard on the knot, turned her hair up into a bun and reached down into the bag at her feet. Inside was a cap with realistic blonde ponytail attached to it. She put it on and checked herself in the visor's mirror. "Powerful people live there. There has to be some level of protection on that street that we're not considering. Are there cameras?"

"No."

"How do you know?"

"Because, I've checked." He turned to her. "I'm putting neither of us in jeopardy for Wolfhagen, Carmen. I could give a shit about him. But just like you, I've been paid. I've done my work and I've checked that street. It's clean. Now we stick to the plan. Just walk at a regular pace. When you bend, do it quickly. I won't be far behind."

"I want that bonus, Vincent."

"We both do. We'll get it."

The van weaved through traffic, Spocatti caught a string of green lights and started uptown toward East 75th Street. He didn't say another word to Carmen and she felt she knew him well enough to know why. What they were about to do next was critical not only because it would take out the one woman who delivered the trial's most damning testimony against Wolfhagen, but also because it would cause a massive, city-wide panic that would allow them to complete their night's work and finish this job for good.

But the downside was beyond comprehension and almost crippling for her to fathom, just as it had been when Spocatti first had the idea. If they pulled this off--and given the planning and preparation that had gone into this particular job, there was no reason for her to believe it wouldn't go off--hundreds of innocent people could die and buildings would fall as a part of Manhattan was wiped off the face of New York City forever.

CHAPTER THIRTY-THREE

9:38 p.m.

While Carmen was busy putting stitches into Spocatti's arm and preparing to kill Ted Yates, Maggie Cain was preparing to talk to a dead man.

Marty handed her his cell, but kept his thumb pressed against the receiver so he couldn't be heard. "I don't know what's going on here or if this person is who he says he is, but I need you to play it cool. Either he's for real or we're being set up. I've never heard his voice before. You should know immediately whether it's him."

She shook her head at him. "What are you talking about?"

He put a finger to his lips and lifted his thumb from the receiver. Maggie took the phone. "Hello?" she said.

"Maggie, it's Mark."

A chill went through her—it couldn't be him. She looked up at Marty in denial, but in spite of the poor connection, she was almost certain it was Mark's voice.

"I need your help."

There was a crackling on the line, a buzz of interference. She put a hand over her free ear and tried to focus on his voice in spite of the sudden racing of her heart. She watched Marty grab a napkin and start to write on it. For a moment, she couldn't speak. Her world was drawing in on itself and then, in a flash, there was only the truth standing in front of her. She stared at it for a moment and then walked into it.

"How can this be you?" she said. "I went to your funeral. I was with your parents when your body arrived from Spain. I saw them lower your coffin into the ground and bury you."

"But you never saw *me*, Maggie."

That stopped her. He was right--she hadn't seen him. He arrived in a body bag. Only his parents were allowed to physically see him. "But your parents saw you," she said. "Your parents would have told me if it wasn't you."

Marty pushed the napkin in front of her. She looked down and read: "Get him to reveal something only the two of you would know."

"My parents know what's happening. They've known from the beginning. Wolfhagen is killing everyone who testified against him. When I was running in Pamplona, I was stabbed by an American. He was dark. Maybe of Italian or Spanish descent. Before he stabbed me, he told me that Wolfhagen wanted to thank me for ruining his life."

Something was wrong. His voice wasn't right. It sounded like him--but there was something off about it. Something raw. "This isn't you. This isn't Mark's voice."

"I've had several operations, one on my larynx. I'm still healing, Maggie. I'm in rough shape."

"Answer a question for me."

"Anything."

"What's my cat's name?"

"Baby Jane."

Anyone could know that. The real test was if he answered her next question correctly. If he did, there would be no doubt in her mind that this was Mark because it was their private joke. "But what do you call her?"

He didn't hesitate. "Blanche," he said. "She's always been Blanche to me."

She put a hand to her mouth.

"She's never been as tough as you think she is. She's a wimp. She's always been a wimp. You got it wrong. You should have named her Blanche."

How many times had he said just that to her? She looked up at Marty and nodded. "It's him," she said. "It's him."

"Find out where he is."

Her whole body started to shake. "Where are you?"

"I was in a Spanish hospital for a week before I was able to reach the FBI and tell them what happened. I've been under their protection since. Their doctors have been treating me for the past several weeks."

"Are you alright?"

"I'll be alright. But right now I'm shit--I'm filled with steel rods. I've got new knees. They had to rebuild my nose. I've got a long road ahead of me, Maggie."

She was fighting back tears. "When can I see you."

"Tonight," he said. "But only briefly. The FBI knows you're working with Marty Spellman on this. They want you both to come in and talk, tell them what you know. Can you do that? I need you to do that."

She told Marty, who nodded.

"Where are you?"

He gave her directions, but the directions didn't make sense.

"Why are you there?" she asked. "Why aren't you in a hospital?"

"You're not thinking clearly," he said. "I'm supposed to be dead. If they put me in a hospital, the media would be all over it and my cover would be blown. The FBI has safe houses all over New York. I was put in one of them. It's critical that I appear dead. It's critical that no one sees me until this is over."

It made sense.

"When can you be here?"

She asked Marty.

"An hour," he said.

She looked confused. They were only twenty minutes away. She was about to speak when he held up a hand. "An hour," he said firmly.

"We'll be there in an hour."

"Why so long?"

Marty moved a hand across his throat, signaling that he wanted her to cut the conversation short. But Maggie didn't want to. She wanted to keep talking to him, but she'd made a deal this evening to trust Marty and to do as he said, and so she did.

"Peter Schwartz was murdered," she said. "We found him in his living room and now we need to make sure we have a safe exit before we leave. Give us an hour. We'll do our best to be there by then."

"I love you," he said.

Her throat closed at the sound of those words. Never did she think she'd hear them from him again. Never did she think she'd talk to him again. It was wonderful and it was surreal. She'd been fighting all this time to find answers, to somehow bring down Wolfhagen for what he'd done. The fact that he hadn't succeeded in killing Mark filled her with an elation that was impossible to describe. "I love you, too. You don't know what it's been like. You don't know how hard it's been."

"It's almost over," he said.

"I need to believe that."

"It ends tonight."

"Can you promise me that?"

"Whatever information you and Spellman have culled is important. The feds are ready to act, but they need to know what you know. You need to tell them everything. And then you need to stay here with me and be safe. I'll see you in an hour."

Before she could reply, the line went dead. She held the phone in her hand for a moment and then clicked it shut. She looked up at Marty, who was staring at her intently. "He's alive," she said.

"You're certain that was him?"

"Only one person would know what he called my cat and that's me. It was our thing. It was our joke."

"Calling her Blanche was nothing he said in front of your friends?"

"No." She thought for a moment and then shook her head. "I don't know. How could I know that?"

"You couldn't," he said. "That's the point."

"Why are we waiting an hour? Why not go now?"

"Because I have to call people. I need to cover our asses. We don't know if that was him. We're not going alone."

He looked across the room, where Roberta was cleaning glasses at the bar. She was looking straight at him. Concern was a mask that covered her face. She took each glass, gave it a thorough wipe and clinked it above her on the rack. She was standing there but she wasn't there. She was reading him. He knew that face, knew when she slipped away. Wipe, wipe. Clink, clink. Her eyes boring into his. He motioned her over. She stopped beside the table.

"I'm going to say a name to you," he said.

"Is this the name of the person she was just on the phone with?"

"It is."

"Then give me the phone."

He gave it to Roberta, who turned it over in her hands and then lifted it to her breast.

"What's the name?" she asked.

"Mark Andrews."

She closed her eyes. When she opened them, defeat had settled in. "You're going to ask me what I saw, Marty, but it's the same thing. Nothing's changed. It's the same thing I saw when you were here last. It's the same thing I saw when I touched her hand earlier. It's so overwhelming, I can't tell you a thing about Mark Andrews. All I see is your death. Over and over, that's what I see. I'm too close to you to see anything else. I wait on customers and watch you disappear. I clean glasses and see you vanish. While you've been sitting in this booth, I've watched your spirit leave you. I've watched someone murder you."

She turned to Maggie. "It's her."

CHAPTER THIRTY-FOUR

10:12 p.m.

Theresa Wu ran.

She ran down East 82nd Street, ran past the Church of Scientology Celebrity Center and then she stepped it up when she saw that the traffic light ahead of her was green and in her favor.

She burst across Madison Avenue, ran past the Adelson Galleries and kept going until she reached Fifth Avenue and the Metropolitan Museum of Art, which cast a magnificent halo of gold against the darker backdrop of Central Park.

She took a hard left and ran down Fifth, her black hair snapping behind her in a ponytail as she weaved through the few people on the sidewalk. The evening air was so humid, she was drenched in sweat, but the run was exhilarating, particularly at this time of night, when the side streets were mostly quiet and it was just her and the city she loved.

Fifth Avenue was another story. Here, the traffic was moving briskly downtown, but she kept pace with it. She passed 79th Street, the Ukrainian Institute of America and checked her watch. She pressed a button and the dial lit up. She was doing well, but not that well, and so she ran faster, determined to beat her best time.

Earlier that morning, Helena had too many errands for her to complete before noon so she could enjoy her meeting with Marty Spellman, so Theresa had to forfeit her run until this evening. But now Helena was asleep and Theresa was free.

And she felt free. And it felt good. She had an opportunity to go out with the girls later that evening and she might just take it. It had been weeks since she'd been out. There was a new club people were raving about downtown. It would be good to have a few drinks and to let her hair down. It would be good to set herself loose on a dance floor. Last week, she'd splurged and bought a hip new dress at Prada, so why not go out?

She decided she would.

She darted left again, this time onto 76th Street. She moved swiftly and easily, crossed Madison again, and then kept running for the final turn that would bring her onto 75th and home. She'd been running for 50 minutes now. When she ran in the morning, she liked to do at least ninety minutes, but it was late and at the very least, she was getting some exercise. If she didn't, given Helena's frequent demands, she wasn't sure how she'd stay fit.

When she turned onto 75th Street, she noted on the other side of the Madison throughway that a van was parked in the middle of the street, near Helena's home and across from Judge Kendra Wood's house. Its lights were on. Though she couldn't hear it at this distance, she assumed its engine was idling.

A woman stepped out of the passenger's side with a large satchel over her shoulder. She moved to the left side of the sidewalk as the van drove ahead. Theresa stood at the corner of Madison and East 75th, jogging in place until the light turned.

Meanwhile, she watched the woman move down the sidewalk. She watched her dip her hand into the satchel, watched her remove something that Theresa couldn't see, and then watched her dip into the shadow cast by one of the many cars parked curbside. She reappeared again, reached into the satchel and bent beside one of the cars. In an instant, she was back up again and walking casually.

Rinse and repeat.

After what had happened to Wood, Theresa took no chances on these streets, regardless of how exclusive they were--and especially when there was something as odd as this going on. Now, the beat-up van was at the end of the street and about to turn onto Fifth. It sat there for a moment, then it maneuvered around the corner and left the woman to reach, dip, stand, continue.

She was attaching something to those cars.

The light turned, but Theresa didn't cross. Instead, she looked left, saw no one coming down 75th and started running toward 74th Street. She made it in time to catch the light and crossed Madison there. She moved down 74th at a slower pace, just a jog, her mind trying to process what she'd seen, her heart catching in her throat when she saw the van turn onto 74th and start moving toward her.

Theresa kept a steady pace. All business, she pumped her arms. The van drew closer. Its high beams flashed on. Theresa lifted a hand to shield her eyes. She kept jogging. The van was upon her. As she started to pass it, she kept her focus ahead of her even though it was difficult to see. She turned to look at the driver in annoyance and absorbed the details. Male, forty-something, good looking, dark hair, turning to look at her from his open driver's side window. They passed each other.

And then, in a shock of red light that illuminated the buildings surrounding her, he hit the brakes.

"Excuse me," he called out.

No single woman at this time of night would stop for that call. Theresa quickened her pace even as the man called after her again. "I just need directions."

She didn't answer. Instead, she broke into a run while behind her, the brake lights turned to white and the van's engine roared to life.

He was backing up.

Theresa sprinted toward Fifth. She jumped over a cat as it strolled from between two cars parked along the street and sauntered onto the sidewalk. She flew over it. The cat looked up at her and hissed.

The man pressed harder on the gas. She could feel him rushing up behind her. She looked over her shoulder and saw that he was leaning partly out of the window and looking backward as he closed the distance between them. But Theresa was an athlete and there was nothing stopping her but her own endurance. She bit down hard and pressed herself as she fled to the street corner and cut right, almost into oncoming traffic.

Car horns blared.

Theresa righted herself and ran toward 75th.

Behind her, a car made an effort to turn onto 74th Street from Fifth, but the van was blocking its way. More horns. The man in the van had no choice but to stop and go forward, where she was certain she would find him again, this time speeding up 75th.

There were people on Fifth. "Call 911!" she shouted as she shot past them. "Tell them to get to 75th and Fifth!"

She stopped just short of the street and pressed her back against the building at the corner. Slowly, she looked around and saw nothing, no sign of the woman or the van. She looked at the car parked directly next to her and saw what appeared to be a medium-sized white brick stuck to the back near the gas tank. For a moment, Theresa couldn't move. Every part of her told her it was an explosive.

Heart pounding, she weighed her options. She should leave here, save herself, but she couldn't. Helena meant everything to her and her home was only five houses down the street. If she could somehow get inside before the van or the woman appeared again, she could call the police herself, take Helena deep into the basement and into Cecil's fortress of a wine cellar, which was well away from the street. They could hide in there. The walls were so thick, they'd be safe from any intruders or explosions.

She reached into her pocket, pulled out a set of keys, got the correct one ready, and peaked around the corner again.

Nothing.

This time, she carefully scanned the block, but there was no movement. The woman was gone. So far, there was no sign of the van.

And so Theresa Wu rolled the dice and ran.

When she did, she was running the fastest she'd ever run. Fear propelled her forward. With each car she passed, she made an effort to look down to see if the same brick was attached to the rear bumper. From what she could see at this speed, in most cases, it was. The woman was rigging the street with explosives. She was planning some kind of terrorist attack.

But why here?

Focus. Just two houses to go. She sprinted. But then, just as the cat had done moments ago, the woman she'd seen earlier slipped between two cars, stood, moved to the sidewalk and stopped in front of her. Blocking her. In her hands was a gun with an extended silencer. She raised it while, at the end of the street, headlights rolled around the corner and shined against the woman's back. It was the van. Its engine roared.

Theresa was running quickly, but not too quickly to think. In an instant, she dropped hard to the ground and rolled toward the woman's feet. Surprised, the woman fired and the bullet went deep into a confetti of concrete.   She made an effort to jump but Theresa was faster. She collided with the woman, who went down like a ten pin and fell hard on her chest.

Theresa leaped to her feet. Helena's house was just up the stairs to her right. In her hand, she still clutched the key. But the van was nearly upon her now. And the woman was on her feet, though one look told Theresa that she was dazed and obviously hurt, though not badly enough to keep her from raising her gun.

Ducking, Theresa scrambled to Helena's house. She ran up the steps and pressed the key into the lock just as the barrel of a gun pressed against the back of her head.

It was the man from the van. She could smell his breath. It was over in an instant. There was a click. A soft "goodbye." A sudden jolt as a bullet bore through her brain and left part of her face stuck to Helena's door. But molecules were still working, still making an effort to connect. She was aware of herself tumbling backward down the steps. She saw bricks rise up in front of her, a fan of tree limbs, a moving sky.

When her head struck the sidewalk, it did so with a sickening THWACK--and then Theresa Wu saw lights of another sort.

CHAPTER THIRTY-FIVE

10:18 p.m.

In his town house on East 75th Street, Emilio DeSoto admired himself in the full-length wall mirror and realized that at last, he had created his master work.

He was now a retro piece of living art. Minimalism was dead to him. In its place was classic severity and brash beauty delivered through the driving force of haute couture.

He held out his arms and then lowered them, allowing the scalloped polyester fabric to flutter in pretty waves. He did it again and then turned in such a way that air funneled up through the garment to create the illusion of weightlessness. He had smoked a joint earlier and his glaucoma was tolerable. Though he had only tunnel vision, if he looked directly at himself, he could see his reflection, and he was thrilled by what he saw.

After months of work on his latest piece--which used his own slender, angular body as its catalyst--he now embodied two art forms, each of which enjoyed a spellbinding link separated by centuries.

When that Spellman person left, he started going through the motions of at last bringing the influences together. And it worked, just as he knew it would months ago, when the idea struck him that soon, minimalism would no longer define who he was as an artist or a person.

After a long gestation of artistic incubation, that day was now.

He always had been a creature unlike any other--it's why they loved and celebrated him--but now he had taken his talents to a new, defining level of greatness.

His face was a shield of Kabuki makeup that consumed his features--there was no trace of them beneath it. While his skin always had been pale, now it was painted pure white. The only other color was bright red, which he'd applied to the corners of his eyes--and to the lower lids--in an effort to make them appear as if they were about to spill over with blood.

On his lips was the same red, painted in such a way that his mouth now looked so grossly small, one would be surprised if words could escape it. Naturally, some critics would look at his mouth and seek connections to his dead body of work. They'd think its tiny appearance was his nod to minimalism, but they'd be wrong. Some would lean toward the great Kabuki artist Tamasaburo and see it as something of an homage, but they'd be wrong. It was, in fact, a post-apocalyptic statement designed to honor the past--and to confuse what DeSoto believed was now a dystopian present.

He turned again in front of the mirror, lifted his arms at his sides and enjoyed the way the vintage Halston caftan moved in sync with his body. It had belonged to Barbra Streisand, he'd bought it anonymously at auction when she had her big 1994 Christie's garage sale, and he wore it instead of the traditional Kabuki dress most would be expecting given his Kabuki makeup.

On his head was a white turban, also by Halston, which harkened back to Emilio's days at Studio 54, where he'd use cocaine in bathroom stalls and on bathroom floors with other celebrities and danced with a freedom that was stolen away from him when he gave himself over to the dead art of minimalism.

Completing the look--and crossing boundaries but not continents--were the tall wooden Geisha shoes that now pinched and bruised his feet. He was click, click, clicking around the room while dipping his head and fanning out the caftan by lifting his arms behind him when one of the clicks sounded like a pop.

He was standing at a tall window that overlooked 75th Street. He looked down at his feet to see if he'd broken one of the shoes and when he did, he caught movement on the street below. On the sidewalk were a pair of legs lying flat between two cars. They were slender and appeared to belong to a woman. As Emilio watched, they suddenly were pulled from sight.

With that Wood woman murdered, instinct made him move to the side of the window, so he wasn't exposed. He was confused and a part of him was frightened. There was a van idling in the middle of the street. Its driver's side door was open. Light pooled from the van onto the street, where a man and a woman, crouched low, were leaving the spot where those legs had disappeared. They hurried to the van, stepped inside and sped toward Fifth.

And Emilio DeSoto, who rarely did the right thing unless it benefitted him, stayed true to himself. There were killers in this neighborhood. The rodents Wood led here had just taken another life. There was no reason to believe that they wouldn't take his.

Removing his shoes, Emilio put his hands straight out in front of him so he wouldn't bump into anything and hurried out of the room. As he moved carefully down his curving staircase and rushed to the phone that was in the living room, the caftan billowed behind him, just as it should. He picked up the phone and dialed 911.

An operator came on the line. "What's your emergency?"

"Somebody is going to kill me," he said.

"How do you know that, sir?"

"Because the rodents just killed somebody else."

"What rodents, sir?"

"Wood's rodents."

"You're going to have to be more specific. Are you in danger now?"

He went to a window, looked out at the street and saw those dead feet tucked between two cars. "Yes," he said. "I'm in danger. Alright? I'm in danger."

"By who?"

And Emilio exploded. "How the fuck do I know?" he shouted. "What more do you need from me? I just told you I'm in danger. They're going to kill me just like they killed her."

"Sir--"

"They're going to kill me because I don't fit their mold. They're going to kill me because I'm different. Because I'm magnificent."

"Sir--"

"They're going to kill me because I'm poised for greatness. They're going to kill me for all those reasons, and if you don't get your ass down here now, I'll be just another dead freak felled by the very rodents you idiots can't seem to catch."

* * *

Spocatti drove to the end of 74th Street, stopped at a red light and was about to ask Carmen if she was hurt when an NBC news van drove past them. It was moving fast--too fast--and each turned to watch it race up Madison and cut left onto 77th Street, where Peter Schwartz lived.

"News is out," he said.

"Literally."

"Cops will be there."

"And more will be coming. We need to move. It's time to finish this."

The light turned green. Spocatti stepped on the gas, drove three blocks east for protection and then cut back onto 75th. There was a parking spot midway down the street. Surprised, he went for it but saw the fire hydrant as he approached. Didn't matter. Cops were busy and about to get busier. He took the spot and turned off the engine.

"Why are we so far back?"

"I'll tell you in a minute. Are you hurt?"

"I'll live."

"She was a feisty one."

"God's telling her that now."

A woman with a dog turned the corner and started walking toward them. She was young, maybe twenty-five, with a bounce in her step and a smile on her face. She said something to the dog and laughed when it barked. They waited for her to pass before speaking.

"There's no failing here," he said. "Let's run through it. What's first?"

"You're on the street with the video camera."

"What's second?"

"I'm on the phone with Pamela Dean to make sure she's home, which I already know she is because I saw her pass a window on the second floor of her townhouse. But I'll double check."

"What was she wearing?"

"Let's just say she's not going out."

"If someone else answers and you need to ask for her, what's your name?"

"Rebecca Stiles. Pamela and I used to work together with Wolfhagen. She was one of his moles and gave him information that helped him bilk billions from foreign markets."

"If her husband answers, what if he doesn't know you?"

"He doesn't need to know me. Pamela and I were lunchtime friends. We ate together once a month. But it's been years since we've talked. We lost touch after Pam took the stand against Wolfhagen. I'm in town. I heard about Wood. I know she lives next to her and wanted to check in to see if she's alright."

"That's so kind of you."

"Rebecca's that kind of girl."

"Do her voice."

One of Carmen's strengths was mimicry. Not long after Wolfhagen was sent to Lompoc, Pamela told her story to "60 Minutes." Wolfhagen sent them the tape. Carmen studied it. She did the voice.

"Nice," he said, and then paused. "I need you to be aware of something. Did you see the black Escalade when you were planting the explosives?"

"The one at the end of the street? Just before Fifth?"

"That's right."

"How could I miss it? Those cars are obnoxious. Why?"

"You know what McVeigh used to blow up the Federal Building in Oklahoma?"

She didn't answer. A part of her froze.

"That's what's in the Escalade."

"But that will take down several blocks."

"Actually, we don't know what it will do. We used only a quarter of what McVeigh used. I know it will level its share of buildings and give us our distraction, but I don't know to what extent. When you're certain Dean is there, I want you to detonate those bombs."

"Who put the Escalade there?"

"I have friends all over this city, Carmen. Who did it doesn't matter. What matters is that he was able to do it." He reached behind him and grabbed the camera. He held it up to his face to see if he could zoom in properly down the street. Perfect. With a lens this powerful, he easily could focus on the events as they occurred, which would make Wolfhagen happy. And that's what mattered.

"Let's do this," he said.

"Just a minute. You say you don't know what will happen when the Escalade blows. But look at us--we're pointed in that direction. What's the plan on getting us out of here?"

He patted her knee. "It's simple. We're going to run like hell in the opposite direction. I have a car waiting four blocks behind us. It's all taken care of, Carmen. You just need to be able to run."

"From an explosion of that magnitude? We're essentially in a tunnel, Vincent. A fireball is going to roll down this street. It will incinerate us."

He stepped out of the car with the camera and moved to the street corner. Over his shoulder, she heard him say, "That's why you need to run fast."

* * *

Emilio DeSoto retrieved his wooden Geisha shoes from the second floor, squeezed his sore feet into them in the first-floor living area and looked out again at the legs that were between the two cars outside his home.

It had been fifteen minutes since he called the police and there was no sign of that they were anywhere close to coming. No sirens. No flashing lights. Nothing.

Twice, he had gone to his door and opened it, hoping to hear something, hoping not to be attacked. But nothing had happened-- the rodents were gone. More compelling, each time he opened the door, he could see those feet, which ignited in him a curiosity that was impossible to stuff down.

Who did they belong to? Who was murdered and why? Was it someone he disliked? He hoped it was someone he disliked.

He went to a mirror and checked his Kabuki makeup. Flawless. He held out his arms and allowed the Halston caftan to fan out and then ripple softly against his sides. Brilliant. He put his hands up to the turban and moved it slightly on his head. Perfect.

If he had time, he would have changed into different clothes and removed his makeup, but time was running out and if he didn't act now, he might miss this moment. Naturally, the police would show up at some point--likely soon--which meant he had a limited window in which to go to the sidewalk and see who was attached to those dead feet before this neighborhood was consumed again by the police.

Awkwardly, he walked away from the mirror, click, click, clicked to the desk across the room and removed the loaded pepperbox he kept there for protection.

He held it at his side, just as Joan Crawford did in his favorite movie, "Johnny Guitar," and made the supreme effort of walking across the room to the front door, which was no easy task given the shoes on his feet.

Still, there was no way in hell he was going to wear anything else but these shoes. If someone saw him on the street--if the paparazzi were there to take his photograph, which he knew could happen at any moment because he was a celebrity--he needed to be seen in this new creation as it was meant to be seen. Nothing else would do.

Stealing himself, he opened the door.

He looked each way down the street, saw no one, and then looked at those feet sagging against each other between the two cars. With his free hand grasping the iron rail, he descended the few steps that lead to the sidewalk and stood there, listening. Ahead of him, over the buildings and a few blocks away, he could hear sirens, but they were stationary and not growing louder. They were on another street.

Emilio frowned, though you wouldn't know it given the upward lift of his Kabuki lips. This was one of Manhattan's finest neighborhoods. What was it coming to? Years ago, as a young artist living in the Village, he'd felt safer in his sixth-floor, one-room walk-up than he did here.

Pepperbox in hand, he worked through his tunnel vision and clicked forward on unsteady feet, ready to shoot if anyone approached him, ready to kill if that's what it took.

There was a breeze on his face and it kicked up the caftan, allowing it to take flight behind him in ways that gave him new ideas about how he'd officially present this when the time was right. He'd use fans.   Dry ice would be employed because of its retro hook and because it would capture that Studio 54 vibe he was going for.

As he stood there, billowing, he thought of Diana Ross blowing kisses in a Central Park monsoon.   Arms open to the breeze, his gun pointing at the house across the street, he let his wings fly as he hobbled forward and stopped at the dead feet.

Because he couldn't see well, he needed to lean almost directly over the body to see the face. And when he did, he saw the ruined face of that pretty Asian slant who worked for Helena Adams. Part of her head was blown off. Emilio put the back of his hand to his mouth and looked closer. One side of her face was missing. She was resting in the congealed fallout of her own blood.

He felt nauseous. Violated. This was taking place on his street? His Geisha shoes took several steps backward. The only other time in his life that he had confronted death was during his black period, when he went inward and explored it with his own vision.

But it looked nothing like this.

He click, click, clicked over to the car to his right, came around it and leaned down again so he could have a better look at the slant's face. But he couldn't see anything. He was casting a shadow. He was about to move so light could slip through when suddenly her face bloomed orange as the cars at the far end of the street began to ignite in a series of rapid explosions.

Emilio moved so he directly faced the center of the street and could see all of it. And what he saw was a horror show. Cars on each side of the street were flipping high into the air and pinwheeling into the buildings on either side of them. Windows smashed, fireballs rushed toward the heavens and, in the vacuum created by the broken windows, he watched fire being sucked into those buildings. Soon, they'd burn.

His pepperbox dropped to his feet. When one car exploded, it caused the car in front of it to explode. And so on. It was unfolding quickly--too quickly--and the lot of it was roaring his way.

E turned toward Fifth Avenue and ran.

Tried to run. Because of his shoes, he nearly tripped. He tried to kick the damn things off but they were too tight. His feet had swelled in them. He struggled to remove the shoes, but it was impossible. And so he hopped and he hobbled, his arms held out on either side of him for balance while behind him, all hell was unleashed as this part of 75th Street was smashed and burned beyond reason.

He tried to scream for help, but all that left his Kabuki lips was a frazzled peep of a shriek. Out of nowhere, a car door flew over his head and smashed in front of him on the street. It was like a fiery comet morphed into something else by the heated atmosphere.

Emilio looked over his shoulder and saw that death was upon him. He looked ahead of him, where the traffic was rearing to the right and colliding on Fifth. People leaped out of their cars. On the sidewalks, others ran.

He was almost there. He could make it. He pushed harder. Click, click, click! Click, click, click! Another car erupted. And another. The sound was deafening. He could hear the vehicles rising into the air behind him. There was a great yawning as metal twisted against metal and melted in the rising heat.

Something caught his eye. He looked down the length of his spread-eagle arms and saw that the caftan, once white, was now glowing orange in the flames licking behind him. He was morphing from a moth into a spectacular-looking butterfly and he wasn't that far gone to realize the terrible beauty of it.

He rounded Fifth, where now masses of people were running down the avenue to what they hoped was safety. He hit the middle of the street and was about to cut left when a fiery tire bounced hard beside him and sprayed liquid flames onto his face before it somersaulted over the sidewalk and jackknifed like a demonic Halloween pumpkin into Central Park.

People were running alongside him. He tried to keep up, but couldn't. The heat was becoming unbearable. Hobble, hobble, hobble. Click, click, click. He watched them look at his Kabuki face and what he saw in their terror-filled eyes wasn't what he expected. The look was unmistakable. What he saw was pity.

And then Emilio burst into a sphere of light.

The tire also had sprayed fire onto his caftan, and now it was he who was erupting. In a matter of seconds, the fire curled up his body, rounded his legs, tasted the edges of the scalloped fabric and raced toward his outstretched wings.

He stood in the middle of the street as the flames consumed him. The polyester caftan melted into him, searing his skin as it sank inward toward the bone. Hands reaching and pulling, he tried to yank the caftan over his head, but he couldn't--it now was part of him. The art he created literally was part of him.

Cars were still exploding, still turning in the air, still shattering the faces of the buildings on either side of them. More debris fell from the sky. Something struck his head and his turban became alight with flame. He batted his hands at it, but the polyester glued itself to his palms, destroying them.

The heat of it all caused his Kabuki makeup to melt. He was aware of people coming near him in an effort to help, but the moment they saw his face, their lips twisted back in horror and they kept running. "Sorry," they said. "Sorry." He was watching them run from him when his shoes hooked a manhole and he fell face first in the street. With his arms stretched out at his sides, he now looked like a burning cross.

"WOAT!" he shouted as the flames seared his throat. "FLAK!"

Something heavy struck his back. He expelled a rush of air and managed to crane his neck around. He was pinned beneath a car's burning hood. He writhed beneath it like a trapped bug. Glass exploded into the street. At this level, all he could see were feet running past him. Why wouldn't they help him?

"SHELP!" he cried. "GLOP!"

And then, as the polyester continued to burn into him and cause him to melt along with the heat from the car's burning hood, Emilio DeSoto, once one of New York's most revered artists, realized through the pain that he was becoming every artistic expression he ever hated.

As his body roasted, his frying mind was aware that he had long passed any kind of impressionism, post-impressionism or realism.

He now was a bloody, sizzling abstract blob, which proved to him again just how cruel life could be and that there was no God.

He was floating, floating. People stepped on him and screamed in the gathering rage of chaos. And then, just before life left him, he was aware of the biggest explosion yet as a vehicle at the end of the street exploded.

But it wasn't just any explosion. It was more like a bomb and its force was enough to flip the hood off him. As his eyesight faded, he watched people lift off the street and somersault weightlessly in the air. Others were vaporized in the ferocious funnel of flames. And then there was something else, something he barely could see.

All around him, the buildings were crumbling.

CHAPTER THIRTY-SIX

10:37 p.m.

Wolfhagen checked his watch, turned on the television, backed away from it and watched New York City burn.

He flipped through the news stations and saw the same thing on all of them--part of the Upper East Side was destroyed. Dozens of buildings had either collapsed or were severely damaged. People were running in the streets. Commentators were calling it a terrorist attack, but all were wondering why anyone would target this section of Manhattan since it was a residential area, which didn't make sense to them.

As he listened, he learned that the explosion had leveled a portion of East 75th Street, with the damage spreading to 76th and beyond to parts of 73rd. Hundreds were feared dead. There was a crater on the corner of 75th and Fifth that suggested a powerful bomb was employed after two rows of cars parked curbside exploded from 75th and Madison and rolled west to 75th and Fifth.

Wolfhagen turned off the television. This was no longer his city. It and its people had turned against him years ago. He could care less about the damage or the dead.

And besides, tonight was a night for many endings.

Earlier, he pulled the glass out of his feet. The vase was too thick to cause any real damage--if it had been more delicate, then he really would have been in trouble as the glass would have cut more deeply into him. It hurt to walk, but he'd bandaged his feet the best he could. Like the pain in his split lip, he could handle it.

He went to his dressing room and changed into something casual--khaki pants, blue polo, comfortable sneakers. Perfect for running if running is what he had to do, though given the condition of his feet, he hoped that wasn't the case.

He stepped into the bathroom, combed his hair and removed a small bottle of makeup from the silver tray to his left. He dabbed some beneath his eyes so he looked younger and less tired, and then stood back and appraised himself. He hated what he saw and reached over to dim the lights. It was magic. Ten years fell from his face. Already, the stubble was starting to show in spite of having shaved earlier, but it was tolerable.

For the past several hours, Carra had held him captive in this suite of rooms. They'd fought earlier--certainly one of their uglier fights, but nothing like the one they'd had years ago in Paris, when he'd beat her so hard with a belt at the Ritz, there was a moment when he thought he killed her. Now, he tried to remember what they fought about then but it escaped him. Like so many things in his life, his memory had nearly given up on him. He had difficulty recalling elements of the past, which probably was for the best given their smothering weight. But it didn't matter.

Right now, for Wolfhagen, it was all about the present.

He moved out of the room and into the bedroom, where the door across from him was bolted shut. Before she left, Carra called her security team and now four men with outsized bodies and brains the size and consistency of rabbit shit were making sure he didn't leave.

When she left earlier, he knew where she was going because Carra made sure he heard her on the phone, just to rub it in. She was out on the town with Ira Lasker, a man Wolfhagen once had trusted everything to, just as he had with Peter Schwartz, Hayes and the rest. At some point over the past year, Carra and Ira had started dating.

Fucking, he thought. *They started fucking.*

Along with everyone else, he'd seen their photographs in Vanity Fair, on Page Six, in the Times, all over the tabs. Usually, their heads were held back and they were laughing in that way that the rich laughed when their only security was money and power, which could slip away from them at any moment. And so they laughed on camera to sustain the illusion of lives others craved to have, but didn't.

He'd read articles about her philanthropy work, which actually was quite cunning on Carra's part because the grotesque amount of cash she threw around lifted her profile in ways that distanced her from him. She was the largest pink ribbon breast cancer awareness ever had seen sweep through its doors. She was PETA's go-to person for the past five years, going so far as to pose nearly nude because God knows, when it came to saving animals, Carra would rather be naked than wear a piece of fur. How she had rebuilt her image was ingenious. She found the correct, high-profile ways to give back. Have an obscure disease that needs funding and attention? Just call Carra!

Lately, in each article that was written about her, she always managed to mention Ira, who betrayed Wolfhagen as so many others had along with him--including Carra--when he took the stand and testified against him. Those people now were being slaughtered and Wolfhagen felt nothing for them.

He smoothed his hand down the back of his hair and thought again of Wood's severed head. He still could see her dead eyes frozen in sightlessness, her blue face crisp with death's rotten imprint and her bloody lips curling up from him as if they'd been dipped in week-old ketchup. The image delighted him. She was one of the biggest hypocrites he'd ever met. She'd locked him away for three years even though she'd been one of the more enthusiastic members of his club. Karma had caught up with her. Karma grabbed her by the throat and took her down. He couldn't help a smile.

Maybe she still has a shot, he thought. *Maybe she won't burn in hell. Maybe God will show her mercy and she'll become one of his little angels.*

With a giggle, he went to the door and knocked on it. There were footsteps, groans and then the door swung open to reveal the four goons. "What?" one of them said.

Wolfhagen sized him up. Years ago, when he was at the very top of his game and the world bended to its knees to service him, often literally, he occasionally used to sleep with men to spice things up. He liked sex and he was nothing if not sexual. To him, a body was a body, and this was exactly the type of body he used to hire to fuck the hell out of him.

The man was tall, thirtyish, masculine, built. Like the rest of them, he also was wearing a black suit because that's how Carra rolled. In this case, he agreed with her. He loved a man in a suit. He loved it when he used to wear one. Wear the right clothes by the right designer and, if you could pull them off, doors opened for you.

"I'm going out for the night," Wolfhagen said.

"No, you're not."

He reached into his pants pocket and pulled out four checks he'd retrieved earlier from the checkbook buried deep in one of his bags. The goons drew closer. "Yes, I am."

The hot one looked down at the checks. "You can't bribe us, Mr. Wolfhagen."

Wolfhagen knew better. "But I have $1 million for each of you."

The hot one cocked an eyebrow at him. "Mrs. Wolfhagen pays us well. She offers nice, steady employment. Why don't we just take the checks and shut the fuckin' door in your face?"

"Because that would be cheating yourselves out of more," Wolfhagen said. "And everyone wants more. It's what the world is made of--craving more. Dying for more. Wanting to be more. And besides, I just want to go out for two hours. That's all. Carra won't know. I'll be quick. When I return, each of you will receive another million for your trouble. And the secret stays with us."

"Why do you need to go out?"

"Can't say. Sorry. Lot's of secrets, some going to my grave. But time is running out. Carra is a late night kind of gal, but let's face it, she's putting on the years and I doubt she can go as deeply into the night as she used to. So, to minimize risk, I need to leave now so I'm back here before she returns."

He held out his hands and, as he did so, each man glanced down at the unsigned checks. Then, they looked at him. "All I need is one of your cars, a cell phone and two hours. That's it. If you agree, I sign these checks alone in the car, give them to you and then I'm off."

They all looked at each other.

And Wolfhagen's shoulders sagged in frustration. "Oh, stop looking so tense, you big lugs--you'll see me again. It's all part of the goddamn plan."

* * *

The car they offered was surprisingly sweet--a black Audi TT. He felt a little rush as he slipped into it. Snug yet comfortable. Beautifully appointed and made specifically for one's lost youth. He couldn't be sure yet, but he bet it was fast, which was perfect for his needs.

"Do you have a pen?" he asked.

The goons were waiting outside the car. The hot one reached into his jacket to retrieve a pen and, when he did, Wolfhagen saw his gun resting inside its holster beneath the folds of fabric.

"Can I borrow that?"

"Borrow what?"

"Your gun."

"You're not borrowing my gun."

Wolfhagen started signing the checks on the steering wheel. "What are your names?"

They told him.

"Make sure they're your real names."

"They are."

He signed each name with a flourish, then stopped at the last check. He looked at the hot one and wished he could reach out a hand to see if he was really packing. But that wouldn't be good form. "$500,000 for the gun. That's $250,000 per hour, plus the million I'm giving you now. Good money, if you ask me. It'll put your kids through college."

"I don't have kids."

"Then think of your wife."

"I don't have one of those, either."

"Then you and I need to talk. Later. My bedroom. When it's just the two of us and a harness."

The man screwed up his face and the goons looked at each other. The tallest of them said in a low voice to the hot one, "If you don't do it, I will."

"Okay," the hot one said. "Write the check for one five."

"Of course." He winked at him. "And what a business sense. You've got a head on your shoulders. I like that." Wolfhagen filled out the amount and then, turning slightly to the window, he said: "First the gun."

The man hesitated, but then he handed to him.

No stranger to a gun, Wolfhagen checked to see if it was loaded. It was. He gave the men their checks, rolled up the window so they couldn't pull anything on him, cut into traffic and roared off to the very place he knew Carra would be.

It was Saturday night. She'd be at her version of The Bull Pen. The club he created all those years ago was back in operation and apparently thriving--the few people who remained friends with him during his awful fallout with the world were members of it. They told him that Carra and Lasker were there once per month on a Saturday night. Though they'd moved the club to a new building after the federal crack down, Carra and Lasker had kept it going in his absence, obviously for the money it brought in, but more likely for the connections it offered.

He wondered if they videotaped the crowd as he used to do. If they did, he wondered how many favors they were sitting on now.

The address he was given would take him to West 83rd Street, which told him all he needed to know. While the location had changed, what was happening inside that club hadn't. These people needed their playtime, but they also needed to play in a location that was safe, upscale, unsuspecting and in which they could do anything they wished in complete privacy. Whether the club was extreme as it was when he ran it was doubtful--Carra was a conservative little cunt. But she also was bright and he knew she wouldn't be stupid enough to tamper with what once had worked so well.

The Bull Pen offered certain expectations.

Tonight, it would see those expectations lifted when he himself murdered Carra and Lasker in front of those who were there. Some would get off on it. Others would wonder why they did. And a few would be repelled.

That is, of course, if anyone was there. It wasn't even 11 p.m. yet. It might be that only a few stragglers would enjoy the show, because like most of the darker clubs in New York, few got started before 3 a.m., which was just fine with Wolfhagen. In this case, the fewer people, the better.

To pull this off, he needed help. And so he took the cell phone the goons had given him and tapped out a number. As the line rang, he rolled down the window and sped uptown, the warm breeze stirring his hair.   In the distance, he could see the orange, fiery glow hovering above the city's Upper East Side.

When it came to murder, Wolfhagen had the best help in the city.

CHAPTER THIRTY-SEVEN

10:42 p.m.

For Carmen and Spocatti, time was smashed by the chaos of what they'd created.

With the clock running against them, they now needed to beat the media, who soon would go public with connections that had become so obvious, it would start what they feared all along--a running of the bulls as Wolfhagen's former bulls left the city.

And when that happened, it would prevent them from finishing their job and collecting the millions in bonuses that came along with it.

And so they moved. They had their distraction. There were people to kill. No time to lose.

They were now four blocks east of 75th and Fifth, where the Escalade ignited and leveled the buildings surrounding it. With only a fleeting exception, they hadn't stopped running until now, when Spocatti slowed beside a car Carmen didn't recognize and popped the trunk.

Sirens sounded everywhere. The night was so heavy with humidity, the smoke from the explosions hung low, choking the air.

Carmen looked at the end of 75th and Fifth, where buildings had fallen into the streets. Fires were burning. Helicopters circling. People were rushing past her and toward the damage in an effort to help those likely trapped beneath the rubble.

She was aware of people screaming. She was aware of her own heart racing. She kept hearing the word "terrorists" being shouted in a cacophony of fear and outrage. She watched Spocatti click the cap off his video camera and offer Wolfhagen a final shot of the devastation. Right now, he was everything she wasn't. He was an automaton. He was cool. He was composed.

But Carmen? She'd be lying if she said she wasn't shaken.

Spocatti stood next to her on the sidewalk. The video camera was poised in front of him, pointing down the street. She looked at him and swore she could see the hint of a smile on his face. He was getting Wolfhagen his money's worth, but they needed to leave before the streets were closed. She'd give him 30 seconds.

Earlier, when Carmen called Pamela Dean, the woman did exactly what they hoped she'd do--she answered her phone, confirming she was home. For the last time in her life, she said "Hello" and listened to Carmen as she sent her Wolfhagen's best. "You knew this day would come, Pamela. You ruined his life, and now he's taking yours. He'll be listening to this. Can you tell him how it feels?"

Before Dean could reply--but not so quickly that she couldn't process what was happening--the cars parked curbside lifted from the pavement and started to flip in a fiery rush. Like dominoes, one car exploded and it set off the next car, and the next.

It was so engrossing, they hadn't wanted to leave. Hollywood should have been there to see it if only because it would have understood that it got it wrong every time--this is how it looked. Better yet, in the midst of all of it, they'd watched a person in a white caftan turn into a funnel of flames as he stumbled toward Fifth. A hail of burning debris rained down on him and those running past him. When he fell, they each turned to run, knowing that the Escalade was about to explode and blow the surrounding area into nothingness.

They raced toward Madison, clipped around the corner and pressed their backs against the buildings just as the street flashed white, the buildings shook and somewhere behind them, other buildings fell. There was a rush of searing wind and then the fireball Carmen feared most whooshed past them down the street, incinerating those caught in its path. Then, with no tunnel to propel it, it lifted in the middle of Madison, rolled high in the wide-open space and evaporated.

There was no question that Dean was dead, so they continued to run, this time cutting through the traffic until they stopped at the getaway car.

She nudged Spocatti. "That's it. We're out of here."

He clicked off the camera and put it in his bag in the trunk. She walked around the car as he pulled out his keys and unlocked the doors. "Who's first?"

"Cohen is closest. We do him, then Dunne, then Casari." His cell phone buzzed in his pants pocket. He removed it and looked down at the number, which he didn't recognize. He hesitated, but answered it, anyway. Wolfhagen.

"It would help if you told me when you have a new phone, Max. I almost didn't answer."

"Sorry. Where are you now?"

"We just did Dean. We're getting ready to do the others."

"They'll need to wait."

"That's a mistake."

"There are two other people I need your help with first."

"We don't have time for two other people. Have you seen the news? Have you looked out your window? We told you this was happening tonight. They'll be blocking the streets. If they haven't already, the media will make the connections and report them. And when they do, the rest will run. If you want them dead, we've got a narrow window to make it happen."

"And you will make it happen. You never fail, Vincent. That's why I hired you and your sweet little conchita. And besides, this one will be quick, it has to be done for critical reasons and I can't do it without you."

"You're going to be there?"

"That's right," Wolfhagen said. "At last, we'll meet."

"You shouldn't be there. It's too much of a risk. Let us handle it."

"Sorry to keep saying sorry even when I don't mean it," Wolfhagen said. "But that old itch is back and with these two, I'm in the mood to watch what happens when someone is stupid enough to fuck with me, to cross me, and to think I won't do anything about it."

CHAPTER THIRTY-EIGHT

9:45-10:42 p.m.

In the hour that had passed since Maggie spoke to Mark Andrews, Marty made a round of phone calls that began with Gloria, who already had talked to the girls and to the Moores, and who was on her way to them when he called.

"Are you alright?" she asked.

He was surprised by the concern in her voice. "I'll be fine."

"Are you safe?"

"That's an entirely different question."

"I don't know what this is about," she said. "But I know it has to do with Maggie Cain. Whatever she's gotten you into isn't worth your life, Marty. You need to know that. You can back out of this right now, just walk away from it, and be safe. Those girls need their father. You and I may be divorced and have our differences, but that doesn't mean I don't need you, too."

"So, it's just you, me, Jack and the girls?"

"And whoever comes into your life. We can make it work. If you've gone this far to protect your daughters, I know you're in a bad spot. I'm asking you to get out of it."

But he wouldn't. That's not how he operated and she knew it. Each job was a risk. It always had been. It always would be. He looked across the table at Maggie, who was looking across the room at Roberta. Just moments ago, Roberta had said to Maggie's face that she was going to kill him. While he loved Roberta, he'd never bought into her belief that she was psychic. He'd always believed that it was part of her shtick, a way to appeal to her customers, another way to make money.

But now things were different. Another part of him couldn't deny what he'd seen in her face--genuine fear, real concern, a premonition of sorts, if that was possible. There was no question in his mind that Roberta believed what she was saying. She believed Maggie was going to kill him.

"What did the girls say to you?"

"They're scared," Gloria said. "They don't understand what's happening."

"How long before you're there?"

"Ten minutes?"

"And you won't leave the Moore's?"

"I know the drill."

"I'll call you later."

"You don't need to do this."

It was as if he was talking to the old Gloria again. For once, she'd dropped her artist bullshit facade and was just talking to him. "Keep an eye on the girls," he said. "Bring Jack with you. Nothing's going to happen on your end. I'll make certain the same is true on my end." He paused. "And thanks."

"For what?"

"You know what."

He severed the connection and, after trying to absorb what had just transpired between him and Gloria, whom he hadn't had a civil conversation with in months, he called Jennifer Barnes. By now, she would be at Peter Schwartz's house with a full crew and soon would go live with her story. She answered on the second ring.

"It's me," he said.

"Ted Yates is dead."

Marty ran a hand through his hair.

"It came over the scanner a few minutes ago. He was having a drink at The Townhouse and collapsed at the bar."

Marty knew The Townhouse. He and Gloria were once members--she'd insisted upon it. He was about to tell Maggie the news when Jennifer said, "There's more. Alan Ross was found in an alley in the South Bronx thirty minutes ago. His neck was broken."

Marty saw the questioning look on Maggie's face and told her the news.

"They testified against Wolfhagen," she said.

Marty held up a hand. "How did Yates die, Jennifer?"

"They're thinking heart attack."

"I'm thinking coincidence. Yates and Ross testified against Wolfhagen. Was Yates with anyone?"

"That's all I've got. You're positive they testified?"

"Is this for your report?"

"It is."

"Then you're about to break the story of the year. I am positive. Start making the links. Mention the Coles, Andrews, Ross, Yates, Schwartz--all of them. Google the others who testified and are still alive. Get the word out now. If you have to go to the Channel One site to report this first, do it so AP picks it up. If they'll give you a news break for a special report, even better. This is going national. You'll be everywhere. Be prepared."

"I owe you one."

"No, you don't."

"Are you okay?"

He looked at Maggie, who was looking intently at him. "I don't know," he said. "But I'll find out soon enough. Are Hines and Patterson on the scene?"

"They're standing next to me."

"Are they working together?"

"Put it this way, they've agreed to go on camera together."

"The end of the Cold War."

"I wouldn't go that far. Do you want me to give them a message?"

Always the sly reporter. "No," he said. "I need to talk to them myself."

"You're not holding back on me, are you?"

He didn't want her to know anything about Mark Andrews or the safe house until he was certain it was legit and that he and Maggie weren't being set up. "There's more to the story, but I can't share it with you yet."

"Why?"

"Because it might be dangerous."

"And your point? I dated Gotti's son, for God's sake. What else do you have?"

"I meant it might be dangerous for me." She started to apologize, but he pushed forward. "You've got a great story to lead with. Let's roll it out with exclusives delivered by you. Once I know more, you'll have more. This story is yours--all of it--just give me time. If I gave you the wrong information, you'd look like a fool. I'll call the moment I know something."

She was nothing if not competitive. A silence passed while he waited for her to say something. She didn't.

"Okay?"

"I'll wait for your call," she said, but the way she said it, he already knew she wouldn't. She'd look for other angles. She'd try something. "I'll talk to you later. And please be careful. I need you around, okay?"

"Jennifer--"

The line went dead.

He called Roz, his contact at the FBI, and hoped she was at her desk and working late. She wasn't. He tried her cell. No answer. He called her home. Nothing. He wanted to ask her if she knew anything about Andrews and a safe house, but obviously she was out and not taking calls. And so he called Skeen to see if he did a postmortem on Andrews. He found him at home.

"When was that?" Skeen asked. "A couple of months ago?"

"A month and change."

"I didn't do it. Somebody else must have."

"Anyway you can find out for me?"

"I can make a call."

"I'd appreciate that, Carlo."

"It's late," he said. "Give me a bit. I'll call you when I know something."

"Next week, lunch is on me."

He called Hines.

"Schwartz looks pretty tonight," Hines said.

"Thought you'd like that."

"I could have done without the maggots, the rubber fetish gear and the smell, but thanks for the tip." He lowered his voice. "And fuck you for also sharing it with Patterson."

"This is big," Marty said. "I need you both."

"Yeah, yeah."

"It's bigger than you think, Mike."

"What's that supposed to mean?"

"Call Patterson over. I need her to listen to this, too."

"Christ."

"Just do it."

He listened to Hines say something to Patterson and knew that Jennifer was correct--they were working together. She must have been standing right next to him.

"She's here. I'm assuming you don't want this on speaker."

Not with Jennifer and others listening. "Can you get to your car?"

"We can do that."

They did that. Marty heard doors open and slam shut.

"Put me on speaker."

"You're on."

"Hello, Linda."

"Spellman."

"Are we friends again?"

"We never were friends."

"Are we talking again?"

"Depends on what your serving."

"I'll let you decide if it's any good. Mark Andrews might be alive."

"Then it's rancid," Patterson said. "Andrews is dead. Everyone knows it."

"Who is everyone? He was run over by bulls in Pamplona. He presumably was shipped home to the States with that written on his big toe. It was never treated as a homicide and because it wasn't, you couldn't have been involved in any way with it."

"The man was buried. It was in the papers. I read the stories, saw the photos. His mother actually agreed to go on the evening news. She was devastated. Her darling son. She bleated like a goddamn sheep while I was trying to eat my dinner. It was nauseating. When they asked her how she'd cope without him, she started bawling like a baby. I shut the fucking thing off."

"It's interesting you say she agreed to go on the news. Would you have?"

"Of course not."

"Why?"

"Are you an idiot? Because my son was dead. He was gored to death. Do you know what that would do to a mother? Do you have any idea how personal...." And then Linda Patterson heard herself, processed what she said and her voice trailed off.

"Are you getting it, Linda?"

"I'm getting it."

"Andrews came from old money. There's a protocol there. She wouldn't have gone on camera. If she had, it would have been viewed as unseemly."

"But if she needed to, she'd do it to help her son."

"That's right."

Hines again. "What have you got, Marty?"

"Someone claiming he's Mark Andrews just called me. He says for the past four weeks, he's been here in the city. He's at a fed safe house. They're taking care of him. My client was once involved with him for years. She's here with me now. She talked to him. She's convinced it was him. Trouble is, I'm not."

"Why?"

"I don't know--maybe we're being set up. Maybe somebody knows we're getting close to figuring out who's knocking off those who took the stand against Wolfhagen. Wolfhagen has been out of Lompoc for two years--long enough to lay low and for people to forget about him. Now those people are dropping dead. Initially, they did it right. They started out slow. Six months ago the Coles were murdered and supposedly a month ago Andrews was murdered. But now, over the course of just two days, we've got Schwartz, Ross, Yates. And God knows who else. I think we can agree it's likely that there's another Schwartz chilling out there."

"Where's the safe house?"

Marty told him.

"Nice neighborhood."

"Your tax dollars at work."

"You were asked to go there?"

"My client was asked. I'm taking her."

"Two for the price of one," Hines said, and paused. "If that wasn't Andrews on the phone, why are they targeting you?"

"Somehow, they found out I'm working the case. They want me out of the way so they can finish what they started."

"No offense," Patterson said. "But you're just a shitty little P.I., Spellman. If they know you're on the job, then they know we're on the job. Why target you before us?"

"No offense, Linda, but you wouldn't know as much as you do without a shitty little P.I. like me leading you to Schwartz and now potentially to Andrews. Neither would you, Mike."

"Your death would be easier to manage," Hines said. "Ours wouldn't. Maybe it's you first. Get you and your client out of the way, then get the rest who testified against Wolfhagen, and worry about us in the meantime."

"Are you seriously playing devil's advocate?" Patterson asked.

Hines let it slide.

"Fine," Patterson said. "What if it's true, Spellman? What if it was Andrews on the phone? What if he's alive?"

"Then we all win. But until I actually see him and know that he's safe, I'm assuming otherwise."

"When are you leaving to meet Andrews?" Hines asked.

"Now," Marty said. "But I can't do it alone. This is part of the same case. If you're going to own this and run with it, I need you both to be there."

But before Hines could answer, Marty heard Patterson scream.

Confused, he heard a muffled sound and then what sounded like doors opening, the cell phone hitting something hard, then tumbling onto something soft. He called out Hines' name but there was no response, even though Marty could hear him shouting to someone. And then Marty heard the unmistakable sound of something else--explosives.

Maggie leaned forward. "What's wrong?"

"Quiet."

He pressed the phone harder to his ear and felt a chill race through his body. It wasn't just Patterson screaming now--many people were. He could hear explosions, he could sense a growing chaos. He slid out of the booth and went into the kitchen, where he could get away from the Moroccan music.

Maggie followed him. Roberta was across the room, fixing something at the stove. She turned to look at him. Steam rose in waves in front of her face. She dropped the spatula she was holding and came over to him.

He held up his hand, looked around the room and spotted a radio. "Turn it on."

"What station?"

"880."

She flipped it to the local CBS news affiliate and turned up the volume. They were recapping the day. Stocks had closed lower. The President was traveling to China. The Middle East was in turmoil again. Marty half listened to the radio and to the tension heightening on the other end of the phone. The newscaster switched to the weather. Clear skies. Heat on the rise. Storms by Tuesday.

And then, on the phone, he heard the biggest explosion yet. He took a step back at the sheer force of it and shouted Hines' name. Roberta reached out to put a hand on his arm, but the moment she touched him, she jerked her hand away as if she'd been scalded.

The cell phone went dead. Marty lowered it in his hand and was about to tell them what he heard when Roberta, her hands to her mouth, said, "Those poor people."

Maggie was standing just inside the swinging door. "What people?" she said. Neither answered. "What's happening?"

The news broke.

Each turned to the radio.

Terrorists had attacked New York City. Bombs had leveled a portion of 75th and Fifth. Buildings were in the street. The majority of the damage extended from East 73rd to East 76th. Parts of East 77th Street also were affected. Hundreds were feared dead. Marty immediately dialed Jennifer's number, but all he got was a rapid busy signal, which told him the very last thing he wanted to know.

At least on some level, the terrorist attack also had reached her.

CHAPTER THIRTY-NINE

10:45 p.m.

Marty swung through the kitchen door, Maggie and Roberta behind him. He moved to the exit, knowing what he had to do. He had to get to Jennifer. He had to make sure she was safe.

"This is just the beginning of it," Roberta said. "Don't go. They'll already be blocking the streets. You won't be able to get near there. There's nothing you can do."

He knew she was right. The streets would be blocked. Already, he could hear the wail of police sirens moving north. Soon, the feds would be there. Then, the National Guard. He'd never get through. He turned to her. "I need you to do something for me."

"Anything."

He pointed to the television above the bar. "Turn it on Channel 1. If Jennifer Barnes goes live with a report, I need you to call my cell immediately. If she has two detectives with her--Mike Hines and Linda Patterson--I need you to tell me that, too."

She nodded.

"You've got their names."

"I do."

"When you touched me in there, what did you see."

"Fire," she said. "People burning. People dying."

And so he grabbed her forearm. "Jennifer Barnes," he said, seeking her face. "You've met her before. We've been here together. I remember you telling me how much you liked her. You told me she was the one." He looked down at his hand. "What do you see now?"

"Nothing," she said.

"What do you mean by nothing?"

"Blackness," she said.

"What does blackness mean to you?"

"Death," she said. "All I see is death."

"Whose death?"

"Yours," she said. "It's your death. Why won't you listen to me? Why won't you believe me?" She pointed at Maggie, who was standing next to Marty. "She is going to kill you and you won't listen to me."

Maggie was about to intervene, but there was no stopping Roberta.

"I saw those fires," she said to Marty. "I was right and still you won't listen to me. If you leave here now, if you go with her, she will kill you. I'm as certain of that as I've ever been certain about anything in my life." She looked at Maggie, whose face had gone pale in the heat of Roberta's words. "You're going to kill him."

Maggie held up a hand. "Look," she said. "I've kept my mouth shut since you've started your barrage against me. I've tried to be polite because he's your friend, but I'm through with it. Stop saying that now."

"I won't. I know what I saw."

"I don't care what you saw. It's ridiculous. I'm not going to kill him."

"Yes, you are." Roberta reached out and touched the back of Maggie Cain's hand. Then, defeated, she dropped her hand at her side. "You're going to shoot him, my friend is going to die and there's nothing I can do to stop it."

CHAPTER FORTY

11:02 p.m.

With the Audi's top down and the warm city air running through his hair, Wolfhagen felt in the moments before he orchestrated Carra and Ira's deaths that he was on the cusp of the greatest rush of freedom he had felt in years. Certainly since he walked away from Lompoc.

Soon, he would be through with them. Carra especially. At last, she would forever be out of his life. And while he loved to watch, a part of him now was considering doing the job himself. He felt that strongly about her death. He should be the one who killed her, not somebody else who wouldn't understand the pleasure of it.

Only once before had he physically taken a life. It wasn't something he hired out, as he usually did. Instead, it was all him. He considered it part of his personal growth--an act that had changed him. And when it was over, there was no remorse. Just another high to fuel the high he already was enjoying.

He thought back to that day, when the feds were closing in on him, the old Bull Pen was in decline and he had used one mother of a knife on one backstabbing mother fucker's throat.

He'd cut so deeply, he almost severed the man's head. But given the weight of the man's betrayal, it was worth it. It also was easy-- too easy--and he had delighted in the man's clotted, piggish squeals while Wolfhagen himself stood drenched in the fountains of blood fanning from his throat and into the room.

He thought back to that night and remembered that the fun hadn't begun there. It had started outside, in his limousine, when he smashed Maggie Cain's head through a window and permanently disfigured her face.

It was one of his finest days. But tonight would top it all. There was, in fact, no question that it would *kill* it.

He was driving up Central Park West moving toward 83rd. He was listening to club music on Sirius and jonesing for a taste of meth, which he'd sworn himself off, at least for tonight.

Need to be clear. Gotta be clear. Have to be clear. Can't fuck this up.

Occasionally, as police cars from all over the city raced down the street with their sirens blaring and their lights flashing, he had to pull to the right to let them pass. But with so much chaos unfolding on the east side of the Park, he didn't mind. It was the distraction he needed. Above the Park was a warm, flicking glow from all of those awful fires he'd seen on TV and the idea of them burning warmed him.

He clicked off the radio, turned left onto 83rd and slowly approached the new Bull Pen, which was housed in an elegant, unassuming pre-war building that looked exactly as it should look-- like a residence.

If Carra had done her job correctly, the entire building would be sound-proofed, including the entrance. If music was playing anywhere inside, you'd never know it by opening the front door because barriers would be in place to keep the sound out.

You'd also never hear the music if you passed the building, or especially if you lived on either side of it. By all appearances, this was the quietest house on the block, which was remarkable given the sheer number of people who showed up late on those occasional Saturday nights when Carra opened.

As he drove past it, he looked around him on the sidewalks. It didn't appear that anyone was waiting for him, but that didn't mean they weren't already here. He could imagine his little assassin minions tucked away in dark corners, watching him. He could feel their eyes on him as he reached the end of the street. He was anxious to meet them, but he was more anxious to either watch Carra get mutilated by the kindness of one of his strangers--or by someone she used to call her husband.

It should be me, he thought. *I should be the one holding her down and gutting her. I should be the last person she sees. Let them take Ira.*

And there it was. He'd made up his mind. That's how it would be. It would be he.

He drove across Amsterdam, shot down 83rd and then turned left onto Broadway. He cruised to 81st Street and took another left. Even if there had been a place to park on 83rd, which there wasn't, he at least wanted to be a block or two over and have the ability to run if he had to. And in spite of how Carra had cut his feet, Wolfhagen could run. He might be older now, but he was fast. If anyone came after him, he was fairly certain that even in this state, he could get to this car with enough distance between them and take off.

He rolled down the street, found a spot that would be too tight for most cars to squeeze into, but this car was tiny and it fit with some maneuvering. He lowered the vanity mirror and checked his crowded teeth. He cupped a hand over his mouth and checked his breath, which smelled of peppermint. He wouldn't look directly at his face. This was as good as it got.

He stepped out of the car and started walking toward the Park, which was two blocks away. When he reached it, he turned left and was surprised by what he saw--crowds of people rushing toward him. When he drove by moments ago, none of this was happening. But word was out. New York was burning. As the avalanche of good will swarmed around him and occasionally threatened to topple him, he shouldered his way toward 83rd and couldn't help being amused.

They were running toward the fires, thinking they could help. They ran past him with the same haunted faces they wore when the terrorists struck the Twin Towers. They actually thought they could do something. They actually wanted to risk their own lives in an effort to help. It was as incredible to him as it was foreign. If a gas main broke, which was possible given the level of destruction he'd seen, some of these people were rushing to their own deaths. It made no sense to him what they were doing. Why die to help a total stranger?

He moved left, as close as he could get to the buildings, and removed from his pants pocket the cell phone the hot goon had given him. He pressed his hand against the side of the light jacket he wore and felt the gun hidden there. In the air was the distinct smell of smoke. All around him, motion, reaction, propulsion. He tapped out a number and waited. Second ring. "Max?"

"You both there?"

"Just waiting on you."

"Did you see me drive by a minute ago?"

"We saw you."

"And not even a friendly wave. I'm on foot, about a block away. I'm assuming there's no crowd or activity yet."

"Nothing yet. But all the shades are drawn."

"It's too early," he said. "They're getting ready. They're probably squeezing into their cute leather suits."

"How is this going to work?"

"I'm taking Carra. You two take Lasker. This needs to be clean and quick so you can have the rest of the night to do your thing. Inside that door will be security. They'll be armed. You stay behind me. Whoever is there will recognize me. They'll be startled that I'm there, which is my moment to act. We'll take him down and check the room for others. If they're not right there, they will be lurking somewhere. Security is tight. Try to take them out quietly. It's our best shot at finding Carra and Lasker, and finishing what we came for."

He rounded the corner onto 83rd. "I'm here."

He clicked off his cell, but saw no one. He moved down the sidewalk and listened as footsteps fell in line behind him. They were good. He stopped and turned to face them. The man came forward first, his hand held out.

"Spocatti," he said, shaking Wolfhagen's hand.

The woman came forward and did the same.

"Carmen," she said. "It's good to meet you."

"You don't look at all how I imagined," he said. He nodded at Spocatti. "I thought you'd be taller, beefier, a real bruiser, but you're none of those things."

"I don't need to be."

"Well, great. I love confidence. And it's nice to meet you, too. Are you ready for this?"

"We're eager for this."

"Then let's do this. Just let the man see my face. He'll be taken aback. That's when we act. My gun doesn't have a silencer." He looked at Spocatti. "Does yours?"

"It does."

"Let me borrow it."

They traded guns and Wolfhagen turned.   The building was soon upon them. They walked up the stairs and Wolfhagen moved his arm behind him, suggesting that they should step far to the right. Spocatti and Gragera did so, pressing themselves out of site.

Wolfhagen cocked the gun, knocked on the door and cupped his hands behind his back. A moment passed, then a huge man in a black suit opened the door slightly.

"Well, look who it is," Wolfhagen said. "Bobby."

The disbelief on the man's face was unmistakable. Years ago, at the original Bull Penn, Wolfhagen had personally hired him.   The door opened wider.   Big Bobby peered out to look around, but Wolfhagen was enough to block his view of Spocatti and Gragera. "Mr. Wolfhagen?" he said. "What are you doing here?"

"I'm here to see Carra and Ira, and not just because their names go so well together. Would you mind leading the way? They'll see me."

"I don't think they will. Shit's changed. You know that."

He needed to get off the street before anyone saw them. "They'll see me, Bobby." In a flash, he drew his gun, pressed it against Bobby's forehead and pulled the trigger. The back of the man's head exploded, but the noise was muffled. Wolfhagen was stronger than he looked.   He hooked his arm under the man's armpit and helped him down while he started to bleed out.

His heart quickening, he looked into the room beyond. It was intentionally small and dimly lit. It was this room that offered the additional sound barrier. Beyond it would be where the real action took place.

He titled his head to the left and saw the door that led to it. He was surprised to find it partly open. With his gun held out at arm's length, he took a step into the smaller room. He could feel Spocatti and Gragera behind him. He eased himself to the door, knowing that anyone could be behind it. Spocatti knew it, too. He went to the door, pressed Wolfhagen back and then got on his own back. He looked up at Wolfhagen, put a finger to his lips and motioned to him that he was going first.

Gragera stepped beside Spocatti and crouched with her back against the door frame. Wolfhagen watched Spocatti lift his knees and push himself forward, so his head was only slightly in the room. He kept his gun near his face, ready to fire if anyone was inside. He looked around the room, then nodded at Gragera, who peered carefully inside and then swung back. She did it again, but took a longer look.

And each relaxed.

Spocatti got to his feet. "No one's in there," he said in a low voice. "Where would they be?"

"At the old club, a good deal of the wilder stuff took place in the basement," Wolfhagen said. "It's still early. If they use the basement here, they could be there, setting up." He shrugged. "But that's a guess. I don't know how this is set up."

"Then we'll take the risk. You follow us." He held his hand out for his gun, which Wolfhagen gave him in return for his own. "Stay behind us. If anything happens, drop to the ground. We'll cover you."

Together, each eased into the room.

Though the lights were dim even here, Wolfhagen could see that the area was large and open. Chandeliers hung from the ceiling, but the lights were barely burning. Leather chairs were in the center of the room. Off to the right were two metal cages. Beside them looked to be a necropsy table, not unlike the one he'd sliced that man's throat on all those years ago. Though Wolfhagen couldn't make it out completely, what appeared to be a bar was to the far left of the room.

And then, as all of the lights suddenly flashed to full brightness, he was certain that's what it was. Just beyond it, he could see Carra stepping into the room. She was wearing a black leather catsuit. Her dark hair swung as she turned to look at him. Wolfhagen took a step back, raised his gun to shoot her and pulled the trigger.

But nothing happened. He tried to fire again, but the gun just clicked. It was empty. He looked at Spocatti, who was drawing away from him while he reached into his pocket and held out his hand--in it were the remaining bullets, which he rattled in front of Wolfhagen before tossing them across the room, where they rolled, jumped, clattered.

He'd been set up.

Now, Spocatti and Gragera were pointing their guns at him. Wolfhagen stared at them in shock as another person entered the far end of the room.

This time it was Ira Lasker. He was slightly hunched over and moving behind something. Wrong. He was pushing something.

Carra rounded the corner and started moving in his direction. In her hand was a whip. She cracked it for effect, the sound reverberated off the high ceilings, which she liked so much, she did it again.

On her feet were black leather boots that stretched past her knees and cupped her thighs. She was the dominatrix he'd turned her into years ago, only this time, she was running the show. Crack, crack, crack. The whip criss-crossing in front of her and ready to strike. She laughed.

"Max," she said. "How's my little bitch pig tonight?"

Wolfhagen looked at her for a moment, and then turned to Lasker as he rounded a corner. The thing he was pushing was a wheelchair. Though he couldn't fully process it because none of it made sense, his eyes didn't lie. It was Mark Andrews in that wheelchair. It was Mark Andrews, who had been pummeled by bulls in Pamplona. It was Mark Andrews, his former lackey who presumably was dead and buried.

It was Mark Andrews, and he was coming straight at him with a gun.

CHAPTER FORTY-ONE

11:21 p.m.

This was her night, but if she was going to succeed in being done with the man who had ruined her reputation and humiliated her for years, she knew she had to move quickly. Soon, Marty Spellman and Maggie Cain would arrive, presumably to come to a federal safe house, where Mark Andrews was waiting for them.

And he was waiting for them, against his will. He also was holding an empty gun on Wolfhagen, against his will. She needed to take care of Max before the focused shifted on Cain and Spellman. They were too close to the truth. Only when they were dead would she feel reasonably confident that she and Ira could walk away from all of this and be safe.

Carra watched as Max looked in disbelief at Mark Andrews.

"How?" he asked her. "Why?"

She told him. Along with Ira, over the past seven months she had devised a plan that had involved the deaths of the majority of those who had testified against him.

It had been simple--hire Spocatti and Gragera and, through Lasker, convince them that they were dealing directly with Wolfhagen. She didn't know them. She didn't trust them. And so if anything went wrong and they were caught, she knew they would spill his name convincingly if they were pressed to do so in the event that they were caught before this was finished. Moreover, if they were forced to take a lie detector test, they'd be telling the feds what they *knew* was the truth. It was Wolfhagen who hired them. There was no reason for them to believe otherwise.

In each conversation with them, Ira had mimicked Wolfhagen's voice and demeanor. Tonight, Spocatti and Gragera were informed that they'd been misinformed. When they arrived, Ira told them everything. They'd never worked for Wolfhagen. They'd only ever worked for her and Ira.

If they were surprised, they didn't show it. They remained the professionals they'd proved themselves to be. For their trouble, Carra gave each their $10 million bonus checks early.

Not long ago, her own guards called warning her that Wolfhagen was on his way. He bribed them, just as she knew he would. They took his money, just as she'd told them to. They warned her that he asked for a cell phone and a gun, and that it was unlikely that he'd come alone. Knowing Spocatti and Gragera were hers now, she asked them to take out Wolfhagen's hired hit men when they arrived.

When they did, they were told that after this evening, they were free to go. There would be no more killing outside of those deaths that happened in-house tonight. Carra had everything she needed-- the tapes of each person's death, which would be sent by FedEx to the LaJolla estate tomorrow morning.

Each tape implicated Wolfhagen. She was working with his assistant, who now was on her payroll. That person had his orders. He lived in an apartment on the La Jolla estate. Part of his duties was to open the mail. When the tapes arrived, he was curious and watched them even though Wolfhagen specifically told him not to. But he did and he was horrified by what he saw. Even though he didn't want to get involved because what he saw frightened him, he knew he couldn't allow Wolfhagen to continue. And, so, he did the right thing. He alerted the police and the media.

Even if no one bought it, Carmen still won. The media would latch onto it. By then, Wolfhagen would be dead and with him, whatever was left of his soured reputation would be finished when the footage was aired and word got out that he had hired two assassins to kill those people who betrayed him on the stand.

People would believe it. It was human nature to believe the worst, particularly when you're dealing with someone who has a past like Max, who once was responsible for the collapse of the stock market and thus for shattering millions of financial dreams.

The public still hated him. This would only fuel their ire.

To stay at her house, he had blackmailed her with the tapes he had from the past, but just as she told him earlier, the more she thought about it, the less concerned she was.

All those years ago, when they secretly filmed the crowds coming undone at his parties, she made every effort to steer clear of the cameras. He assumed she was on those tapes, but she knew where the cameras were hidden and kept clear them. Be he was on those tapes, along with everyone else he wanted to hang if they didn't come through with the inside information he wanted. Carra was so certain of this, she was willing to bet on it now as she prepared to take him down.

"How are you alive?" Wolfhagen asked Andrews.

"Well, let's see, Max. Obviously, I didn't die. Doesn't that suck? People got to me in time. I was taken to the hospital Gregorio Marañón in Madrid and was brought back from the dead. And now it looks as if I'm about to bite it again."

"That's because he made a mistake," Carra said. "When Spocatti drove a knife into his side, he told him that he was being taken out for taking the stand against you. Three weeks ago, he reached out to me because he knows I hate you. He thought I'd want my own revenge and that we could help each other. What he didn't know is that I already had taken out the Coles and that I already tried to kill him."

"So, why are you waiting?" Andrews asked.

She thought of Maggie Cain. "Because you called at the right time. Because I'm using you as bait." She snapped her fingers. "And then you're gone, too."

"Why did you kill Wood?" Wolfhagen asked. "She put me away. You should have been thrilled by that. Why take her out for it?"

"I didn't kill Wood. Her death is as much a shock to me as it is to everyone else. I've given it some thought and the only thing I can think of is that someone you burned knew you were in town. It likely was a past member of your club, probably someone you threatened with one of your tapes. They saw an opportunity to nail you for whatever you did to them and they acted on it."

She shrugged. "What better way to implicate you in her death than to cut off her head, put it in a Tiffany box and send it to you at the Plaza? Some would think you were in danger. But others know your reputation. They'd see another angle. They'd think you sent it yourself because it's the last thing a murderer would do. They'd think you did it so you could hide in plain sight. They know how crafty you are, Max, and I have to admit, it is good. If you weren't going to die tonight, somebody was betting that by sending you her head, you'd be crippled by it. Just know that I didn't kill Wood--and that we might never know who killed her. Life always doesn't give us answers, but I do know this--you've got plenty of enemies who want to watch you burn. I'm just one of them."

* * *

While Carra ticked off all the brilliant ways she'd pulled off this operation, Spocatti ticked off all the ways he should get out of it, but not without a brilliant shot of retribution of his own.

He'd been lied to. He'd been tricked. By the expression on Carmen's face, he knew she was as angry as he, but they refused to let it show. Their faces were blank slates.

Occasionally, they looked at each other--communication in a glance. What he saw in her face was clear--she wanted revenge. She wanted Carra Wolfhagen and Ira Lasker strung up and quartered because they'd actively put their lives at risk by not coming clean with who they really were and what their true objectives were from the start.

But what did she see in his face? Age and experience told him to hold off as long as possible while considering every option before acting. Safety was paramount. Getting out clean was key. He knew what Carra had in mind next and it was so twisted, he'd be lying if he said he didn't want to see it go down. But at what cost? How far was he willing to go for his own taste of revenge when and if he was able to turn her own plan against her?

What Carra Wolfhagen and Ira Lasker didn't understand is that right now, he and Carmen owed them nothing. Their deal was broken the moment the truth was revealed.

They'd signed a contract to work with Maximilian Wolfhagen, not Carra Wolfhagen and Ira Lasker. They'd gone into this job with the belief that they needed to murder those people on Wolfhagen's list in a controlled environment manufactured only by them.

They'd never agreed to the unnecessary, amateurish complication they were facing now. And they never would have taken this route because it could have been handled so much more professionally.

He knew others were coming. He knew there were plans for them, too. An idea occurred to him on how to turn this when Carra called over to them. "Are you ready?" she asked.

Ready for what, he wondered. Ready to scrap this deal and get out now? Or did he and Carmen have time to pursue other options? He didn't know.

"We've been ready," he said. "You've been wasting valuable time."

She tilted her head at him. "Then let's finish this."

CHAPTER FORTY-TWO

11:36 p.m.

When they left Roberta's, they drove in silence. The safe house was on the Upper West Side, far and away from the orange glow they could see flickering above the East Side of Manhattan. Traffic was thick. They were barely moving.

Maggie was looking out the passenger-side window, obviously reeling from Roberta's repeated insistence that she was going to kill him.

Did he believe it? No. Could he explain how Roberta had seen the fire and the people burning before it was announced that terrorists had attacked the Upper East Side with explosives? No. But he did know one thing--Maggie Cain was not a killer.

She was someone doing her best under difficult circumstances. She was alone and she was frightened. This was beyond what she'd expected. After her experiences with Wolfhagen, which literally disfigured her, she had difficulty trusting people for good reason.

Marty understood her now. She was the first to see a connection when the Coles died, and then presumably Andrews. Though she couldn't be sure about it, she hired him to watch Wolfhagen, likely thinking he was somehow behind it. But now that Mark Andrews might be alive, they had to at least scope the safe house and see if it was true.

He called Roz again at the FBI and had yet to hear from her.

He called Hines, but since the explosions had yet to reach him.

He reached out and squeezed Maggie's hand, which she squeezed back. He tried to call Jennifer again but it still was a rapid busy signal.

His mind went through a mental check list. Gloria was safe. His daughters were safe. But right now, he knew he was on the cusp of something that was either going to lead to more answers and a better direction, or possible death if they entered the safe house and it wasn't Andrews.

His cell phone rang.

Startled, each looked at it in his palm. "It's Roberta," Marty said.

He answered it. "Was she on the news?"

She wasn't. "It was another woman," Roberta said. "She interviewed a few police officers, but no one by the name of Hines or Patterson."

"Did you see her anywhere in the background? Maybe she was making the rounds for a larger story. She's their top reporter. Did you see--"

Roberta interrupted him. "There's no best way to tell you this."

A car rushed past them, horn blaring. He wasn't focusing. He righted the car and slowed for the red light ahead of them. "Tell me what?" he said.

"She's missing. You haven't seen the images I've seen. That woman reporter went on air and the last thing she said was that the Channel One family also was affected. They mentioned Jennifer. They're searching for her, but they can't find her. When the buildings let go, they lost her. They said there's too much rubble. Too much chaos. I'm so sorry. They've put out an alert that if anyone does see her to please contact the station immediately."

CHAPTER FORTY-THREE

11:36 p.m.

"Get rid of Bobby's body," Carra said to Spocatti and Carmen. "Wipe up his blood. He's been there awhile, so he's probably stuck to the floor, poor thing, but clean it the best you can. There are towels at the bar. He can't be there when Spellman and Cain arrive."

"*If* they arrive," Spocatti said.

"Oh, they'll be here," Carra said. "Love is a funny thing. Maggie Cain now knows her beloved is alive. They had a lovely chat. She's flooded with hope. When they come in, take them out, then finish off Andrews."

She looked down at Mark. "Sorry," she said. "But you've seen too much. And do you really want to be stuck in a wheelchair for the rest of your life?"

He didn't answer.

"I didn't think so." She looked at Spocatti. "Then we do what we discussed earlier--call the police and get out of here. Each of you has your checks. You'll never have to see us again. Just cash them in and move on." She bowed her head to them. "And, thank you. We couldn't have done any of this without you."

"We mean that," Ira said.

"Our pleasure." He looked at Carmen. "Let's get Bobby. We're losing time."

"Why are you doing this, Carra?"

That stopped Spocatti. It was Wolfhagen who posed the question, and now Carra was coming over to him to answer it.

"I'll keep this brief," she said. "When we were married, you never once told me you traded inside information. You lied to me, you kept it all from me, and yet when it blew up in your face, it also blew up in mine. Do you have any idea what my life has been like for the past five years? It's taken years to rebuild my name, and I'm only halfway there. As long as you're alive, they still see you in me. The stink won't go away until you go away. So, guess what? You go away tonight."

"Right now, I'm a guest at your home," he said. "The media has been chronicling it. People saw me at your party. How are you going to explain that?"

She reached out the tip of her whip and ran it along the curves of his face. "I'm going to tell them the truth. We had an argument over the home in La Jolla, which is mine and which I've decided to sell. If they want to--and they will--they'll document your phone call to me just as they'll document that soon after it, you booked an immediate flight to New York City.

"Because you live there, you threatened me not to sell. You flew here to tell me to my face that you weren't moving. You told me that if I sold, you'd hire someone to set fire to the house, which belonged to my father. I took you in as a guest because it was better to keep you close while I figured something out."

She paused. "It's only been a day, Max. And guess what? I have figured something out. In the meantime, how could I have known that you had an ulterior motive to be here in New York? How could I known everything you were doing on the side? All these deaths captured on film." She shook her head at him. "You're not a very good person. The world knew that once. They'll be reminded of it again."

She looked at Spocatti. "Bobby," she said. "Then the rest. Move."

He turned to Carmen--communication in a glance. He began to step past Wolfhagen and Carra. "You said there were towels at the bar?"

"They're at the far end. There should be enough, but Bobby was big, so who knows?"

"Right," he said, and as he passed her, he swung violently around, dipped his hand into his holster and removed his gun. Carra sensed the rush of motion and turned just as the butt of Spocatti's revolver came straight at the side of her head. She ducked and he missed. Missed! She stumbled back and he swung again, but not before her whip whirled around and struck him hard across his face.

Stunned by the blow, he shook it off while she ran across the room. He charged after her. She was quick, but not quick enough-- those boots she wore were a bitch and they didn't give her the traction she needed. As she ran past Wolfhagen and toward the bar, where he knew there'd be a staircase, he saw Carmen swing at Wolfhagen's head. He collapsed on the floor just as Ira Lasker started for the door.

"Door!" Spocatti called.

Carra was running faster now. She skidded as she rounded the bar. He heard a thump behind him and knew it was Lasker. He heard footsteps running his way and knew it was Carmen. And then, suddenly, Carra turned to face him.

She swung the whip at him again, but this time he was prepared for it and caught it with his free hand. He yanked on it and pulled her close into to him. He could feel her breath on his face. He could see wild fear and rage in her eyes.

"What the fuck are you doing," she said. "You've got your money!"

"You lied to us. You never should have done that. There are repercussions."

She started to struggle, but when Spocatti slammed his gun against the side of her head, her eyes rolled back and she went down at his feet in a heap of unconscious sleep.

Carmen looked down at her. "I want that suit and those boots," she said. "They're fantastic." She looked up at Spocatti. "But don't worry, I'll get them later. What do you have in mind?"

Spocatti glanced across the room at Mark Andrews, who hadn't moved because he couldn't move. He stepped farther away from the bar and onto the staircase that was on the other side of it. She followed him and he quietly told her.

"We have time for all that?"

"I think so."

"But what's the point? We should lock them in one of those cages, get out of here, make an anonymous call to the cops and be done with it."

"The police are a little busy right now, Carmen. We've got time. We finish this our way, then we call the feds, the cops, the media."

"They could die if we do this."

"Not if we do it right. And we have to do it right. I want them in jail. Death is too easy. I want a spectacle. I want something people won't forget. And don't think I'm not thinking about our own safety. That comes first. We do have time for this. Cain and Spellman aren't here for a reason. They can't get through. The streets are either jammed or blocked. Enough time has passed for them to be here, but they're not."

"They could be close."

"Then we lock the door and deal with them if I'm wrong."

"Cain is good. You saw what she's capable of. She took me down and she shot you. Don't forget that."

"She also had surprise on her side," Spocatti said. "This time, we'll be ready for them." He holstered his gun. "They're coming," he said. "And so will everyone else. But Carra Wolfhagen and Ira Lasker lied to us. They deserve what's coming their way. Let's really give the world something to talk about. Let's crank this into the stratosphere. Let's fuck with people's heads. You with me?"

"Well, when you put it like that, how can I refuse?"

A knock came at the door.

Worse, a knock came at a door that might be unlocked.

Carmen immediately came across the open space, wishing the lights weren't on. She pulled out her gun and held it on Andrews. She put her finger to her lips and pressed the barrel to his temple. All over her face was one message. *If you say one fucking word, you're dead. I will kill you. You will die. There's no option.* And then she pushed him across the room, to the very spot where Carra lay unmoving.

Spocatti pulled Bobby out of the entryway, into the large room and behind one of the cages. The man had almost completely bled out. Behind him, he left a broad swipe of congealed blood.

There was another knock on the door, this time more aggressive.

Carmen lowered the lights and now Bobby's blood, while sticky, appeared black on the dark floors. As another knock came, this one the most impatient yet, they quickly moved Lasker and Wolfhagen behind the bar.

They looked at each other. It was Spellman and Cain, they were sure of it. They rushed across the room and moved to the curtained window to peer outside, but they couldn't see anything. The tall hedges on either side of the entrance blocked their view, though not of the street, which was teeming with people. Some were running. Others were on their cells and walking quickly. All were moving toward the Park.

They couldn't see who was knocking. And then the knock came again.

Spocatti went to the door while Carmen moved in place just behind the wall that separated them. She drew her gun. She heard Spocatti put his hand on the doorknob. And then she heard a voice the moment he opened it.

"I'm Jennifer Barnes," a woman said. "Channel One. I apologize for knocking so late, but I noticed your lights are on and this is important."

"What's the problem?"

"I think I was given the wrong address," she said. "I was sent to 11 West 82nd Street, but it doesn't exist. I've been walking all over this neighborhood and saw that you're 11 West 83rd, so I thought I'd stop to see if this was the correct address."

Carmen pressed her back against the wall. Her gun was poised and ready. She could hear the people on the sidewalks in ways that she'd never heard them in this soundproofed house.

"Who are you looking for?" Spocatti asked.

"It's complicated."

"How can it be complicated?"

She hesitated. "It has to do with a federal investigation."

"Ah," Spocatti said. "What did you say your name was again?"

"Jennifer Barnes. I'm a reporter at Channel One."

"And how did you get this address?"

"I'm working with Detectives Mike Hines and Linda Patterson. They gave it to me."

"Who were you hoping to find?"

Another hesitation.

"I'll need to know, Ms. Barnes."

"I'm here to see Mark Andrews."

"I see," he said. But he said nothing more.

"I think I've made a mistake," Barnes said. There was an edge to her voice. "I'm sorry if I interrupted. I think I might have the wrong address."

"Actually, you don't," Spocatti said. "Ms. Barnes, you're at a federal safe house. If you'd like to see Mark, step inside. But I'll need you to stay with me in the entryway while I phone my superior. Before we go any farther, he'll need to question you."

"Show me your identification."

And Carmen knew the moment Barnes drew a sharp breath that what Spocatti showed her was his gun.

CHAPTER FORTY-FOUR

12:17 a.m.

The streets of Manhattan were so clogged, it took them ninety minutes to reach the safe house on West 83rd. When they finally got there, the building, a gorgeous pre-war limestone with large casement windows and an impressively grand entrance, appeared to be in darkness.

But it wasn't.

As they passed it, they could see a slant of light beyond the heavy curtains that shielded the windows. People were inside. Mark Andrews might just be waiting for them.

This was their second go around the block and as they drove past the building this time, Marty took it slower, looking for any sign of life inside. But all he saw was that sliver of light and those heavy, almost industrial-looking curtains. He lingered on those curtains and had to admit that if this was a government safe house, they'd fit right into the equation given the privacy they offered.

He tapped out Jennifer's number again and still got a rapid busy signal. He tried Hines and Patterson and got the same thing. The pit of worry in his stomach now had grown into a vine that wrapped itself tight around his chest. If anything happened to Jennifer, he wasn't sure what he'd do. He was in love with her. He was scared for her. But when they'd left Roberta's, he knew he'd never get close to East 77th Street--or to her. And so they came here. They needed to see if Andrews was alive or if they were being set-up.

On 82nd Street, they found a parking space that wasn't a parking space. It was reserved for hydrant access, but perfect for his needs. Given what was unfolding on the other side of the Park, it was unlikely his car would get towed tonight, and so he backed into the space, righted the car, shut it off and looked at Maggie.

"Are you ready for this?" he asked.

She nodded. "It was Mark's voice," she said. "I've thought about it ever since we left the restaurant and it was his voice. I know you have reservations, but there's no question. It was Mark on the phone."

"You have your gun?"

"I do."

"It's loaded."

"It is."

"Even if it was Mark and he is alive, you're aware that this might be Wolfhagen. Somehow, he might know we're onto him and he's setting us up."

"I'm aware of it."

"You're prepared to take that risk?"

She nodded.

And so was he. "I need you to follow my lead. I've seen you shoot. I know you're trained and capable of protecting yourself. But if he's got a team in there, we're in the shit. If you do see Mark at the start, I want you to remember that they might have planned it that way to get you inside. They'll be expecting you to go to him, but you can't. Is that understood?"

"It is."

"You need to follow me and just do as I say."

"Alright."

"The moment they open the door, I'll know whether we're dealing with the feds. You always can tell a fed. I've been around enough of them to smell them. If I think it's something else, I'll tap my thigh once, but we play it cool. We're grateful that they reached out to us. We just want to see Mark." He paused. "And once that door closes behind us, we act. We take the motherfucker out quietly and get ready for the onslaught. We keep them at bay as long as we can and, if we fail, we run. Is that clear?"

"What do you mean by quietly?"

"We pistol whip him and ease him down onto the floor. No gunfire. They know we're coming and they'll be ready for us, but anything could happen. If for some reason they're distracted when we arrive and only one person comes to the door, all the better for. Slim chance, but you never know."

"Got it."

Because of the street lamp above them, he couldn't see her face. It was in silhouette. But in her voice was something else--cold determination. She'd waited for this. She was ready for this. "You're clear on everything?"

"I got it, Marty. I'm following your lead. I'll do what you want."

While that's certainly what he wanted to hear, why did he feel her emotions were going to get the best of her and, if she did see Andrews, that she'd screw it up?

* * *

On the sidewalk, the walked side by side. They moved briskly and kept pace with each other. Maggie's hair swung but the rest of her was rigid. Marty was focused and running every possible situation he could think of through his mind. Neither said anything to the other. They could have been a pair of automatons.

Save for a few stragglers, most people were either on the other side of Manhattan, trying to assist, or they were in their homes watching the situation unfold on television. Except for the faint wail of sirens off in the distance, the streets were relatively quiet, the only exception being the heaviness of their footsteps.

They rounded 83rd and started toward the safe house. In spite of the warmth, Marty still wore his blazer. He'd given Maggie the light windbreaker he kept in his car. His gun was concealed in his holster. Maggie kept hers tucked in her waistband at her back.

The building was now in front of them. So was a young woman coming their way. She passed them with her head lowered. They could hear her sobbing. Instinctively, they slowed and watched her over their shoulders. She never looked at them. She made no attempt to reach for a cell phone or something worse. She was legit.

They took the steps, exchanged a glance. Then Marty knocked.

The door edged open.

Surprised, each took a step back. Marty held his hand out behind him, keeping Maggie back, and drew his gun. He listened but could hear nothing. He maneuvered his head so he could look through the crack, but it wasn't wide enough.

He knocked again, harder this time, his gun held low at his side and ready. The door gave a few more inches. *This isn't right, this isn't right, this isn't right.* He put his hand on the handle and gave the door a gentle push. It swung open. *This isn't right, this isn't right, this isn't right.* He looked back at Maggie and saw that she had drawn her gun. He motioned for her to lower it lest they be seen by anyone who might pass on the street. She did so, holding it close to her thigh.

There was no other way to do this but to step inside. So Marty eased into the oddly shaped, narrow front foyer. There was a door to his left and to his right, but only the door to his left was open. The lights were on inside. The floor was sticky. He listened and thought he could hear something. It sounded like feet scuffing against wood.

He moved closer to the open door and pressed his back to the wall. He waved for Maggie to join him. When she did, he motioned for her to close the door. But before it latched shut, he stopped her. Keep it open. Don't make a sound. Leave it slightly ajar, just as they'd found it.

Again, they listened. Something or someone was in the next room. They strained to hear anything that would give them a clue, something telling, and this time they heard what sounded like scratching. And then they heard a tapping.

And then, without warning, something or someone gurgled.

Marty and Maggie crouched down. With an outstretched hand, he kept her back and took the chance that could end his life. He peered into the room.

The space was massive. Two metal cages to his right. Leather furniture positioned around the room. No people that he could see. He swung his head back, waited a moment and looked again. This was the room that he'd seen on Schwartz's tape. He checked the details and saw it all. This wasn't a safe house. They were being set-up, just as he feared.

He was about to rear back when he saw them.

Unbelieving, Marty stood and turned the corner so one eye was exposed. What he saw was a horror show.

At the far end of the room, three people were hanging from ropes just above the bar. They were clawing at nooses fastened to their throats. Their feet were kicking, reaching, dancing on the counter top, sometimes sticking just long enough to allow each to release the tension and take a breath.

Tap, tap, tap.

Marty looked up and saw that each rope was strapped to the beam above them. It was too dark to see their faces. Tentatively, he took a step into the room. And then, above him, came the sudden sound of footsteps hurrying about on the second floor. Something heavy thumped against the ceiling. A muffled voice came through the plaster ceiling. It was a man's voice.

There was no time to waste. He looked at Maggie and motioned for her to follow him to the bar.

They were naked now, completely exposed. They dipped in and out of shadows. They could hear the doomed gasping, their feet slipping, exhaustion setting in.

Hunched low, Marty and Maggie kept moving across the room until something caught Marty's attention and they stopped.

It was Mark Andrews.

He was at the far end of the room, near one of the windows. He was in a wheelchair and he was pointing up at the ceiling. Behind Marty, Maggie gasped but she didn't run to him. She held out an open palm to him. Andrews put a finger to his lips and, with his other hand, he made a motion for them to hurry.

And so they did. They went to the bar, looked up--and saw all of it.

Hanging from the ropes were Carra Wolfhagen, Ira Lasker and Jennifer Barnes. Their faces were turning blue, the fight to live was leaving them and as Marty watched them swing and twist before he sprang into action, he knew all of them were mainlining toward death.

CHAPTER FORTY-FIVE

12:31 a.m.

Marty scrambled behind the bar, leaped onto it, put an arm around Jennifer's waist and lifted her up so the pressure was off her throat.

"Stay with me," he said, reaching into his pocket and pulling out a jackknife. He clenched it between his teeth and with his free hand, he pulled out the blade. "Stay with me. Don't leave me. Stay with me."

Her hands were tugging sluggishly at the rope around her neck. Saliva was running out of her mouth and down her chin. Her eyes were boulders bulging under the pressure. Her body trembled against him in spasms. She was trying to breathe, but it was almost impossible. And then, with a quick sawing motion, the rope snapped, but it didn't go down as Marty had hoped. Instead of her falling back into his arms, she fell so heavily against him, they each went over the bar and toppled to the floor below.

Stunned, they lay there. Jennifer was on top of him. The noose was tight around her neck. She wasn't moving.

Maggie came around the corner and took the blade out of Marty's hands. He watched her sprint to the top of the bar and quickly cut the ropes that bound Lasker and Carra, who now were hanging lifelessly.

She wrapped her arm around their waists and eased each body to the floor. She jumped down and loosened the rope around Carra's neck, patted her face firmly, then turned and did the same to Lasker, whose eyes were open and staring up blindly at her.

Carra groaned behind her. Maggie turned to look at her and saw her eyes fluttering. She'd live. She put her ear to Lasker's chest and listened. She licked the back of her hand and held it over his mouth. And then, as Marty lifted Jennifer off him and shook her until her own eyes flickered open, Marty watched Maggie slam her fists down hard on Lasker's chest. She did it again while Carra Wolfhagen turned onto her side and loosened the noose just enough to pull it over her head.

On the floor above them, they could hear footsteps coming their way. At first, they started off slowly at the front of the room, near the building's entrance, but now they were picking up speed as they raced to the back of the room, where they were.

And then Mark Andrews' voice, loud and clear, rang throughout the room. "He's upstairs," he called. "He's armed. Be careful."

And the footsteps stopped. Quietly, they started to retreat. And Marty knew--if whoever was upstairs didn't hear movement soon, they'd know they'd been tricked.

He held Jennifer's face in her hands. "Are you alright?"

She nodded.

He kissed her on the forehead. "Stay here. Don't move. Don't you dare move." He gave her his cell. "Call 911. That's all I want you to do. I know you're in pain, but try. Tell them where we are. Tell them this is linked to the explosions across the Park. Tell them to hurry."

He looked at Maggie, who had been administering CPR and now was feeling for a pulse in Lasker's neck. There was none. "He's dead," she said.

Above them, a creaking. Someone listening.

"We need to get up those stairs." He looked at Carra Wolfhagen, who had sagged against the bar and was rubbing her hand over her throat. What the hell was she wearing? Not the little black dress Jennifer told him about earlier. "Who's up there?" he asked.

"Max," she said, in a voice low enough so Mark couldn't hear. "He did all of this. He lured us here. He tried to kill us just like he's killing all those people who took the stand against him. He admitted it to us. He said we were next."

"It's just him upstairs?"

"Yes," she said.

He cocked his head at her. "And he strung all of you up by himself?"

"No," Jennifer said. Her voice was barely audible. There was a faint wheezing sound when she spoke. "There were two others."

"He had help, but they ran," Carra said cautiously. She looked down at Lasker and then crouched to press her hand against his cheek. "They killed him. They helped Max do this and they ran when they put those nooses around our necks and hoisted us up." She motioned toward Jennifer. "When she came to the door, they knocked her unconscious and dragged her in here. I saw it happen."

Marty turned to her. "Is that true?"

She nodded.

Again, Mark Andrews: "I'm fine," he said with an irritated voice. "Get your hands off me and go upstairs. He's there. The staircase is just behind the bar. Move!"

Above them, a retreating.

Marty looked at Maggie. "You ready?"

The determination in her voice was as clear as the gun now clutched in her hand. "I'm ready."

"Then let's do this."

* * *

Wolfhagen stood in the center of the sprawling second floor, where most of the walls had been knocked down, likely by Carra and Lasker, to provide for a more open, free-flowing space. Essentially, this was a replica of the main floor. A second bar was here and in a broad nod at the old Bull Pen, painted above it in money-green was a giant bull with a ring through its snout.

He could hear them down below. The police. He'd heard Andrews shout orders at them twice, warning them that he was up here and waiting for them. And the cripple was right. He was waiting for them and he would kill them. They wouldn't take him again. Wolfhagen was either walking out of here or he'd die here.

In this dim hollow of dark fetishes, Wolfhagen found exactly what he'd use on them when they took the stairs. He went to it, grabbed the bottle of 150 proof vodka he found at the bar, and started dousing the object until it was sheeted with liquid. And then he retrieved a second bottle of vodka and soaked it again until the liquid leached inside the cavity and dripped from every corner.

Like Carra, Lasker and the reporter, Wolfhagen also had been strung up. But he managed to break free and take the gun Carra's assassins placed on the bar before they left. They put the gun there and said that freedom was just below should anyone want it. What they really meant is that whoever broke free first could have the gun, kill the rest and escape before they were found out.

Wolfhagen was that person. He was taller than the rest and found enough footing on the bar to lift himself up, remove the noose, topple to the ground and grab the gun. He came up here to find a grislier way to kill them all when he heard a commotion, the sound of bodies dropping, and then Andrews directing the police.

Carra was wrong. He wasn't afraid of death. If it came, it came. What frightened Wolfhagen more than anything was not leaving a mark.

Since he had transformed himself at Yale, it's what he always feared--the idea that he might slip back and become that nobody freak everyone loathed when he was growing up. Now, if he could pull this off correctly, he had a chance to not only take out the police, but also everyone else in the room below.

After that, he faced the challenge of getting out alive, but if he could manage it, all Wolfhagen needed to do was get to the front door. Run out into the night. Disappear forever into the world.

* * *

Marty and Maggie moved around the bar and came to the grand staircase that led to the second floor, which was in darkness. Maggie ran her hand along the wall to the left searching for a light switch while Marty darted across the staircase and did the same on the right wall.

The switch was on the left.

They stepped back into the first floor's main room, tucked their bodies against the wall and looked at each other, their guns poised and ready.

Maggie tapped his thigh.

Gingerly, Marty reached out and snapped on the lights. He jerked his hand away and listened. Light was now fanning down the stairwell toward them. They listened and, at first, could hear nothing. There were no footsteps. There was no movement. And they wondered. Was Wolfhagen waiting at the top of the stairs for them? Was he waiting for one of them to peer around so he could blow a hole through their head?

Quietly, Marty dropped to the ground and got on his stomach. He positioned his gun in such a way that it was pointing up the stairs. Maggie inched forward and leveled her gun in front of her. The barrel was about an inch from the end of the wall. If Wolfhagen shot at Marty, she'd swing around and take him out.

He looked up at her, saw that she was ready and eased his head so he could look up the staircase.

Nothing.

He motioned for her to look. And when she did, nothing changed to something.

The floor started to creak. They could hear the distinct sound of something rolling. It was coming quickly, so quickly, in fact, that Marty got to his feet and looked up at the staircase with Maggie. And when they did, there was the sound of something igniting, a fresh blast of heat rolled down the staircase, and then a large bloom of fire mushroomed toward the second-floor ceiling as it came into view.

What they saw was a grand piano. It was engulfed in flames and it stopped just short of going over the staircase. Behind it was Wolfhagen, his face caught in the curling cascade of flames.

He was grinning down at them. Maggie took a shot at him but missed. Marty ran to the other side of the staircase to see if he could get a better view, but it was worse here. Wolfhagen was hidden behind the growing fire.

And then came Wolfhagen's voice. "You want to fuck with me? Then you better have the balls to fuck with me. Tonight, I win."

Maggie took aim and shot again just as he gave the piano a massive push.

* * *

It was as if it came from hell.

Ablaze and dripping liquid fire onto the staircase's old carpet, which quickly caught with flame, the piano teetered for a moment at the top step before it started to thump and bump down the staircase. Flames sprayed and sparks flew as it shook the building and built momentum. And then there was the sound it made-- thousands of notes playing at once, wires snapping, wood splintering. It was a concerto of the damned and the music it made filled the space as if a madman was directing it.

Transfixed, Marty and Maggie watched it come toward them. They watched it jump over stairs and gather speed as it flew through the air like some fiery, misshaped, musical comet. In the vacuum of heat building within it, the piano's lid blew off and shot toward the ceiling, where it hung in the air just long enough to catch the ceiling on fire before it smashed back onto the piano.

"Run!" Marty shouted.

The piano slammed into the wall at the base of the stairwell. The force was so great, it blew the piano apart, but the fire remained and it quickly spread, licking the old wallpaper and moving with surprising speed up the walls, over the ceiling and into the room on the second floor, where Wolfhagen now was trapped and would bake if he didn't get out soon.

Maggie looked at Marty, who was peering up the stairs, and when she did, she saw Carra Wolfhagen's face emerge faintly in the room behind him.

Given the veils of smoke, the debris and the fire billowing up from the piano, Carra appeared to be an orange ghost hovering behind him in the dark room. At first, Maggie wasn't sure why she was here. Was it to see her husband burn? But as Carra drew closer and Maggie saw that she was holding a gun, she knew differently and took position.

The next few moments were a blur.

The flames were growing. Pieces of the ceiling were crackling down onto the piano and the stairs. It was difficult to see clearly. Worse, Marty couldn't hear Carra walking behind him because of the fire's roar and the falling plaster.

Carra was an encroaching funnel of orange light. She looked across the haze at Maggie, cocked her head at her and then quietly

lifted her gun to Marty's head.   A large chunk of the ceiling gave
way and smashed onto the piano.   Hot air and flames fanned out,
creating a blizzard of smoke and ash as Maggie took aim at Carra's
chest.

But too much smoke was blowing into the room.   It was almost
impossible to see.   Time slowed.   She held her hand as steady as she
could and fired at Carra just as another piece of the ceiling
dropped.   Marty turned away from it and moved into Carra's path.

And when he did, the bullet cut through him, he sank to his
knees and fell hard on the floor.

* * *

For an instant, Maggie stood there, unbelieving.   She shot him.

For an instant, Carra looked down at Marty and then through
the smoke at Maggie, unbelieving.   She shot him.

Carra turned to run, Maggie fired off a shot but missed.

She was about to run after her when she heard footsteps
running across the second floor.   She looked up at the staircase and
watched, stunned, as Wolfhagen leaped from the top step and fell
through the smoky air.

His legs scissored beneath him.

For balance, he kept his arms held out at his sides.

In one of his hands was a gun.

His shock of white hair turned increasingly orange as he neared
the fire.

He was heading straight for the center of the burning piano,
where the lid was burning.   She reared back when he smashed on
top of it.   The lid broke but Wolfhagen was invincible.   He leaped
out of the pit and into the room.   He came face to face with her
and lifted his gun, which she swatted away with her own.   She
punched him hard in the face with her free hand and then hit him
harder with her gun against his left cheek.

He stumbled back, but Wolfhagen was nothing if not quick.   He
fired at her and missed.   The room was smoky, he couldn't see.
Neither could she.   Eyes and lungs burning, she pointed her gun
where she thought he was standing and fired.   She listened but

didn't hear him fall. Instead, she heard him running toward the door that was across the room. Freedom was there. They both knew it.

But she wouldn't allow him freedom. Rage drove her forward. At the front of the room, the air wasn't as smoky. There was a distinct breeze and the sound of traffic mingling with the sound of flames. And Maggie knew--Carra Wolfhagen was gone. She'd run out and left the door open.

Maggie ran faster and as she did, she began to make out all of him. He turned over his left shoulder to see how close she was. His face appeared to her--that face that she hated. He was breathing hard, panting like the animal he was, his crowded teeth bared into a tight smile of triumph. He knew he was going to make it. She could feel it. She swung around one of the tables in the center of the room, lifted her gun and steadied her aim.

She heard Mark say something behind her, something about the smoke. But he wasn't her focus. This was her chance. She was taking Wolfhagen. He charged forward and then turned toward her again. "Love your face," he said.

"Love yours more."

When she fired, his head exploded. But she was running so quickly, she ran straight through it as it exploded. She felt blood and brains and bone collide against her face. He went down and she jumped over his falling body. One look told her what she needed to know. He was dead.

At last, she was rid of him.

* * *

But what of Marty?

She shook and wiped off Wolfhagen's remains. She turned the corner and sprinted into the other room. She screamed for Jennifer to get herself and Mark outside. She could see Marty glowing from the fire at the far end of the room. Next to him, the piano was snapping, crackling. Marty was in a heap. The building was going up quickly. Too quickly. If she didn't hurry, either the second floor would collapse on top of them or the smoke would kill them.

She stopped beside Marty, pulled him away from the heat and saw that her bullet had hit him in the chest. He wasn't moving or breathing. She could hear Jennifer rolling Mark forward. They were coughing. She called to Jennifer and told her to get an ambulance.

With a chest wound, she knew the procedure of reviving him had to be done differently and so she lowered her mouth to his, covered the wound with the palm of her hand and forced air into his lungs while Roberta's words rolled through her head: *You're going to shoot him, my friend is going to die and there's nothing I can do to stop it.*

But the dead could be brought back.

Applying more pressure to the wound and aware of the sound of sirens coming near them, Maggie spoke to Marty between breaths. She knew he was dead but she wouldn't stop. She breathed air into his lungs and was aware of the blood seeping up through his chest each time she did so.

And she knew. His lungs were filling with blood. He was drowning.

Before each breath, she spoke to him.

"Don't die," she said with a raised voice. "You come back. I know you can see me. Jennifer is safe. You don't have to leave. Come back."

All around her, the walls were starting to give. Chunks of the ceiling gave way and smashed to the floor while fire on the second floor started to reveal itself and tumble down from above. Jennifer and Mark were at the door now. They stopped to look inside and then Jennifer started to run toward Marty.

"Go!" Maggie said. "Get him out of here. Don't come back-- you won't have a second chance if you do. Marty's fine, Jennifer. I'm getting him out of here now. Wait for us across the street on the sidewalk."

Reluctantly, Jennifer stopped.

"Come with us, Maggie."

It was Mark. She found him and now she was certain she'd lose him again. The building was going to give way. She knew it. She felt it. It took everything she had within her to say, "Just go. We're right behind you. I promise."

"I love you," he said.

"I love you, too."

They left.

She gave Marty another shot of air, but nothing was working. She increased pressure on the wound and then, in her despair, she realized she was crying. All around them, pieces of the ceiling continued to fall. The house was shifting, weakening. The walls were alight with flame. The heat was intense. She leaned over him and held his face in her hand. She gently shook him. "Come back."

The police, fire department and EMTs broke into the building. Maggie looked at them as they raced toward her. She turned back to Marty. "You're not going to die," she said. "Your girls need you. Do you hear me? Your girls need you. You can't do this to the girls."

And then, in spite of the smoke closing down on her, she pressed her scarred cheek to the hot floor, took a lungful of clean air and breathed whatever life was left inside her straight into him.

EPILOGUE

SIX MONTHS LATER

AMSTERDAM

Smelling of cannabis and feeling a bit high because of it, Vincent Spocatti left the Speak Easy Coffeeshop on Oudebrugsteeg, where pot was smoked as freely as the coffee was poured, and took a right on Warmoesstraat, a narrow street whose origins began in the 13th century.

As such, surrounding him was a bizarre hive of the old and the new. This was a popular street and now, on the tip of dusk, it was teeming with clutches of people walking close and in the midst of chatter. He listened to them as they passed--a cacophony of Dutch voices lifting and lilting.

He loved it here.

It was February, he was bundled against cold, there was a loaded gun in his pocket and his two marks were walking ahead of him.

One was an international banker pushing sixty, the other was his international mistress pushing thirty. Back home in the States, the banker's longtime American wife was pushing to have each murdered by nightfall.

He could smell the Amstel river in the distance and he could hear the familiar clatter of the Central railroad, which occasionally made the pavement tremble when a train passed. And then, in his pocket, he felt a vibration of another sort--his cell phone.

He reached for it, saw that it was an email and opened it to a photograph of Carmen, who was in Bora Bora resting in a hut that reached into the South Pacific deep. She was on a deck, in a bikini and looking tan and fit. Beneath the photo were a few words:

"Paradise ending. New job tomorrow. This one's big. You might hear from me."

He turned off the phone and looked ahead of him, where his marks were walking arm-in-arm, her head on his shoulder. She was blonde and she was pretty, with a smooth complexion that was just this side of pink given the chilly air. He heard her laugh and, as she turned her head to whisper something in the man's ear, he saw just how delicate she was, just how fine her jaw line.

He had orders to get a photo of her face after he'd blasted it into nothingness.

Carmen.

The last time he'd seen her was in New York, when they decided to be nobody's fool and turn the tables on Carra Wolfhagen and Ira Lasker when it was revealed that they lied to them and put them at risk. And so, just for fun, they found rope, put nooses around their necks and strung each up by their throats above the bar.

Wolfhagen and the reporter joined them.

When they left them behind, scrambling and gagging and choking as they fought to stay conscious, there was a sense of redemption. Maybe they'd live, maybe they'd die--neither he nor Carmen cared. What mattered is that Carra and Ira have time enough on those nooses to know why they were there. They'd think about their mistakes and wish they'd been straight with them from the start.

Later, Spocatti read in the Times how the scene unfolded. Carra Wolfhagen was caught by the police when she ran out of the building and down the street. The next day, Mark Andrews identified her and Lasker as the masterminds behind framing Wolfhagen. She now was facing prison. Spocatti read that Lasker died in the fire, as did Wolfhagen, who was burned so deeply beyond recognition, his remains were identified by his crowded set of teeth. All in all, a good ending in which he and Carmen learned valuable lessons while pocketing millions for their trouble.

Now, the day had tipped into night. Storefront windows illuminated the stone sidewalks. Above them, street lamps flashed and created warm umbrellas of amber light. Tonight, he would end this job, likely by busting into their apartment and taking them by surprise, and then he'd move back to New York City, where another job was waiting for him.

Two years ago, he had been involved in a coup to take down the billionaire George Redman and his family, among others. Things hadn't gone as planned and now Spocatti was being brought back to finish the job thanks to a provision provided by a man's will. He was so intrigued by the situation--at the sheer freshness of it--that he agreed on the spot to take the job.

He would finish what should have been finished, and in the absence of one man's ego and unwillingness to listen, he'd be free to kill in ways that were efficient, precise and, if he was in the mood, likely creative.

* * *

NEW YORK

The cat, Baby Jane, walked across the piano keys to the sound of her own music.

She stopped in the middle of the keyboard, reached out her paw and pressed down on one of the keys. Curious, she did so again, this time more firmly. And then, delighted that she possessed the gift of music, the cat reared up on her hind legs and crashed down in an eruption of sound.

Maggie Cain swept into the room and hooked the cat with one arm. "You're no Chopin," she said. "You do, however, have the aggression of a young Rachmaninoff. But do me a favor and work it out later, when I'm not writing." She scratched the cat's chin. "Okay?"

Unfazed, the cat squirmed out of Maggie's arm and ran across the room to the window. She leaped onto the sill and looked out at the falling snow. New York was in the midst of a Nor'easter. They were predicting eighteen inches, but as Maggie moved behind the cat and looked out at the barren street, she knew they were in for more because the snow already was that deep. But she didn't mind it--right now, everywhere she looked was bright and white and seemingly brand new.

She went back to her office and stared at the words on her computer monitor. Her new novel, a thriller, was nearly finished. She'd never attempted the genre before but given what she'd experienced six months ago, she felt uniquely qualified to give it a shot. And she was enjoying it. Three more chapters, a second and a third draft to hone the text, and then it was off to her agent Matt, who encouraged her to write it.

The phone rang. She glanced over at the lighted dial and saw that it was Mark. She weighed whether she wanted to be interrupted by him, and decided that she didn't. She let him slip into the gray world of voice mail and waited for him to leave a message.

"It's me," he said. "You up for company? I could grab a cab, stop by the market and get the fixings for a roasted tomato, basil and garlic soup. Let me know soon--I know you're probably writing and haven't eaten. The soup would do you good."

He severed the connection and she looked back at the screen. She tried to concentrate, but it was difficult. He was making every effort to win her back. What still surprised her is that he even had to try. If she had been told the night she found him alive in that safe house that there would be any question they'd be back together again, she would have scoffed.

But then Mark went to Wolfhagen's funeral and when he did, a part of her saw him in a different light. Regardless of what Wolfhagen had done to her and to the millions of people whose financial lives he ruined in the stock market crash he helped to create, Mark still revered the man, which she couldn't accept or understand.

When she confronted him with it, he shrugged it off-- Wolfhagen once meant a lot to him. He taught him what he knew today. He forgave him for what he'd done in the past. She should, too. After all, he'd done his time. He wasn't responsible for anything Carra and Ira did. It was healthy to move on.

But for Maggie, that wasn't the case--her scar wasn't just emotional, it was physical. And how could Mark overlook the fact that Wolfhagen tried to shoot her?

She dropped Mark then. Months passed without a word. And then, two weeks ago, he called with an apology and asked if they could work this out. He told her that he loved her. He said that he missed her. He wanted them to be together. But in spite of the fact that a part of her still loved him, another part of her wondered if she was for him. Not knowing, she built up roadblocks. She still hadn't agreed to see him.

Words on the screen. She read them again and added a sentence. He was pulling out all the stops with that soup. He knew it was her favorite. And the weather was perfect for it. She typed a line of dialogue, screwed up her face when she read it and then deleted it. Words on the screen. She stared at them so long, they went out of focus. For a moment, they could have been ghosts.

And then she knew exactly who to call.

She reached for the telephone and, holding it between her head and her shoulder, she opened her computer's browser, searched for a number, got it and dialed. Given the heavy snow, she was surprised that the line was answered.

"Tarot Cafe."

"Roberta?"

"Lotta."

"Is Roberta there?"

"She's in a trance."

"Oh. Is it rude to break her from it?"

"Depends on what she's seeing. Hold on and let me read her face."

Maggie waited.

"I'm seeing a darkness."

"Maybe we should interrupt."

"This important?"

"It's critical."

"Hold on."

It was a moment before Roberta came to the phone. And when she did, her voice was reduced to a hush. "Is this you?"

"Excuse me?"

"It is you. Why are you calling me? Did you cross over? You must have crossed over. But why? You weren't supposed to do so until tomorrow at six."

"Roberta, it's Maggie Cain."

"Who?"

"It's Maggie."

"Maggie? Why the hell didn't you tell me it was you? I thought you were someone...else. What's up, cookie?"

"Can I ask you a question?"

"A question! Well, it's about time. The non-believer is now a believer."

Maggie laughed. "That's right."

"What's your question?"

"This is going to sound stupid."

"Everybody says that."

She felt like an idiot. "I want to know if I should be with Mark Andrews?"

And when Roberta spoke, she changed the course of Maggie's life. "No," she said gently. "Mark isn't the one for you, sweetie. It's not in the cards. I saw it when you stopped by to visit a couple of months ago. I saw something else in your future. Someone else. It wasn't Mark."

"Who was it?"

"The one," she said. "Give it some time. Give it till summer. Then come and introduce me to the man you'll be marrying. We've already met on another plane, but I'd like to meet him in person."

- * * *

LAS VEGAS

Jennifer Barnes fed a twenty into the machine, cracked her knuckles and hit the button marked "Maximum Bet." Four cards appeared on the screen. She was at the Wynn playing an aggressive game of Black Jack. A martini was in one hand. A lit cigarette was clenched between her teeth.

The game was aggressive because she was losing--big time. This twenty was it for her, which she'd said to herself about two hundred dollars ago. But this really was it. She swore to herself that if she didn't win now, she'd walk away.

As the cards revealed themselves, she smiled.

On the left side of the screen was her hand--an Ace and an eight, giving her nineteen. On the right side of the screen was half of the computer's hand--a four. The other card was hidden. Still, with a four, the odds were in her favor.

There was only one way to play this. She held on nineteen, hit a button, took a sip of her martini and watched. The computer's hidden card was a seven, which gave it a eleven points. Her stomach sank when the next card was revealed--a Queen, which totaled twenty-one points, meaning she lost again.

Tight-ass motherfucking machine.

She downed the martini, snuffed out her cigarette, checked the time on her watch and saw that it was past two, though the casino was still packed. She walked through the perfumed air, had an itch to play something else as she walked past the inviting machines with their inviting sounds, but she kept on course. She was calling it a night. She walked across the floor, showed security her room key as she breezed past them to the elevators at her left, and then zipped up to one of the penthouses.

She entered her room and, in the wall of windows opposite her, was met with a grand view of the Strip. It was beautiful.

To the right of the windows was Marty. He was sitting at a desk, his face bathed in the light of his laptop. He looked up at her as she stepped in. "Win big, kid?"

"You're funny."

"Lose big, kid?"

"You could say that. And I assume by this 'kid' business that you watched 'Casablanca' while I was out?"

He started typing. "Just out on Blu. Looked amazing. While you were throwing money at Steve Wynn's feet, it was just me and Bogie."

"How's the review going?"

"I've actually moved on to 'Hamlet'."

"Doesn't everyone die in that?"

"That's generally the case with Shakespeare."

She walked behind him and put her arms around his chest. "And here I thought you'd be writing about happy movies with happy endings, if only to strike a balance given the year we've had." She leaned down to look at the screen. "Which version of the movie are you reviewing?"

"The Gibson one. Also just out on Blu."

"In this case, I'm glad Hamlet dies."

"I'm conflicted."

"Oh, please."

"The man gave us 'Mad Max'."

"Are you forgetting 'The Beaver'?"

"For every 'Beaver' there's a 'Lethal Weapon'."

"Sort of like his mouth."

She took off her shirt and walked across the space to their walk-in closet. She looked over her shoulder and wondered if he needed a distraction. He was healthy now. In the months that had past since Maggie Cain accidentally shot him, he had fully recovered, but had yet to take another job, even though offers came in. In the meantime, Jennifer took a leave from her own job, which she would return to in the next few weeks. For awhile, this would be their last vacation. Each knew they needed to get back to work or they'd never move forward.

But were they ready for work? She thought he was ready, but she wasn't sure about herself. When the explosives ignited two blocks over on 77th, she grabbed Hines and pleaded with him to tell her what Marty wouldn't--that he was going to a safe house on the city's West side because there was a chance that Mark Andrews might be alive.

Convinced that this was the core of the story, she left the scene with the sense that she was exchanging one nightmare for another. Six months passed and still she couldn't shake that night, what that man and woman did to her, and that she nearly lost Marty.

But she had to try.

She slipped into the closet and opened one of the drawers. She found something see-through and sexy, and put it on. Moving quickly so he couldn't see her, she dipped into the bathroom, brushed her hair and her teeth, grabbed a bottle of perfume, sprayed it into the air and walked through the mist.

She stepped out of the room and looked across at him. She loved him. Better yet, she was married to him. No fuss--just a quick trip to the Wynn's wedding salon. When he proposed to her on the plane, he gave her a four-carat diamond solitaire and told her that she meant everything to him. The next day at Cartier, they bought their rings. And then, within hours, it was official. She was Jennifer Spellman. To her surprise, when Marty told the girls, Gloria sent flowers and a note to Jennifer. "Dinner when you return. The kids are eager to meet you. So is Jack. We're a family now. Brace yourself."

The telephone rang.

Marty looked over at her and his eyes widened when he saw what she was wearing. "Tell me I don't have to answer it."

"You probably should," she said. "It's past eleven in New York. Something might be wrong with one of the girls."

That made him pick up the phone. "Hello?"

"Marty Spellman?"

It was a woman's voice. He looked over at Jennifer. "Who's calling?"

"I need your help."

"How did you get this number?"

Jennifer walked over to him.

"Your ex-wife, Gloria, gave it to me. We're friends and she said I should call you. I know it's late, but I'm in trouble and I wasn't sure where else to turn. I know you're the best."

"Who is this?" he asked again.

"Leana Redman."

"George Redman's daughter?"

"You could put it that way."

"What's the problem?"

She told him and Marty closed his eyes as it came pouring out. Though he didn't know her, he suddenly feared for her.

"I'll be back in New York in two days," he said.

"Can we meet then?"

They agreed on a time, he told her to call him if anything changed and hung up.

Jennifer stood next to him.

"That was Leana Redman," he said.

"Is she alright?"

"Not even close."

"A couple of years ago, I covered what happened to her and her family. It was awful what happened."

Leana's words ran through his mind. Already, he was wondering how he'd get her out of this. Considering who they were dealing with, he wasn't sure that he could.

"This time it's worse."

###

Read Christopher Smith's thriller "Fifth Avenue" to find out about Leana Redman and the Redman family--and just why this time, it's gotten worse.

Made in the USA
Lexington, KY
07 September 2013